A Novel by GS JOHNSTON

The Cast
OF A HAND

Based on a True Story
of Love and Murder
in Second Empire France

AUTHOR NOTE

The mass murder on which THE CAST OF A HAND is based took place in France, in 1869. Monsieur Antoine Claude, the celebrated Paris Chief of Police, led the investigation. Such was the height of the public's outcry, the case is often referred to as the first thunderclap in the fall of Napoleon III and The Second Empire.

PROLOGUE

Hortense came to.

The darkness caused her no fear, nor the pain or the bone creaking cold, so cold, not even the dirt about her mouth.

She couldn't hear the children.

She held her breath.

Listened. Listened to the sound in the fields.

A spade sliced the earth. She was sure.

The sound ceased. She could hear nothing now, not a solitary sound.

She dared to inhale a shallow breath. The air moved like molasses yet burned like whiskey all the way down her throat. She must breathe. Confine her breath to the apex of her lungs. That she could bear.

Her torn basque covered her head, a pocket in the earth. She arched her aching fingers, pressed them into the soil above her.

She tried to move her head but there was no room, just crushing pain. She opened her mouth, thrust out her tongue. Rotting vegetation in the dirt made her nauseous. She opened her eyes then closed them quickly, soil snared under the lids.

Where were the children?

What had happened?

Why?

What could she do?

She held her breath again, listened again but heard no cry. The slightest murmur would reach a mother's ear, attuned to the crib. The children were obedient to the last. But she'd failed to protect them, failed completely, utterly.

The loam sat heavy on her chest. She was going to die here.

Was she six feet down or thrown in some cursory grave?

Would anyone ever find her?

Would there be a marker with letters carved deep in gray stone?

Rests here Hortense Juliette Joseph Kinck
née Roussel
Deceased September 19, 1869
Pray for her.

Why was she forsaken?

Such thoughts were futile. She must find her children, press her hand to theirs. Touch warmth.

Not dirt.

CHAPTER ONE

It was already mid-morning when Monsieur Antoine Claude, the Paris Chief of Police, strode across the Pantin field on the outskirts of Paris—and stopped dead. Good God. Streams of women lifted their hems high through the rows of lucerne. Men in black top hats and business vests stumbled in the furrows. Away from them, patchwork crowds roamed the reaches of the field, covering it as if some great fête were in progress.

Damn them. This was murder, mass murder, a blood bath. Claude removed his hat. Evidence had surely been lost, traces of the crime trampled.

If only there'd not been a delay in the police prefecture's getting the news to him. Surely his superiors knew travel plans would cause him no hesitation in returning to duty. Catherine, bless her, had "unpacked" many a holiday without having left the apartment. *Damn them.*

He continued across the dewy field. Ahead of him a mob ringed a flimsy barrier erected at a small distance from the grave, people pushing, jumping to catch a glimpse.

"Who's done this, Monsieur Claude?" a voice yelled.

It was a journalist from *Le Petit Journal.* His question set off the pack, yapping quicker than any mind could follow. The police saw Claude approaching and parted, arms raised to deflect the journalists and let Claude through.

Officers, some down on hands and knees, combed the narrow periphery of the communal grave. The earth had been removed, the loam piled in a corner. He hoped someone had taken note of its state. Was it packed solid or loose? Moist from the dew or dry? Such details would help fix the time of the event. At the far perimeter, a young policeman vomited violently.

Claude took his pocket note book and walked forward. The grave was shallow. He drew closer. The woman was in her early forties. The children ranged from a small girl of two or three to a boy in his mid-teens. Five children. Four male. The woman had dark hair, her dress of dark fabric torn about the basque. She could be any middle-class woman in Paris. She wore a wedding ring. Her eyes were open, wide with unimaginable horror. Blood caked over her chin and across the white undergarment covering a huge belly. She must be the mother—a pregnant governess was unlikely.

The children were neatly dressed, well kept. One boy's mouth hung agape at a grotesque angle—he'd left life in terrible pain. Not that they all hadn't. The little girl's hair was dark and still coiled but her light smock was soaked in blood.

A photographer gingerly set a tripod on the uneven turf near the grave. Claude pointed him out to the nearest officer.

"Is he police?"

The officer scuttled towards the man, who had no identification.

"Get him out of here," Claude said. "And anyone who isn't authorized."

To the side of the grave, the farmer who'd discovered the bodies was recounting his story. Claude opened his note book.

"It were daybreak," the farmer said after giving his name. "I was walking to my plot."

"Why did you see this?" Claude pointed to the single rut track at the side of the field. "It's away from your path."

"I don't know, I guess… the furrows I'd ploughed had been disturbed. The mound caught my eye. I knew it weren't there yesterday evening. I was annoyed someone had been on the plot overnight."

"Annoyed?" Claude made a note.

"People come to the fields, gypsies and the like, help themselves to whatever they want. This is my living."

"Of course. What happened then?"

"I walked towards the mound, saw a trail of blood leading to a handkerchief so I went closer. There was blood on the handkerchief. I kicked about in the soil and … and…" Claude made another note. "It were dark but I kicked… I found a hand." Again he stopped, and when he resumed speaking his voice shook. "A little human hand. And him."

He pointed to the far edge of the patch, where the smallest boy lay with his hand extended away from his body.

"He were stone cold and I ran to the authorities."

Claude thanked the man, then turned to an officer.

"Do any of the local police recognize the woman?" he said.

"No one knows anything."

Claude left the farmer as the police prepared to exhume the bodies. The crowd surged forward. An officer trying to push them back was forced into the grave, his foot barely missing the little girl's chest. He touched the woman's cheek.

"The flesh is warm!"

The crowd waved forward again.

"Stand still."

Claude's voice, a full baritone, dry and even, arrested the crowd.

"You must stay back," he said. "This isn't some fairground attraction. You're destroying evidence." He fixed the crowd with his pale gray eyes. "Come now," he said in a friendlier tone, "something terrible has happened here. We owe this woman and the children some respect."

There was a moment of standoff. And then, as if a sheep dog had motioned the right command, a small retreat waved through the crowd.

A doctor ushered to the grave lifted the woman's wrist. Claude squatted next to him.

"She's alive," the doctor said. "But only just."

The woman's eyes were open wide, as if stuck, but the iris contracted and relaxed. Claude felt her hand, warm yet offering no return of pressure. Her lower lip trembled. He moved his ear towards her mouth. There was no sound, just the faint warmth of breath on his cheek.

"Who are you?" he said.

He heard nothing. The doctor held the metal of his fob watch near her nostrils.

"Her vital signs are gone."

"But she's warm," Claude said.

"She was alive, undoubtedly, when she was first uncovered."

Claude sighed heavily. The poor woman. If he hadn't been delayed…

"Check the others."

As he walked from the shallow grave a man retched behind him. At least something was human in this field. Rows and rows of workers' cottages stood not a hundred meters away from it. The area was populated with Prussian and Alsatian laborers brought to Paris to work on Haussmann's rejuvenation. Surely someone had heard something.

"She wears a fine wedding ring," a male voice said. "She's not been murdered for her jewelry."

Claude recognized the voice. It was Adolphe Desbarolles, standing at the edge of the excavation. Desbarolles' work sought to link the characteristics of a criminal's hand to crime. Claude took this with some seriousness though many dismissed chiromancy as parlor entertainment, a judgment reinforced by Desbarolles's earning the major part of his living from reading bourgeois women's palms. On a normal day Claude wouldn't have minded his presence but he'd not authorized it and the laxity annoyed him. Still, Desbarolles was an acquaintance—a perceptive, highly intelligent acquaintance. He looked closely at the children's bodies, even more closely at the woman.

"What else do you see?" Claude said.

"All the children were alive when they were buried but died from injuries. Except the one who died from the single blow that pierced his forehead."

Claude could see that one boy was marked by an ugly mid-forehead gash.

"What leads you to that conclusion?"

"Their contorted bodies. They fought for air, fought to dig themselves free. An examination of their fingernails will confirm. And the woman was in labor."

Noting the pregnancy was one thing, but why had Desbarolles thought to look further?

"The mound has moved lower on her belly," Desbarolles said.

"If you continue with such clear observations," Claude said, "I may suspect you for being at the scene of these murders."

"I witness events but not in such a base manner."

"We may assume she's their mother, but we can't be sure as yet."

"But my friend, she is. They have the same inherited features in their hands."

Claude looked at the small hands of the little girl. She still held a piece of sausage, her little thumb pressing it to her palm. The hand of the boy next to her was twisted with what look like dislocated fingers, the other boy's hands were lacerated. But there *was* something, some commonality between them—what did Desbarolles's tuned eye see?

"There's a similarity," Claude said. "But I can't name it."

"And neither will I."

For a moment, Desbarolles's soft eyes rested on Claude. Then he nodded his head, clipped his heels in a salute, and left the enclosure. With his refined gait, he all but glided across the field—the starkest of contrasts to the rattling, cleaned but still stinking empty dung carts now arriving to remove the bodies to the Paris Morgue. Was no more dignified transport available?

Claude wouldn't watch the children being put into the carts. Best return to his office and commence the investigation.

CHAPTER TWO

"See that man? Take a break, take a look!"

Hortense stopped her sewing machine and looked up at Martine, who stood near the doorway, pointing to the shop. The other half-dozen women and their machines rattled on without missing a beat. Martine was a gossip. Who could possibly be so interesting?

But when Martine beckoned Hortense, she walked along the line of machines and joined her.

"I've seen him here before," Martine said.

The man in the shop was Hortense's age, in his mid-twenties, well dressed. In fact, he was trying on a long coat she'd stitched last week. He *was* handsome—dark chestnut hair and thick eyebrows, a high forehead and high cheekbones that gave him the appearance of nobility—but she'd not paid particular attention to his looks in the brief time they'd seen each other.

"He lingers to catch a glimpse of someone."

"He does nothing of the kind." Hortense couldn't stand tomfoolery. "You can see, he conducts his business with Monsieur Noël."

"He tried that coat on last week and it fit fine. Unless he's changed his weight in a week, he's here to see someone."

"He may linger, but what interest is it to me?"

Hortense returned to her machine. But the other, prettier girls fluttered around the doorway, passing and repassing it to catch a glimpse of the man.

Monsieur Noël appeared at the door and ordered them all back to their machines.

"Except for Hortense," he said.

Why should she be singled out when she wasn't caught ogling?

"You sewed that coat?" he said.

"The dark navy? I did, Monsieur."

"Then come with me."

She felt their eyes on her but seized her pins, scissors, and a marking block. The man remained standing on the plinth. He nodded his head, and she thought she detected the smallest trace of a wry grin before she averted her gaze.

"Monsieur would like the waist to sit a little more… comfortably." Monsieur Noël looked at her. "I don't think that's possible, now it's been cut."

The waist? It was already cut tight. Before she began stitching the coat she'd asked Monsieur Noël if the cut was correct—the proportion of shoulder to waist seemed extreme. Now she looked at the coat. She walked to the rear. The coat hung well, the fabric dropping from the man's square shoulders. And Monsieur Noël's pattern had been correct. The man had a fine figure, slender and taut, and the coat encompassed his waist most comfortably.

"If the waist is taken in, it will buckle here… and here." She pointed to two seams. "But if I increase the packing slightly in the shoulders, it would give the illusion of a tighter waist."

Noël looked at the man for a moment, then raised his eyebrows slightly and nodded.

A thunderous crash rang out from the workroom.

"Forgive me," he said and hurried away.

The man took off the coat and said something—she had no idea what–as she raised her hands to accept it.

"I'm sorry," she said.

He repeated it, his accent as thick as undercooked choux pastry. What did he want? He was a foreigner, not from Nord-Pas-de-Calais.

"Would-you-like-to-join-me," he began, then continued with each word individually placed, "at the Café Magot? Tomorrow evening?"

She gasped. Her face flushed. Though unsure what to say, she didn't want Monsieur Noël to hear. She'd long held a flame for Monsieur Noël, a flame he'd neither fed nor starved. The easiest path was to agree to join this bold man, if only to get him out of the shop and not give Monsieur Noël any cause for suspicion.

She nodded.

He smiled.

Monsieur Noël returned, apologizing, and she fled to the workroom.

"I knew it was you he wants to see," Martine said, her faced squeezed with delight.

Hortense was scowling.

"Who is he?"

"That's Jean Kinck," Thérèse said. "He has his own factory. Wealthy, very wealthy."

Jean Kinck was a fine-looking man, anybody could see that. And rich. He could have any woman. Any! So why on earth was he interested in her?

CHAPTER THREE

In the middle of Paris—in the middle of the Île de la Cité to be precise—Claude stood at the window of his third floor office at the prefecture of police. He gazed down on the square, busy with people, busy with the business of the day. He'd inhabited the same small office his entire career while one by one his contemporaries had been offered something larger, higher and quieter in the building. But he liked this small office, and not just for the view. It was filled with memories of triumph and disappointment, with the knocks of professional life.

From the corner of his desk, he took the dossier of recently reported cases. It was a ritual when he entered his office, the dossier updated through the day, a quick way of keeping abreast of new cases. And there it was; Woman and Five Children Slain in a Pantin field. If only one of those fools had noticed that poor woman was breathing. If only he'd been called to the field earlier. Children. Five murdered innocents. He sighed deeply. Mutilation was one thing, but he'd not been prepared for what he saw. Who were they? The farmer had walked past the site close to sunset and returned just after sunrise. At this time of year there was just under eleven hours of dark. Six murders, eleven hours.

He opened his notebook: *Why were they in the middle of a farmer's field in the middle of the night on the outskirts of Paris? Mother and children? Then, where was the father?*

Pierre Souvas came down the hall—Claude recognized the sound of his assistant's gait, irregular in its rhythm when he rushed.

"I'm sorry I'm late," he said. "I only just got word of this."

Souvas, a tall man in his late twenties, flopped a pile of papers on the desk. Claude looked at the clock. It was nearly midday.

"There goes your holiday," Souvas said.

Claude had told the prefecture he and Catherine were going on a walking holiday but in fact they were going to the Auvergne to look for a small parcel of land for his retirement in the not too distant future.

"My wife is disappointed." Claude shrugged. "What do we have?"

"Somewhere here…" Souvas rifled through the pile of papers. He was normally organized but the case notes were in a mess. He pulled a sheet from the pile, unfolded it, and leaned his large frame over Claude. The drawing detailed the grave site, three metres long but only half a metre deep, an outline of each body, the positions of the bodies, their limbs. Claude briefed him on what he'd observed.

"The bodies have been searched," Souvas said. "There's nothing to identify them." He opened another paper. "In the children's clothes we found seven francs in copper coins, three clay marbles, and a small doll." He looked up at Claude. "A wooden rosary was in the earth sifted from the grave."

"The mother had no bag of any kind?"

"Nothing. We've searched the field."

"And she wasn't robbed." Her wedding ring, a not ungenerous collection of diamonds around a ruby, hadn't been taken. "There's no obvious motive."

"What motive could there be?"

"Rape is unlikely, with the children present. Robbery is possible but we have no idea what was taken or why the thief left a valuable ring. And why kill her and the children? Evil for evil's sake? Revenge? It's all guesswork at this point."

Why let his mind run on motivation? It *was* all guesswork.

"One other thing," Souvas said. "Some distance from the grave, we found part of a small photograph."

He handed the remnant to Claude. It was a portrait shot of a person with dark hair and a high forehead, the type kept in a locket or wallet. But it was ripped in half above the level of the eyes.

"The hair on the top is thick and wavy," Claude said. "The person may be young." He pointed to the side of the head, above the ear. "It's cut close, do you see? It's probably a male." Souvas nodded. "No one of that description among the cadavers?"

"It mightn't even be related to the murders," Souvas said. "Dropped by someone else."

"A photograph is expensive."

"Her dress was silk, very well made, same with the children's clothes."

Claude sighed. Whomever they were, they were bourgeois. He couldn't remember a case starting out this frustrating.

"Police have been to the surrounding cottages," Souvas said. "No one can report any disturbance."

"Good lord! There must be fifty laborers living within earshot."

"They often don't want to get involved. This occurred at night. Or perhaps the bodies were killed elsewhere and brought there."

"There would be evidence of a cart. Or movement across the field. Damn those crowds. If only the whole area had been cordoned off…"

Now Souvas sighed. "The autopsy has started. They'll work all night to finish a draft. The lack of an adult male… "

"I know. If they're a family, we need to find the father."

A junior came into the office.

"The bodies were followed to the morgue," he said. "The place is over-flowing, surrounded, nearly a riot."

The Paris Morgue was open to the public to view unidentified bodies. Distraught relatives, English and American tourists, searched for friends or family members, bloated bodies dragged from the Seine, the poisoned, hanged, shot, or stabbed. But a much larger band of ghouls came in droves. Chaste bourgeois women tittered at the naked corpses. And the men? God knows what perversion drew them. The whole business infuriated Claude, who'd long advocated closure even though the Paris Morgue was listed in American tourist guidebooks. Damn it, these mutilated woman and children deserved privacy.

"Close the morgue."

"You can't," Souvas said. "They must be identified. And there'll be ramifications—"

"There always are. Close the building to the public. Anyone who thinks he—or she—knows them must supply good detail as to their suspicions. Then they'll be allowed to look."

The junior officer said, "The woman's black silk bore a tailor's label, Thomas du Roubaix."

Roubaix was a small manufacturing city in the area of Nord-Pas-de-Calais.

"Many garments are made there," Souvas said. "Sold all over France."

"We've got little else to go on," Claude said. "Dispatch a message to the police prefecture in Roubaix. Tell them what's happened."

What else could be done?

With no forewarning, Joseph Piétri, the Prefect of Police, stood at the door. How long he'd been there, how much he'd heard, Claude didn't know.

What the devil did he want?

Unannounced.

By instinct, the junior officer slipped away. Souvas remained. Claude stood, nodded and then turned to Souvas.

"When missing person reports come in," Claude said. "Any at all, we're to know immediately."

Souvas gathered some papers and left. The two men watched the door as his swift, uneven gait echoed away in the hall.

"We don't often see you down here," Claude said.

Piétri, younger than Claude, a small knotted man of fifty, continued to stand. His eyes, deep set and dark, moved slowly over the few documents on the desk.

"Damn, ugly mess," Claude said, returning to his seat. "The fields of France reduced to a shambles."

Piétri closed the door. "What have you got?"

"A woman and five—"

"I've been briefed. Where are you starting?"

Claude detested his tone. Piétri had risen to his position through astute political ability rather than good policing practice.

"This must be solved…" Piétri considered his next word. "Swiftly."

Claude waited for some more edifying remark but nothing came.

"Of course," Claude said. "Swiftly. And accurately."

Piétri grimaced. "Perhaps you're not completely grasping the situation."

"Then, perhaps you could enlighten me?"

"When the evening newspapers run the story, this viciousness, in a laborers' neighborhood, will send the populace mad."

"Why does the neighborhood increase the spectacle?"

"The woman was clearly bourgeois and odds on she was attacked by a laborer."

Piétri had heard his discussion with Souvas.

"I don't see that's necessarily so. And what makes you think it was one person?"

Piétri withdrew slightly, pulled his expression tight. "What makes you think it's more than one?"

"I've made no such conclusion. But the sustained savagery points to many hands."

Piétri slowly shook his head. "Will this happen again?"

"Another murder? I can't see in to the future."

Piétri breathed out slowly and moved to the office door.

"I support you closing the morgue," Piétri said. "Souse the public outcry."

He stepped in to the hall but turned back to face Claude.

"Swiftly," he said. "For everyone's sake, execute this swiftly."

He left the door ajar, his heels firm and determined in the hall. Claude sat back in his chair.

What the devil…? Of course, unless the culprit was apprehended there was great chance of another attack, or set of attacks, but why on earth wouldn't he solve this as quickly as possible?

This wasn't going to be easy. The newspapers would wind people wild, the resulting dervish reporting all manner of people missing, all manner of culprits, all manner of crimes. They'd have to sift through the chaff. But he wouldn't play second fiddle to the newspapers or anyone else in the police prefecture. Damn them. Damn them all.

CHAPTER FOUR

Hortense told her father she'd catch a later omnibus that evening from Roubaix to Tourcoing, pleading extra work because it was the week before the Feast of the Ascension. She didn't want to lie but it was half true—she'd convinced herself that Jean Kinck wanted only to speak of his "ill-fitting" coat.

He arrived on time. The other girls distracted Monsieur Noël. He said nothing beyond his initial greeting, for which Hortense was thankful. As they walked in the streets of Roubaix she felt spring arriving, the gray winter sky blooming to a fragile blue. Because of her years waiting for Monsieur Noël, she'd never stepped out with a man before. She turned a handkerchief again and again around the fingers of her left hand. She prayed no one she knew would see her—but then who would believe she was seen walking with such a man?

They stopped in a café, where he ordered a pot of tea while she scrutinized him. His chestnut hair was velvety. Her friend Nathalie would say his high forehead was a mark of great intelligence. His clothes were of finely spun wool, Roubaix's best. He was handsome. Very handsome.

"You say very little," he said.

"I'm sorry." It was her nature to listen. "I have difficulty understanding you."

He blushed.

"I'm sorry—my accent is strong. I'll speak slower. I come from Alsace."

Alsace was to the east, that was all she knew. She felt embarrassed to admit such unworldliness.

"Why have you come to Roubaix?" she said.

"There were few… opportunities in Alsace. Great unrest."

No work? Alsace didn't sound appealing in the least.

"Early in my life I concluded I'd never make my fortune there. I've lived here… it's 1852, so that makes it… My lord, nearly eight years."

"I could never imagine leaving my family." The very thought made her shudder. "I'm content with what I have."

"We have a Bonaparte in power again. A stable government. My manufacturing business is small. But each year it's achieved growth through nothing but my hard work."

What could she ask a man like him, so steadfast and industrious and focused on his future? What could she tell a man like him? Across the broad cutting table with Monsieur Noël they spoke of bolts of fabric and metre upon metre of seams and she had never to think. She would have a good long life with Monsieur Noël if only he would act. What did she know of government? It was the realm of men. Only they voted. Her father talked endlessly of this and now this man expected some pithy remark. This had been a folly, accepting his invitation. She should stand and walk, return to Monsieur Noël and never turn her head.

"Do you like to read?" he said.

She felt the heat in her face, was sure it had turned scarlet. "I can't."

His face remained impassive. She might have told him she couldn't play the cello.

"It's a useless thing for a woman," she said.

"Then tell me of your life."

She couldn't answer him. She had to answer him.

"There's little to my life you've not already seen. I work for Monsieur Noël. My father is comfortable but self-educated to a high degree and…well spoken. As to my ambition…" She grappled. "I've nothing as interesting as you."

"Your family?"

"We live in Tourcoing. It's nearby." Of course he knew that. "I have two brothers, one older and one younger."

He nodded as if she'd said something interesting, then looked at his fob watch.

"I'm afraid I must leave you."

She drooped in the chair. All along she knew her plain nature would be the end of any attraction. What could such a man want from her?

"Can we meet again?" he said.

"Will you return to this place, Alsace?"

"Not today." He laughed. "My office is in the center."

He smiled but she felt confused and lowered her eyes to the table.

"I've no future in Alsace," he said, his tone warm. "My life is here."

She pressed her lips to a smile and raised her eyes to his.

"Now I've established myself financially in Roubaix," he said, "I want to marry and start a large family."

She just couldn't keep the blush from her cheek. She caught Jean's smile and returned it.

Outside the Café Magot, something uncomfortable settled between them like the pressure of a coming summer storm. He motioned toward his office, the same direction as her omnibus. She lowered her eyes to the pavement. The silence rocked until she could stand it no more and looked up.

"I shall go, then," she said.

She raised her hand to shake his but he put it on her shoulder and leaned in. His lips touched her cheek. A thousand tiny pins slipped in under her skin. Before she could pull away he'd done the same to her other cheek, and while it still tingled he turned and walked away.

She stood and watched and finally let out the breath she hadn't realized she was holding. Her cheek seared with the intensity of a cut, but the sensation was all pleasure. Whatever Jean Kinck sought from her, she didn't care. She hoped he found it in abundance. She watched until she could see him no longer, heedless of prying eyes who might have seen what just happened.

CHAPTER FIVE

Claude decided to walk the short distance from the police prefecture to the Paris Morgue on the eastern tip of the Île de la Cité. The day still held light, and after reading and rereading a first draft of the harrowing autopsy report he wanted to clear his mind before confronting the bodies. On the Place du Parvis Notre-Dame, endless tourists gathered around a commander jabbering away in some foreign language or other, gesticulating wildly at the cathedral. Other people, in singles or small groups, ambled towards the building, gathering for Vespers.

Claude looked to the higher reaches of the cathedral's western facade, the grand round window, the flushed and cool colors muted in the evening light, the small statues of Mary and child and angels and the demon grotesques, always he admired the hunchback grotesques. Despite all the turmoil Paris had endured, the Kings and Queens, the revolutions and coup d'etats, the up and the down beats of Republics and Empires, this building remained, sacrosanct, immune, guarded. When he'd first moved to Paris from Lorraine, a provincial young man of nineteen, he often came to regard this beating heart of Paris. Baron Haussmann's renovation of Paris had energized the boulevards, torn away the clutter. The building stood tall and proud, the sun gracing the lower reaches. A man could step back and admire the grandeur. The empire smelt like a rose, at least, Paris did now, her effluent swept away by the fresh network of underground sewers. Credit where credit was due but the Second Empire's constructions would outlast the Second Empire.

How had such magnificence been engineered some seven hundred years ago? And how was it that each visit created a hunger for more and closer inspection? It was far too long since he'd been inside. He should make his way to the morgue, but the building drew him in.

The setting day streamed through the western windows. The quiet of the interior, the scent of decades of incense and contrition candles, the sense of the ceiling as another sky—all flooded him with calm, this feeling of his youth. It was why he came to this building, not for the rhetoric of the mass he'd long ago questioned to destruction but to see the sunlight stream through the eastern window in the morning or the western portal in the evening. Such design, such thoughtfulness, the hand of God firmly clasping the hand of humanity. Less than twenty-four hours ago a woman and five children had walked across a field to their deaths. Where was the hand of God?

Someone nearby coughed, the sound disappearing without answer, swallowed by the vault of the building.

Moments later he was on rue du Cloître Notre Dame, past the southern transom and the visceral buttresses, turning into Quai de l'Archevêché. Outside the morgue, crowds spilled from the footpath to the road. He'd done well to spare the victims a veritable flood of these ghouls, but his edict had riled the crowd to the point that many were yelling insults at the unyielding building or screaming to be let in.

Give us our daily bread.

Along the footpath, the vendors selling oranges and apples and "the lightest pastries in Paris" stood by their ignored stalls. The morgue was low-slung, a symmetrical triptych. The central section, higher and broader, contained the public viewing area. Its three large wooden doors, arched like those of Notre-Dame, were bolted, a tight line of police in front of them as if at any moment the crowd might lunge forward to seize access to the sensation they sought.

"When will you reopen the morgue to us?" a man cried above the jeers.

Claude knew him well. The poor soul was convinced he was already dead and came each day in search of his body.

"You just yelled to me," Claude said. "I've answered you. Therefore you're still alive. Go home."

Police formed a corridor for Claude to pass through the crowd, which erupted in taunts (Are we safe? How long till he kills again? What are you doing?) that thankfully receded when the doors closed behind him. If he'd ever doubted it, the public and Piétri, the prefect of police, were synchronized. The air was chilled. A weak light came through the high casement windows.

The six bodies lined the far wall, laid out on five marble pallets, tilted forward. The line was closed in behind sheets of glass for the sake of hygiene and to keep the odor of rotting flesh from the public viewing area. Despite this contrivance the air was acrid, almost intolerable with the bite of lime.

He'd not been prepared for the sight and stood at a distance to draw his breath. The corpses were arranged in descending order of size. As was usual, the bodies had been stripped naked except for the morgue's leather loincloths. The small boy and girl shared the last pallet.

A morgue attendant approached him.

"I would imagine you want to view the bodies more intimately."

Claude didn't want that at all—what he *wanted* was to leave the room. Why did this crime so affect him? Murdered bodies, decaying, bloated, bloody… they were his stock in trade. Murdered children were not uncommon.

They passed through a small side door into a series of short corridors, eventually emerging inside the display case. The woman's dark eyes were open and looking to the right.

"I'll leave you." The attendant bowed his head and withdrew.

Claude watched the shut door for a moment before slowly turning towards the bodies, approaching the pallet from the left, away from the mother's glance. Her mouth was parted in a half-smile. It was a smile, Claude convinced himself, and not a grimace as he'd first suspected. She was plain and solid. Her hair was thick and dark, as were her eyes, her hips broad, made for birthing. Had she seen the policemen who'd uncovered her, tried in vain to gain their attention?

The autopsy stated she'd sustained a total of twenty-nine stab wounds, all but one delivered from behind. Two had pierced her lower back and ran clear through each kidney. The depth and size of the cavities confirmed the wounds resulted from the same long knife.

But one wound was to the front of her neck. Although the line of the cut was quite clean, the surrounding skin contained smooth bulges, causing the surface of the skin to buckle and crepe. Air had entered between the layers of the skin. The autopsy report noted that if these areas were palpated, the pockets of air would disperse causing a characteristic crackling sound as the air moved about, further splitting the lower layers of skin. Claude could see the cankers. He felt no need to touch them.

Through this wound, the murderer had forced his hand, grabbed her larynx and pulled it free. It hadn't been found at the site. Claude was dumbfounded, couldn't imagine why someone would inflict such a wound amongst so many blows. At first it seemed senseless, but then it was no wonder there'd been no reports of cries. And no wonder she'd been unable to form words in her last few moments of life.

The autopsy confirmed Desbarolles's assertion of her pregnancy, estimated between six and seven months. The attack had forced her into labor, the fetus lodging in the cervix, asphyxiated by "uncoordinated contractions of the various groups of muscles." The unborn child was female. As Claude saw it, this was a seventh murder. Already another death the newspapers would relish and Piétri scorn.

The woman's hands were folded over her belly. He lifted the cold hand, long and slender-fingered. He rubbed his thumb across the palm. The hand, slightly roughened, had worked, the skin worn hard and dry about the edge of the palm. She was middle class but without domestic help. Odd. Even he and his wife had domestic help. Claude moved closer. The nails were jagged and serrated from her attempts to dig free from the grave.

Had these hands touched her assailant? Of course they had, as she struck out. What could they tell him? There was most surely something there—a hair, a shred of fabric, a layer of skin lodged beneath these appalling nails. He narrowed his eyes to focus. And even if there was some sign, how should it be read or linked to an attacker?

His eyes began to water, blurring his focus. Eyes were a blunt tool but the emerging forensic science was only marginally better. He noted what he saw in his book, ignored his frustration and moved on to the next pallet.

The state of the largest boy's lungs, which were filled with a reddened frothy liquid, showed that he'd been strangled by his own scarf. And yet he'd also been hit about the head with a flat object causing a section of the skull to hang open in a flap, revealing the gray spaghetti ball of brain.

The second largest boy had been killed with a single blow—directly through the forehead, as Desbarolles had asserted. The shape of the gash suggested a weapon with a long, thin proboscis. A pickaxe? Perhaps.

The third boy had also been strangled, then beaten by some sharp object, not a knife. Also a pickaxe? Gashes in his chest, the back of the shoulders, and the head suggested a pickaxe.

The little girl had been hit in the stomach—only once, the pink tube of her intestine spilling the moment she was cut open.

The forensic report drew special attention to the wounds on the youngest boy's hands. The deep gores made the picture all too clear—he'd grabbed at the blade, tried to hold it tight as it cut into his flesh. His brave resistance had won the little boy a reprieve, only to be attacked again from behind with the pickaxe whose blow had finished him off.

A surge of nausea surprised Claude, who forced down bitter acid. He'd seen many cadavers but never so many young ones together. The autopsy report concluded in an odd tone—apparently he was not the only one unusually affected by viciously murdered children's cadavers. *Never was slaughter made by a more terrifying and assured hand.*

But not a single hand—of that Claude was certain.

He moved away from the pallets. Their clothes and artifacts were on a side table. The boys had worn gray trousers and a black jacket. The little girl a blue dress. It was silk. The children's socks were hand knitted, a gifted stitch, a low brown color. Had those hands made them? He sat at a small table at the far side of the room, out of view. He wrote the extensive list of wounds in his book, needing to see them in his own hand. Once this was complete, he allowed his hand to run, almost automatic writing.

Where did the wounds come from?
What can they be reduced to?

The weapons must be a long knife, something flat like a spade, and a pickaxe. Most definitely a pickaxe. Both the spade and the pickaxe were needed to dig the grave. Perhaps the murderers had only initially armed themselves with a knife but in the struggle resorted to the other items? But the murderers were organized, bringing the wherewithal to dig the single shallow grave.

This was planned.

No gun. This too points to planning. Such a weapon would have alerted the nearby cottages.

Even in a frenzy of killing it's unlikely one person could control all the children, then methodically kill them one at a time. There were no signs the victims had been bound. Are there other children who escaped? Wounds came front and back.

<u>*There was more than one assailant.*</u>

How many people were involved? It's impossible to say as there's no indication as to the period of time the attacks took place. The autopsy states they died at various times. Perhaps this supports Desbarolles's assertion they were all alive when buried. But the viciousness of the attack, some hundred and seven wounds in all, supports the assumption there was more than one person. No one has that strength.

The murders were premeditated.

The woman and the children had been lured to their death for some reason. Robbery? There was no money about the bodies. But how much money could she have been suspected to carry to justify such frenzied killing? And her jewelry was untouched.

There was no sign of rape.

<u>*The woman and the well-dressed children walked willingly to the place they were killed.*</u>

Claude underlined the sentence—he was sure of it. She and the children trusted the attacker. They'd not been killed in a fit of panic or anger. It had all been planned.

But what motive, what viciousness and determination to kill, what animal strength by how many was needed for such a sustained attack, rending flesh so heartlessly?

Claude closed his notebook and placed it in his coat's inside pocket. From this secure distance he looked back at the bodies. He couldn't approach them again. His stomach wouldn't allow it. He called out to the attendant, who escorted him back to the public area. The large central door opened, the jeers of the crowd flooded in.

Souvas ran unevenly across the morgue's entrance hall.

"Monsieur Claude! We've found someone."

"Who?" His heart raced. Souvas was panting.

"On Sunday night, a police foot-patroller saw a coach crammed with five or six people, it's only licensed for four…"

"Take a breath," Claude said.

Souvas took two.

"He noted the company's name and tracked the driver to prosecute him for overloading. The driver confirmed he'd taken a woman and five children to a field outside Pantin."

Claude said, "There are indeed good minds in the Paris police force."

We wouldn't be going home tonight to Catherine. She would understand. Together he and Souvas walked towards the bolted morgue's door.

Bardot, the coach driver, sat forward on a chair in Claude's office, bouncing his clasped hands between his knees. He was in his mid-twenties, a large man who with Claude and Souvas stretched the office's space to capacity.

"What time did you pick them up?"

He mumbled something Claude couldn't understand.

"Damn it, man, answer the question."

"I'm not sure."

"You'll lose your license for overloading unless you cooperate," Souvas said.

The threat worked on his tongue like a vat of beer.

"I picked them up from the railway station at about ten-thirty in the evening."

"What was their mood?"

"They seemed jolly but they were in a great hurry to meet someone."

"Who?"

"I don't know. On a number of occasions, the young man —"

"Which young man? The eldest boy?"

"No. There was a young man with them. The woman, five children, and a young man."

Claude gripped his pencil tighter, the lead powdering on the page.

"Was he intimate with them?"

"I can't say."

"But they knew one another?"

"Oh, yes."

"Were they family?"

"I assumed the woman was the children's mother. They obeyed her."

"But the young man?"

"The children fussed around him."

"Like an older brother?"

"Yes."

"But the woman?"

"I don't think she spoke to him." Bardot rubbed his forehead. "He bribed me to carry them all. I told him there were too many and look where it's put me."

"It's put you nowhere to fear if you tell us everything you know," Claude said. "We need your help."

"He leant out the window and demanded I drive faster."

Claude sat forward but kept his expression as relaxed as he could make it.

"At the Quatre Chemins, he yelled to stop."

Near the Pantin field.

"They stayed in the coach talking for a few minutes, I couldn't hear. After a while the young man, then the woman… let me think, I really wasn't paying attention… right, the man and woman and the two smallest children got out of the coach."

"And the others?"

"They stayed. The three boys, yes. The young man said they'd be back in a few minutes and I was to stay with the other children."

"What did the young man look like? Take your time, give us a good description. You're an important witness."

Bardot, no longer frightened, took time to think.

"A solid build, but he was short. Thick dark hair. Maybe in his late teens, eighteen, nineteen at the most."

Claude thought immediately of the half photograph in his desk drawer, the existence of which he'd kept from the press. Nothing connected the photograph to the case.

"He spoke with a strong accent."

"Where from?"

"I've no ear for accents."

Claude was careful not to show the slightest disappointment, wanting to keep Bardot in his helpful frame of mind.

"What did you do while they were away?" he said.

"Climbed down to smoke a cigarette, talked to the boys—wait! They said they'd come to Paris to meet with their father and older brother."

"So the woman was definitely their mother," Claude said. "Do you think the young man was another brother?"

"No. Well, I suppose he could have been, but he wasn't no son from the way he acted, and she didn't say nothing to him."

"Did they say where they were from?" Souvas said.

"Ummm…" Bardot took off his cap and ran his fingers through to the roots of his dark hair. "I think it was the north somewhere."

"Roubaix?" Souvas said.

"That's it!"

Souvas left the office.

"He's gone to alert the Roubaix prefecture," Claude said. "You're aiding our investigation—please tell me what happened next."

"Nothing for maybe twenty minutes, then the young man come back to the coach, but by himself—said they'd decided to stay. At Pantin."

"How did his mood strike you? Did he seem different?"

"He was still jolly enough. And the children were happy to go with him, they ran ahead while he paid me."

"You were near him. What were his clothes like?"

Bardot appeared confused.

"Were they disheveled in any manner?" Claude said. "Did he appear to have exerted himself?"

"No. He were just the same. There were no sign of blood."

Claude sat closer to Bardot. "What were the names?"

Bardot met Claude's gaze. "I can't remember." His eyes moved from Claude's. He shook his head slightly. "For the life of me I can't remember… but I'll try."

Claude sat back in his chair. His deduction was correct. The woman and the children had walked calmly, fearlessly, to meet their deaths. But he'd never suspected they were lured to the field and quite possibly killed by an older brother and their father.

One hundred and seven wounds.

CHAPTER SIX

Perhaps Hortense made too much of this. She told no one, not her mother or father and especially not Martine, who would go on and on about it without discretion or mercy and in purposeful earshot of Monsieur Noël. A handful of times they met in secret and as they parted Jean kissed her cheeks and she felt the same breathless sensation but each time amplified. Despite its industry, Roubaix was a small town—it wouldn't be long before some innuendo reached her parents, and Jean kept asking questions about them. What could she do but invite him for Sunday afternoon tea?

The news of the arrival of a suitor, the very first in the house, caused considerable consternation. Hortense's mother raised her hand to her daughter's burning cheeks, as if to cool them. Her father knew of Jean Kinck and nodded his head vigorously. As the evening settled, Jean told stories of his work and plans, many memories of his life in Alsace, entertaining everyone until late. Hortense sat next to him, not really listening, just wanting his eyes to leave her mother or father or brothers and return to her. Whenever it did, his gaze warmed her, like nothing she'd felt before. Was this love? If it was, then it was very different from any love she felt for her family. It made her feel like tissue, as if the slightest weight would make her tear and fall apart.

Later that evening when Jean had left, her father came to her.

"Jean works as steady as a mule."

"He is industrious," she said.

"One day he'll be a great success. By marrying him, if you were to be asked, you'll be well cared for."

She felt a wave of panic. What had he and Jean discussed as they sat alone in the front room?

"But Papa, I've so little in common with him. With Monsieur Noël—"

"Monsieur Noël? But he has… he's never made any suggestion. Has he?"

"No. But our conversation is easy. Jean asks me things I have no mind for."

"Jean could speak of worse."

"He's from Alsace. What if he wants to return to his people?"

Her father looked at her sternly.

"All his plans center here—were you not listening to him? No other man has asked for your hand. You're twenty-five. You'll soon be past a marriageable age."

She had no desire, no conception of leaving her family and her home. She'd wither and die.

And yet… had Jean not told her that he was established in Roubaix, that Alsace was behind him? Had he not himself mentioned marriage and children?

Excitement, fear, confusion, disbelief, hope—all these feelings now fought one another. Her father saw the war in her face.

"Stop fretting," he said softly. "He won't forsake you. All will be as it should."

She didn't trust herself, especially now. But she'd always trusted her father.

A few days later, Jean and Hortense sat opposite each other in a Roubaix café. She felt as if a weight had been lifted, now that her parents approved of Jean and they no longer had to scuttle about the city. He spoke with such formality he might have been conducting a business contract.

"I would like to marry you."

A proposal. Not at all romantic, at least not in the sense she'd imagined as a young girl, but the shock—the pleasure—of it all but felled her from the seat.

"Does the idea displease you?"

"No," Hortense said.

"Will you tell me what you think?"

Her mother had taught her a woman should never express an opinion. And what words could she summon with this racing heart? This breathlessness? She looked down at the table.

"I promise to consider it."

Jean sighed and sat back in his chair. "This wasn't what I expected."

"I'm not doing this for coquettish effect."

"Then it distresses you."

She tried to shake her head but it wouldn't move.

"No."

What was she to do? Jean had agreed to expect no dowry. She reduced her concerns to one.

"You talk constantly of Alsace. I think you miss it. Greatly. What if you want to return?"

Jean's brow relaxed.

"All my business and prosperity are here. In the coming years, the economy is said to flourish to heights we've never seen and I aim to prosper greatly. I'd be an utter fool to leave."

He smiled and cupped his hand over his mouth but then, as he started to laugh, pulled it away to reveal a generous smile.

"I wish to marry a girl from this area. It will be a secure anchor." Now he spoke softly, tenderly. "I don't want to leave. I'll take care of you."

Her skin tingled, swarmed in at her, as if the softest down drifted along her flank, teasing and tickling. Could she balance these arguments any longer? Monsieur Noël would never act. This may be her chance. She could choose. The height of the sensation was dizzying. She so wanted children. That couldn't happen without a husband. Jean was a good man. What more? Their marriage would start on an equal footing. Her husband would countenance her opinion. In return, she would obey his decisions as if they spawned from her own desire. She couldn't keep a smile from her face. Calm washed over her.

"Then I'll marry you, Jean Kinck."

Jean moved his chair around the small table, closer to her. Although she felt the eyes of the café patrons, she dared not look away. He took her hand in his, knitted his fingers into hers, held their two hands in his lap.

"You know I only came back to Monsieur Noël's to see you."

She knew no such thing.

"Why would you do that?"

Her audacity elicited the broadest smile yet.

"Time will show you." He leaned towards her. "I will give you a good life."

Nothing—no embarrassment, no awareness of onlookers—could have made her move. His lips, ripe with good health, grazed hers. The most fleeting contact created the most tingling sensation. He remained near. She felt his tea-scented breath on her cheek. Was he tempting? Having created this hunger, would he not sate it? They stayed so suspended. With no sense of propriety, she leaned forward and pressed her lips to his, much more forcibly than he had a moment ago. She felt his lips harden, clamp together. But as she made to pull away, they softened, caved. His tongue parted her lips and entered her.

CHAPTER SEVEN

It was only 7.30 a.m. and the square was almost empty. Although still autumn, Claude could feel the coming winter on the tip of his nose. He'd had a few hours' sleep—on the floor of his office, where he kept a thick blanket and a pillow for such occasions. He'd worked late into the night pondering the little information he had and hoping something new might arrive. It hadn't.

The morning papers would howl this case, telling the story in lurid detail so as to induce as much fear as possible in the public. Beware—this could happen to you. On a number of occasions Catherine had brought this kind of coverage to his attention.

Catherine. Damn it.

He'd forgotten to send her a message about staying at the prefecture. And when the news of the murders arrived, they'd been about to leave for the Auvergne. She'd given him *that* look—her expression as blank as she could make it, her sharp glance saying nothing and everything. She simply took off her hat. She was tired of this choice. And she'd made her opinion known. There was no disagreement between them—more than ever he wanted time alone with her. He was sixty-one, nearly sixty-two. But his work was like a wave. Even when it receded, it dragged at him.

Who was he fooling?

The woman was always two or three paces ahead of him. She knew where he was and wouldn't worry. She had better spies than the Paris police. They were both in good health. There was still time. She'd forgive him.

No sooner had he received a café au lait and brioche (Catherine forbade pastries) than Souvas burst in.

"I thought you might be here."

"What's happened?"

"Yesterday evening, a police spy reported a shopkeeper near the Pantin field sold a pickaxe and a spade to a young man the day before the murders."

"Why wasn't this reported to me earlier?"

His voice boomed in the café and the crowd fell silent. He shouldn't have drawn attention to them, but this lag time in reporting information was infuriating. Souvas waited for the café chatter to rise again.

"The items agree with your conclusions."

Claude stood. "We'd better go and talk to him."

He walked away from the table.

"Monsieur," Souvas said. "Your breakfast, the newspaper?"

"To hell with them."

He felt a familiar sting. Perhaps this had just been some dozing minion's oversight, but competitions and conflicting loyalties riddled the prefecture and for years he'd felt he was on the losing end of them. Piétri must know of such inefficiencies and yet he demanded nothing but a swift solution.

"It's not your fault," he said as they walked to the coach.

"What isn't, monsieur?"

"The delay in my receiving this information. I know it's not your fault."

"Perhaps it was," Souvas said once they were seated and on their way to Pantin. "I've been somewhat... distracted."

"Murder cases are hard to endure. I'd like to say they become easier but this one has unsettled me."

"Yes, but there's something else. I've been interviewed for a small promotion."

Claude regarded him. He'd heard no talk of promotion. And he'd never felt Souvas experienced any great desire for it. But recently he'd indeed been distracted, late for meetings, mislaying papers...

"It's a double-edged sword," Souvas said. "For one thing I'd no longer be working with you."

"You sound unsure it's what you want."

"Unfortunately I won't know that till I have it. Or haven't."

Claude appreciated this youthful dilemma when choices spread out before a man, choices made in a maze.

"If this delay wasn't my fault," Souvas said, "whose was it?"

Claude had never discussed his suspicions with anyone at the prefecture.

"Almost ten years ago in 1860," he said, "A judge Poinsot was murdered in a railway carriage on the Eastern Railroad, shot through the brain and heart. He carried a small amount of rent money and papers containing state secrets. Both were missing."

"Was it robbery or assassination?"

Claude smiled. Souvas's mind was working.

"As evidence came to hand, I believed Poinsot had been assassinated for the papers. They concerned a network of Prussian insurgents ensconced in Alsace who sought to stir up the Protestants against the Catholics in the hope of annexing Alsace to Prussia. I suspected an Alsatian man named Jud but failed to apprehend him.

"When I reported these findings to the prefect, I was told to back off."

Souvas gaze snapped to Claude. "Why would he do that?"

"It was political. I didn't stop, but there were consequences. Amongst other things I've experienced these… delays ever since."

Souvas looked away from him to the view. For a few minutes they rocked together in silence save for the rhythmic sound of the horse's hooves on the street.

"Promotion brings envy," Souvas said.

"Worse than that—it brings higher forces of control. Watch your back."

Again Souvas turned his head away from Claude, making it impossible to read his expression.

"If there's anything I can do," Claude said, "anyone I can speak with, let me know."

"That's most kind."

"Nothing has been heard from Roubaix?"

"I dispatched a telegram." Souvas sighed. "I've had no reply. You'd think someone would have missed them."

"Perhaps not. If they'd come to Paris for some purpose, a holiday, and as yet weren't due to return, no one would be the wiser."

"Everyone in France must know of the murders."

"The woman's hands were roughened," Claude said. "She worked. Maybe they lived in the country? Maybe they don't read newspapers? Maybe they don't read?" He rested for a moment. "Maybe they are not French."

As they walked through the shop, Claude was encouraged by the small size. Perhaps the sale would be memorable.

"I thought you'd come," the proprietor said before Claude had introduced himself. "After that spy was asking all those questions."

The shopkeeper was a weedy man, tall but thin in the core.

"We investigate everything," Claude said.

"Good to see you're all on your toes. Not like the news-papers say."

Claude let the jibes fall. He'd no need to defend the police's reputation, which the newspapers eviscerated in spite of anything he said or did.

"What can you tell us?"

"I don't remember a lot, just that when your spy was here yesterday I was reordering stock and I noticed there were a pickaxe and a spade missing. It jolted my memory—you know how one thing leads to another. The newspapers said they was what was used in the field to kill those poor buggers."

"Were the items stolen?"

"I sold them."

Claude heard the defensive tone in the proprietor's voice.

"Of course you aren't accountable for their use," he said. "Tell me about the man who bought them. What did he look like?

"Young…"

"How young? Thirteen, sixteen, twenty?"

The man thought for a moment.

"No… his voice were deep. He had peach fuzz on his face. Maybe sixteen, seventeen. Not much more."

"Did he say anything?"

The man lowered his head.

"It were late in the day… No. He just asked for them. Knew what he wanted."

From his coat Claude took an envelope with the small section of photograph found at the site.

"Could this be him?"

The man studied the photograph piece.

"I can't rightly say—it's hard without the eyes." He looked closer, squinted. "Perhaps… Yes, I think he did look a bit like that."

Despite all manner of prompting, the shopkeeper could remember little more. The young man had bought the items in the late afternoon. They discussed nothing. He did nothing to make the shopkeeper suspicious.

Claude and Souvas made their way back to the prefecture.

"It sounds as if he's the same person reported by the coachman," Souvas said.

"What makes you say that?"

"The description is similar, similar estimation of age."

"Yes…"

Claude looked out at the passing streets. The children had come to Paris to meet the father and an elder brother—but where were *they*? If they were innocent, they'd come forward to claim the bodies. If not, why would a father and son murder so many? A father, driven by the right motivation, sickened jealousy, was capable of such an act. The same with a son, but what could make them act together?

They crossed the Seine by the Pont Notre Dame, turning from the rue de la Cité into the expanse of the prefecture's courtyard. Despite their activity, the morning was still early and little moved in the yard. In silence they walked towards Claude's office, only to encounter a small commotion at the far end of the corridor when they reached the third floor.

"I need to see the chief of police," a man said to an officer. "I have information."

"Concerning what?" the officer said. "What information do you have?"

The man moved his hands about his face as if shooing off a fly. In the wake of bizarre crimes, especially when the newspapers created a frenzy, unbalanced people besieged the prefecture with blurry conspiracies of one kind or another.

"I'll not talk to anyone but Monsieur Claude," he said.

"He isn't here. You can speak with someone else. Your name?"

Claude walked up to them.

"I am Monsieur Claude."

The man turned to face him.

"I'll say nothing more in public. I have information for you."

"Follow me, please."

In Claude's office, the man perched on the seat. He was in his fifties, well groomed and dressed, no outward sign of mental disturbance. But he was agitated, highly. Claude placed his notebook on the desk.

"What's your name?"

"Rigny. I own a hotel in the area of Pantin."

"What is it you have to tell me?"

"I read this morning in the paper that the woman found in the field wore a dress from Roubaix."

He stopped, as if he needed Claude to affirm this fact. Claude raised his eyebrows and nodded quickly.

"About eight days ago, a young man registered at the hotel. He'd given his address as 22 rue de l'Alouette, Roubaix. And in the coming days, a good quantity of mail come for him from there."

"What was his name?"

"Kinck. Jean Kinck."

"I'm sure there are many people who stay at your hotel. What makes this man so memorable?"

"On the Sunday night, the night of the murders, at about six o'clock in the evening, a woman and five children come in and asked for the man. Jean Kinck."

Claude's heart accelerated. He wrote down the name, his pencil carving into the lower layers of paper.

"Kinck were still staying at the hotel," Rigny said, "but he left earlier that afternoon on some outing."

"What did the woman do when you told her?"

"Said he was to have reserved a room for them, but he hadn't. She was annoyed. Worried, even. She booked a room and paid."

"What was her name?"

"She just gave it as Madame Kinck. I don't think she could read. She signed with an X."

"Did she say anything?"

"No. She was annoyed, agitated. She looked exhausted. I didn't ask anything." His gaze remained fixed on Claude. "It's my habit."

"How much money did she have?"

"Let me think….I did see her wallet. She were flustered and didn't try to hide the money. Possibly as much as five hundred francs."

She had been robbed, or the wallet had been lost in the scuffle.

"Why didn't you report she was missing?"

The color drained from Rigny's face.

"The rooms was paid for. In advance. They still are. I don't like to ask a lot of questions." He lowered his head and voice. "Many of my clients only rent for a few hours…."

As if Claude wasn't aware people rented rooms for licentious encounters.

"She left some bags," Rigny said.

"Did she return?"

"No. But he did. Around two-thirty in the morning. Woke me up—I heard him on the stair. Two people."

"But not the woman?"

"At first I did think it was him and her, but it were two men. The footfall was heavy on the stair."

Claude felt a wave of agitation and looked at Souvas.

"I think we'd better go and look at these rooms. Before more time is lost."

Young men leaned against the walls of Rigny's hotel smoking cigarettes, shoulders hard up against the bricks, their hips forced forward and caps pulled down low on their foreheads. As Claude and Souvas passed he heard one comment in German that they were police. They didn't seem troubled. Now that Haussmann's vision of Paris was nearly complete, these laborers, mostly Alsatian, were largely left idle. Some had returned to their homelands but others hung about, unemployed and causing trouble, perhaps hoping the emperor or Haussmann would dream some more.

The building was run down, as Claude expected. The hotel, the street, even the suburb wasn't a place a bourgeois woman with five children would be likely to venture.

They searched the woman's room while Rigny watched, even more agitated now. Three bags had been left in the corner. Nothing had been unpacked. Souvas placed the bags on one of the beds and began going through their contents.

"Just trivialities. Clothing, a few simple toys. No identity papers."

"Where's the other room?"

"Down the hall."

A suitcase sat on the bed. Claude opened it: a few shirts, a pair of pants. He pulled everything free, searched the pockets of the garments but again there were no identity papers.

Souvas opened the cupboard.

"Nothing in here." He leaned in deeper. "Hang on a second."

He stood, holding a bundle of white cloth tied together with a thin rope. He unraveled it.

"Well, well," he said as he unfurled a white shirt, stained blood red on the front panel and the left sleeve. He lifted a pair of blood-stained trousers, splattered with mud.

He looked at Claude, who looked at Rigny, who shrugged his shoulders.

The hairs on Claude's neck prickled. He picked up the shirt. The stains were fresh, still red. The piece of rope could have been used to strangle. Perhaps the soil stains could be compared to the soil in the field.

There wasn't anything more they could do but ask Rigny to leave the rooms as they were, then return to the prefecture.

Claude would have Souvas telegraph Roubaix for information. This time about a young man called Jean Kinck.

CHAPTER EIGHT

Within a month of their wedding, a fine day in mid-September, 1852, Hortense left her employment with Monsieur Noël. It was a hard decision but Jean encouraged her. She would miss the company of the other girls, their daily gossip, even their arguments. For nearly ten years this workroom had been her social life, not just her work. But marriage changed everything, and it was inevitable she would leave.

She stood by her machine. Where had the years gone? She'd come to Monsieur Noël when she was only sixteen, and she was now twenty-five. She had no confidence and he sometimes yelled at her, but she knew her stitch held sure. With time he'd become more patient, more appreciative of her work.

She walked away from her machine. The girls gathered at the workroom door. They were in tears and she fought to stop the tears welling in her own eyes.

"We'll never see you," Martine said.

"Don't be like that," Thérèse said. "She's better out of this place."

"Goodness," Hortense said. "Please don't cry."

She too began to cry. It was just change but she hated that so.

"I'm not moving far away," she said. "We'll always see one another."

"Goodbye, Hortense," Monsieur Noël said from the far end of the room.

His overdone nonchalance confirmed her suspicions. He harbored feelings, even now.

"Goodbye, Monsieur Noël," she said. "Thank you for everything."

Jean was to meet her on the street—where was he? Punctuality was as much a part of him as his blue eyes. She stood, her hands by her side. The constant noise of loud clattering in the road seemed to assault her. But her father always said traffic noise was a sign of industry, and without industry they would all—

Suddenly everything went dark. She clutched her face. Fabric.

"Hortense."

"Jean?"

Her heart raced.

"Don't touch the blindfold."

What in God's name was he doing? Slowly she lowered her hands.

"I have a surprise," he said.

Once her hands were at her side, she felt him tie the blindfold in place—so tight it hurt a little. She relaxed her shoulders, tried to smile, despite the discomfort she felt. He spun her around as if she were a child at a party.

"Jean? Jean! Stop, please, I feel so giddy."

Suddenly he wasn't touching her. She stopped the circles and rocked to find her balance, firming her feet to the pavement. Why was he doing this? She couldn't feel his presence, hated her reeling disorientation.

"Jean?"

She could see nothing, again felt assaulted by the traffic noise. Where was he? This was a folly. What was he doing? She raised her hands in front of her, cast them about in the open space.

"Trust me," he said, his voice a hard tone she'd never heard.

She steadied herself. He took her, one hand on her shoulder and the other at the opposite elbow, a blind woman and a guide. They began to walk. She had no idea if they went towards the canal or away from the shop. Maybe even across the road.

"Where are you taking me?"

Jean said nothing. She felt unnerved not seeing where he was leading, where she was placing her feet. She tried to trust, she truly did but each blind step into the dark frightened her. Why was he doing this? Where was he taking her? And what would passersby think?

"Jean," she said, her voice tight with fear. "Please, can we stop this?"

But his grip tightened on her elbow and her breath would only come shallow, despite great need of air. What was he doing? She raised her hand to the blindfold but before she graced the fabric he grabbed it with such force his fingernail pinched into her palm. She pulled her hand away. She concentrated, on her step, on her breath, anything else to allay the tide of fear she felt.

They were now in a quieter place, the clatter of traffic more distant. The heat of the day fell away, the air on her skin cool and moist.

He grasped her, reined her in like a dray horse, stopping her advance.

"Where are we?"

Still Jean said nothing. He let her go. She raised her hand to the blindfold and again he took her hand and lowered it slowly to her side. Her heart pumped in her ear. She strained. She flinched at the beat of wings—a pigeon's? She heard no footsteps. Metal on metal.

"Jean. I'm frightened." She felt a cry rise in her throat. "Stop this. Please."

He took her hand and led her forward. The sound changed, lessened, echoed slightly. She heard a door shut. She could stand no more and the cry she'd suppressed flew out, her nerves strung taut and too tense.

He pulled at the knot of the blindfold. The light rushed at her, blinding. She swung round to face him.

"Where are we?"

She raised her hands to her face, her cheeks moist with tears.

His smile was sweet and radiant.

"Why are you crying?" he said.

"You…" He'd truly frightened her. She breathed deeply. "I'm just overwhelmed."

She looked from left to right. To one side of the hall there was a parlor and to the other a dining room. The hall led to a staircase and a passage through to a large kitchen at the rear of the house, spacious with a huge central work table, leading directly to a garden.

She cried the tension she'd felt. Why had he done this? Only to please her? Only to please her.

"Why are you crying?"

"You frightened me."

"Frightened? Are you scared of our home?"

She breathed in. "Home?"

"Where did you think I was taking you?"

He smiled again. How could she not trust that smile? He took her hand and kissed the back of it and together they ran to the upper floor.

"Four bedrooms!"

She couldn't contain her excitement and rushed to the two front rooms with views of the rue de l'Alouette— she recognized it—and then to the two rear rooms looking over a smallish garden courtyard.

"It's all ours?"

"This room will be ours," Jean said. "And this will be for… Henri, Aymeric, Stephane, Achille—"

"But they're all boys' names."

"You're right." Jean smiled. "This room will be for the boys' little sister, Marie, named after your mother."

She laughed and laughed.

"Do you like the house? It's near my office."

"Yes."

"I know you wanted to be near your family…."

It was not so very far away from them, and having this lovely house near his office would greatly aid Jean. She'd be able to take him lunch. He could return late.

"We will start our life in the rue de l'Alouette," she said.

She laughed and threw her arms around him and kissed him. She'd married a man full of sweet surprises and treasures.

"We'll lose one another in all these rooms," she said.

"Perhaps we may," he said.

The pleasure of the moment vanished from his face. He turned from her. What had displeased him in an instant? He took her hand and led her through the house to a stone bench in the garden.

"I should have told you this before," he said. "But… I've suffered great losses in my life."

"What do you mean?"

"My family—my parents are both dead."

He'd said they couldn't afford to travel to the wedding, but when she implored him to pay for them, he said it was too far for them to come. And they'd sent no gift, not even a letter of congratulations. In the end she'd sensed there was some wrong between them and thought it best to leave the subject alone.

"Why didn't you tell me?" she said.

"I don't like to talk of it. My father died when I was only six." He sighed. "And my mother died when I was sixteen."

She placed her hand on his, an inadequate gesture.

"Life was hard for my mother." He turned to face her. "I've no one, except you."

"I see," she said.

And understood. He hadn't wanted to admit this truth to her. It was a fragility, something that could undo him in an instant, unravel him like a skein. She admired this, his need to maintain control. It was the gift with which he strode through his business. And now she knew the seed from which this characteristic had grown. He'd told her. Nothing more need be said. In essence, he was a simple man.

"There's something I need to tell you," she said a few moments later.

He looked at her, his eyes wide with fear. She lifted his hand and placed it on her belly.

"Something has changed in me," she said. "I'm pregnant."

Jean gasped and snatched his hand away. Hortense laughed.

"You won't damage it."

She took his hand again and placed it on her belly. He snatched it back.

"Are you sure?"

"My mother is convinced."

"It frightens me."

"Look at me." She smoothed her hands to either side of her wide hips. "Surely you've noticed. I'll be fine."

"I'm happy, of course." He tried to smile. "But I worry… Something might go wrong—I couldn't bear to lose you."

Her heart tightened and she squeezed her eyes to repress the tears. Who would have thought a man so capable, so able in the world, could become so dependent on her? She had none of his worldliness, none of his abilities. But she provided him with something he'd not had, something he'd searched for but never found. She could make him a home in this wonderful house. And she could make him a family. She had that power, a woman's dominion. A large family, each child replacing some part of the parents he'd lost, of the comfort and security he'd lost, when he was so young.

CHAPTER NINE

As silently as he could, Claude turned the key in his apartment's door. He'd left on Monday morning and here it was Tuesday evening, well after eleven. He was too old for such long days. In his youth…   But then all things were possible in youth, when drive and ambition swept away tiredness, drove the need for sleep into another day. And in his youthful nights, sleep always came. Now he careered after it.

Catherine came to meet him in the entrance hall, her long silver hair loose around her shoulders. She looked sleepy— no doubt awakened by the sound of his key in the door. He kissed her warm cheeks, inhaled her scent.

"I'm sorry I'm so late."

"You were later last night…" She thought for a moment. "In fact, you didn't come home."

"I *am* sorry. I've been busy. The murdered mother and children—terrible enough in itself, but what we have so far is confusing. You shouldn't have waited up."

She wound her hair to its usual steadfast roll, sweeping herself into the air like a swan with her elongated neck and long body. He loved the way she did this, he always had. At times he pulled the clasp free, just so she'd refix it.

"I was neither concerned nor waiting up for you. I'd been reading."

Her book lay abandoned beside her armchair. She looked at his face and waved her hand.

"You *will not* practice your investigative skills on me," she said. "I fell asleep. Arrest me. Have you eaten? Clara has prepared something."

Had he? He was so tired he felt no hunger so it didn't matter if he'd eaten or not.

"Perhaps some tea," she said.

She passed from the front parlor towards the kitchen, their many bookshelves rocking slightly to her step despite the lightness of her footfall. The shelves gave the hall and the parlor something of the feel of Claude's cramped office. But whereas Claude's shelves were full of his handwritten notebooks, hers were filled—in no order whatsoever—with the great writings of French and Russian literature. She'd read and reread them all and then found more to read. The haphazard order of her shelves, from which only she could find a title, amused him.

After washing his hands and face, Claude came to the kitchen. She brought the tea to the table and sat opposite him.

"I've been to cancel the trains," she said. "Tomorrow I'll write to the hotels in the Auvergne."

She'd spent months of research, booking a series of hotels for them to walk between. They would view the land, find where they could settle.

"I'm so sorry," he said.

But more than sorrow he felt regret. They were approaching his retirement. He pushed it off and pushed it off. Time was running out. He wanted that time together, time unsullied by death and crime.

"After this case," he said, "we *will* look for the land."

"Yes, after this case."

"You're angry with me."

"The land will wait for us. We'll have another holiday." Her eyes still held the clear blue of her youth but this evening they lacked warmth. "Père Hyacinthe has published a public letter."

She was changing the subject but he wouldn't fight it. Catherine maintained religious rituals, unlike him, but often said they were in need of serious reform. From the pulpit of Notre-Dame, Hyacinthe Loyson opposed the church's resistance to the empire's rising tides of rationalism, liberalism, and materialism. The emperor had made moves to release some of his control. The First Vatican Council had been convoked to deal with these issues but the convocation had already excluded many voices.

"Hyacinthe's caused a stir," she said. "The letter denounces their excluding so many liberal voices."

"A brave man." Claude set down his tea cup. "He risks excommunication."

"Risk is necessary," she said. "Now, what have you learned about your case?"

Claude told her everything, sparing no detail. A squeamish woman couldn't have stayed married to him for thirty-four years.

"Why would someone disembowel a small girl, stab and maim and kill others who could only be innocent? The poor woman…" She threw her hands in the air. "And for what purpose?"

"I don't know."

The two fell silent.

"Something beyond the obvious is bothering you," she said finally.

"Bardot, the coach driver, stated he picked up the woman and the children at ten-thirty in the evening from the train station and took them to the field. This doesn't tally with hotelier Rigny. He says they arrived at his hotel from the train station around six."

Catherine thought for a minute. She was a good listener.

"Why would she return to the train station only to leave from there again?"

"Exactly."

"Something happened between leaving the hotel and leaving the station some three hours later."

"But what?"

He had no idea and Catherine offered no opinion.

"At least we have a name," he said. "Kinck."

"You think the son met them at the station and took them to the field."

He looked at her. Of course she'd read the heart of his confusion.

"The Roubaix prefecture sent a description of Jean Kinck," Claude said. "He's forty-six years old. A wealthy manufacturer. He's not a young man."

"Then who is this young man?"

"Kinck's eldest son, Gustave, fits the description of the young man in the cab, the shop, and at the hotel. And the driver said the family was going to meet their father. I believe this young man to be Gustave Kinck."

She sat back in her chair, looking into his face.

"And you think he's responsible?"

Did he? He closed his eyes.

"I don't know," he said, as much to himself as to her.

"From what you've told me," she said, "these murders can't have been managed by just one person."

"I agree. But a father and a son?"

Her sigh contained his.

"The public are outraged by this," she said. "In the market today it took forever to buy a fish because everyone was talking."

"The brutality of the murders, the fact that children were killed—it's disturbed people everywhere."

"But what's more disturbing is it's taken *this* to disturb them. People are murdered every day. Why are they so taken with this?"

"It's a whole family, the cornerstone of life."

"I don't understand someone who can kill a little girl in such a way," she said. "But I can no more understand how anyone can take any life. The public should be outraged every day."

She didn't mean to be hard. All life, to her, was sacred. How keenly she felt their lack of children.

"After I'd been to the field," he said. "Piétri came to my office. He told me to solve this quickly, worried there'll be another attack."

"And you intend to dally? Impudent bureaucrat." She fell silent. "But he's not wholly incorrect."

"And I don't feel this pressure?"

"I didn't come to your office suggesting you don't."

"I'm sorry. I'm very tired. But the insinuation I wouldn't act with all human speed—"

"These murders are inhuman."

"Piétri hasn't seen their bodies. Children torn apart. How could I not be fearful?"

"You must stay calm."

"Why come to my office to say it?"

"Someone higher has leant on him."

They were both silent.

"Be careful," she said.

He looked up at her. "What on earth do you mean?"

"The emperor promised not to forsake the public in return for their allegiance. An horrendous crime ruptures this neat contrivance—it's a highly visible sign that all's not well in the empire."

Catherine and Antoine Claude were old enough to remember the years of turmoil – the 1830 end of the Bourbon restoration, the 1848 abdication of the July Monarchy and the return of exiled Louis-Napoleon Bonaparte and the rise of the Second Republic. In late 1852, almost in awe, they'd watched Louis-Napoleon build to a plebiscite. How bloodlessly he emerged from a chrysalis, instating himself as emperor, and spread wide the vainglorious wings of the Second Empire.

The anvil of easy credit forged the empire's first prosperous decade, powering the remodeling Paris, levelling the warren of tight streets to broad boulevards, the gas-lights clearing the night sky and the sewers draining the filth. But in the second decade, silkworm eggs withered, phylloxera attacked the roots of grapevines, the American civil war made cotton scarce, gelding the country's hungry looms. Close at hand, threats of war, Italy, the Schleswig-Holstein affair, Prussia clattered at the borders. The tide of fortune had turned. Credit dried like grapes on a rootless vine.

At length, Catherine and Antoine discussed the cracks in the Second Empire's façade but Catherine maintained the prosperity had silenced the far left *and* the far right. The bourgeois slept, lulled by poppies ripened by material wealth.

But the young, those now demanding change, had no such memories and flexed newly enervated muscles, calling for liberalization. The empire's roots strained. In the recent 1869 May election, the emperor had lost an enormous number of votes.

"He's still won," Claude had said.

"Only just," Catherine responded.

Rumors ran that he was tired, gored by kidney stones, aged and all vigor gone. After nearly two decades, his quiet tyranny lacked a clear chain of command, his thirteen year old son too young to assume power.

"The Pantin field is covered in people," Claude said. "People gawking at another spectacle, like it's a department store. Everyone does as they please. Where is society, self-control?"

"You must find an answer before the questions become hysteria," Catherine said.

She was right. Ironically, as late as a year ago in an effort to rein in the young, the emperor had allowed the newspapers to critique the empire. And in the last two days they'd spared no punches. It wouldn't be long before they questioned the moral state of an empire that allowed such an atrocity. If there were another murder… If the investigation dragged on, questions would be raised about the efficiency of the police. And it was only a matter of time before Piétri made greater demands and leveled accusations at him. The emperor had already issued public statements outlining his distress about the case. A scapegoat was needed. It wasn't out of the question that the emperor would chastise Claude in person.

"My instinct tells me there's more to this than the obvious," he said. "Much more."

"It's beyond the petty tyrannies of Piétri and the prefecture. It's political. Although the emperor might not know it. Yet."

That night Claude slept lightly but woke heavily. It wasn't a nightmare, just an unsettling dream that demanded his return to consciousness to escape it. Two nightjars had sat in a tree, watching something. The light was silvery, a full moon. Though it wasn't a lucid dream he knew he was frustrated—there was something out of his view, something these birds could see but he was restrained in some way and couldn't look at it.

What did the dream mean? What had the vision nurtured in him? Nothing. Just that he was now awake and it was only half past three. He wouldn't go back to sleep. Catherine's breath was light and regular. He slipped out of bed and went to the kitchen. With a glass of milk he sat with his notebook, thinking.

> *Jean Kinck-a man with great business acumen.*
> *If I'd murdered my wife, what would I do next?*

This was pertinent, a better aperture through which to view.

> *Paris is an unfamiliar city. Despite being a metropolis, someone would notice him. If he moved to a hotel or an apartment, someone would speak with him. Someone would question who he was, why he was there. He's from Alsace, he must have an accent. He's not a laborer. He dresses well. Someone would ask where he came from?*
> *Clearly, he wouldn't return to Roubaix. Nor to Alsace. He would go where there were many strangers.*

> <u>*He would leave France.*</u>

Claude banged both palms against his forehead. How could he have not seen this? But success wasn't scored by plain deduction. It involved risk, jumping into the void.

He returned to the bedroom. Catherine had the lamp burning and an open portmanteau on the bed.

"Brutal murderers such as these will try to flee," she said. "You should go to Le Havre."

"I've reached the same conclusion."

The horror of these murders had engaged her. Across the room, he smiled at her, then turned his attention to the suitcase.

"Antoine," she said.

He looked up. The warmth had returned to her eyes.

"Earlier this evening… I was churlish."

"We will find our land," he said. "Just not now."

"Be gone with you. There's work to be done."

He went to her and kissed her lips ever so softly. He would leave Paris first thing. He'd not even tell the prefecture. He needed none of their interference. As Catherine packed his case he felt a certainty, as he'd always done. She too believed in the importance of his work. She shared his desire to mine the truth. Having to choose between finding a piece of land and the answer to these murders gave her no qualms.

CHAPTER TEN

Within days of moving into the house, Hortense had planted a small herb garden at her back door in a patch of all-day sun. She had furniture brought from her parents' house. Of the upstairs rooms she furnished only their bedroom, one of the smaller rooms at the back of the house. She had seven more months to furnish a nursery but she was sure Jean would agree to the child sleeping in their room.

Each day at midday she walked to his office with his lunch, which allowed him to continue working. She would carry soup, bread and cheese, cold meats, simple fare. But she quickly noted it was best she took nothing warm as he was often distracted, barely saying hello to her and not eating until later. If she took cold things, he could nibble at them all afternoon.

And in the evening he'd return home, sometimes bringing men with him for another meeting. She fed whoever came, delighting in the company, pleased to help in any way. She could follow little of the discussions as work stretched into the late evening, simply understood that Jean met with the men at home so he could be with her even if they were unable to talk. And the men were all appreciative of anything she did, pleased not to stand on formality, pleased by the warmth of her kitchen and the simple food she cooked for them.

Unlike her father Jean moved constantly, always thinking, always reading and planning. He was up before the birds and awake with the owls. His industrious nature made her proud. And he had good ideas, like the one he proposed to work colleague, Monsieur Viller, who sat at her kitchen table one night with Jean while she prepared the meal.

"You're not thinking clearly of what we should do to maximize profit," Jean was saying.

"Make fabric?"

"I have no eye for fine fabric and the fickle trends of Parisian fashion could ruin a business overnight—"

"If you want another type of business, go to another area. Tariffs will soon be dropped, clearing greater trade with Britain—"

"I want to produce something more universal."

Hortense's father had worked with fabric all his life and the designs of the big houses did change with each season. Not that she would ever be as bold as to agree with Monsieur Viller.

"If there's one thing the fabric industry needs," Jean said, "it's the quick and efficient repair of its machines. If a machine isn't working, the mill loses money."

Monsieur Viller was silent. She moved the gravy over the flame and stirred.

"But people bring machine bits into the area from other places," Viller said. "The machines aren't broken for long."

"A day is too long. Even a couple of hours. If I were to make these parts locally, all that time to order and transport them—sometimes weeks, even months—would be unnecessary."

His colleague said nothing.

"If I could do this, I would… treble my business. At least."

Hortense glanced at Viller's face.

"And if there are changes in fashion, there will still be cloth. I'll be immune."

"Jean Kinck," he said, "you're as cunning as a fox."

Jean was right. If he repaired the mill machines, they were exempt from the whim of fashion. No change would harm them.

CHAPTER ELEVEN

Travelling incognito, Claude was content to walk. To take a cab would alert someone of his presence in Le Havre and first he wanted to mingle in the markets and cafes, see and hear what he could hear and see. He left his portmanteau at the station.

It had been many years since he'd travelled to Le Havre and at first glance he was unsure of the direction he should take towards the centre and asked a porter. He pointed to the north-west. He thanked the man and declined any further help, sure he'd soon recognise a landmark and his sense of direction wouldn't fail.

Le Havre was a watery city, run through with canals and docks. An endless stream of men, women and children came and left, but, moreover, trade, that golden item of the Second Empire, flowed through the port. And the city had changed considerably, wide boulevards replaced the warren of tight streets, gas streetlamps stood at attention waiting the evening and the air smelt sweet, the effluent drawn away by a buried sewer. All the modern convenience of Paris but the network of water, canals cordoned off with high walls, reduced the street traffic and noise, a quotient of Venetian hush. But as he walked, the landmark he'd been so sure he'd orientate himself around, didn't appear. He would walk a little more and if nothing became apparent he would bury his pride and ask.

Along the canal, a whistle sounded, high and repeated blows, its tone standard issue for the French police force. Some two hundred metres ahead of him, a young man had pulled away from a police officer and was running along the canal's footpath in his direction. The police officer and another man pursued but already had some distance to make up. Claude could probably block the young man but he was moving at a pace. The officer continued to blow the whistle. Claude squared himself to the young man, still some metres away. But the young man stopped, looked over his shoulder to the pursuant police officer. In an instant, he raised his hands to the wall and like a cat vaulted, standing erect and perfectly balanced on top. Claude started to move towards him but in the same instant the young man's knees bent and he jumped, up and out into the air, then descending below the line of the high sandstone wall.

Claude stopped. For some moments there was nothing. The policeman had stopped the whistle. Then a thundering splash rang out. Claude moved to the wall, raised his hands and hauled himself up, his toes pressing in to the base for some added support. There was nothing, no sign of the young man, just eddies in the dark water. Claude stayed so suspended. He looked along the wall. The police officer and the other man were also hauled up looking over the wall. The seconds passed, ten, fifteen, it must have been twenty and there was no sign in the water. Claude looked towards the sea, in the direction of what little current there would be. Could he have got under something? The retaining wall descended into the water. Then he burst the surface, torpedoed by some great force. He collapsed back into the water but surfaced, whopping for air, his eyes large and feared. He wasn't a young man. He was only a boy.

A caulker on a nearby boat threw a floating device, landing it in the water beside the boy. Barking for air, the boy looked at it, pale and terrified, but made no effort to take it. And then he disappeared, slipping below the surface as if by volition.

The caulker, already stripped to the waist, plunged into the water, swam to where the boy had disappeared, and dived down. For a long time nothing on the surface changed. They've both drowned. But then the two broke the surface. The caulker held the boy tightly to his big chest with one arm, incapacitating him. Slowly they made their way to the ledge at the side of the canal.

The police officer and the man hurried to the base of the wall. Claude followed to the stair and by the time he'd reached the lower wall they'd dragged the boy from the water. His lips were blue, his fingernails blue. He just lay. Nothing happened. The police officer looked at Claude.

"I'm the Paris Chief of Police," he said.

The officer acquiesced, so driven by adrenalin he didn't question such a bizarre presence.

Claude looked at the boy. He was little more than a boy. He knelt at his side, lowered his face to the boy's. No sign of respiration. But as he pulled back, water shot from his mouth, as high as you like in the air, falling back to his face. Claude motioned to turn his body on its side. He felt his rib cage expand.

"Take off his coat! Loosen the collar."

The officer tore at the shirt, the buttons firing from the fabric. Together they raised him slightly and pulled back the jacket from his arms. The young man moaned and then vomited a good quantity of bilge over himself and the officer. But his lips, whilst still pale and dire, were no longer blue.

"He'll live," Claude said.

Still pulling away the coat, a leather wallet fell from the inside pocket. The officer picked it up and opened it.

"You said his name was Fisch," he said to the other man, who'd retreated, back against the wall.

"That's what he told me."

"It says here his name is Kinck. Gustave Kinck."

Claude snatched the identification document from the officer's hand. Despite being wet and some of the ink blurring, the name said Gustave Kinck. Claude looked again at the face. Now some life had returned, the dark auburn hair color, the age, fit all the descriptions he had of Gustave Kinck.

This was remarkable.

"I ain't got no involvement in this," the man at the wall said, so famous was the name.

Under heavy police guard, the boy was taken to the hospital. Claude and officer Ferrand and the man, Courson, went to the police prefecture. After he'd washed and tidied himself, Claude met with Ferrand.

"How did you know?" Ferrand said.

"What?"

"That he would be in Le Havre."

"I deduced the Kincks would attempt to leave France. Le Havre would be the most obvious port of departure."

"That's remarkable."

Police are often jaded but Ferrand seemed genuinely impressed. Claude had encountered this type of reaction before—especially outside Paris, where his reputation stretched out less fettered.

"Who is this Courson?"

"He's local. He claims to know nothing. Never travelled beyond the harbor. I tend to believe him."

Claude followed Ferrand through the building to a large office. Courson, who had a broad powerful physique and looked to be in his mid-twenties, sat at the table. He jumped up when they entered. Claude motioned him down and they sat opposite him. He worked as a tout at *La Femme Sans Tête,* one of the many cabarets around the harbor. He'd met Fisch, as the young man was calling himself and he continued to use, a few days ago. Claude took his notebook and pencil from his pocket and began to write.

"Says he's Prussian," Courson said. "His accent was so heavy I could hardly understand him."

"When exactly did you meet him?"

A strain appeared on Courson's face.

"I guess it was Tuesday. Midday. I went to have an ale at the cabaret. He came to speak with me."

"What about?"

"Just chat at first. He'd left Prussia in a hurry. Kept banging on that the French emperor was in trouble. He was convinced there's to be a war with France. But I knew what he wanted."

"What was that?"

"Same as everybody else in this city—to get away. But he'd left Prussia in such a hurry he'd left his papers behind. He asked if I knew someone to help him… get some new ones."

"And you helped him?"

"He was to leave tomorrow for America. He was so full of hope about it. Said if I could get the papers fast he'd pay for me to travel too."

"You organized the papers?"

"I knew a forger…."

Courson stopped himself, as if he'd just realized he was in a police station.

"We're not concerned about your involvement with forgers," Ferrand said. "Please continue."

"The best," Courson said. "Fisch showed he had money and the willingness to part with it. But he'd disappeared, the forger. I'd not been able to find him."

"I was doing my rounds of the cabarets," Ferrand said. "As you'd know, there're a lot of people in Le Havre without documents. Fisch couldn't produce any papers, despite Courson's urging. So I told him he'd have to come to the prefecture for verification. The three of us were walking along the canal, he broke free. Athletic little bastard. In one vault, he mounted the wall and jumped. No hesitation at all."

"I saw," Claude said.

"Straight into the water. I doubt he can swim. Quite a while before he came up."

"Yes. Yes," Claude said. "Was he travelling with anyone else?"

Courson thought for some moments. "No. He couldn't have been."

"Why's that?"

"Since we met, I've been with him all the time."

Courson lowered his face into his hands. These illusions society held to the nature of these couplings were never close to the truth. Claude felt no judgment. He wanted only to arrive at the truth. Find the father before he fled.

"Even at night?"

Courson remained fixed.

"You stayed at his hotel?" Claude said.

"Yes." Courson lowered his hands. "Yes."

"You've done nothing wrong," Claude said. "Nothing will be said. Take me there."

In silence, Claude and Ferrand followed Courson through the maze of streets. The hotel was mid-range but even so the price was beyond a young boy. But Jean Kinck was a wealthy man and perhaps he'd paid for it. The hotelier stood in the doorway while they searched the room. Courson made to remove some of his clothes but Claude demanded he leave everything as it was. There was nothing, just a few items of clothing. No documents. Not a whisper of Jean Kinck.

"How long has he had the room?" Claude said.

"He's been staying since the…" The hotelier checked his memory. "Arrived on the Monday evening, the twentieth."

"Did he have contact with anyone else?"

"No. Not that I know of."

There was only one bed in the room.

Downstairs in the hotel office, Claude checked the hotel register. No one else had arrived that evening. No single males under any name. He described what he knew of Jean Kinck's appearance and the hotelier shook his head.

Outside the hotel, he checked Ferrand had Courson's details and allowed him to leave. At the prefecture, they were met by an officer who'd returned from the hospital. Gustave was breathing well but had not said a word.

"Once he was stripped," the officer said. "We found some other documents."

"Documents?"

"Strapped to his body."

In another office, a small desk was covered in books, weighty tomes placed in an even grid pattern. With great care the officer stacked them to the side, revealing sheets of blotting paper. He peeled back the top sheets. The drenched documents were too delicate to touch. Some of the ink had run, but they were unmistakable.

Here were the legal documents of Jean Kinck's life. A bill of sale of a house in Roubaix, valued at 8000 francs. A mortgage deed, births certificates for Jean Kinck, his wife and children, a gold watch, and some 200 francs.

With a sense of pride Claude walked the bleached corridors of the hospital, his shoes squeaking on the tiled floor. The sunlight poured in through columns of sashed windows, some open to the afternoon's air. He was under way to solving this mystery before Piétri or the newspapers had time to make any complaint.

He entered Gustave's room, his step heavy across the floor. A bed was situated on one wall. Directly opposite was a small window under which an officer sat guarding both the boy and the unbarred window lest he make an escape or another attempt on his life. Claude motioned for the guard to leave the room.

The boy lay utterly still, making no acknowledgement that someone had entered the room. His head was partly covered by the white quilt drawn to the bridge of his nose. Claude inspected him at a closer range. He recognized the bold forehead and the wave of dark hair in the photograph found at the murder site. Two large eyes, wide with fear, stared unblinking, perhaps unfocused. Claude too hadn't blinked.

"Gustave," he said, softly but forcefully.

Under the bed covers, the boy's limbs appeared stiff, held rigid. Claude had witnessed this type of response to a traumatic event many a time. The stillness would last a day or so then descend into repetitions of certain movements.

He leaned closer, his shadow now over the planes of the boy's face. Still no response. His eyes were dark, so dark they appeared to have no differentiation between the pupil and the iris. A crow's eye. His lips were parted. Claude watched, waiting for his inhalation. None came. Had he stopped breathing?

"Gustave?"

Still no response. Claude moved a little closer.

His eyes flicked to Claude.

He bit the air with a percussive tshhh.

Claude held himself still, resisted the urge to jump back. This movement, no matter how small, was a threat, a warning. The eyes that glared at him were cold, the darkness profound. Claude, knowing he would never get the upper hand if he showed fear, slowly moved back from the boy whose eyes remained fixed on him in some passive form of intimidation.

Claude didn't have time to wait. He needed to locate Jean Kinck. Immediately. The boy, in this condition, wasn't going to provide him with any information no matter what question he asked. He was alive and safe from self-harm.

Outside the room he asked a medical officer when he would be fit to travel.

"There's no water damage to his lungs," the doctor said. "Tomorrow morning, I suspect."

"I'll return at eleven to collect him."

He knew how to shock the boy to speech.

CHAPTER TWELVE

The production of bespoke screws and brushes for the Roubaix mills grew Jean's business at a pace he'd failed to anticipate. Within two months his turnover had quadrupled, orders coming from all over the district. When he couldn't produce an item quicker than it could be ordered from somewhere else, he'd say so.

"Even if I can't make what they want, next time they'll come to me," he told Hortense. "They'll trust me. In the long run, that's worth much more."

But the expansion demanded long hours, each day stretching into the night. And as Jean's business swelled so did Hortense's belly. By early July, just after her twenty-sixth birthday, a great listlessness came over her with the summer heat, and she passed her days at her parents' house. She hadn't wanted to go there. Despite her size and breathlessness there were none of her quotidian tasks she couldn't complete though they might take more time and effort. But Jean was busy and he argued as only he could that it was foolish to risk being on her own when her time came. But for over two weeks nothing had happened save exhausting false contractions.

"If this baby doesn't arrive tomorrow," she said to her mother, "I'm returning home."

Her mother glared at her. "The contractions are stronger. And they come more often."

"I'll never have this child. The doctor says it will be next week."

She felt she'd be pregnant for the rest of her life.

"We should send for Jean," her mother said. "It will be tonight,"

By mid-afternoon the contractions were regular and stronger. Once her waters broke, this rush of water that caused fear and exhilaration, they sent word to Jean—but by eight in the evening when the midwife arrived there was no sign of him. The contractions came in waves of pain that came and went and then just came. Jean was by her side. Then he wasn't, then he was. Her mother was there. The midwife was there. The moon at the window fled and sunlight poured into the room with such intensity her mother drew the drapes.

"Her womb is in spasm," she heard the midwife say.

Pain and exhaustion took her over. She felt her shoulders held down. Someone mopped her brow with a cool cloth. Her gown stuck to her. She was numbed by pain.

"You must try," she heard the midwife cry, crouched between her legs. "Push with all your strength."

"I have none left."

"You must."

She bore down. At least that's what she thought. Whether her body obeyed her command she had no idea. But she'd never felt it before, this giving way, as if she'd been disemboweled and yet somehow born. She heard a sigh from the midwife. She heard a mewing cry.

"It's a boy."

She felt his weight on her belly, felt his warmth, felt his first flickering movements. With what energy she had, she raised her hand to the baby, felt his hand and fingers. Her son was whole and his cries ever so soft but sure. The midwife raised the child for her to see—

"His forehead. His cheekbone."

They both bore a mark, raised and an angry red.

Her mother placed her cool hand on Hortense's forehead.

"He was in the wrong position," the midwife said. "His face was pushed down onto your bones."

Hortense looked at his face, grazed as if he'd slid along a rough path.

"With the application of some olive oil," the midwife said, "in a few days there'll be nothing."

"Are you sure?"

"Quite sure."

The baby was cleaned, swaddled in a light blanket, and placed on her breast. The small lips opened, puckered, drew back. The midwife took Hortense's nipple between her fingers, roused it, and guided the tiny mouth forward. How sensual the sensation, though she'd been told there wouldn't be milk for a few days.

Jean stood in the room's doorway.

"Come," she said. But he was frightened. "Please, come and see your son."

Slowly he approached the bed. But even then he wouldn't avert his eyes from hers to the child held content in the crook of her arm.

"Are you all right?"

"I'm fine. Tired but everything's all right. He's a fine little boy."

He glanced at the child and gasped.

"What's wrong with his face?"

"It will heal."

"Are you all right?"

"Jean…" She did her best to laugh but even this sounded exhausted. "It was hard work but I'm very much all right. Just look at him!"

Jean's contracted face relaxed, and now he looked at the baby and smiled.

"He's too precious. Too fragile."

"What shall we name him?"

"I don't know…"

"Would you like to call him Jean?"

"He should grow with his own name."

"What name would you like?"

Jean was quiet for some moments. In all the time of the pregnancy they'd not discussed names.

"Gustave," he said.

She considered the name, studied the child.

"Gustave… yes. I like it. Gustave Louis Joseph."

"I like that too. After your father."

She looked at him and smiled with a full heart. He knelt next to the bed, for the first time caressing the little battered face with the tip of is index finger.

"Such a hard start to life," Jean said.

"The hard part is done. His life will be blessed."

"I thought I was going to lose you."

"You've not lost me," she said. "You've gained a son. Now you have the two of us to worry about."

He leant forward and kissed her mouth, his lips cold from fear, then kissed Gustave's forehead and looked at him with an intensity that took her breath away. He brushed the fine tuffs of hair covering Gustave's head. It was as if she'd disappeared. Poor Jean had been so scared. He was a gentle man and he would help their son become a gentle man too.

CHAPTER THIRTEEN

Claude looked from the train carriage window as it ground into the Gare Saint-Lazare. He'd sent directives to the prefecture that he was bringing Gustave Kinck to Paris with an order that the transfer be kept top secret. But evidently this directive hadn't been followed or had been leaked to the press. Half of Paris grappled for a vantage to view this spectacle, a living specimen more enticing than those at the morgue.

He felt a wave of anger quickly replaced by a wave of panic. How could they ensure Gustave's safety? If he was taken into the crowd, they might tear him limb from limb.

Claude went back to the first class carriage, whose blinds had been pulled down. The boy sat still, his head slumped forward till his chin touched his chest. At that moment, he looked utterly innocent. Though he'd reached puberty, he appeared to be poised on the cusp. His arms and chest bespoke great strength but his face bore only the first marks of hair and was held in an expression of childish fear.

Claude made his way to the senior officer.

"We weren't prepared for this mob," he said. "You'll have to remain here with him. Possibly we'll have to go to another station to disembark."

Now that the train was stopped, the crowd began to roar.

Claude made his way towards the rear carriages, and then got off with the second class passengers. A row of police had moved in to cordon off the area around the front carriage. Porters swarmed over the platform and escorted passengers and their luggage, even those with lower class tickets, away from the train. At least there was some overture to organization. People close to the carriage jumped high in the air to catch a glimpse, but nothing could be seen.

A group of three officers came up to Claude.

"What the devil is all this?" he said.

"We don't know how this became public,' one of them said. "The carriage waiting to take him to Mazas Prison is through that door over there." He pointed towards the rue de Rome. Claude looked back to the train and again to the door, a distance of a hundred meters. It would take time to move the train to another station and the crowds would move unimpeded through Haussmann's broad boulevards.

This was it, the crowd again a result of lax security he would interrogate Piétri about. He told the officer to create a path to the door and have other men form a ring around Gustave. Amongst the melee he caught sight of Desbarolles headed his way, smiling.

"How the hell did you know this was happening?" Claude said.

"My maid had it on good authority from the market—"

"Your maid! It was meant to be a bloody secret."

"I decided to see for myself. It's quite a turnout."

Even the maids of Paris knew the police's machinations. These notions of equality and liberty and fraternity had run too far.

"How did you know to travel to Le Havre?" Desbarolles said. "I was impressed."

Clearly the maids reported even this.

"To anyone else I would simply say it was the result of clean lines of deduction. I built an image of Gustave and Jean Kinck. If they were to avoid detection, they would leave France."

"And to me," Desbarolles said. "What would you say?"

"I would say something only a man like you would countenance." Claude stepped closer. "It was part deduction but moreover a leap of faith. A gamble."

Desbarolles nodded.

"Your assertions at the grave were accurate," Claude said. "How did you know those things?"

Desbarolles smiled. "Deduction."

Claude returned his smile. More and more he liked this man's wry humor. Although their motivations were diffuse, their method of analysis coupled with verve was the same. They understood one another.

"Let's see if you can deduce again," he said. "Gustave won't be taken directly to Mazas Prison. If you want, come with me to the Paris Morgue."

Desbarolles raised his eyebrows slightly and nodded.

The murmurs of the crowd fell as if they'd caught Claude's secret. A contingent of police gathered around the carriage door. Gustave was led to the platform, handcuffed, his head covered with a scarf like a Bedouin tribesman, a small slit for his eyes. Mouths swung agape, eyes trained on the prisoner without blinking as two officers held him by his elbows and forearms. Claude could hear the swallows in the station's ceiling. Thus surrounded, he looked trifling to Claude, just a boy.

The police encapsulated him, linked their arms together, and other police moved ahead to part the crowds. The party made their way unimpeded, the crowd stunned into near silence as the entourage passed onto the street and into a heavy metal van drawn by four powerful horses. The carriage moved off towards Boulevard Haussmann, a mob pursuing it. Claude and Desbarolles headed for the Paris Morgue.

"This case has piqued your interest," Claude said.

Desbarolles turned in the cab to observe him.

"No more than many others."

A few years ago Desbarolles had published in a journal of criminology an article on the emerging discipline of forensics. Claude held an open mind to all things but felt the article impetuous, published without enough rigor to support the theory in the storm of criticism it evoked.

"And your work?" Claude said.

"I still read palms, if that's what you're referring to."

Claude felt a sting. He'd not meant this. Desbarolles's book, *Les mystères de la main,* had been well received and Claude knew he worked on a new compendium, *Révélations completes.* But to support himself, Desbarolles read the palms of bourgeois women at twenty francs a session.

"And what do their hands tell you?"

"That the bourgeoisies are bored and have too much money."

They arrived at the morgue ahead of the police entourage. A small crowd, held at bay by police, still called for the morgue to be reopened, unaware of what was about to transpire.

The solid police carriage wasn't, as Claude had feared, followed by a mob. Gustave emerged, slowly straightening his body to his full height, still with his head covered and his hands cuffed behind his back. He was hurried into the building, his shoulders raised high and pinched together.

His handcuffs were removed but when the officer tried to remove the scarf from his head he raised his hands in protest.

Two officers took him to the long purification room at the back of the building, a private viewing area. The room was dark and cold with a sound of slow running water, a moist chill, and a sour smell in the air. Gustave kept his head lowered.

The six bodies lay on the raised pallets along the length of the far wall.

"Please, lift your head," Claude said.

At first, it seemed the boy hadn't heard. Claude spoke again in a harsher tone. Gustave lifted his head little by little towards the bodies. He drew his breath quickly and audibly.

Claude felt his own breath catch in his throat. What could this boy be feeling, confronted by the slaughter? He steeled himself. This was the only path forward.

"Do you recognize them?" he said.

Gustave stood firm. He looked slowly along the line. He advanced a few small steps, scratched at his ear, the hand cupped into a fist, moving back to front. He shrugged his shoulders, then half turned around to face the waiting men.

"Yes, monsieur," he said. Then, pointing with his forefinger, "That's Emile, that's Henri, that's Alfred, that's Achille, and that's little Marie."

He looked at them without uncovering his head, so Claude couldn't see his face. But his voice was firm.

"And the woman?" Claude said.

His body shook. He nodded his head, as if this was all that was needed to affirm her identity.

Claude let him rest for a moment. He had to conjure a gamut of emotions— grief, pain, anguish, regret—allow them to surge, then send them crashing like a geyser and spew forth a complete confession. But Gustave looked again at the bodies and then back at Claude and the others. He shrugged his shoulders as if to ask, "What more do you want?"

Perhaps time would erode his control. His head, still covered, moved about the corpses, one to another, back again in various combinations.

"What do you know of the bodies?" Claude said.

No response.

"Do you know how they came to be murdered?"

No response.

Claude looked at Desbarolles. He glared at the boy then at Claude and shrugged his shoulders. Claude remembered his own mother's corpse, pale and lifeless but laid on soft silks in a coffin surrounded by the heady scent of flowers, every color of spring. How harsh this was, Gustave's mother bare, only her loins covered by a leather strap. What could he be feeling? What depth of emotion did he fight so valiantly to subdue?

Claude could stand no more. He ordered the boy to be led away from the bodies to a smaller office, where he was asked to formalize his identification of the bodies by signing the *proces-verbal*.

Desbarolles moved closer. Gustave sat in front of the transcript. He removed the scarf from his head. Gently, he blew some specks of dust and dried ink from the paper. His hand was large, considering his size. He picked up the pen, tested the nib on his thumbnail, leaving parallel dark lines along its ridges. The thumb was most unusual, stretching in length to the last knuckle of the forefinger. What would Desbarolles see in this hand?

"I never struck them," Gustave said.

Claude raised his hand to silence the others.

"It's true. I pushed them into the trench but I didn't strike any of them. I only held them."

"Then you had accomplices?" Claude said, moving to face him.

"Perhaps," he said without raising his head. "But you'll never find them."

He looked up at Claude and then at Desbarolles.

"I'm enough for you."

He picked up the pen and signed his name with a neat hand. He blotted his signature and placed the pen back on the stand. Claude looked at the signature:

Jean-Baptiste Troppmann.

"What are you doing? Why have you written this name? Who is this Troppmann?"

The boy, eyes cast down to his lap, said nothing.

"Are you not Gustave Kinck?" Nothing. "My God! Who are you?"

The boy gave no visible reaction. Claude knew he'd retreated—there was no point in questioning him in this room full of men watching them. He'd take him to the prison and continue the interrogation there.

Outside the morgue, a large crowd had gathered. Claude wasn't sure, but he thought he heard a man shout "Troppmann!". The ink of the signature was barely dry. The boy was brought into the daylight, his head no longer covered. The crowd roared. He stood rooted to the spot, squinting, brittle, and anxious. The officers cleared a path to the van, but the mass lunged forward, hands thrusting to touch him. Some hurled insults. His head twitched as it moved from side to side. The van drove away at a walking pace while the crowd banged on the side, causing the horses to lose their rhythm.

Desbarolles stood next to Claude.

"Congratulations," he said.

"On what?"

"You have your man."

"I'm not so sure," Claude said. "He's intimated others were involved—"

"It's in his hand. As I expected."

He faced Desbarolles.

"And what on earth was your expectation?"

He handed Claude a sealed envelope.

"Early this morning, before I knew you'd arrested him, I drew his hand. He has a murderer's thumb. It's the marker of a psyche prone to violent breakdowns. Such people might appear to be mild-mannered, even polite and courteous, but under pressure they'll lose all control. Under great pressure, they'll murder."

Claude looked at the drawing and shook his head.

"I have no opinion of such a thing. But this connection you draw between his hand and his behavior is far too tight."

"The loss of control may only manifest as crying in men or hysteria in women, not necessarily murder. But given other sets of circumstance, murder may well result."

"But to intimate our fates are completely sealed at birth—"

"Not our fates but our disposition."

"Experience shapes us, teaches us."

"Our experience gives us opportunities to act. Examine the boy's hand. You'll see I'm quite accurate. It's not motivation you should look at but disposition."

Desbarolles bid Claude good morning and walked away along the Quai de l'Archevêché towards the left bank.

Claude felt battered, by the assertions but more so by the events of the last few hours. The sure course he'd set himself had derailed.

For now, he wouldn't think of this. He needed to concentrate on this young man. Kinck, Troppmann—whoever the hell he was, he held the answers to what had occurred in the Pantin field.

CHAPTER FOURTEEN

Just as Hortense felt herself giving over to her first *petite mort*, Jean withdrew. She sighed heavily, the tension she'd teetered on subsiding. Jean's hips continued their rhythm, rubbing himself along her inner thighs to this unshared pleasure. She tried to separate her legs but Jean pressed them together. He shuddered, spilling the warm seed onto her inner-thigh and the under sheet. He lowered himself, rolled from her to his back.

"You shouldn't do that," she said though a woman shouldn't talk of such things. "It's a sin."

"None of us are without sin."

If she became pregnant again he feared he might lose her in the birth. She harbored no such fear. Gustave was her first, the subsequent ones would be easier. And Gustave slept and ate so easily and walked before she knew. She dropped a mixing bowl when he first uttered "maman". She felt none of the tiredness or terror of which others spoke. Having one child created nothing but a desire for more. Many more. She'd labored like a milkmaid to rouse Jean, but always he withdrew before he thought his seed was loosed in her. And now, awakened by her husband–her husband!— she couldn't lay her own desire to rest, was left with it, urgent and unspent.

"It's been two years since Gustave was born," she said, but he'd already fallen asleep.

Yet despite him, she suspected she was pregnant. It was seven weeks since her period and her breasts were tender and she felt nauseous most mornings. She welcomed these unpleasant signs. Jean, of course, hadn't noticed any change in her.

"How can that be?" he said, when she told him.

Why were his eyes filled with fear?

"I don't know."

"I was told if I… removed myself you wouldn't fall pregnant. A priest told me."

She took his hand and pressed it to her belly.

"Please don't worry—I'll be fine this time. I feel no concern at all."

And indeed, their second son, Emile Louis, was shed easily.

With this ease, with two children, Hortense began the happiest period of her married life, filled with hard work and frugality that yielded the sweetest pleasures. She ran the home with economy, diplomacy, and love. And now Jean had overcome his fear of loss, soon followed Henri, Achille, Alfred and Hector. They were all so different; some wouldn't eat, some cried all night, some at dawn, some spoke, some quiet, some naughty but they were all hers and lovely. They thrived as other children born of healthy women withered. That is, all but Hector who wasn't strong and lasted only a few months. The loss cut her, seared with pain but as if in some great answer, she was soon given little Marie. By the time Gustave had reached his sixteenth birthday they had six vital children. Gustave, Emile, Henri, Achille, Alfred, and Marie.

After all these years and children, Jean worked like a draught horse. It seemed to Hortense he labored without thinking, not for pleasure but for survival. He had purchased his fourth domestic property and banked over a hundred thousand francs.

"He's home!" the children would shout when he returned in the evening, tired from the long day.

"Hello, my little darlings," Jean said. "How are you all tonight?"

"I have a cut on my hand," Emile said.

"I won a race this afternoon," Achille said.

"Come," Hortense said from the kitchen. "Your father is tired, leave him for a little and tell him these things at dinner."

"I *am* tired," Jean said. "But I've worked all day to see you all."

The children glared at her. Jean took off his coat. She kissed his cheek, hung the coat in the hall cupboard, and returned to the kitchen. From the front parlor she could hear their loud voices, Jean's the loudest. In their presence he forgot all the business's worries.

On Gustave's sixteenth birthday in 1869, he started work amongst the mounds of ledgers and figures in his father's office. Perhaps she'd wanted something more for him. But it was a start in business and would give him training in the ways of that world. And she would miss him in the home. No matter what she asked him; to bring in her washing at the first sign of rain, to refill her bottle of cooking oil, to check the chickens for eggs, he put these tasks on his list of chores and each evening they were done.

"Emile," Gustave said, calling up the stair to him. "Come and I will show you how to chop the wood."

Gustave went back to the woodshed but when there was no sign of Emile he returned again to the base of the stair and called up to him.

"Perhaps he is too young to wield an axe," she said.

"He just has no concentration."

Perhaps that was so and Gustave had diagnosed Emilie's dreamy behavior. And although he was now tired, in the late evening he would still read to her. She enjoyed these florid tales, always stories of great adventure, people drawn far from their homes to resolve some crisis and return.

"It's best to stay amongst one's people," she would caution.

She would miss him now he would work, her perfect child.

One evening after the children were in bed, Jean and she sat at the table as they always did, Jean moving from the head to be closer to her.

"In two days' time," he said, "we'll all travel to Paris."

She looked at him and blinked, her mouth open.

"To *Paris*?"

"I've made an appointment. We're to have a photograph made."

He sat back in his chair and smiled. She had no idea what a photograph was, and even when Jean explained they would sit in front of a machine that would engrave their image she was no wiser. She didn't know which part frightened her most, travelling to Paris—which only made her think of revolution and heads sliced off by a machine—or the machine that would "take" her face.

"Like a painting," Jean said, "but it will look real."

"A painting?"

"The children have grown so quickly," he said. "I wager you can't even remember what Gustave looked like when he was Alfred's age."

But he was wrong. She could picture them all at any age. And this idea of a photograph seemed a folly for the rich. Why was Jean convinced this was for them?

"But to Paris… It's so far, Jean. It will cost so much money."

This got her a heavy sigh.

"The price is none of your concern. We'll leave on Wednesday. We'll be gone until Sunday."

Two days later they took the train to Paris. The children were excited and Jean helped keep them all controlled. Paris was so ripe with noise and scents Hortense felt overwhelmed—and here was Jean pointing out the innovations of the "new imperial Rome," the wide boulevards clogged with people and traffic, the serried apartments rising five floors above the ground with balconies that jutted out like petulant children's jaws.

"Do people live there?" she said.

"Of course."

"How would you sleep? How would you breathe?"

Jean described their hotel as very grand but she found the rooms not very clean, small, and noisy. Sounds came from the boulevard, from water running in pipes all around them, from other rooms. She could hear a woman laughing, something wicked in the tone.

The next morning they visited the photography studio of Charles Segoffin. They were shown to a large room with high ceilings and tall windows and white walls. Such a quantity of light poured in it was as if there was no room at all. The men were so brisk and brusque in positioning the family in front of a white sheet she felt they were a source of irritation. She and Jean were on chairs, Alfred and Marie on her knee, the other children standing around them. They were ordered to remain still and she marveled at the effect the photographer and his machine had on the children. They remained fixed, staring at the device in front of them that would somehow take from them their heads, their faces.

While the man worked on various aspects of the machine, Jean examined the other devices in the room.

"What is this for?"

He pointed to a device like a pair of glasses but connected at some small distance to a flat screen that faced it.

"That's a stereoscope. One views the photograph through it and it becomes dimensional, more like reality."

When Jean continued to look at the device, the man came and showed him how to use it. Jean gasped, removed it from his eyes and scowled.

"It's the emperor. He's sitting in the thing." He looked at the small screen and then again through the device. "He looks alive."

"It's a recent photograph."

Jean looked again into the device. "You can see his thumbs so clearly, as if he twiddles them. It's magic."

"It's not magic but it's expensive. There's no magic money can't buy."

Jean raised the device to his eyes again.

"Most impressive." He looked at the photographer. "Make our photograph like the emperor."

Some weeks later the photographs and the viewing device were delivered to the house. Jean came home from work. After he'd viewed the pictures he raised the device to her eyes. The glimpse she caught of herself was like a mirror. She pulled back but Jean assured her there was no sorcery and so she looked again. There she was, her hair in its usual roll, her gaze diffident. Jean and the children glared out at the photographer except for little Marie who looked at her brothers, confused by what was happening.

With great gusto, Jean showed all who came to the house the photographs and the device, all the while linking words like glamourous, abundance and beneficent to the emperor.

"His power wanes not. His empire is a march of miracles."

She could see no such thing in the device. She barely recognized Jean. These new machines, each with its own task and most of them showy and offering no more than bare hands could achieve. The machine was little more than unnecessary. She had no idea how much it cost but people seemed to know of its worth and were amazed.

Hortense understood that Jean sometimes stayed late at his office, only because he could use the uninterrupted time to achieve amounts of work that would otherwise take twice as long or more. But over the last month or a little more the frequency and lateness of these evenings increased to the point that he returned home after all the children were in bed more often than not. And if they were awake he dismissed them. No excuse was given, he would just wave a hand and they were gone.

What had changed? Many times she asked, only to have him dismiss her or change the subject to something banal. One evening the office boy stopped on his way home to tell her Jean was still at work. She set herself to repair a mound of the boys' socks in the front parlor. Finally, at ten o'clock, Jean arrived home.

At first she said nothing. Was it her place to question his work? But as they sat in the parlor engaged in trivial conversation, her fingers working a needle through the thick seam of a trouser leg, she stuck herself hard in the base of her thumb and spoke without thinking.

"You're very late this evening."

"What are you saying? I arrive home at this time most evenings."

"But in the last month, it's been a little later every night."

"It's business."

"And that… "

"What?"

"That manner of yours. You dismiss me. You dismiss the children."

"I'm tired."

"Yes. You're tired."

"What would you have me do?"

She stopped her work and looked up at him.

"What you've done all our life. What I do. I overcome my tiredness for the sake of the children."

"If you're tired, hire someone to help."

"I don't want a stranger in my house. I'm not the problem. I'm not the one ignoring the children."

"I don't ignore the children."

"That's right. You don't ignore them. Little Marie comes with a drawing and you tell her to go away. Henri needed a little help to add up some figures—"

"Be *quiet!*"

"And now you yell at me. The children move away from you before you yell at them. You weren't like this, just over a month ago. What's the matter?"

"I have thought to return to Alsace."

He said no more that evening, remaining seated at what was now his usual place, the other end of the table.

CHAPTER FIFTEEN

Claude made his way from the morgue to Mazas Prison, the large gallery on Boulevard Diderot.

He was both right and wrong.

The young man who rented a room at Rigny's hotel eight days before the murders, who bought the pickaxe and spade, who'd commandeered Bardot's cab with the woman and her children to the Pantin field wasn't Jean Kinck. Nor was it his son, Gustave Kinck.

Who was this young man, this Jean-Baptiste Troppmann? As he'd carried young Kinck's identity papers, he's *assumed* he was Gustave Kinck. After all, his features, age, and coloring were close to those described in the document. But how easily deductions ran awry if one step was faulty.

Had the young man signed his correct name in error? He was exhausted, disorientated. Had this stripped away all artifice? Had he meant to maintain he was Gustave Kinck? Christ only knew, but Claude would assume the boy was Jean-Baptiste Troppmann unless evidence to the contrary came to light.

He looked again at Desbarolles's sketch of the hand. Not only had he outlined the shape of the thumb, long like a finger, he'd detailed the palm's creases. The idea that character could be read with such precise detail from a hand as if it were a book was a contrivance. But then Claude remembered an incident from when he first moved to Paris to work as a clerk in a law firm.

His job amounted to little more than carrying boxes of files between the law office and the courts of the Palais de Justice. He was asked to attend a dinner to celebrate a young man, Pierre Lacénaire, beginning work at a renowned notary's office. Claude knew few people in Paris and leapt at the opportunity to make acquaintances.

Lacénaire had been involved in a duel in which he killed his opponent. Everybody at the dinner hailed him a hero, but Claude wrote in his notebook: *An odor of blood exhales from his pores. It intoxicates me far more than wine.* In the course of the evening, Claude's companions noticed a change in his demeanor.

"In spite of his smiling face and verbosity," Claude said, "I see no good."

"He's provided a good meal."

The others laughed.

"Behind the mask of a gentleman," Claude said, "lies the face of a wild beast. I've seen him as he is—an enemy to society."

"He's quite a handsome fellow."

"His features are handsome but their expression is horrible." All in earshot were listening. "If his head is deceptive, his hand, which I've examined, is not. That hand, with its thin, flat fingers enlarged at their extremities like the feet of reptiles, exhibits the cruelty of the individual. That man won't enter the notary's office next Monday." His audience rumbled in protest. "And I tell you, before long you'll hear much about him. He's killed and he'll kill again."

"I think we'd best be getting you another drink—"

"Or a cab."

The men laughed. Claude felt slapped and regretted what he'd said. He must learn to hold his tongue. He had no idea what he'd based this conclusion on, knew only that he felt it profoundly. Who was he, a lowly office clerk, to make such statements?

But come Monday, Lacénaire didn't enter the notary's office, and on Tuesday morning an attempted robbery was discovered. A few months later Lacénaire was arrested for the robbery and eventually thrown in jail, where the thugs in the Parisian prison served to school him in the subtleties of the art of crime. Having paid his debt to society, he emerged from the prison chrysalis to become the brutal assassin of rue Montorgueil.

Stories of Claude's perspicacity reached the head clerk of the Criminal Court of the Tribunal of the Seine—who offered employment, such intuition always in demand. And so Claude's life at the prefecture began, thanks to nothing more than an unschooled reaction to the shape of Lacénaire's hand.

And in the light of this memory—in this cab on this journey to interrogate this young man—who was he to judge the worth of Desbarolles's work?

A wall twelve meters high ran along Boulevard Diderot, its constancy marred only by the gawping-mouth archway and three-window eyes on the entrance. A dark plume rose from Mazas's long chimney. What did they burn day in, day out that gave off that constant deathly color? The authorities would have one believe the single- pallet cells, designed to isolate the prisoners, forced them to contemplation and confession. Claude knew better: the place was an incubator of crime.

Free of his constraints, Troppmann had crawled to the corner of the wooden pallet and curled himself into a tight ball, knees to his chin, both hands tucked into his armpits. He looked nothing more than a frightened boy. How could Claude reach him?

"Jean-Baptiste," Claude said. "Is there anything you need?"

He remained entwined in himself without acknowledging Claude's question.

"Is there someone you'd like me to contact?"

Again, nothing. Claude sighed heavily.

In this light, his face uncovered, the boy looked older than the sixteen years of Gustave Kinck's identity papers but not by much. Through his clothes, his arms were muscular, as were his thighs, drawn up so his chin rested on his knees. The ripe, solid power of a man. Yet his shoulders were narrow, unripe, almost those of a young girl. He'd barely begun to shave the light dusting from his face. He *was* only a boy, almost at war with his body.

He'd wedged his hands into his armpits, the pronounced muscle and sinew almost forming an external ligature. Best not ask him to show them.

What would entice him to talk? Who could he appeal to?

"Your family, perhaps," Claude said. "Where are they?"

No reaction.

"It's been quite a day," Claude said. "I'm tired. Exhausted. You must feel far worse."

Still no response.

"I'll leave you. They'll bring you food. Something warm in your stomach… It will make the night shorter. I'll come in the morning. We'll make a fresh start then."

Claude wanted to touch him. Might that begin the thaw? In front of Troppmann's eyes, Claude opened his hand to a flat palm and slowly lowered it to his shoulder. Felt his warmth, felt the muscle and underlying bone.

But still there was no response.

From the cell Claude marched to the prison governor's office, where he asked that Troppmann be transferred to a larger cell with two pallets.

"He may try to kill himself again. Dress a guard as a prisoner and have him share the cell."

A trusted man was given a name and a hastily-put-together crime of house theft and his subsequent arrest.

"You'll tell him the details," Claude said to the guard, who was ten years older than Troppmann but looked young. "Even if he appears not to listen, tell him your story and try to draw his out of him any way you can. Indulge him. I want to know everything."

Claude thought of Troppmann, scared beyond belief. A confession wasn't going to come easily. Claude focused on the guard's eyes.

"Use whatever's at your disposal."

The guard was quiet for a moment. "I've worked within the walls of Mazas for a decade," he said. "I've encountered all degree of perversion."

Claude nodded. "Whatever transpires won't be broadcast beyond the most discreet circle. You'll be rewarded."

He returned to the prefecture to catch up on correspondence he'd missed while in Le Havre. Having not eaten well for days, he dispatched a junior to a nearby restaurant. As much as his digestion would object, he would eat and work. He scanned the dossier of recent cases. How quickly these paper mountains accrued on his desk, in under forty-eight hours. Most of it was nothing, just acknowledgements requiring his signature but he still had to read them. He stood to accelerate the weak gaslight flame. Joseph Piétri appeared at the door. They observed one another. Not a word. Piétri stepped towards the desk.

"My faith was well founded," Piétri said.

"What can you possibly mean?"

"You've apprehended him. In record time."

"He panicked and gave himself away."

"Your modesty is appealing." Piétri paused, rocked on his heels. "Call it what you will. I can only suggest you expedite the path to trial."

"He's not yet confessed. And he's intimated he had accomplices. I need to find the father and the eldest son."

"Where does he say they are?"

"He's not spoken."

"If he's not spoken, how can you be so sure others are involved?"

"He's young. Very young. Docile. Gloomy. Weak. I find it hard to believe he did it all. And for what?"

"Profit."

"But he left more value than he took."

Piétri raised his right hand to his mouth. "This will calm the newspapers, the public. He can't kill again."

"Why is calm suddenly more important than truth?"

Piétri's dark eyes fixed Claude. "Since the emperor was routed in the May election, the… public turmoil has increased. The emperor needs calm. This incident has inflamed things."

"Calm resides in truth."

The aroma of roasted pig flooded the office. Piétri glared at the junior and the covered tray.

"I wouldn't suggest anything else. Expedite the truth." Piétri fixed Claude again. "I'll leave you to your work."

The damn suggestion. In the grand scale accuracy stood ahead of speed. Method. Process. Justice. It wasn't the fault of this Troppmann boy that the empire was near its knees. While he ate, he half-mindedly read and signed papers, fuming over Piétri's impertinence.

Before he returned to Catherine, he left Souvas a note.

First thing this morning, bring the shopkeeper, the hotelier Rigny, and the cab driver Bardot to Mazas Prison.

CHAPTER SIXTEEN

A restless night did nothing to salve Hortense's distress. She avoided speaking to Jean, had to steel herself even to look at him. She bustled the children through their morning but once Jean had left the house made her way to her parents in Tourcoing, pouring out her heart to her mother.

"I won't move," she said. "Papa must make him see."

Her mother looked at her from across the large work table of her kitchen.

"You can't make your father responsible—"

"Only he can put pressure on Jean's honor."

"Jean has provided you with everything—"

"I don't want everything. He must keep his promise to stay."

"All men need a dream to follow. It doesn't necessarily need to become real."

"All men?"

"All men."

"Then Papa, what's his dream?"

Her mother glared at her. After some moments, she shrugged one shoulder.

"You have some time. Jean's business will keep him in Roubaix. Replace this… dissatisfaction with satisfaction."

"What on earth do you mean?"

"Ohh…" Her mother stood and turned away from her to stoke the fire. "You can't be so ingénue. Don't talk to a man of what he's feeling. Open your eyes, Hortense. Inhale." Her mother crooked her face towards her. "These are the first days of spring. Everything is busy with satisfaction."

It was true, these days brought warmth. Scents missing since last summer drifted on the candescent breeze. Although Jean came later and later from work, Gustave would return early and report his father was very busy.

"There's something new afoot," he said.

She felt herself tighten. Alsace. "What would that be?"

"He's bought a property, next door to the factory."

She felt a ray of hope. "Is he expanding?"

"I'm not sure what it involves."

Despite wearing his woolen suit, he picked up her empty wood basket and went to the woodshed. She had an ally, a set of eyes in Jean's office.

Hortense would have the children in bed and share a meal with Jean, nudging the conversation away from Alsace to anything she could stretch—what the children had done that day, whether he'd enjoyed the meal, even such mundane topics as what clothes she'd managed to repair.

And later, upstairs in the dark, she enticed him as she'd done years before. At first he hesitated and she allowed the hesitation. If she knew one sure thing about her husband, control was paramount. But after some weeks of this pleasure, when he moved again to withdraw himself she lowered her hand, held him, and guided him back into her. His face remained impervious. What did he make of such boldness? She flinched her hips. He winced, sucked in his breath. And then he moved his hips and thrust forward, slowly at first, gaining pleasure and assurance with each second.

In this manner, spring unfurled. But during this confluence, one evening Jean returned home after midnight.

Without any words of approval or disapproval, she took his coat and hat, hung them, and motioned him to the parlor.

"There's something I must tell you," she said.

Jean looked at her, his face a mix of fatigue and confusion.

"Hortense, I'm tired. Couldn't this wait?"

"What I have to say has to be said."

She poured two cognacs and sat. He sighed but sank into an armchair.

"I am pregnant."

Jean eyes bulged. He lowered his glass from his mouth without taking a sip.

"Are you sure?"

"Quite."

Without removing his large eyes from her, he sipped his cognac.

"Does it displease you?"

"Displease me…?" He paused. "You're over forty. I thought… because you allowed me… that this wasn't possible."

"Marie was only born two years ago and I've felt no great change. The doctor is unconcerned."

Jean retreated into his thoughts. What could she say? Admit to him she'd become pregnant to distract him?

"It's just…" He hesitated. "I thought you knew."

"Knew what?"

"My business… It's not as certain as it was."

She'd never thought Jean would link a baby to his business.

"What do you mean?" she said.

"France is not as it was. There are wars. The civil war in America, even though it's over, there are still problems with the supply of cotton. Roubaix hasn't yet recovered."

"But you said you were immune."

She recalled the night at her kitchen hearth when he laid out his plan to Monsieur Viller.

"That was over fifteen years ago. The political situation has changed. To the whims of fashion, perhaps, but not to downturns in production."

"You're saying we can't afford another child."

He looked down into his lap, retreated to his own thoughts, his countenance weighed. Had she miscalculated? She'd not thought to add more stress to his situation. She'd assumed… but why would she not assume they could afford another child when she hadn't been told to economize?

But then he raised his face to hers, the light in his eyes returned.

"Then it will be an indulgence," he said. For the first time, he smiled. "A sweet indulgence."

He came to her, took her hand and kissed her. She relaxed. He felt as she did and there would be no concern.

"It will be sweet," she said. "Like caramel."

"The May election will see, the emperor put right, France restored." He kissed her softly. "I will just have to make more money. I have faith in the empire, moreover in the emperor. He will provide for this child."

And with this news he did indeed begin to work with the vigor of youth. And with the hard work came calm, long glimpses of his old self. His talk of Alsace receded – to the point Hortense began to agree with her father. Jean had experienced a period of nostalgia and homesickness that started to subside once it was voiced. Despite his financial concerns, perhaps even the joy-filled reality of another child had replaced his need to dream. But although she'd defeated one foe, she'd released another.

CHAPTER SEVENTEEN

When Claude returned to Mazas in the morning, the spy-prisoner guard was removed from the cell—but despite all his efforts Troppmann hadn't uttered a sound. The whole night he'd sat on his bed in the corner, his knees pulled to his chin.

"I told him the stories we planned. Prattled on like a madman. I asked him questions, friendly, you know. He didn't even seem to hear me."

"There was no reaction at all?"

"Only to one thing… I touched his thigh, near his crotch. He glared at me." The guard looked down at his feet and then back at Claude. "But he didn't tell me to take it away."

Claude wished the guard had pressed for a definite reaction. Troppmann had used unnatural coupling with Courson in Le Havre to get the papers he needed. But if it was part of Troppmann's makeup, he wanted to know. But when quizzed further, the guard blushed and said he'd nothing more to report.

Claude and Souvas escorted the shopkeeper, the hotelier, and the cab driver to the cell. The guard was just about to open the cell door when Claude decided on another course of action. He opened the small viewing aperture. Troppmann lay on the pallet, staring at the ceiling, unaware he was being observed.

After they all watched a few minutes Souvas took the three men away to the office for written identification statements. Troppmann had bought the implements, been at the hotel and caught the cab.

When Claude entered the cell, Troppmann made no movement despite the noise the heavy door made.

"Are you feeling rested?"

Nothing. Not even his eyes flinched. His breathing remained regular.

"I've a few questions. If you answer them I'll leave you in peace."

His silence irritated Claude, but he kept his tone ingratiating.

"Where is your family?"

Troppmann's hands lay at his side, palms facing the ceiling. He answered none of Claude's questions: how he'd become involved in the murders, why he had Gustave's papers, the Kinck family's papers, the whereabouts of Gustave and Jean Kinck. Claude kept his voice even, inviting. What could he do? How could he unlock this mystery unless they found Jean or Gustave, preferably both?

He asked more questions. He asked the same questions different ways.

Silence.

He took Desbarolles's sketch from his pocket. Remarkable. Desbarolles had encapsulated the muscular architecture, the lack of fat, the tendons and sinew laid bare. And the proportion, the size of the large wrist to the larger hand and the full breadth of the span from thumb to little finger, these he'd captured as if Troppmann had sat for him. But most startling was the thumb. Desbarolles had drawn it almost as a finger, long and slender, its tip reaching up past the second knuckle of the first finger. Claude had never seen a hand like it, containing elements of great power—and yet the thumb, so fine and slender, embodied an odd delicacy. He shook his head. What could this mean?

Troppmann was a young man, and generally speaking, young men had families.

"Is there someone we should contact? Where is your family?"

No response. Claude, having reached the end of his patience for the moment, was about to tap the door for the guard when the boy surprised him.

"I was born on October fifth, 1849, to Joseph and Françoise Troppmann, in Brunstatt. It's a small town, Haut-Rhin, Alsace."

His voice was automatic, without emotion. His Alsatian accent was strong but he spoke with surety.

"Murdering Madame Kinck and the children was Jean and Gustave's idea."

He sat, spun his legs from the pallet to the floor, facing Claude. Claude moved the chair and sat opposite him with his notebook open.

"Jean didn't want to live with his wife any longer. She was a greedy woman. He believed she was having an affair with a rich industrialist in Roubaix. He accused her, said none of the children were his, except for Gustave."

"But the children were born over a long period, over sixteen years."

Troppmann looked at the floor.

"He took measures yet she continued to conceive."

The remark caught Claude off guard. For Jean Kinck to tell such a personal detail to a young man, they were intimate.

"But why would Gustave kill his mother?" Claude said. "That's hard to understand."

Troppmann looked at Claude, his face open. Claude was finding it hard to believe this face.

"He was disgusted by her behavior. His brothers and sister weren't truly his. He was angry."

Troppmann swiveled back towards the wall, pulling his knees in tighter to his chest, protecting himself.

"And what was your role?"

"I only helped. I pushed them into the graves but I didn't strike them. Jean and Gustave dealt all the blows."

He said this so coldly. Could a husband and son act in such a manner? Could the wife and mother's betrayal actually drive them to murder not just her but her children? This was a story.

"It was Gustave," Troppmann said, "who bought the spade and the pickaxe from a man in Pantin."

He stared at Claude.

"We've interviewed the shopkeeper," Claude said. "He's identified you."

"He's mistaken. Gustave and I look quite similar. Even you were fooled. Gustave bought them."

Claude softened his eyes. At least the young man was talking.

"I've been a policeman long enough to know eyewitnesses are often mistaken, he said. "Now please tell me, where are Jean and Gustave?"

"They've left France. The evening of the murders, they left Pantin for Le Havre and took a boat to America. It was all planned."

Claude scribbled a note.

"Don't bother checking the records," Troppmann said. "They're under false names. False papers. You'll never find them. As I said, it was all planned."

"Yes, I see it was well planned. Where were you to meet?"

"In New York City. We were to travel to New Orleans to make our fortunes. One can speak French there."

"And yet you had all the family's papers?"

"Jean gave them to me. He thought it was safer if he travelled without them."

Something had loosened Troppmann's tongue. But it was now too loose—Claude doubted its veracity. The confession was cold, no sense of regret or empathy. Taking him outside the direct question and answer game, Claude allowed silence. But Troppmann met it head on, unruffled by the unfilled void between them that stretched on and on.

Claude broke first.

"We found blood-stained clothes and a rope at Rigny's hotel."

"They were Kinck's. After the murders we returned there. Kinck had to change before they left for Le Havre."

This corroborated Rigny's assertion he'd heard two people with heavy tread on the stair. But the shopkeeper had been quite sure that Troppmann had bought the pickaxe and spade.

"Why did you attempt suicide?"

"Death was preferable to jail." He gave Claude a hard look. "It was a cheap stunt to put that guard to work on me last night."

Claude felt himself color as if he'd been unmasked by some young coquette. And Troppmann wasn't done.

"I'd have thought the Chief of Police would have more sophistication."

"Perhaps it was base," Claude said, "but surely you understand I must find Jean and Gustave."

"They're already in America. The murderers are in America."

He lowered his head between his knees as if this bleak confession had drained him of energy. Any further questions about their location were met with morose silence.

Claude closed his note book and left the cell. The newspapers would have a story. The emperor would be safe. This boy would be a challenge.

Walking through the maze of corridors and bolted doors and check points, back to the sunshine of the Mazas's courtyard, Claude felt annoyed with Troppmann. He'd blamed the bulk of the crime on people he declared to be out of reach—a cheap ploy.

There must be another answer. He would concentrate his efforts on the search for Gustave and Jean. Although disguised, there must be some record of their leaving Le Havre. Damn it, he'd send word to New York City, check the lists of arrivals. Piétri would object to the cost but this had to be established. He would send word to authorities in Alsace, to the small town of Brunstatt. He needed to know more of this Troppmann, where he'd come from, what he had and hadn't done, the realities of his life.

This was the only available path, playing into or out of Troppmann's hand.

CHAPTER EIGHTEEN

Jean was late. Gustave had returned home earlier and didn't know of any reason for the delay. In the lamplight she darned the endless holes in the boys' stockings, then at midnight decided to wait no more and go to bed. But as she climbed the stairs, Jean opened the front door. He looked up at her and started speaking but Hortense couldn't understand a blessed word. He normally spoke in a methodical manner, but this voice was vivacious, the strange words tumbling out.

"I can't understand a word you're saying," she said, raising her voice above his din.

He stopped and looked at her, then began to laugh, a boyish giggle.

"I'm sorry," he said. "I forgot myself—I was speaking my language."

"Where have you been? It's very late."

By now he'd taken off his hat and coat. She kissed his cheek, inhaling deeply but sensing only a trace of alcohol. He walked into the parlor, shaking his head at his folly. He poured two cognacs.

"I met someone. He's in Roubaix installing a machine. It's his father's invention. Imagine that." He turned to her, his eyes wide with excitement. "He needed a part modified. He's a charming fellow. Enterprising. It's years since I've felt so engaged by one person." Jean stopped speaking. His eyes glazed over. "But I guess that shouldn't come as a surprise." He looked directly at her. "He's from Alsace."

"Alsace…"

The word fell from her like lead.

"He's coming for dinner," Jean said, smiling at her, the joyful intonation of his patois entering his French. "Tomorrow night. I want him to meet you all."

At a little after eight, Jean and the Alsatian arrived. Hortense was in the parlor with Gustave, having sent the other children upstairs. Jean entered the room and Gustave rose to greet his father, whose voice brimmed with pride introducing him to their guest. But when Gustave stepped aside, she gasped at what she saw. She couldn't help herself.

He was no more than a boy, a handful of months older than Gustave, not a man at all. He had the same chestnut brown hair, the high forehead. She felt a sense of disappointment, that this feature she so admired in Gustave might be common in the area of Alsace. His eyes set close together were dark, whereas Jean and Gustave's were both a beautiful blue. This disturbed her. He was of small frame and slope-shouldered. The first traces of soft chestnut down covered his face. He wore a worker's coat, the fabric thick and coarsely spun, and work boots.

He stood, fixed, near Jean.

"This is Monsieur Jean-Baptiste Troppmann," Jean said. "This is my wife."

He looked toward her, then around the room, then he flicked his eyes back at her—well, around her—his gaze confident yet haphazard.

A tumble of children came down the staircase. Jean exerted no control. Troppmann laughed with a childish glee that matched their innocent cries. He raised his hands high above his head and as if by magic they all fell silent. He scrutinized them as a group, long and hard, then each one in turn.

"This is Emile," he said, his voice flecked with Jean's accent only heavier and coarser. Troppmann extended his hand. For a moment Emile scrutinized the hand, confused with the formality of the gesture. Troppmann jolted his hand slightly in mid-air until Emile raised his, then Troppmann's hand swallowed Emile's completely.

"He's thirteen years old," Troppmann said, "and fond of reading books of adventure and romance."

Emile's face flushed but he burst out laughing.

Troppmann then looked about the group, deciding who next to set upon.

"This is Henri," he said. Without the slightest hesitation Henri reached out for Troppmann's hand. "He's ten years old and very, very lazy."

And so it went on—Achille, seven and serious, Alfred six and the most handsome of them all.

"But where's Marie?" Troppmann said. "Where is little Marie?"

He scanned the room while Marie raised her hand and giggled at his failure to notice her. Finally, when her exasperation grew too great, she ran to him and jumped into his arms as if he were a brother.

"There she is," he said, laughing as loudly as Marie. "The littlest and already the prettiest of them all."

Hortense looked at their faces. With these accurate descriptions he'd set each of their faces aglow. She caught a glimpse of her own face, perplexed and fearful, in the mirror above the chiffonier. She hardly recognized herself.

"Dinner is ready," she said. Food would bring the children back to her.

"But we've not had an aperitif," Jean said.

"It's later than usual," she said. "The children are hungry."

"Let's eat," Troppmann said, rubbing his hands together theatrically.

Throughout the meal, the children and Gustave competed to tell stories of great adventures. Normally Jean wouldn't tolerate the noise, but this evening? His eyes never left Troppmann or when they did he'd look at Hortense and raise his eyebrows and smiled.

Troppmann ate his soup with such a noise, dragging the spoon across the plate towards him. He gulped his wine as though it were ale.

Once they'd finished the meal, she asked Gustave to help get the younger children to bed. Amid hails of complaints, they left the table.

"Don't worry, my little friends," Troppmann said. "We'll meet again soon."

He smiled, showing teeth ragged and unkempt, and waved both his hands in the air beside his face. She climbed the stair behind them. Jean and Troppmann, left alone at the table, reverted to their patois.

"He's such an interesting man," Gustave said as the two of them closed the last of the doors on the children.

"Do you think so?"

"Why… Don't you like him?"

Gustave's eyes narrowed, searching for clarity. She inhaled deeply. What could she say? That she didn't like this young man because he wore working boots to her table?

"I've formed no opinion," she said. "But he's a boy, like you, not a man."

Gustave was in a hurry to grow and saw any older boy as someone to look up to. She sighed heavily as he bounded down the stair. She had no words, no sure feeling, just that she felt most disquieted by this young man's overpowering presence.

She returned to the dining room. Jean had moved from the head of the table and was sitting next to Troppmann.

"You're the image of an Alsatian," he said to Gustave, sitting opposite them.

Hortense shivered. Gustave was a handsome boy. He didn't look like the other boys of Roubaix. She looked from Gustave to Jean to Troppmann. There was a similarity between them, variations on a theme. With each of Troppmann's compliments, Gustave's confidence grew. And if he wasn't making Gustave's face light up, it was Jean's. He fidgeted under the table. What could he be doing? She peered to the side. His hands held a small section of rope, some forty centimetres long. Without attention, he moved the ends over and under one another, pulling them to a knot. Then he reversed it, flipped it back to a length and started on another configuration.

"A foreigner achieving such a level of success," Troppmann said, "must have annoyed the good people of Roubaix."

He smiled at Jean.

"I've led a lifetime of being overly friendly so I could succeed."

Troppmann said something in their patois. The two laughed. Gustave laughed too though Hortense doubted he understood.

"But your business," Troppmann said. "It must have suffered. These times are not good."

"The emperor will right things."

"Are you so sure? He's older now."

"He has vitality."

"And a thirteen year old son to succeed him."

A fear appeared on Jean's face. It lingered for some moments but then Jean released it.

"He still won the May election," Jean said.

"But his vote was severely reduced."

"The emperor will right things."

The evening continued, Jean and Gustave focused solely on Troppmann, Troppmann solely on them. Jean showed him the photograph and the viewing device. Troppmann barely glanced at the photographs. The device itself was enough to impress him. It wasn't that Hortense felt excluded, she simply wasn't there. She stood from the table. Even this didn't disrupt their conversation.

"It's late," she said. "I'm tired."

Jean and Gustave looked up at her. Jean smiled briefly. Troppmann's eyes remained fixed on the table.

She walked towards the stairs. The three laughed. She lay in bed listening to the noise, laughter, and competition to tell stories that came from the dining room for hours. Troppmann hadn't even thanked her for dinner.

She detested the young man. She detested the roughness of his clothes, his heavy manner. His accent—sharper than Jean's when they first met. He wore working boots to her table. The children were sponges and consumed anything different around them. Especially Gustave, who was at a vulnerable age.

And his hands were so common, large and cumbersome. His life would be far better spent in some rigorous hard labor for which he'd been built. And that fiddling with a rope. And what was it that Jean and he found to spend so much time talking of? He was only a boy. His life was so different from Jean's. What had they in common other than Alsace?

Her anger tumbled out the following day in front of her father.

"He's an actor. Like some skilled magician, pulling stories from his sleeves to entertain the children—"

"You're overheated," he said. "Come and sit for a while."

They sat in silence for some minutes. Blood pounded hard in her temples, but gradually her father's calm took hold of her.

"Can you imagine what it would be like to be a foreigner?" he said.

Her calm evaporated. She rose from the chair and reminded him of Jean's promise.

"I won't countenance living in another place."

"What do you think it's like for Jean?"

She hadn't thought of the situation from this angle.

"What do you think he discusses with this boy? All countrymen when they meet at some foreign crossroad talk of their origin, no matter how unfairly they may feel it's treated them. They discuss the weather in that region, they discuss a shop that sells local pastry and is situated near a post office, a chapel's bell. They search for mutual friends, families held in common. It's done out of remembrance, romantic illusions of things that might have been. Nostalgia. It's no wonder, my child, that Jean's bewitched."

She felt a twinge of guilt at how unwelcoming she'd been.

"Troppmann is a mirror for Jean," her father said. "Wasn't Jean about his age when he came here? Even though he has lived in Roubaix for over twenty years—twenty prosperous years— he must still feel himself in exile."

"But he's accepted here."

"If the Prussians invade Alsace, or if the Alsatians show any support for their captors, there would be problems for Jean and perhaps he would lose all his customers. His ability to earn…"

Over the years Jean had spent living in Roubaix, his accent had become diluted. Perhaps it was an attempt to blend in, perhaps it was unconscious.

"If what I've told you hasn't helped to calm your heart, there's only one other thing I can say. I've heard of the machine the young man is here to install. Once his work is finished, Troppmann will leave the area and your life."

She left her father with a lighter heart.

There was no long-term problem.

All would be resolved and be as it once was.

She must be generous. She would school herself to overlook everything she felt about this young man.

CHAPTER NINETEEN

After lunch, Claude stepped from his coach onto the Pantin field. The long drive had done nothing to settle his stomach, acid flaring into his mouth. After the frustrating interview with Troppmann, he'd taken refuge in a heavy *langue de boeuf* and was now suffering the consequences. But far more bilious was the sight confronting him.

Families arrived with picnic baskets, meals taken on the crime scene's soil somehow more succulent. A carousel of wooden ponies was largely unused. Untethered children ran around the perimeter of the grave enclosure. A tour group, mainly women sailing under bright parasols, stopped near him. They'd paid to be escorted through the site as others paid to be guided through Notre Dame.

"Just here," the guide said, 'it's believed the father ate the heart of the mother."

His words unfurled with wonder. He pointed to the ground. His followers gasped.

"Her heart was untouched," Claude said. "Who told you that?"

The entourage regarded this dissident voice with suspicion. The guide waved his blood-red cravat in the air and walked on, followed by his faithful.

"Read the autopsy report!" Claude yelled.

But none of the group heard—or cared. This spectacle surpassed Le Bon Marché and Folies Trévise.

A week had passed since the murders of Madame Kinck and her children. Despite extensive searches of Le Havre departure records, no trace of Jean and Gustave Kinck or anyone resembling them had been found. In their absence, people could say whatever they wished about Jean Kinck.

Claude sighed. Why had he come to the field? What had he hoped to find? Without advancing to the grave site, he turned back to his coach. But en route to the prefecture he stopped at a café where he ordered a chamomile tea to settle his stomach and read the newspapers.

In the days after Troppmann's arrest, the press had run stories on Hauguel, the Le Havre caulker who'd plucked Troppmann from the canal and certain death. They anointed Hauguel a quick-witted "national hero" who stood in perfect contrast to Troppmann, his body large and masculine where Troppmann's was sinewy and small. He'd risked his own life whereas Troppmann sought to end his. Hauguel had brought a criminal to justice whereas the highly paid police force had failed to protect its citizens.

It was the first whiff of Catherine's prediction. The Republican opposition would turn the brutal murders into another example of the emperor's failure to administer the country properly. Perhaps the emperor himself felt this gathering against him. In the last few days, the Empress Eugénie had travelled to inspect the site.

"Does she expect to find something I've missed?" Claude asked his wife.

"There's very little she's seen in the past, so I'd think not."

The empress, stirred by the Kinck family relatives' grief, adopted a niece of Jean Kinck. They were born on the same day of the year and in these passionate times that was link enough. The press lapped it up: noble empress and poor Alsatian girl.

Claude finished his tea. The adoption was a master stroke. The empress and the emperor were made again magnificent. Stories about the national hero Hauguel, the inefficient police force, the emperor's waning control would all disappear from the newspapers for a few days. But there were new stories: an offer of ten thousand francs for a photograph of Troppmann, rumors he'd commenced a hunger strike—ideas Claude hoped wouldn't fix in Troppmann's mind. Should he deny him access to newspapers?

When Claude alighted from the coach at the prefecture, Souvas raced to meet him.

"Where have you been?" Souvas's face was red, his breath short. "Another body's been found."

"Bodies are found every day," he said. "Why does this one excite you so?"

"At the Pantin field."

Claude's face blanched. "I was just there, nothing was—"

"The news just arrived. I'm going there now."

"Is it a copy murder?" Claude said.

"I've no idea."

The two hurried to a coach and urged the driver to go as fast as possible. Claude remained silent. It could be a copy crime, the field could become a dumping ground for corpses. The empire couldn't stand another family annihilated with such ferocity. Piétri would be livid. But how could Troppmann be involved? He'd been behind bars.

At the field, a crowd had massed around another site, some seventy meters from the first enclosure. The police had cordoned off a large area, much larger than the main site. Claude and Souvas pushed their way through. The stench was strong.

Claude raised his handkerchief to his nose and felt his stomach turn. The body lay in a shallow grave, in fact far shallower than the others. A man, wearing a gray suit with a plain knitted vest. The body lay prone on one side. The face was caked with dried blood, the hands tied behind his back. A large kitchen knife was embedded deep in his neck. An eye hung from its orb. The age was hard to ascertain.

Claude approached the people who'd found the body, a middle-aged woman and a young boy with a terrier.

"I was walking with my dog," the boy said. "She ran to smell something in the bushes. I called and called but she wouldn't come. Kept digging at something."

"I was out for a walk and heard him calling," the woman said. "I went to see what it was and smelt the most awful smell. Repulsive."

Claude was holding his handkerchief to his nose.

"What happened then?"

"I went closer. The dog was flinging dirt everywhere. I saw something, an eyeball. Just an eyeball. I fainted."

She'd received more of a thrill than she'd bargained for.

Souvas pointed to the stockings. They were the same as the other children. The knitted vest was a similar design to the oldest boy's. This was Gustave, he felt sure.

"When did the woman and children die?" said a doctor examining the body.

"A week ago."

"He's been dead at least three or four days before that."

"Christ almighty. How the hell did they miss this?"

"He fought, too. Hard." The doctor pointed to the side of his head, large patches of hair missing. "The cuts to the hands, the arms, that slash on his cheek–he defended himself."

Amongst the rotting leaves and the half-turned earth, the bound arms and hands lay stretched out from the body. The hand clutched something. Claude collapsed to his knees, peered at it. A clump of dark chestnut hair was caught in the body's clawing hand, only a dozen or so strands, long enough to sway in the light breeze—the last thing he'd gripped in life. This was the attacker's hair.

Claude asked Souvas to collect the hair and left the field. He would play a hunch.

A heavy guard escorted Troppmann from a police van through the main chamber of the Paris Morgue. He had been told nothing. He walked ahead of Claude to a smaller purification room at the rear of the building.

The body lay on a marble pallet, tilted forward. The hands were untied. They'd been fastened by a specialized handcuff knot, secured by an overhand knot. Whoever had tied them knew what they were doing. The stiffened arms lay at the sides as naturally as could be achieved. The body had been washed, the caked blood removed from the face, the eyeball returned to the socket, the knife removed from the throat.

He was a young man of Troppmann's age. His hair was a similar chestnut color with the same fullness. His forehead was high and proud, the forehead Claude had seen in the small fragment of photograph. Hortense Kinck had carried a photograph of this boy.

For a long moment Troppmann stood silent. And then he took a large handkerchief from his pocket and began to sob. The sight made Claude tremble.

"Poor fellow," Troppmann said, regaining some control.

"Do you recognize the corpse?" Claude said, to satisfy the official purpose of identification. A police officer transcribed every word.

"It's Gustave Kinck."

Claude felt a swell of sadness, regret, even confusion. It was the first time Troppmann had shown any emotion for the victims. Claude must exploit the vulnerability, but for now they stood before the corpse, linked by their sadness at the sight.

"I have to ask this—did you kill him?"

Troppmann turned to Claude.

"How can you suggest such a thing?" There was a note of hysteria in his voice. "No, I didn't." He breathed out in something of a growl. "His father has killed him."

"Why?"

He shrugged. "Fear he'd talk about the murders."

Claude motioned to an official to cover the body.

"This boy's been dead longer than the woman and the children."

Troppmann remained silent. Claude observed his eyes. No longer that fixed-in-the-middle-distance gaze—his down-turned eyes darted about.

"This weakens your story," Claude said.

Troppmann met Claude's gaze, his face impassive. Then his eyes darted away.

"Where is Jean Kinck?"

"He was to leave for America. I don't know how this happened."

"When were you to meet in America?"

"Around the middle of October."

"Where were you to meet in America?"

Troppmann narrowed his scrutiny of Claude.

"I need the address, the time, the place. We could have him arrested. It doesn't help you in any way not to tell me these things."

Troppmann looked down at the floor.

"Do you still maintain Jean and Gustave Kinck killed them?"

He nodded.

"This isn't possible. Who killed Gustave?"

The demand had no impact. Feeling his temper rise, Claude took a deep, calming breath. It didn't help much.

"Take him back to prison," Claude said.

The guards approached but Troppmann motioned them away. Claude turned and began to leave the room.

"If I could only be in his place," Troppmann said.

Claude rebounded, coming between him and the body. Troppmann lowered his eyes.

"What do you mean?" Claude kept his voice neutral.

"He's only a young boy."

"So are you," Claude said gently. "So are you."

Troppmann looked down at his feet.

"You wrote to your father, on Monday, the twentieth of September," Claude said, taunting him with information he'd received from authorities in Alsace.

Troppmann's face darkened. "Likely enough."

"The day after the murders."

Troppmann's eyes darted away.

"And you sent him a lot of money, didn't you?"

Troppmann stared.

"You must answer me!"

"I did," Troppmann said, his voice hissing. "Don't ask me another question. I won't say another word."

"Where did the money come from?"

"For God's sake! A father's murdered his sweet son—"

He nodded towards the body.

"I don't believe you."

Troppmann shrugged his shoulders.

"He's with his mother..."

Troppmann's face drained to a gray-white. He pulled his bottom lip in under his top teeth, his stare again fixed in the middle distance.

The passivity enraged Claude. He signaled to the officers, who ushered Troppmann from the building.

Souvas and Claude stood together on the Quai de l'Archevêché and watched the van.

"Where the hell is Jean Kinck?" Souvas said.

Claude sighed. "Dig up the entire fucking field."

CHAPTER TWENTY

Each evening Hortense prepared a meal for nine as if the child in her belly already sat at the table. She stirred the stew and wondered how many it would be serving. Some nights neither Jean nor Troppmann came but more often they arrived together, engrossed in each other. She heard the front door close, dried her hands, and walked to the entrance hall.

"Welcome," she said, smiling the most benevolent smile she could muster. She took Jean's coat and hung it in the closet. Jean walked to the parlor. She offered to take Troppmann's but he shook his head. He wouldn't be parted from his coat, even wearing it to her table.

"How was your day?" she said.

"All right."

He averted his eyes. With only the slightest whiff of Troppmann, the children arrived from all directions, all noise and questions.

"They'll eat you alive," Jean said and laughed.

The younger ones took his hands and walked him to the parlor. She watched him. Although he combed his long hair, layering it neatly down, his cheekbones jutted from his face. And then he looked as if he'd lived for months on stale bread and thin soups. He was appallingly thin, his cheekbones caved and eyes shadowed. But he'd eaten well at her table more nights than not. And for many weeks. If only for his own mother's peace, she resolved to add some weight to his bones.

"You're feeding him the wrong things," her mother said.

"He eats as well as everyone."

"I would imagine a lack of one's own cuisine would have a bad effect on anyone's mood."

"Jean has never said anything."

Her mother glared at her. "Has he not spoken of returning to Alsace?"

Hortense couldn't keep the horror from her face. It was true—all their married life, Jean had eaten well and never gained weight. Perhaps she'd not fed him appropriate fare.

"What would one eat in Alsace?"

Her mother pondered.

"Heavy food, taking from the Prussian. Rich meats, pig and geese."

Hortense felt renewed. If she couldn't win Troppmann's words, she'd have his stomach.

She roasted pig until the salted crackling was brittle. She skimmed set goose fat from pots of cooled bouillon and ladled it into sauces for his meat, followed by egg-rich custards. But she fumbled, sauces stuck to saucepans, equivocated when she should act, burnt rather than browned, a debutante in her own kitchen. In all the uproar, she mislaid her favorite knife, a present from Jean, his first she believed. Small but sharp and swift, a bone handle worn to her hand, like her needle, her hand's extension. She'd looked in every drawer and on every shelf. Without it, she hacked at meats and couldn't remove an apple's skin in one long, easy coil. But she needn't have worried at her lack of artifice-Troppmann consumed everything placed in front of him with the same swift ambivalence as if nothing had any taste at all, sweet nor sour, well butchered or not. Jean made no comment on the change of fare.

"Is there anything in particular you'd like me to cook?" she said. He looked up from his plate. "What's your favorite meal?"

He shrugged his shoulders and lowered his face to the plate. He never thanked her for her effort and over time the fat did nothing to fatten, the custard nothing to sweeten his conduct to her.

He kept his large hands washed, the nails clean. Always after he'd eaten, he tied and untied knots. She figured it soothing, like rosary beads. But there was a small tear above his pants pocket. She looked closer. His felt coat and shirt were missing buttons.

"If you like," she said. "I can repair your clothing."

He looked at her blankly and nodded.

"What a magnificent idea," Jean said. "Change into some of Gustave's clothes."

Gustave took Troppmann upstairs and after some time the two returned, Troppmann dressed in Gustave's fresh pants and shirt and a colored woolen vest she'd knitted for his last birthday, the whole garment a struggle but the weave pleasing in completion. Gustave wore it often and it suited him, a treasured possession.

"This vest suits you," Jean said, straightening the seams along the shoulder and the side. "It was made for you. It's yours."

No! But what could she say without seeming mean-spirited? With Troppmann, Jean knew no boundary. And Gustave looked so happy, smiling at Troppmann.

"It does suit you very well," Gustave said. "Far better than me."

Troppmann looked down at the vest, turned over the fabric to view the lining. He looked into Hortense's eyes.

"Your stitch is fine," he said. "Almost as fine as my mother's."

Although she resented the loss of the vest, she'd found a flaw in Troppmann's armor. She'd win his respect through appeals to his mother. For now she worked quickly to repair his clothes, her needle as accurate as was her beloved knife once.

CHAPTER TWENTY-ONE

Claude strode along the rue de Rivoli, intending to turn at Boulevard de Sébastopol and head back to the prefecture. He stopped at a newsstand, where he cast his eye over a particularly appalling headline: WHAT DEMON IS UPON THE EMPIRE?

Hysteria was one thing, but these headlines?

"God damn them," he said. He had a mind to go to the editor and—

"Damn whom?"

He turned to see Desbarolles. He handed him the newspaper and against his better judgment paid for it. Desbarolles glanced over the article.

"You had the whole field dug up," he said.

Claude winced. Nothing had been found. "Piétri chastised me, called the expense a reckless waste of the empire's purse, amongst other things." Claude had been hard pushed to defend himself. "Perhaps it was exaggerated," he said, "but how else was I to respond to such inefficiency? The autopsy's confirmed the body was there four days before the others. *Four days.* The grave was shallow, it as much as had a beacon and no one found it."

"Why are you fostering this hysteria?" Desbarolles said. "Go to trial."

Claude shifted to his back foot. Piétri argued the same, as if a return to order and calm were more vital than who was responsible for it.

"I can't. I won't. Not until Jean Kinck's located."

"Troppmann can't deny involvement."

"In Gustave's murder, he does. Despite the fact it occurred before the others, despite the fact I found a clump of hair similar to his in the boy's hand, he says Kinck killed him."

"And the woman and children?"

"He maintains he only dug the grave, pushed them into it, but he didn't strike a blow."

"And you believe him?"

"I believe he can't have struck *all* the blows."

Claude appreciated Desbarolles's interest in the case. A pure intellect formed a clear sounding board, not swayed by petty concerns like the cost of the investigation or the public outcry.

"It wasn't possible for him to commit all those murders in the allotted time. Therefore, he had accomplices. He claimed they were Jean and Gustave Kinck. That I didn't believe. And after the discovery of Gustave's body…"

"If you don't mind my saying, I think you're wrong. His hands are large. He has the strength to kill quickly, efficiently, possibly two children at the same time."

Desbarolles moved his arms from his side, formed collars with his thumbs and fingers.

"It was dark," he said. "He separated them. He worked swiftly. They wouldn't have known what happened to the others."

"But at the morgue, he intimated accomplices."

Desbarolles met Claude's eyes. "You're being played by Scheherazade."

"But to what end? Each piece of his story does nothing to fortify his innocence."

"Go to trial."

"Not yet. I'd only get him as an accessory. I need more time. I need to find Jean Kinck. I need to find the accomplices."

"And the police in Alsace?"

"They've interviewed Troppmann's parents. The day after the murder of Madame Kinck, Troppmann sent a gift of money. He admits it but refuses to discuss where the money came from."

"What have they said of Kinck?"

"His parents are both dead. What remains of his family report that Troppmann and Kinck were in Alsace but went to Paris for urgent business."

"When was that?"

"About a month before the murders. There's no report of them in Alsace that month. Where they went, I don't know. If nothing useful comes in the next few days, I'll travel to Alsace and command the operation."

Desbarolles's face puckered.

"Is that really necessary? I can only repeat, you have the murderer. You need to break him down."

"What do you think I've been trying to do?" Claude sighed. "I will say your drawing of the hand was quite accurate."

"I've no doubt it was. What would convince you of the truth of my theory?"

Claude gave his friend a penetrating look.

"What I've asked for all of my life—reproducible proof."

"If I could give you that, would it bring you rest?"

Under a microscope, modern forensic scientists had compared the hair found in Gustave's hand to a sample of Troppmann's. They agreed it was the same color, the same length, each strand the same diameter, but couldn't confirm it was Troppmann's, not to a level that would hold up in court. Claude thought of the frustration he'd felt standing next to Madame Kinck's body in the Paris morgue. Perhaps it wasn't science that would elucidate the signs *on* the hand but Desbarolles's art of chiromancy that would read the signs *within* the hand?

"Perhaps," Claude said.

"Then bring me a criminal, someone unknown to me. I'll analyze his hand. I'll tell you of his character and crime, even of the past that formed him, in which you place such faith. Then, without prior knowledge, one of my students will analyze the hand. The readings will be the same and accurate."

Claude stared at Desbarolles. Why did this proposal unnerve him?

"I've not a lot of time—"

"Friday evening?"

Claude sighed heavily and nodded. He walked away from Desbarolles, along Boulevard de Sébastopol towards the Pont au Change.

He wished he could be so certain. He'd no desire to travel to Alsace but the area played on him in an inarticulate rhythm. Both Troppmann and Kinck were from Alsace but had met on the other side of France. In Paris, Troppmann had stayed in an area frequented by Alsatian workers, lower class men prone to solve any dispute with a knife. But Troppmann was not of that social class.

Of course he felt a connection to the Poinsot case of so many years ago. Perhaps this wasn't intuition but oversensitivity and he should ignore the sensation. But he couldn't. He'd tried but couldn't resist poring over maps of the area of

Troppmann and Kinck's birth, reading reports of the political unrest, that Prussian loyalist wanting the area to secede.

He recalled the bitterness of those months after he'd laid the Poinsot case to rest at the prefect's command. Once back in his office, he took his note book of the case from the shelf.

> *This silence, which I was warned to keep "in my own inter-est," produced a most painful impression upon me. I began to see our empire and the emperor were strong in appearance only, and that France was being made to pay for its return to despotism by subservience to foreign nations, namely Prussia. For having, in memory of a glorious Napoleon, delivered herself over to a crooked nephew, France was now in the power of foreign despots more cruel and far more able than Napoleon III.*

With a heavy hand Claude had buried the official case files of the Poinsot murder, all the implications of Prussian insurgents ready to act against the emperor, in the bowels of the prefecture.

But the "extreme position" he'd taken damaged his professional standing. He missed a promotion. He was given cases of murdered prostitutes and the endless line of bloated bodies pulled from the Seine.

And even in this case, he'd been called late to the Pantin field. Yes, that morning he was to leave for the Auvergne, but this was a massacre and he was the most qualified to investigate it. He should have been notified immediately. Instead there was a delay. If they'd truly been concerned for his holiday, why contact him at all? Why not let him remain ignorant, give the case to some aspiring young officer? But no. They waited—just an hour, two at the most, defendable—and then told him so he would have to play catch-up.

There was a delay in his getting the information from the police spy who'd found the storeowner who sold the pick-axe and spade. He'd entrusted the command of the search of the field to the local police and Gustave's body, badly buried but obvious to a dog and a bourgeois woman, hadn't even been found. And the chaos at the arrival of the train from Le Havre at Gare Saint-Lazare had been no spontaneous eruption. The information had been leaked. It had been engineered. In anger he'd ordered the whole field dug up and then been chastised about the cost.

Who knew what else had been missed?

Damn them. He shook off his anger. He breathed deeply to restore his vigor. Despite them he would persevere, chase out, *ad infinitum,* every aspect of these murders. It wouldn't finish until there was no stone unturned. He would persist with Troppmann—if anyone knew the truth, it was him. Damn them, he'd even ignore his intuition and go to Desbarolles on Friday evening and see what he saw in a criminal's hand.

CHAPTER TWENTY-TWO

The house cat was fat and Hortense knew they'd not had that many mice. In the woodshed off the kitchen, at the back amongst the rows of logs, she'd wound herself in the sawdust and woodchips making a smooth round nest. The evening this was discovered, the children rushed Troppmann through the house to the woodshed. Troppmann picked her up. She'd never let Hortense touch her but she lay still and content in his arm. He placed a hand on her belly.

"Her time is soon," he said. He applied a slight pressure and the cat reached out a paw in caution. "Even as close as tonight."

"How can you tell?" Emile said.

"What time?" Archile said.

"How many kittens?" little Marie said.

Troppmann massaged the cat's belly.

"Let me see," he said. "There's one, two…" He raised his eyes to the ceiling. "There are seven, one for each of you and one for me."

The children cried with excitement.

"We won't be keeping them," Hortense said. "I've enough to look after."

Hortense left the woodshed and returned to the hearth but not before she heard Marie asked where they would all go.

"We'll find a nearby home for each of them," Troppmann said.

If Troppmann didn't come home with Jean, Jean would arrive late. The next day someone in the market might mention seeing the two drinking at a cabaret the previous evening.

"I know," Hortense would say, never letting the slightest concern show in her face. And soon the reaction wasn't feigned. In her heart, she'd known already.

Now that she'd refurbished Troppmann's garments, she felt they'd established some communication. Clearly Jean and Troppmann shared a love of mechanics but she had no insight into this. And Jean shared this with Monsieur Viller without this intensity. There was a love of something else she couldn't see. She asked about his youth, the house he lived in, about his family, thinking he might enjoy talking of them. He would answer yes or no or at best "I suppose so." But of his life, she did glean a few small points from what she overheard.

Troppmann was the youngest in his family, and perhaps he enjoyed being the eldest of their six. His father and mother still lived in Alsace in a village quite close to Jean's.

"My father's much the same as you," Troppmann told him. "But he invents."

"I've no such insight," Jean said. "Invention takes a fertile mind."

"He invented a small clamp to seal large burlap bags. It was a great success, strong and secure yet easily released. But its best feature was it could be unfastened." Troppmann raised his large hand in the air and clamped his thumb up to his fingers. "And refastened, used again and again."

"But isn't it more profitable to sell something that can only be used once?"

"To develop the idea, my father took on a business partner who had the money and the contacts to find a manufacturer. But he tried to steal the invention for himself."

"Partners are harder than a marriage," Jean said.

Hortense glared at Jean, who didn't even know he'd offended her.

"For this reason alone I've never taken one," Jean said. "I'll always remain in control."

"The two fell into litigation," Troppmann said. "After a long battle, my father won the rights to the invention but then found it impossible to find the money to make it. He was left ruined, bankrupted."

"The law's an unequal beast."

"We lived in this shadow. He worked as a mechanic but always the risk we would topple into poverty hung over the family. He was robbed by a business associate and he shouldn't have had to pay for a crime he didn't commit."

"But he's recovered now, with this new device."

After his bankruptcy, Troppmann's father had established another company to market his new invention, a small papier mâché funnel used in the machines that dyed yarns and fabrics. Hortense's father had praised the mechanism.

"Someone who could invent this funnel must be very smart," Jean said.

"We grew up lacking so many things," Troppmann said. "He's owed something better."

Troppmann cast his hand in a grand arc encompassing the room, as if to suggest all he'd been denied. Hortense felt the wave of envy stem from his hand. Did this young man think all these objects had materialized through nothing more than a magical wave? Jean had worked hard, *she* had worked hard to extend every franc to the maximum. She had no maid, no cook, and she'd reared six children. All this saving had gone to buy the finer crockery, the lined drapes, even the mahogany table from which Troppmann ate. Why did Jean not…

She stood from the table but when no one acknowledged her she did as her mother had taught her, buried her anger and left for the kitchen. She stoked the dying embers to heat water but the fire was dead. And Gustave hadn't replenished her wood box. She called out to him. A bolt of laughter erupted in the dining room. He wouldn't come. She took up a candle and went to the woodshed.

In the flickering light, she found a log of sufficiently small size. The cat mewed, a solitary cry. She turned the dim candle to the far corner. The cat lay stretched, a sea of small tawny and auburn heads bobbing at her nipples. Hortense counted the line. Six good ones. The seventh, a runt, was sure not to last. By the morning, the cat brushed it aside. Of course Marie's heart went to its plight and Hortense explained it was just the way of it. But that evening Troppmann lifted it from the litter.

"We shall feed him," he said. Marie's eyes dilated with joy.

He asked Hortense for milk which he warmed in a small glass in his hand.

As quiet as a mouse, Marie stood at his side with one hand on his arm and another on his knee, transfixed by the kitten on his lap. He soaked the corner of a kerchief in the milk and placed this near the kitten's mouth.

"His fur is the color of my hair," Troppmann said.

Marie smiled.

The kitten took the cloth as if it were a nipple. Hortense never would have believed such a thing. With infinite care, Troppmann repeated the patient action until all the milk was gone, the sated kitten asleep in his lap. Jean, of course, smiled at him and only nodded his approval to her.

With this new task, Troppmann came to the house two or three times, sometimes as much as four times a day, coming and going as he pleased.

"He grows," he said.

Marie smiled and clasped his arm in both her small hands.

"He's small and yet powerful. But with his blue eyes, he's more like Gustave. Don't you think?"

Marie nodded her ever-willing head.

Having Troppmann, having anyone for that matter, so often in her kitchen irritated Hortense. But she was amazed at his care, pleased at how much joy he took from pleasing Marie.

One evening when the children were asleep, he came to the kitchen from the woodshed.

"The mother tries in vain not to mother," he said.

"She's rejected it."

"That she has. But he's shrewder than her sneering."

"What on earth do you mean?"

"He avoids her regard but seeks the warmth of the litter. He'll outlast them all."

"The warmth is no concern to her."

"A good mother cares for the young."

Hortense sensed more. His mother. He'd never spoken of his mother, a subject she'd never explored.

"Your mother must feel your absence."

"I love her dearly," he said. "I wish her every good blessing."

"No one can replace a mother," she said.

"No," he said in a cold voice, with such certainty that she felt he'd issued a warning. Then he said, "You're soon to be a mother again."

She was now far enough into her pregnancy that her swollen belly couldn't be hidden.

"I would have liked my mother to have another child, but because of my father's woes, I was her last."

"Motherhood is a constant task."

"The kittens – you don't like them."

She was unprepared for such a remark. "The children... They're good for them. For me, I have no opinion of them. They're just more work. We can't keep them. The children will object to them being sent away."

At night she lay awake and traveled the road of her father's explanation. Troppmann and her husband were kinsmen. She had to admit that with Troppmann's arrival there had come a sense of peace in Jean. Even if Troppmann didn't return with him to the house, one of the children need only mention him and Jean was light-hearted and playful in a way he hadn't been for a long while. Perhaps this was all he'd needed, an Alsatian countryman.

She would have appreciated this light-heartedness had it not come at the price of her exclusion. Although her pregnancy advanced, in the past they'd found ways to pleasure one another. She couldn't remember when they'd last made love.

In her half sleep, she would walk a narrower lane of thought. Jean had begun to counsel him, give him advice on how to proceed in the world. The affection between them was like that between Jean and Gustave. In many ways Troppmann now had the successful father he felt he deserved. She might have accepted the relationship between father and surrogate son had it not been for the fact that, to her vexation and loss, Gustave was included.

Something evaded her, something she couldn't put into words. Jean was one thing. Troppmann another. How did they come to be so intimate? All night, she lay awake convinced she was missing something important. But an answer remained ahead of her, hopscotch one step, two steps, three steps from her grasp.

CHAPTER TWENTY-THREE

Claude returned again and again to Mazas. The guards reported Troppmann's mood, some days surly and some improved. He read popular magazines, exercised incessantly, and had written a letter to his mother and family. It contained vague references to his present predicament, only said he'd been detained over a misunderstanding. He asked about his brothers and sisters, then ended it: *I hope you take care of yourself and don't listen to these lies.* Claude elicited two responses; evasion and silence.

Claude ordered the release of the seven bodies for burial. The Roubaix prefecture sent word that Madame Kinck's parents, Madame and Monsieur Roussel, would travel to Paris to collect them. Detailed photographs had been taken that could be presented in court. The state would pay for the funeral, and a bidding war erupted between various municipal councils over which town should stage the funeral and where the bodies should be buried.

Claude was appalled, commerce striking at the heart of grief. He met with the parents, their sad air filling his small office like a vase of lily of the valley. He expressed his condolences, for which they seemed pathetically grateful.

Monsieur Roussel said, "Roubaix argues they should bury the family since they lived there—"

"Lille argues it's the largest city of the area," Madame Roussel said.

"They could provide an adequately grand funeral," her husband said, "but…"

Monsieur Roussel stopped, unable to continue. He was a calm man, his spirit was damped. Her hands, long and slender-fingered just like her daughter's, fidgeted in her lap. What contrivance had modeled the daughter's hands to her mother's so exactly?

"What would *you* like?" Claude said.

"We want them to rest in Tourcoing," Madame Roussel said, "so we can visit and tend the graves when all the hoopla has subsided. But now the city of Cernay in Alsace wants the family returned to the soil from which they grew. They want it as an attraction."

Of course they did, for the hoopla wouldn't subside. The cities knew there would be great fanfare around the burials.

"It's not for them to decide," he said. "The bodies should be turned over to you and returned to Tourcoing for burial. I'll write letters to the appropriate officials demanding this be done."

They both thanked him, their sleep-starved faces perhaps a touch brighter.

"Monsieur Roussel," Claude said, "could I speak with you, in private?"

The couple looked at one another, their expressions calm and united.

"These events have shown me I'm not a weak woman," Madame Roussel said. "Anything you need to say can be said to me."

Damn. He'd been insensitive.

"What do you know of Troppmann?"

"We've never met him," Madame Roussel said.

"I'd heard of him, apart from Jean," Monsieur Roussel said.

"Heard of him?"

"He and Jean met thanks to a machine he installed and struck up a friendship."

"What did Hortense think of him?"

The two looked at one another again.

"She wasn't fond of him," Monsieur Roussel said. "She'd spoken quite openly about it."

Claude thought about Troppmann. His manner was less refined than the Roussels but he wasn't without grace.

"Why did he displease her so?"

"It's odd…" Madame Roussel said. "She felt he'd infiltrated their home. He'd befriended the children."

"He liked them?"

"I think so," she said. "Children know whether adults really care about them or are pretending, and they all adored him. And Jean saw no wrong in it at all."

Claude had thought Troppmann might have ingratiated himself with the children to gain Kinck's favor, but he now felt certain the friendship with them was sincere.

"But Hortense saw something else?" Claude said.

"She felt excluded," Madame Roussel said. "He ignored her."

This rested uneasily with Claude. If Troppmann and Kinck had sought to liquidate all the family's assets and leave France, why would he draw attention, create an adversary in Hortense? The better strategy would have been to coddle her. He knew how to ingratiate himself.

"And there's something else," Monsieur Roussel said. "It appeared Troppmann had rekindled some desire in Jean to return to Alsace."

"It had been a condition of their marriage that they'd never leave Roubaix," Madame Roussel said.

"You can't restrict a man like Jean Kinck," Monsieur Roussel said. "I knew in my heart when I first met him, when he asked for Hortense's hand, that he'd eventually want to return to Alsace despite all his assurances to the contrary."

Claude sat forward. "Tell me about Jean."

"In every way, he was the best husband for my daughter," Monsieur Roussel said.

"He loved the children," his wife said. "Doted on them. But of late he'd been withdrawn."

"How?"

"For many years he'd been content," Monsieur Roussel said. "Although lately he'd lost long-standing contracts."

"Why?"

"No practical reason. His work was always top quality. But he felt something had changed… He was a foreigner to the area. And there was another change in him. No one ever said anything, but I saw it."

"What on earth do you mean?" Madame glared at her husband.

"He'd become… I'm not a man of words, but he'd become more… showy. He wore more expensive clothes. He bought every type of frippery."

"You're right," Madame Roussel said. "Yet he maintained his business was bad."

"Did Hortense share this change?"

"No," Monsieur Roussel said. "Not at all. She resented it."

Claude sat for some moments. Could an altercation over where they would live rise to murder? People had murdered for far less.

"You think Jean killed them," she said.

"In his absence, it's easy to jump to such a conclusion." He was quiet for a moment. "Can you think of any reason Jean might kill them? Troppmann has asserted Jean suspected your daughter of having an affair."

"Ridiculous! She had six children and despite my insistence kept no maid. She had no time for another man and she was already six months' pregnant."

"Are you sure the child was Jean's?" Claude regretted this harsh assertion.

"We live in a small town, not a metropolis," Monsieur Roussel said. "Affairs are hard to conceal. And even if Jean discovered she was pregnant by another man, why would he kill all his children?"

"Quite. But Troppmann maintains Jean believed only Gustave was his."

"Drivel," Monsieur Roussel said.

"She couldn't have maintained an affair for sixteen years," Madame Roussel said. "It simply isn't possible."

"Troppmann maintains Jean took… measures against conception."

The two gawped at Claude.

"How would he know such a thing?" Madame Roussel said.

Claude sat back in his chair. He'd crossed a line.

"Did your daughter ever mention why she thought Jean wanted to return to Alsace?"

"She'd no idea," Monsieur Roussel said. "She came to me for answers. He had a new business proposition afoot in Alsace. Jean never discussed his business with me."

Helpless, Claude looked from one lost parent to the other. Monsieur Roussel's lips began to quiver, his eyes filled with tears. He collapsed his face into his hands, his wife reaching to touch his shoulder.

"I fear I've killed her," he said. "I urged her to follow Jean. If I'd not…"

"We need an end to this," Madame Roussel said.

"Now Gustave is dead… He was her favorite. Where will this end?"

Claude's mouth dried. He had no words. There were no words. Nothing but action would abate this anxiety. He maintained Madame Roussel's gaze, all he could to meet her sorrow.

"It will not end," Claude said, "until I have found the truth. Your daughter and her children deserve justice."

"Our whole family…" Monsieur Roussel said. "Murdered…"

"We would like to see the bodies," Madame Roussel said.

The deep gouge at Gustave's neck reared into Claude's mind. His first instinct was to protect them, tell them they couldn't, but that would achieve nothing.

"I'll arrange a private time."

Claude watched them walk from his office, down the prefecture's long corridor. They walked apart. Monsieur Roussel gait slowed, the even steps maintained with effort, his shoulders weighed down. Madame Roussel's spine was straight. She walked as if she slowed herself not to leave her husband behind.

How could people bear such sorrow?

Madame and Monsieur Roussel endured the French bureaucracy and with Claude's help won the battle for the bodies.

Two days later, Catherine handed him a newspaper. At the small kitchen table he read of a long, solemn procession that allowed fifty thousand people in the streets of Tourcoing to catch a glimpse of this wrecked family. Factories closed for the day to enable their grieving workers to attend. The

Tourcoing authorities established a subscription to pay for an epitaph.

"The poor souls," Claude said.

"That poor Troppmann boy's caught in forces he's no idea of," Catherine said.

Claude regarded her for some moments, struck by the intensity of her empathy. His work was a cold game—strategy, deduction, verve. She allowed emotion in.

"You must save this boy's life," she said.

"He gives me very little help."

"Remorse is your key."

"He displays hardly any."

"I can't believe that. He was involved with this family. He must have felt something for the eldest boy. And he's said the younger ones were innocent."

Her attitude took Claude by surprise.

"Why are you so keen? You think he's innocent?"

"That's your concern, not mine. But he must not be murdered too. The guillotine is barbaric. And despite all the slicing, crime marches on."

"Tonight, I'm going to Adolphe Desbarolles's apartment."

She turned on him. "Why? Have you read his papers on criminology? I have. Can we view all behavior as predestined? We're far more complex than that."

"He's promised proof."

"He'll argue this boy was born to perpetrate these killings by some crease or such like on his hand. I've read of this murderer's thumb. Phfft. Chiromancy… Tyromancy, why don't you investigate that?"

"What the hell's that?"

"People look into the curds of cheese and tell the future."

"You're being crude—"

"At least you'd make cheese. Desbarolles work is weak, at best."

Exasperation rose in Claude.

"You've asked me to save Troppmann's life. He gives me very little help. Perhaps this evening will reveal something, however small."

"Examine his past, not his hand. You'd do better to travel to Alsace than Monsieur Desbarolles's parlor."

Damn the woman. It was easy for her to demand a resolution, as it was for the newspapers and damn Piétri and the Roussel parents and the memory of Madame Kinck and the whole of France, let alone the pressure he felt himself. Easy for all of them. He had to pull together the evidence. He near buckled. Now she wanted Troppmann proved guilty and innocent. Damn her. He'd seen murder so clearly in Lacénaire's hand.

"I don't subscribe to Desbarolles's theory any more than you but I'm at a loss. I'll go to Desbarolles and trust that some connection, some light can be shed on these obscene crimes."

"The sooner we can leave Paris the better," she said. "There's trouble coming. I don't want to be in Paris."

What was she talking about? They *were* going to leave Paris. Both were tired of the noise, the heat in summer, the press of people, the directionless tourists, and the savage beat of modern life. This was established, deferred but established.

"What trouble?" he said.

"The empire's outlived its use," she said. "I don't want to see the final act. "I'll go to the Auvergne."

He turned to her. "What?"

"The hotels for the end of our trip are still booked. I'll take the train to Clermont-Ferrand." She regarded him for some moments. "You can go to Desbarolles—"

"You're being truculent—"

"Don't look like that. You don't need me here and I can make some preliminary inquiries."

"But I do need you."

She stood from the table.

"You're the chief of police, not I."

She left the room.

How foolish he'd been. Once her mind was set he'd no power over it. And neither did he want that. Only once he'd opposed her, sought to overpower her, and only once had he nearly lost her love. She'd go to the Auvergne. Sure as the sun would rise in the east. But not just to find land. She was annoyed with him, tired of policing and angry with delay.

CHAPTER TWENTY-FOUR

Gustave, Henri, and Emile washed and dried the crockery and cutlery. In the pantry, Hortense poured olive oil from a stone storage bottle to a glass bottle. At the height of summer, the oil ran smoothly with only the slightest need of incline. Hortense demanded the children help about the house, seeing this work as a form of instruction in frugality. Hortense enjoyed her time with them, although from the pantry she could hear Gustave telling more Troppmann stories.

"One afternoon," he said, "Troppmann was in a forest near his home. In a small clearing he spotted two men fighting."

Henri and Emile had stopped work and were, of course, transfixed.

"From a distance, he watched them," Gustave said. "They were big, stripped to the waist. They fought without skill, like kittens."

Henri and Emile laughed. These weren't Gustave's words. He was recounting Troppmann verbatim.

"Finish your work," she called out.

She heard the clink of the crockery, but it wasn't long before Gustave continued.

"He didn't know why they fought but as one of them gained an advantage, the other pulled himself free and escaped into the woodland. Troppmann advanced towards the remaining one, an impressive size. He wasn't scared. 'He thought I was an easy mark,' Troppmann said. 'My size disguises me.'"

"He's sneaky," Emile said. Henri gave an excited giggle.

"And smart," Gustave said. "Troppmann let him strike—fell to the ground as if he had no strength at all. And then, when the fellow couldn't have expected it less, Troppmann took charge of him, from behind. He linked an arm through his and took him by the seat of the pants and threw him from the footbridge into the river."

The children laughed. Hortense inclined the bottle too acutely. Oil blurted from the neck, gushed over the bench to the pantry floor.

"That's enough," she said, striding from the pantry. "Emile and Henri, go to your room."

"But we've not finished—"

"Go to your room."

The younger boys frowned and gazed at Gustave, who looked dumbfounded.

"Go."

She pointed to the door. The two younger boys weren't wont to disobey and wiped their hands and left the kitchen. She turned to Gustave.

"You've always been considerate, sensitive to how your actions would affect me."

His stare chilled her. She'd seen the same on Troppmann's face.

"Why do you tell them such a story?"

"Because it's true."

His voice was surly. She glared, unable to find any words to remonstrate him.

"Help me clean the oil."

In the pantry she scattered sawdust on the floor, which changed to a darker brown. She swept this up and began to scrub.

"He was a long time coming to the surface," Gustave said.

"Who?"

"The man Troppmann threw in the river. He slipped beneath the water and was never seen again."

She inhaled sharply. "Why do you go on with this?"

His eyes narrowed.

"Because you hate him."

She met these eyes.

"Get me another cloth."

She placed one hand over her stomach, the other over her mouth lest some heartfelt gasp escape. Troppmann had watched the poor soul drown in the stream. Did she believe the story? Perhaps he'd made it up to impress Jean and Gustave. But why would someone tell such a tale? Why would he think this would impress Jean and Gustave? What type of man would say such things? And now Gustave was repeating them…. Did she hate him? Had her actions, her manner, left her so unmasked?

"Gustave," she said, taking his hand and dragging him down to her on the floor. She searched his eyes for a sign of him. "Promise me you won't finish this story in front of the children." His eyes dulled. Had he lost all sense of decency? "You understand why such a thing shouldn't be told to children?"

For a fraction, she saw in his countenance her loving Gustave, the one who'd only ever sought to please her. But without enthusiasm, he nodded his head.

Once they'd finished cleaning the floor, he left. She sat alone at the work bench, her head in her greasy hands.

Horrified. She'd never heard such a thing. She didn't want to think of it. This was no tale to tell her father and injure his opinion of Jean, who wasn't the kind of man to associate himself with someone proud to have murdered. In these weeks of Troppmann's presence, amongst Jean's ledgers and Troppmann's tales, Gustave had grown and gone. It was inevitable. Now she looked at it, she'd known this day from the moment first he lay on her stomach – she would become obsolete. His journey, this thing reserved for men, had begun. What role she would play was unclear but she must not take his considerations for granted.

That evening when Jean finally came to their bedroom, she waited for him to undress and lay with her.

"Troppmann told a most disturbing story."

"I can't imagine that."

He rolled his back to her.

"Don't you want to hear it?"

"I'm very tired. Perhaps in the morning."

His breathing grew regular. This was the worst of it; blinded as he was, Jean wouldn't countenance any concern. She'd be happier if he refuted the truth of the story but he didn't even want to hear it. She had no one. No one would speak of this.

The next morning, she dreaded Troppmann's arrival to feed the runt. She hurried the children, shuffled those she could from the house. Marie remained at her side but when it was well after eight and there was no sign of him, she went to the woodshed. The cat was gone. The kittens were all gone. The nest scuffed away to sawdust and woodchip. The cat brushed against her leg, staring at the destruction as if to say her kittens were still too young to be given away. She felt drawn in to a drama she had no liking for. She'd been against the cat. Against the kittens. Why did this bring her such unease?

That evening, the children, plump with sorrow, explained to Troppmann the kittens' disappearance.

"Oh well, your mother said they had to go."

The children turned to her, Gustave and Troppmann the only ones to look away. How dare he! This had nothing to do with her. She wouldn't defend herself. Not here. Not in front of him. She left the table, returned to the kitchen and wept silently, this sense of being disliked or mistrusted in her own home overpowering. No one came to her. Was Jean uncaring?

When the children were in bed, Troppmann sat alone in the drawing room. Jean had gone to say goodnight. He read a magazine and although she'd stood for some moments he made no sign to mark her presence. She asked him what he knew of the kittens. He looked at her with newly dulled eyes and shrugged his shoulders.

"Perhaps a dog took them," he said, returning to the magazine.

Perhaps.

Perhaps a wild beast.

"You did something," she said. "Was it swift?"

"I cared for them. The children know you didn't like them."

She steadied herself. She'd not be thrown. "I'll report you to the police."

He laughed. "*Scheißfrau.* They have more to do than investigate the disappearance of kittens."

"That they do, like murder." He faced her. "You threw a man from a bridge. In Alsace. Watched him drown."

He studied her. "You've no proof of that."

"Someone in Alsace must be looking for him. It wouldn't take a great mind to put the two together."

He looked down at the magazine.

"I've misjudged you," he said.

"You have. I am Jean's wife. I won't have you in this house again."

He closed the magazine, laid it next to him. He jumped to his feet. He meant to frighten her but she remained so. He walked slowly to the front door, opened it and turned back.

"Say goodnight to Jean for me."

With that, he left and closed the door with a good solid bang.

CHAPTER TWENTY-FIVE

Desbarolles performed his professional work in this room, away from the formal parlor and stripped of all superfluous furniture. Deep cupboards with tall glazed display cabinets lined the walls. In the low lamplight, Claude saw stored leathery-looking masks—the faces of dead criminals. Death masks they were called, many believing that after execution the faces of criminals were removed of artifice and the true character written on their countenance.

On other shelves, hands cut free mid-forearm stood in glass jars suspended in dulled preserving fluid. The flesh was tatty about the cut, the skin an un-living white, rendered human only by the dark hairs covering the backs of the hand and forearm. Metal molds, mounds of wax, devices for heating, the paraphernalia of molding were stacked on a large wooden bench.

A bell jar occupied the center of the bench. Inside was a completed cast of a hand. It rose vertically from an enameled base, the long forearm placing the hand at the height of the jar, caught in the gesture of an imperial wave, the thumb and forefinger erect, the other fingers curling over in a whorl. To Claude's eye the hand was unremarkable, painted to simulate the color of living flesh, the fingernails covered in an opaque lacquer. What was it that had so intrigued Desbarolles to make this nondescript cast?

Two policemen stood behind Claude in the shadows of the dimly lit room to protect Claude and Desbarolles and to deny the criminal any chance of escape. In order to obscure further the criminal's character, Claude had covered his head with a burlap bag. Desbarolles moved about the room gathering books from a shelf, drawings of hands, charts and rulers and magnifying glasses, he didn't once glance at him. It was irrelevant. The criminal had sat for nearly a quarter of an hour, his head twitching at the slightest sound, his hearing made more acute by the denial of sight.

Finally Desbarolles sat at the table near the criminal.

"Please, place your hand on the table," Desbarolles said.

He raised his hand from his knee. Desbarolles took the hand in his, pushing back the rough-spun sleeve only enough to reveal the wrist. He ran his hand over the palm as if to straighten a piece of crumpled fabric.

"It's a fire hand, the palm longer than the fingers. The man is energetic. Relentlessly so."

Claude began to write.

"This man has a most ambitious character." Desbarolles peered at the hand intently. "The long index finger is a true mark of leadership. He is trustworthy, loyal, the strength of his ambition such that he wouldn't allow himself to marry. But there's something cunning."

Desbarolles released the hand. He took up a book from the few he'd brought to the table and flicked through the pages, read something, and returned to the hand.

"Most people would think he was born to follow and not to lead but in fact he desires most strongly to be a leader of men. His sense of political cunning makes him loyal to the highest power."

"But what of his crime?" Claude said, impatient to proceed to the crux of the matter.

"Yes," Desbarolles said. "What of his crime?" He moved the hand closer to the lamplight. "Beyond the petty acts we can all be accused of, this isn't the hand of a criminal—in fact, it's quite the reverse."

Desbarolles looked up from the hand and sat back heavily in his chair. Claude returned his gaze, attempting neither to reveal nor deny the assertions.

"I'll leave the room," Desbarolles said. "For added stringency, one of your policemen should accompany me. I'll remain in the parlor. At nine, my student will arrive."

With no further word, he walked out of the room.

Claude turned towards one of the policemen and nodded for him to follow. He heard their steps across the wooden hall into the front parlor and the sound of that door closing. The three men who remained in Desbarolles's workroom were silent.

The sharp ring of the apartment's bell startled Claude. The hall clock began to chime nine o'clock. After a few quick steps on the hall floor, the door of the workroom opened.

Madame Thérèse was a compact woman in her late fifties who conveyed a sense of purpose. She wasn't at all what Claude expected. She wore a long silk dress, a dark color that shot violet when it caught the low light of the room. Her dark hair brushed through with gray hung in tight curls around a face that at one time would have been described as cherubic.

Claude nodded to her. Not a word was to pass between them. She strode to the vacant chair.

"Let's begin," she said in a firm contralto.

She took the hand in hers.

"This man has a most ambitious character."

Again Claude began to write. She too detailed the index finger as a mark of leadership. Unlike Desbarolles, she spoke a jargon, words referencing the lines of heart, head, life, and fate, frayed lines, intersection, dissections, origins, and crosses. Finally Madame Thérèse looked up from the hand.

"This hand reveals a mind intent on investigation. I would say, as I'm sure Master Desbarolles did, this isn't the hand of a criminal. You've played a trick. This man is a detective or at the very least a policeman."

Claude stopped writing. Desbarolles had caught him out, identifying the hand as the opposite of a criminal, by inference a detective. But Madame Thérèse had gone further than her master. Claude admired her verve.

He pulled the bag from the subject's head. Souvas ran his hands over his face to remove the clamminess. Madame Thérèse was examining it when Desbarolles reentered the room. He looked at Madame Thérèse, Souvas, then Claude.

"Why did you deceive us?" he said.

"I couldn't get permission to bring a murderer here," Claude said. "Besides, the important thing is, both your readings were the same."

"And accurate. Are you convinced?"

Were they accurate? Whilst they'd identified him as a detective, he didn't feel either had grasped Souvas's personality correctly. Despite his interview for a promotion, Claude had never considered him ambitious.

"I'm impressed by the duplication," he said.

"Then you agree you have the murderer?"

Claude resented being backed into a corner.

"I'm moved somewhat more to your belief."

Late the next evening as Claude prepared to leave the prefecture, he received a communiqué from the Mazas governor demanding he come to the prison.

He dispatched an aide to cancel a dinner appointment. The day had threatened rain, and as he left the prefecture it started to pour, unseasonable sheets of water. His coat was soaking wet, and he felt uneasy. What had happened to provoke such an alarming message?

At the prison he was ushered to the governor, who told him Troppmann was agitated, talking, babbling, some of the words not even French. Claude ordered a physician be brought to the cell and went to him.

The heavy rain rumbled and groaned in the high reaches of the galleries. Water poured, an untempered cascade from the roof to the courtyard. Troppmann paced the floor in his undergarments, his face flushed, the dark of his eyes reduced to pinheads.

"What's the matter?" Claude said.

Troppmann continued pacing, glancing at Claude, the floor, the objects of the room as if he'd never seen them before.

"What do you want? What's the matter?"

"I am… off to the side of the road. The cream is fresh in this dairy."

He appeared dazed by his surroundings. Perhaps the enormity of his situation had finally sunk in.

"The children," he said. "The children…"

"Tell me."

"They should have stayed in the coach. Damn woman, they were to stay in the coach. They weren't to be touched."

"Who said they weren't to be touched?"

Troppmann turned towards the pallet, plunged his hand under the mattress. He had a knife, a small blade. His arm crossed his chest, the blade at his own throat.

"Don't," Claude yelled. "For the love of God, no."

"God?"

Distract him. "Who said the children weren't to be touched?"

"My mother." And then he babbled feverish nonsense.

With his eyes fixed on Claude, Troppmann leant his head back. His neck's arteries pulsated. Claude lunged forward, got his hand to Troppmann's wrist and pulled. Claude grabbed his other wrist. Troppmann flexed his arm but Claude pushed his weight forward. Dazed Troppmann, unprepared, toppled, the two conjoined crucified, careering to the floor. Claude landed on top of him, felt his breath rush out.

He'd winded him. Not a bad thing.

Still crucified, Troppmann moaned, turned his face to Claude. Their eyes met, so close.

"Who said that?" Claude yelled.

"The moon rises in the south..."

Claude raised the knife in Troppmann's hand and crashed it down, sending the small knife spinning across the floor to the pallet. He yelled. Troppmann yelled. The guards came. One secured Troppmann's hands to the floor, the other helped Claude to his feet.

"Who?"

The physician entered the cell, a strapping man in his mid-thirties. Troppmann rolled into a fetal position, low guttural sounds. The physician ordered the guards to leave. Claude stood to the side. The physician knelt, repeatedly smoothed his palm over Troppmann's head. After some moments, with Claude's help, they raised him to his feet. The physician's presence quieted Troppmann enough to remove his shirt. He stood still but his arms fidgeted. The exertion caused the muscular plates of his breast to heave up and down, his diaphragm drawn out like a bellows.

The physician moved his hands over the skin. He cupped Troppmann's jaw in the palm of his hand. He looked into Troppmann's eyes, opened his mouth and regarded his teeth, his tongue. With a flexible tube stethoscope he listened to his chest and heart, comparing the beat to his fob watch. Through all this Troppmann was compliant.

"Turn around." He tapped on Troppmann's back. "Please remove your pants."

Troppmann complied, folded the pants neatly and placed them on the bed. His nakedness had some further tranquilizing effect on him. He stood still before the physician, who warmed his hands by rubbing them together then cupped Troppmann's genitals in his hand. For such a young man, his member was large. But his testicles, now cupped in the doctor's palm, were extraordinarily large, bull-like.

"Turn around. Bend over, please. Spread your cheeks."

Troppmann's large hands spread over the orbs of his buttocks, the thumbs splayed out high, almost to the small of his back.

"Thank you. You may dress yourself."

The physician packed his instruments and asked to speak with Claude outside the cell.

"He's in good physical shape," he said. "His heart rate is highly elevated–could be the cause or the effect of his agitation—I can't say. There's no sign of sodomy."

"He had a knife. He meant to kill himself. What's disorientated him?"

"I'd say he's obtained or been given something, ingested it."

"An opiate?"

The physician glared at Claude.

"An opiate would cause depression, sluggishness. Normally one naïve to such a substance would vomit."

"Then what?"

"His irises are dilated. The stimulation… I'd suggest it was strychnine."

"A poison? Then someone has tried to kill him."

"Not necessarily. In a high dose, it's a poison. But a low dose will induce stimulation, a type of euphoria."

"So was the dose high or low?"

"Well, he's not dead. It was fairly low, the effect is waning. A few hours more… He can't hurt himself."

"Who would give him such a thing?"

"He may have acquired it for himself. Like the knife."

The thought was disquieting. Troppmann had minimal contact with the prison guards, a priest he refused to talk with, no one else. Of course, the guards were easily bribed, coin not the only currency. But the physician maintained there was no sign of sodomy. And the knife… If he committed suicide, he'd no longer be a problem.

"I'll prescribe an emetic and a strong purgative."

Claude called the guards back and ordered a search of the cell—the bedding was ripped apart, the mattress upended, the few magazines and papers whisked about. Troppmann shrieked, jumping up and down like a tormented ape, his overly large hands hanging, thrown up open-palmed to beat at the air.

Nothing was found, no drug or contraband alcohol. After the search had concluded, Claude stayed. Troppmann sat on the edge of his pallet, still babbling. He leaned forward slightly, pressing a hand to his stomach as if he was in pain, twitching his head like a bird.

"What did you take?"

Troppmann babbled something that was in no way an answer to his question. Was this another attempt at suicide?

Or perhaps someone seeking to harm or kill him had sent him the drug, which might point towards accomplices who wished to silence him. But the dose wasn't lethal. It had been given to him by someone to show how easily he could be reached. It could be a warning not for Troppmann but for him. It pointed to accomplices.

"Who gave it to you?"

Silence. And Claude knew Troppmann would remain so no matter how urgent his questions. What if he had taken his life? If he died without a trial Piétri and the whole establishment would be most unimpressed.

He simply must find Jean Kinck

He would renew his efforts, send forces from Le Havre to Alsace, to the east, the west, and the north of France. But to understand it all, he had to find a key to unlock Troppmann. What had nurtured this boy?

As he'd gone to Le Havre, it was time to travel to Alsace.

CHAPTER TWENTY-SIX

The children ran through the house, some tumbling down the stairs, some from the garden, all towards the entrance hall. In the kitchen, Hortense dried her hands. She would let nothing show. Despite what she had said, Jean and Troppmann were home and she would go as she always did to collect their coats and welcome them.

In the entrance hall, the children stood still, staring at Jean who was hanging his coat. Gustave was with him but stood apart, his hands linked together in front, his eyes lowered to the floor.

"Where's Troppmann?" Emile said.

"Is he coming later?"

"He was to bring us a surprise."

Jean turned to Hortense. "Silence the children."

The abruptness caused the children to stare at their father. Little Marie pressed herself into the folds of Hortense's skirt. Jean walked past them, into the parlor. He hadn't been like this for months.

"Come, children," she said, stretching her voice as light as possible. "I need all your help in the kitchen."

Together they prepare the meal, each taking a serving dish or plate to the table. Jean remained in silence, glaring at the plate as he chewed his food.

"Father," Alfred said. "What's wrong?"

Jean kept chewing, the muscles of his jaw and cheeks flitching with each grind. He said nothing. How could he be so thoughtless with the children? Alfred turned to her.

"Eat your dinner," she said.

Under this cloud, the meal proceeded. When they were finished the children asked to go to the kitchen and their chores. She collected some plates and as Jean made no motion to speak she went to join them. Gustave remained like a lieutenant awaiting instruction, his mood a reflection of Jean's.

"What's the matter?" she asked Gustave later in the evening.

"Troppmann has left," he said.

She felt herself go cold, such was the contempt in his eyes. He closed his bedroom door.

He has gone. He has gone. He has gone.

Had her words really had this effect? No. Surely not but she felt a thrill nonetheless. He'd waxed into their lives and now he'd left. He'd completed his mechanical business and like some untethered gypsy had moved on.

Gustave was saddened. Perhaps with time he would return to her, recommence his considerations. And with time and the new child, Jean's mood would lift, but she resented the way he treated the children. She was five months' pregnant. Little Marie had moved constantly in her womb, as this child did, and she hoped it too would be a girl. She was forty-two. This was her last child.

She resolved to ignore any mention of Troppmann by the children and to distract them as best she could. They washed and pressed the baby clothes, friendly blankets, and colored sheets she'd packed away, too fond of memories they held to part with them, hoping one day to use them again. Henri sometimes used language he'd learned from Troppmann, but for the most part he'd gone. He'd gone from their lives.

A week or so later, two at the most, Jean called her to the parlor. Her heart filled with concern, she perched on the sofa's edge.

"Tomorrow, I'll leave for Alsace."

If she'd been struck dumb by Troppmann's departure, she was crushed by this news. All lightness evaporated.

"We plan to establish an industry in the area—"

"An industry," she said, breathlessly. "What industry?"

"I've received a letter from Troppmann. He's found a site near Bollwiller, in Alsace, which is perfect for our requirements."

"What business?"

"I can't say. It must be kept secret."

"So secret you can't tell your wife?"

Never before had she so directly demanded information. Jean's gaze remained icy.

"If my wife trusted me, she'd stop these questions and pack for me."

"What a neat contrivance!"

"If the site he's found is suitable, I'll remain in Alsace and establish myself. In some time, you'll follow with the children."

She couldn't stand. She felt so many thoughts, thoughts a wife shouldn't utter unless she couldn't help herself.

"I don't approve of this person and have no desire to leave Roubaix."

"You don't approve—"

"You haven't even consulted me on this. May I remind you of your promise when we married?"

"May I remind you that you're pregnant? How do you expect to pay for it?"

"It?"

He exhaled savagely. "I'll have no trouble from you."

Something snapped in her.

"What trouble have I ever brought?"

"I've told you my plans. You're my wife. You'll obey."

Jean left the parlor and then the house. She sat frozen. She'd been foolish to think she banished Troppmann. He simply acted, pulling strings, from afar.

What was a wife to do?

She gathered herself and went to their room. With her heart fit to burst and her head throbbing, she packed clean shirts and pressed trousers in a small case. She prayed the building Troppmann had found would be unsuitable and Jean would return discouraged at establishing such easy success in another part of France. But amongst his possessions she found two pieces of paper that even she who couldn't read knew were blank cheques. Emile confirmed her suspicions. Jean had already freed the money to pay for this building. She had no control, none.

But she was his wife.

With her stoppered anger, she couldn't bring herself to speak with him and he kept any conversation with her to the most perfunctory details. So many questions she had on her mind: how long would he be away? Would he return for the birth? Would he sell their properties in Roubaix? But late that evening, just when she had all but given up hope, Jean came to her.

"I no longer feel confident of my life in Roubaix."

Her heart contracted. Perhaps she could make him see reason.

"We have everything here. This is our home."

"For how long? A local man has opened a business in opposition to me. He does exactly what I do and each month he's gaining on me. I've lost orders, long-standing customers."

Her anger turned to concern.

"What did they say? What reasons did they give you?"

"No one has said anything. I know these people, local men. They choose my opposition."

"Why would they desert you?"

"The world is changing. People are scared. I'm a foreigner."

She didn't comprehend the affairs of men. "You said the emperor would put things right."

"Don't misquote me. The situation has changed. Once I'm established in Alsace, you can visit your family."

"I don't want to visit—"

"The trains are so fast now and in the future they'll only go faster. We'll have so much money you and the children will travel first class a number of times a year."

She didn't want to travel first class. She didn't want to travel.

"I'm happy with what we have and covet nothing more. If times are hard, I can make some economy."

"No amount of economy will overcome little income. You're with child—"

"But you said we'd survive."

"I have to earn more money. What wife stops this?"

"I want the children to live here, to marry and have their children here where they're at home. I don't want them to be foreigners in a foreign land."

"Yet I must remain so?"

She felt confused. So easily he turned anything back on her. His face hardened.

"And that boy—" she said.

"This is the heart of it, your hatred of Troppmann."

"How can you blame me? He's surly and withdrawn—"

"He's an inspired man."

"He's just a boy. The story he told Gustave…"

She placed her hand over her mouth. Jean walked two steps towards her, his eyes narrowed.

"What story?"

She recounted the story of the man thrown in the river.

"He's little more than a murderer," she said. "I won't have him near the children."

"He was just telling a story." Now Jean smiled, and his voice softened. "I've watched him. You've seen him with our children. With the kitten. He's a gentle person. He couldn't hurt a fly."

"I won't leave Roubaix."

He glared at her, his nostrils flaring.

"We'll see about that!"

At this point she'd never felt more acutely that the worlds of men and of women were something completely different, as if they were separated, one living inside a small sack of fluid that cushioned the blows and blurred clear vision. The other carried this soft cell within.

For the first time in many, many years, she thought of her old life at Monsieur Noël's. Each morning the day ahead was planned, one cut, one stitch at a time, each cut and stitch tiring but never this deep-seated tiredness she felt in every moment. She scoffed. Waved her hand in the air. How easy it was to remember the past without the pain in her knees from kneeling to pin almost endless hems and the ache in her shoulders, tense from hours hunching over the sewing machine. Lifting the bolts of heavy felt.

Life was divided. Jean could be self-contradictory and she couldn't. He had no need to explain. Driven by something or other, he could simply show no real concern for her feelings.

In the morning, Jean focused on the details of his departure. It was a breathless summer day. The questioning faces of the children, her silence, had no effect on him.

On the platform, the children uttered few words. Jean kissed and embraced each of them. Finally, in front of Hortense, he offered his hand. Gustave glared at the airborne hand. She didn't take it.

"Very well," he said. "We'll see one another in a few weeks in Alsace."

Jean turned and walked to the carriage.

The children stood beside her and with no enthusiasm waved goodbye. Gustave stood a few metres from them, his hands together at his front, facing the direction of the receding train. They watched until they could no longer see a trace of the long white column of steam and smoke.

That night, little Marie and Alfred began to wet their beds.

CHAPTER TWENTY-SEVEN

An honorable family of limited means had nurtured in Claude the foundation stones of duty, courage, and faith. With these great three he'd shaped himself from the age of nineteen in Paris where he fit snugly. It was many years since he had crossed France to the east. In Lorraine, he felt acutely foreign. Little he remembered from his young life still existed.

And Alsace was further east, where the Germanic overtones became more pronounced. He expected punctuality. In Alsace he found people obsessed by the arrival of a train to the point where a few minutes either way caused near apoplexy.

By mid-morning he approached the Troppmann's, a half-timber house set apart from the village. What was it he'd expected to find? Something sinister? It was nothing more or less than ordinary, small, neither neglected nor well kept, one of the vast numbers of such houses dotting the countryside. He knocked and soon heard a shuffling sound, the footsteps slow and measured.

"Can I help you?" The soft voice came through a closed door.

"Madame Troppmann?"

"Yes." He waited a moment but the door remained closed.

"I'm from the police. I'd like to speak with you."

"What is it you want?" she said, finally opening the door.

She was shorter than Troppmann, thin like him but frail, her grayed hair pulled back under a white cap. Her powder-blue eyes gave softness to a heavily lined face. The air about her smelt of talc.

"You're not from those newspapers," she said. "One of them come last week and told me he was from the police and wrote the most terrible things about my son."

"I'm Monsieur Claude, the Paris Chief of Police." He took his identification papers from his wallet.

"You needn't bother with them papers. I can't read."

"I'd like to ask you some questions—"

"I've told everything I know, time and time again."

He looked past her to the depth of the kitchen. Sunlight poured in through two south-facing leadlight windows.

"What a lovely room," he said.

He followed her into the kitchen. The tools, bowls and whisks and wooden spoons lay in line on a sturdy table at the center of the room, beyond them a large hearth. Four eggs, a jar of flour and butter were on the table. Claude remembered the kitchen of his parents' house, the sound of the cupboard door opening and closing, the scent of food.

"I've interrupted your work," he said. "Forgive me."

"I were only making biscuits," she said, her tone softer. "I could do that if I was blinded. Come in and I'll make you tea."

Along the windowsill grew ferns and other exotics, reliant on the warmth of her hearth. Every object in the room served a function, the hearth for cooking, the butter churn, a large copper for boiling clothes. There was no fat to this room, beyond the plants. Her life was hard, much denied.

"Have you seen him?" she said, continuing to move, never looking in his eye.

"Often. He's quite well." It was a white lie.

"There's nothing I can tell you." For some moments she stood looking into the empty tea cup on the table. "I know nothing of what they say he's done."

He breathed in the warm smell from the oven.

"What biscuits are you making?"

The corners of her mouth lifted—almost a smile.

"They're Jean-Baptiste's favorite."

Claude found himself oddly moved. He only ever called her son by his surname.

"When he was little I made biscuits in the shape of little men. I'd hide them from the other children." She looked up at a clay crock, high on the sideboard shelf. "No one knew our secrets. When the last of the children left for school in the morning, I took down the crock for him. If it were empty, I'd bake more right away."

"I could take him some," Claude said. "I'm returning to Paris tomorrow—they'll still be fresh."

She brought a chair to the head of the table for him. She had thawed. Claude took out his note book.

"What was he like as a child?"

She looked at him, no trace of hostility in her expression now.

"With all the questions, no one's asked me that." She thought for a minute. "He were a blessing. After five children, I never thought to have another and with all the others at school or work, I could do as I pleased with him for the whole day. He played under this work table. He'd no fancy toys—the lid of a saucepan, a wooden spoon—but he'd play and beat the floor tiles with my singing."

She poured flour from a jar to a bowl and in her hand cut a pat of butter with a sizable knife, the small pieces falling to the flour. The easy precision of a cook always entranced Claude. She then rubbed the butter, the fingers of each hand shearing against the tip of her thumb. Her hand was small, delicate, the thumbs in proportion. Surely for Desbarolles to be correct there should be some seed here of Troppmann's hand but there was none, no sign at all.

"He were always small." Claude wrote as she spoke. "I gave Jean-Baptiste extra food, never from the other children, never the scraps left over as I prepared the meal, always from my own plate. All at my table was fed despite that my husband's fortunes weren't what they should be, if this world were fair. Jean-Baptiste grew strong."

For a long time, she'd kept him away from school. She told the older children to bring their books home and teach him, arranging a table close to the hearth. Claude asked her why.

"A school is a place where they beat children, mold them against their will. I've seen it with all my other children. I didn't want for him to go. The authorities made him."

"How did he find school?"

"He were the eldest in his class but the smallest. The other boys picked on him without mercy."

A new boy, arriving late and small for his age, was sure to meet such a fate. Madame Troppmann had done her son a grave injustice.

"I know a mother shouldn't have favorites, but he's mine."

"Did he settle in?"

"He come home with the skin around his eye purple and red. The larger boys teased him about his height, anything they could find. With one blow to the head, Jean-Baptiste struck one of them to the ground, left him with his ears ringing."

Madame Troppmann rolled the mix, adding walnut pieces, and arranged it on a shallow tray she settled in the oven.

"Would you care to see his room? It's as he left it."

Claude followed her through the dark center of the house into an odd room, stuffy and damp with no direct opening. There was a door to what looked like a cupboard but was in fact a small staircase. She started up, negotiating the steep ascent with ease.

Troppmann's room under the high eaves would be hot in summer and cold in winter. He'd inherited his mother's neatness, the room tidy, the blanket and cover pulled tight over the metal frame of his small bed. A chest of drawers stood against the wall opposite an attic window over a small desk and bentwood chair. On the desk were pieces of equipment, a mortar and pestle, glass phials, retorts, a spirit burner. There were two books, Quinet's *The Wandering Jew* and a book on elemental chemistry. Claude opened the chemistry book, stamped the property of the local municipal library. Troppmann had stolen it. He knew nothing of Troppmann's interest in the subject.

"I see he studied chemistry."

"Is that what you call it?" With some pride she looked at the pieces of apparatus on the desk. "He were always working at it. His father is an inventive man and Jean-Baptiste inherited it. He taught himself from that book."

Claude noted an improvised distillation apparatus fashioned by placing one retort inside another, cooling one piece with a wet cloth and heating another with the spirit lamp. Troppmann's ingenuity was impressive.

"He used to sit with me while I sewed," she said. "Now it were me sitting with him while he worked. Strange the way things turn."

At one time, a plague of rats invaded her kitchen. Jean-Baptiste synthesized some chemical and destroyed them in under a week.

"Be rich, I'd say to him. Be inventive, like your father. This were his invention."

"What was his mood when he came back from Roubaix?"

"Pleasant enough. Despite the fact I'd missed him greatly, I could see he'd grown for the good."

"In what way?"

"He were a man now. He had his own money. He'd paid someone to repair his clothes. He were a man."

"But didn't you miss the young man who'd gone away?"

"It's a mother's job to miss." She looked at the desk. "He came here with that man."

"Jean Kinck?" She nodded. "When was that?"

"Let me think…. Around the end of August."

"How did you find Kinck?"

"He were obviously a man of money, the clothes he wore, his manner. But there were something about him…. He came from this country, yet I felt he wanted to deny it."

"How was your son?"

"He were happy. He and Monsieur Kinck had some great plan afoot."

"What plan?"

She turned to leave the room. "No one would tell me such a plan."

In the kitchen she allowed the biscuits to cool. She offered Claude one with another cup of tea. They were warm and soft, a thin crust on the outside, flaky within. Exquisite.

"To harm someone is simply not in his nature," she said, unasked by Claude. "He's written and told us it's a misunderstanding and will soon be resolved."

What could he say to her? Was she aware of what her son was accused? Should he tell her he faced the guillotine? It was too brutal.

When Claude spoke, his voice was as warm as her biscuits.

"He needs to tell me everything he knows."

"He can't tell you what he doesn't know."

"Why did you name him Jean-Baptiste?" Claude said.

She glared at him.

"I know my scripture. I know what you are thinking but like Jean the Baptiste, he's innocent."

What could he say to such an odd response to an ordinary question? He made for the door of her kitchen.

"Thank you for the tea."

"You need to find that man, Jean Kinck."

"A lot of questions will be answered when we find him, Madame Troppmann."

She nodded her head.

"Where is your husband's factory?"

She gave him directions and a package, wrapped in brown paper, of the biscuits she'd just made.

"He'll be happy to get these," Claude said.

Having cleared the strictures of bankruptcy, Joseph Troppmann owned a small foundry geared to manufacture small items. The building struck Claude, paint peeling, dust clots and refuse about the floor. Claude felt the blast of heat from the forge near the rear of the warehouse, heard a shrill hissing sound erupting from the rear corner, saw the cloud of steam men raised as they plunged heated metal into water.

Troppmann had started work here when he was fourteen.

From the cloud of steam, a man emerged carrying an out-sized pliers-like device, something still steaming caught in them.

"Could you tell me where Joseph Troppmann is?"

The man motioned to an office at the side of the main entrance. The office was small, cluttered, two desks and messy piles of paper. A man in his early thirties sat at one of the desks, dressed in worker's clothes and engaged in paperwork.

"He's out for the moment," the man said. "You from the police?"

Clearly this path had been beaten.

"From Paris."

"He should be back. Things have been a bit chaotic round here, as you can imagine."

The man, whose name was Hesse, had been interviewed by the Alsatian police although Claude didn't recall reading the report.

"You knew Troppmann?"

The man scowled. "Of course. I've worked here for years"

"Was he a good worker?"

"He wasn't a bad worker." He reclined in his chair. "For the boss's son."

Claude pulled his note book from his pocket.

"I take it you weren't friends?"

"My opinion of him doesn't matter but when he first started he was a bit of a milksop. The men called him all kinds of names, 'shorty' and 'sissy' the mildest. Sure as hell embarrassed Edmund, his older brother what worked at the factory too. When young Troppmann got too hot-headed about it, sometimes we'd chuck him in the vat of water."

"How did he react to that?"

"There was fire in his eye. But if there's one thing I'll say for him, he's smart. He soon figured out he'd have to put up with the taunts."

Interesting.

"Did he advance here?"

"Well… he's the one what went traveling to install his father's invention."

"You don't think he was qualified?"

"What would I know? He's his father's son." Hesse was quiet for a minute or two. "Here, now—something I just thought of. After he was here a few months, he worked up incredible strength. He's got these huge hands. Have you seen them?"

Claude nodded.

"He started lifting all the heavy stuff, things the larger men did in pairs. Back then I thought he was doing it to stop the taunts, win himself some favor."

"But you don't think that now?"

"Maybe, but I think it might have been a warning to the other men he could defend himself."

"Did he ever defend himself?"

"Not that I'm aware. Despite everything I might feel, I wouldn't be honest if I didn't admit being indebted to him."

Claude looked up from his notebook.

"Early mornings in winter, ice often covers the foundry floor till the forges breathe again. One morning I slipped near the axle of a main power shaft. It was unguarded, despite us complaining regular about it. I struck my head against the floor, near knocked myself out. The sleeve of my coat brushed against the spinning axle, and the axle started eating it up. Troppmann jumps over a trestle and grabs my wrist, pulled with everything he had until the fabric tore. It come away clean."

He pulled up the sleeve of his coat to show a scar. Despite Troppmann's quick response, a bit of skin on the inside of his forearm had ground against the spinning axle.

"He saved my arm."

He clenched a fist to demonstrate. While Hesse was genuinely grateful, Claude felt, Troppmann showed off his swiftness, his strength, but more important his ability to think quickly.

Joseph Troppmann appeared at the office door. He was as short as his son, his thin hair grayed and pushed back high on his forehead.

"What do you want?" he said, glaring at Claude.

Hesse rose from the desk and left.

"I'm tired of this disruption," Joseph said. "I've a business to run."

"I'm Monsieur Claude from—"

"I know who you are. Another officer who wants to remove my son's head—"

"I want to save your son's life."

At the moment he said it, Claude realized it was true.

"My intuition tells me he was involved," Claude said, "but didn't commit the murders."

Joseph stared at him.

"In my line of work…" Claude stopped himself. "I guess it must be the same for you at times, with your inventions. Certain facts point me in one direction. But something, some small kernel at the back of my mind points me in another. Something isn't right with the facts I have."

Joseph sighed, his breath reaching Claude. He'd been drinking and not just a glass, stale alcohol mixed with fresh. He collapsed into the desk chair, raised his large hands, reddened by working a forge, scarred and distorted by misplaced blows, to soothe his face.

"What is there I can tell you?" he said.

"I desperately need to find Jean Kinck. I believe your son knows his exact whereabouts but for some reason won't tell me."

Joseph opened a desk drawer and produced a bottle of whiskey and two glasses. He motioned towards Claude, who nodded even though he didn't want to drink.

"I only met him once," Joseph said, slugging back the whiskey. "Here at the factory. He came with my son to tell me my invention was well received in Roubaix. Can you imagine how golden those words were to me?"

He seemed to savor the sweetness of this moment until some tart thought caused him to grimace. He poured another drink. Claude sipped his.

"I found Kinck conceited at his own success," Joseph said, drinking the whiskey and pouring a fresh one. "Bad men with money roam the country stealing inventions to claim as their own."

"You think that's what Kinck was doing?"

"I assume all men do it."

"How was he with your son?"

"Not like a father—if that's what you're thinking, I saw no evidence of it."

Interesting, since for young Troppmann, Kinck was the successful version of his father.

"Then what was the attraction?" Claude said. "There's a large age gap between them."

"I'll not hazard a guess."

Claude, his finances modest but planned and secure, couldn't imagine the sting of bankruptcy. He sensed that Joseph Troppmann still felt it most acutely, left burning, irrationally fearing and distrusting all others, even those most intimate to him.

"Your wife said they had some plan afoot?"

"I know nothing of such a plan. What plan? My son's not capable of such things. He was soon to leave to install another machine near Paris."

"What can you tell me of your son?"

"I wish I'd not sent him to Roubaix." The whiskey had loosened his belligerence. "There were complaints about his work in Paris. I should have called him back after he'd finished. There are a dozen men who could have gone to Roubaix and completed the task."

"What complaints? I've had no reports of complaints."

"That he was careless. Unfocused. Life usually only gives you one bite. I'm most fortunate. After my bankruptcy, I grew sharper teeth. With this new invention every legal requirement was in place before I started. He asked to be sent on to Roubaix. His mother insisted he should be given the opportunity."

He poured another whiskey, unconcerned that Claude hadn't finished his. How distressing it must be for a father to dissect a son in this manner.

"I think you still have some power over him," Claude said, infusing his tone with warmth he didn't feel. "He's written to you, many times. Write to him! Urge him to name his accomplices, or—"

"I don't have the spirit. He'd never listen to me."

As Claude left, the sun was near the horizon, the western sky streaked with orange and peach. He felt eager to return to Paris and resume his interrogation of young Troppmann. His father might blame others for his bankruptcy and further misfortune, but Claude was sure the source of the latter, at least, lurked in the bottle.

CHAPTER TWENTY-EIGHT

Jean had been away only a few days, but Hortense felt he'd been gone a year. The children were generally well behaved, and in their father's absence Gustave chastised them if they were too loud and made sure they helped with the chores. She took great comfort in this – with Troppmann's absence he'd become his old self again. She took great pride that at the office he worked long hours, arriving home late. Hortense would cook his meal and serve him in the warm kitchen.

"The office is chaotic," he said.

"It would be without your father."

"He left it in chaos."

This surprised her. Jean was fastidious.

"How do you mean?"

Gustave listed details she had no idea about but high-lighted them as things that had been untended for months.

"And the more I look, the more I find."

Perhaps Jean was testing Gustave's abilities. It didn't seem possible he'd go to these lengths, especially now he had com-petition. Gustave was only a boy. It wasn't fair to put him under even more pressure. Jean must have left someone to help him.

"What does Monsieur Viller say?"

"Monsieur Viller?"

"He works for your father."

"He left. Some months ago."

Jean had never mentioned this to her, though he had always confided in Viller.

"Your father will return soon," she said, forcing a reassuring smile.

"I hope so." Gustave looked at her. Although his face was filled with concern, she saw her young boy. Despite his bravado, all the silliness he'd recited after Troppmann, he was still her boy.

With Jean's absence the baby grew more restless, tossing and turning all day and even more so at night. What woman would mind this? The baby was strong and healthy and each move made her sure it was a girl. The boys had all lain silent in her womb, only little Marie had kicked and tossed in this manner. But it left her often awake at night with her troubled mind. How could Jean have left the office disorganized? With this rival, he should run an even tighter ship.

One afternoon she tidied the papers in Jean's home library. She never discarded anything, just neatened the papers, dusted the ornaments and desk and rubbed bee's wax into the leather border of the ink blotter. Amongst the papers she found a letter. That evening, she asked Gustave to read it.

"I won't read father's mail."

"Read it to me."

"It's not right—"

"I don't care." She extended her hand. The pages flapped about. "Read it."

It pained her to speak so forcefully. He took the letter from her hand.

"Who is it from?"

He looked at the last page. "Troppmann."

"What does it say?"

Gustave regarded her for a long moment, then lowered his eyes to read while she paced the room.

"It's the letter father received telling him to travel to Alsace. There's nothing very interesting, just particulars of travel, which trains he should take."

"What else?"

"It finishes with, 'I have found a room in which we can do everything we want. Come to Alsace, bring money, and I'll show you.'"

"A room?" She stopped pacing. "What room?"

"I don't know." He flicked through the pages. "The letter finishes there."

"But your father said it was a building. Why would he travel to Alsace just to see a room?"

She seized the letter from Gustave's hand and looked down at the scrawl of lines and curves and dots. Gustave pointed to a word.

"Room," he said. "It says room."

Why would they need a room, a secret room?

After many more days, in the morning's post she received a letter she presumed from Jean and summonsed Gustave to read it.

"It's addressed to you and he hopes we're all well. Everything proceeds in Alsace and he considers Troppmann's find most suitable for their enterprise."

The baby kicked hard and she sank into an armchair. All her ill wishes for the enterprise had been for naught.

"He's made an offer for the building...." Gustave looked up at her. "He says it's a building. He's made an offer that's been accepted."

Included in the letter was one of the blank cheques from the Caisse Commerciale—Jean had made it out to withdraw 5500 francs. There'd been some problem trying to cash a cheque for this amount so far from Roubaix, so Jean instructed her to cash the cheque at the Roubaix office of the bank and forward the cash to him in Alsace.

"All that money," Gustave said. "He wants you to mail it to a Poste Restante at the Guebwiller Post Office."

So. Jean had made up his mind to buy this building without consulting her, with no concern for her feelings.

"Leave me," she said. "Go."

Gustave rose slowly from his chair. For a moment he stood looking at her face, his eyes cold. Then he left. Her head ached, as if a band had been placed around her temples and tightened. How could Jean be so heartless, forgetting all his promises to her? How could he spend all this money? How had her life taken this path? Had Monsieur Noël asked her to marry, would she have accepted? He still ran the shop and was still without a wife. What life would they have had?

To think like this was idiocy.

But to send this money... Had Jean taken leave of himself? This was crazy. She wouldn't do it. She went to Gustave and commanded he write a letter saying so.

"I refuse to write such a letter," he said.

"Don't disobey me."

"If it wasn't for you, there wouldn't be a problem."

These words knocked her. "How can you say such a thing?"

"Because you can't read, father made me stay. Troppmann wanted me with them. This crisis wouldn't have risen, if I'd been there."

She felt showered with stones, heavy with her child, such words she'd never heard. Her heart raced. Slowly she sank into a chair.

"You talk of obeying," Gustave said. "What a nerve. You have the audacity to disobey him. You should bloody-well do as you're told." He picked up Jean's letter and the cheque. "This is what he wants. You're wrong not to do this. I'll do it for him."

"You will not."

"I have the authority. Tomorrow morning I'll go to the bank."

He took the cheque and left the room. She remained seated. What was she to do? She had no power over Gustave. That began to evaporate the day Troppmann came to their home.

She lay awake. She thought of those first feelings, how she was linked to Jean from that day she looked at his waist while she adjusted the new coat. Life gave no turning back. It was what it was. She breathed deeply, and with the air, a window opened in her mind. She'd promised to obey Jean. She wouldn't turn that to a lie. Had he ever led her where she didn't want to go? No. He'd never failed her. He'd provided her with a fortunate life. He wanted something more. Did it matter she couldn't understand what he wanted? She was pregnant. If he desired this change, then she must trust they would have a better life in Alsace. Despite Gustave's awful words, he was sure of his father. Why would she doubt that? And she wouldn't allow this to come between her and Gustave. And if Gustave went to the bank, the manager would know of her discontent and this would stir the local gossip even harder and deeper.

She turned in the empty bed. The realization brought with it a modicum of peace, however momentary. Not that she wasn't still torn, still troubled. But the thought that she had every reason to trust Jean pulled tight her resolve, like an astringent herb.

The following morning she dressed in a black silk dress Jean had bought her and left for the bank, accompanied by Gustave as her reading eyes and wisdom. Although still early in the morning, the day was already extremely hot, the silk dress, tight over her belly, barely breathing and heating her further.

The bank manager, Monsieur Rémy, greeted them cordially in his large office and seemed unconcerned at the sizable withdrawal.

"So Jean has found his property," he said. "And quickly."

She nodded and even managed to smile, her heart and head pounding. Jean had discussed this venture with the bank manager but not with his wife.

Through his monocle, Rémy scrutinized the cheque's signature, compared it to documents stored with the bank. The money, five neat piles on a tray, was brought to the office. It panicked her. She'd never seen so much.

"We'll be sorry to see you all leave Roubaix," Rémy said.

She dragged her mouth to a smile. She'd done as her husband asked.

At home, she wrapped the money in brown paper, sealed it securely and lashed it with string for good measure. Gustave addressed the package to Jean, care of the Guebwiller Post Office. They walked to the post office and paid the postage. It was the 28th of August. On the way back to the house, Gustave bought a pouch of tobacco. She'd never seen that before.

CHAPTER TWENTY-NINE

When Claude arrived at the prison, Troppmann was asleep. The groan of the cell door roused him.

"I'm sorry I woke you."

For some moments he regarded Claude, blinking, then sat up on the pallet. He wore only undergarments. He looked tired, his eyes surrounded by dark circles.

"I've not seen you for a few days," Troppmann said, a quick edge to his voice. Claude sat and took out his note book.

"I'm sorry. I've been busy."

The cell was cold. Troppmann began to dress.

"You were poorly, last time I saw you," Claude said. "Do you feel better now?"

Troppmann finished dressing and turned to face him.

"These walls, that door… they can be hard on your nerves."

"Then tell me the truth."

"The truth won't protect me any more than *that* will," he said with a nod toward the door.

"Last time we met, had you taken something?"

"What?"

"The physician thought you'd taken a drug."

Troppmann sat down on the pallet opposite Claude.

"I hadn't. You can trade almost anything in prison."

"For a knife?"

"You know how easy that is to procure."

"But to take your life?"

"My life is taken."

If the incident was a warning to Claude, perhaps Troppmann had been a pawn, the low dose of bitter strychnine hidden in some sweetened food.

"Last time, you mentioned the children."

"I don't recall.... "

Claude read from his note book.

"'They should have stayed in the coach. Damn woman. They were to stay in the coach. They weren't to be touched.'"

"I never said that."

"You did. They were to stay in the coach—you seemed most troubled they hadn't."

"No..." He thought for a moment. "I don't recall."

"The issue isn't if you recall saying it, but if it is true."

He thought again. "I don't know what Kinck intended."

Claude cleared his throat.

"Did you like working for your father?"

Troppmann smiled, which surprised Claude.

"I didn't mind the work. School learning gave no future. I enjoyed the hard labor."

"And your colleagues, how did they receive you?"

"What do you think?"

"I'm asking you."

"You're testing me. Comparing what I say to what you've been told, what you've written in that little book of yours."

Had someone told him he'd gone to Alsace? Why would someone leak that information to him?

"They resented me." Troppmann lowered his eyes to the floor, then looked back up at Claude. "They thought I had no strength and a silver spoon lodged in my gullet. The foreman, Hesse, said he would 'forge a man from this Benjamin.'"

"What did that make you feel?"

"Perhaps my mother should have sent me to the merchant navy to perform such a change." He pressed his mouth to a smile and raised his eyebrows. "I was pleased she'd left me near her, although in unworthy company… Hesse should kiss my ass. I saved his arm from an axle."

Claude said nothing, his silence admitting he knew this story.

"In jumping to that cur's aid, I burnt my hand on a machine, but I felt nothing." He opened the palm of his outsized hand. "After that, they were nicer to me, scared of me."

It served no function to stir this bitterness.

"I came to Paris at your age," Claude said. "Nineteen. I was in awe."

"Paris was kind to you?"

"Not at the start. I knew no one. I worked for next to nothing for an attorney. I carried files to the Palais de Justice. Not like you–you came to install your father's renowned invention."

"Yet you stayed," Troppmann said.

"I was very lonely. But at night I walked the embankments of the Seine, crossed every bridge a dozen times and stared at the wonder of the cathedrals."

"Why did you stay?"

"I met my wife. I found opportunities. I advanced." Claude thought for a moment. "What did you feel when your father asked you to come to Paris?"

He shrugged his narrow shoulders.

"I was pleased to be away from the factory. My father doesn't think much of me but his design was perfect. Once I'd completed the installation, I stayed in case of problems. There were none, nothing I couldn't fix. I stayed a month."

"But how did you find Paris?"

"As I expected, full of people who believe they'll make a lot of money from hard work and in return the emperor will care for them. They can't see they'll never prosper."

"But… did you enjoy the city? Weren't you intrigued by her scale, her majesty? The possibilities?"

"Paris is full of Alsatians working on Haussmann's boulevards and sewers and great buildings. I spent my evenings with them. I may as well have been in Cernay."

"You must tell me the whereabouts of Jean Kinck."

Troppmann laughed. "He's in America. But he's killed poor Gustave. This wasn't planned. Something else has happened."

"What?"

"Something I don't know about."

"The autopsy established Gustave was dead before the others."

"Your learned men are wrong."

"This obdurate manner doesn't help you."

"The rich don't want the poor to share their wealth, Monsieur Claude. Of all the things my father said, I'm most sure of this."

"Jean Kinck appeared to be helping you."

Troppmann looked around the cell. "I can't see how this has helped."

Without any outward display, Claude churned. He needed to knock Troppmann from his perch, and arguing with him would get him nowhere.

"Tell me about the children…"

"I did nothing to foster their love but they adored me. They were innocents."

"Murdered innocents."

"Not by me. Not by me."

"But you were there."

He bowed his head as if examining his conscience. Claude had to provoke him, break this measured calm. He handed him the brown paper parcel. With no outward sign, Troppmann peeled back the paper.

"Biscuits," he said, offering them first to Claude. "Did your wife make them?"

"No, and they're all for you. There are biscuits in every Parisian cafes for me."

Troppmann smiled and lay the package on his bed.

"Are you sure?" he said, mouth half full. He stopped. His expression darkened. "These are my mother's."

He chewed again. He spat the chunks to the floor.

"They are," Claude said.

"You have been to her."

"Yes."

"You must not go near her."

"Why not?"

"She's not to be involved."

"She's worried about you. Where is Jean Kinck?"

"Do not go near her."

"She thinks you're innocent. Prove her right."

"He will kill her."

"Then you believe he's still in France."

"No." Troppmann hurled the biscuits at Claude. "No. No. NO!"

A guard entered the cell and attempted to restrain Troppmann, yelling for help to curtail his flaying arms and legs.

"Tell me where Jean Kinck is," Claude said.

"I will not."

"Tell me."

"NO!"

The guard held Troppmann's arms behind him.

"You're not an imbecile but you behave like one," Claude said. "Don't you understand your situation? They'll cut off your head if you don't tell what you know."

Claude immediately regretted his outburst. Troppmann remained as he was, his face defiant, his arms restrained by a guard. Had he already accepted his fate? Claude couldn't stand to look at him any longer and made his way from the cell, crushing the biscuits underfoot.

To calm himself, he decided to walk from Mazas to the prefecture along the Seine's embankments and sent his coach away. The day's cool air stirred, pleasing on his heated cheeks. Catherine maintained this would be a savage winter. The interview frustrated him but in all the discourse, one thing stood out; the boy was infuriating. And his trip to Alsace hadn't gleaned the information he'd hoped and stood as something of a misjudgment. No doubt Piétri would remind him of the cost and the loss of time. Time tick-tocked heavily.

Once Claude sat at his desk, he felt a moment of calm, cocooned in his office. Somehow the desk felt unfamiliar. Perhaps it was just his absence but no-something had changed. There was a backlog of papers to read and sign. That was expected but something was different. He turned the key in his desk drawer and opened it slowly. The stack of paper wasn't its usual neat pile. He leant down to the drawer. There was a foreign scent, slight and unmistakably present. He moved some of the higher sheets. Had they been rifled through? Perhaps he was mistaken. Who would go through these? Anything of any importance was in his note book and that was always with him. And the drawer was locked. He breathed out slowly. He was tired and imagining things.

He started reading through the papers, letters concerning facets of other cases, requests for information, access to old files, Piétri's estimates of costings for various elements of the Troppmann investigation. Tawdry. Such bureaucracy. Pen pushers ratifying their own jobs with meaningless statistics. All this could wait. He looked across his desk for the dossier of recent reported cases. Keeping abreast of events in the prefecture was much more important than this piffle. The dossier wasn't on its usual corner of his desk.

"Souvas?" he said.

He reshuffled the paper. Souvas appeared at the door.

"Where's the dossier?"

"I updated it this morning."

Claude looked around his desk. "It's not here."

Souvas came to the desk and moved some of the pieces.

"I'm not sure… It was definitely here… How odd. I'll go and get the morning's alerts."

Unevenly, Souvas hurried down the hall. Why the devil wasn't this on his desk? Never. Never had this occurred. Damn delays. He read and signed more of the papers until Souvas returned.

"I'll find the dossier," Souvas said.

"I'm sure it will turn up."

Claude went through the reports, a bloated woman pulled from the Seine, pregnant, suicide, no doubt. A man had been shot in the Jardin du Luxenborg, his face badly disfigured. A body found in the sewer. Evidently it had been there for some time, but discovered when it moved and blocked one of the passageways. It was a male. Murdered by stab wounds to the throat. Suspected knife. Estimated age mid-forties.

"Did you see this report?" Claude said.

Souvas read over it. "No. It wasn't there this morning. Why?"

"I don't know… The way the man was killed. The wounds are similar to Gustave Kinck. His age…"

"Which part of the sewer is it in?"

"The nineteenth arrondissement."

Souvas paused to think. "That's damn near Pantin.

"You think it's related?"

"I think it's worth going to see," Souvas said. "It might be Kinck."

"Good man. You trust your instincts."

CHAPTER THIRTY

A sharp knock at the front door interrupted Hortense's solitary morning housework. Gustave was at the office and Emile had taken the younger children to their grandparents for the day. She expected no one. She walked to the parlor window, shielded by the lace curtain. A large black closed carriage stood in the street. She knew no one with such an ostentatious vehicle. She hurried to the door.

She gasped, held a hand to her mouth and stepped back. Troppmann smiled, his sharp teeth in full exposure, standing as close as possible to the doorstep. She could find no breath, unable to speak.

"How pleasing to find you at home," he said, stepping inside.

She stared at him. He wore a fine suit. He moved with an elaborate arrogance, replacing his awkward boyish manner. She'd not seen him since she'd dismissed him from the house. She made no overture to invite him in but there he was, taking a seat in the parlor. She sat across of him, not out of politeness but because she feared her legs would no longer hold her up.

"Is Jean with you?"

"He's in Paris."

She gasped. Before she could protest he produced an envelope from his coat and handed it to her. He knew she couldn't read. He smiled, almost a snarl. Her mind swirled. She was lost.

Someone came through the front door, and in seconds Gustave stood in the room.

"I couldn't believe you were here," he said, addressing Troppmann. "Where's father?"

"In Paris."

"How did you know he was here?" Hortense said.

The two looked at her, both with contempt.

"He sent his driver to fetch me," Gustave said.

Troppmann turned back towards him.

"Everything has proceeded according to plan," he said.

Hortense held the letter out to Gustave.

"Will you read this to me?"

He glanced at Troppmann and seized the letter. This arrogance had returned to him, blown in from the street.

My dear family,

The time has come to disclose my secret. I had commissioned Troppmann to deliver these letters, for I cannot leave Paris. I'm far too embroiled in our business to travel. Troppmann will explain in person better than I can in writing. At the completion of this work, I will earn half a million francs.

Gustave must travel to Guebwiller in Alsace to collect the money that was sent there. Our business commitments in Paris forced us to leave before it arrived at the Poste Restante.

Enclosed is a procuration letter. It authorizes you to collect the package. The mayor of Roubaix must sign it. Get the papers ready before you leave. If you need money for the journey, get it from the bank. Enclosed is a cheque for 500 francs to cover these expenses.

I have given all explanations to Troppmann. In turn, he'll explain everything to you. You must do everything he tells you.

Your loving father,

Jean Kinck

She felt woozy, her heart racing with the knowledge and the lack of knowledge. Gustave joked with Troppmann, discussing the particulars of his travel as if it was already decided.

"But why must Gustave go to Alsace to collect this money?" she said. "Why didn't Jean pick it up?"

"Unfortunately, we were called away from Alsace," Troppmann said, "before the package containing the money arrived. Business moves swiftly. Gustave must retrieve it. Once he has the money, he'll bring it to us in Paris."

Gustave eyes were bright with the prospect of adventure.

She asked for the letter to be read again.

"There's no time," Troppmann said. "I must return to Paris."

"Paris? What happened to the building in Alsace?"

Troppmann turned on her. "How many times must I say? Business moves quickly." Then, in a more civil tone, "There've been many changes of plan."

"But Paris?"

He handed to Gustave the procuration letter and the cheque for his expenses.

"Now I must return to Jean in Paris," he said to Gustave. "So it's up to you to collect the money and bring it to us."

He ruffled Gustave's hair the way Jean did.

"I'll leave immediately," Gustave said.

"No hasty departure will occur!" she said. "It will take time to prepare the documentation." She stood and met Troppmann's eyes. "Jean's letter says you'll explain. I've many questions."

"And I've said I've no time." He ran his hand over his forehead. "You'll just have to trust your husband."

Gustave followed him out of the house. From the parlor window she watched him mount the closed carriage with all the flair of a marquis or vicomte.

"There'll be no problem," Gustave said.

"My dear friend, I can only hope that's true."

Troppmann disappeared in to the dark recesses of the carriage which quickly sped away.

Gustave stood waving.

CHAPTER THIRTY-ONE

Nowhere had the Emperor and Haussmann danced such a tarantella as the grand sewer of Paris. Planned to reach nearly 600 kilometres, Paris sewage now drained from the newly minted twenty arrondissements to the bowels of the Place de la Concorde. Black city boulevards under city boulevards, a network of sandstone arches disappearing into the darkness, dank, running and dripping and foul.

Claude and Souvas entered the system in Boulevard de Sébastopol, their guide escorting them to below the nineteenth. Like their over ground counterparts, to the sides of the streams were footpaths, small bridges crossing intersections. The water ran determined but thundered like a waterfall, each ripple repeatedly echoing and summing off the hard walls. An intermittent row of yellowy gaslights flickered in the dark. Claude raised to his nose a handkerchief soaked in perfume but the odor was invincible.

The body had been found by a guide, paid to escort tourists through the lengths of effluent, another thrill only the Second Empire could provide; the wonder of excrement. Fortunately only the guide had seen the body and managed to let it remain in the shadow, shepherding his flock to another branch of archways. This was something to be grateful for; if it was Kinck, with a slice of luck, in the short term the discovery could be kept from the newspapers.

After some twenty minutes of walking, Claude felt an air of disorientation. How this guide could negotiate this catacomb was beyond him. Eventually in the distance they came upon a half-dozen collection of police officers standing on the paths at the fork of two streams. Claude and Souvas remained at a distance. It was not his investigation, not at this stage at least, but the commander, Renard, acknowledged Claude. The body had lodged in a grate as if it sat in a warm bath, the water eddying around his waist in a pleasing manner. From what Renard said, apart from the difficult physical positioning, the body was in such a bad state of decomposition the officers were concerned if moved it would break up, dissolve and be lost through grate and the sewer.

From this distance, Claude could see it was male and indeed had been in the sewer for some time. The face, apart from being badly bloated, was battered, the flesh dark and rotting, slipping from the bone. Claude had seen a photograph of Jean Kinck, the memory of which before this rotting man was of no help. The hair despite the filth was dark as Kinck's was, and the high forehead and moustache and pared back goatee, a version of Napoleon III Imperial, were similar to the photograph. The photograph however was some years old. Did Kinck still wear facial hair? Claude didn't know. The build of the body, the bold chest of a tenor, the firm build were what he'd glimpsed in the photograph.

His eyes watered from the perfume and he abandoned the handkerchief to the sewer and moved closer. The neck wounds gaped so similar to Gustave's. It was impossible to tell if there were other wounds to the body which was still clothed, too stained brown to differentiate deteriorating blood from any other type of human waste. But these were worker's clothes, the jacket felt. Poor quality. Hardly Kinck's sartorial elegance. Perhaps he'd taken a disguise. Anything was possible.

"The hands," he said to Souvas.

Souvas looked to the corpse. "I can't see them. They're behind the back."

"Exactly. With all the movement created by the water, they would move about. They must be tied."

"Gustave's were tied."

"Correct again."

Renard came to them. "That's something this brilliant sewer can't remove. You think it's Kinck."

"It may well be," Claude said. "Can this be kept quiet?"

"I'll try but…"

"At least until the autopsy is done."

"Unless there's something on his person, it's going to be next to impossible to identify him."

"Please, keep me closely informed."

In silence, they followed their guide back to Boulevard de Sébastopol. Even in the open air the stench continued to burn his nostrils and he resolved to burn the clothes. Souvas looked pale and dusted himself off.

"I doubt that will help," Claude said.

On the other side of the street, some men caught Claude's eye for no other reason than they were slouching against a wall and looking in their direction. They were workman, felt jackets and fabric hats, dressed not dissimilarly to the corpse.

Why on earth were they so intent on them?

"Quickly," Claude said, crossing the boulevard.

The men straightened. Claude quickened his step and they turned, walked a few paces and disappeared into an alley. A fleet of carriages left Claude at the boulevard's center, unable to pass for some seconds. He made for the alley but the two men were some distance away and had broken into a light trot. Souvas caught up to him.

"What the devil's happening?"

One of the men turned back and saw Claude and Souvas and raised his hand to the shoulder of the other man to urge him faster.

"Follow them," Claude said, starting to run.

His ease wasn't what it once was and quickly Souvas caught him. The end of the alley branched in two opposite directions and the men separated.

"You go that way."

Claude ran down the right lane. The man was ahead of him, but he was much younger and easily pulled further away. Claude worked on, sucking air into his lungs, none of the grace he'd once run, alarm on people's faces who swerved and danced out of his way. The alley opened into a small square. The younger man stood on the opposite side. He knew he had the best of Claude. Claude heaved for breath. The young man turned away and almost skipped to the next alley and then broke into a run. Claude had lost the chase.

Slowly, he made his way back to Boulevard de Sébastapol, recovering his breath. Souvas was already there.

"I lost him," Souvas said.

"So did I."

"Who were they?"

"I don't know. They appeared not to want to be interviewed by us."

"Are you all right?"

Claude nodded. As if he needed a reminder he was too old for this. He should be walking the Auvergne with Catherine not running blind alleys in Paris. In silence, they walked to the prefecture.

Fortunately most people had left the upper levels of the prefecture building for the day and he made it more or less unimpeded to his office. Later in the evening he was to meet Catherine at the theatre, a booking made months ago. As a consequence, he'd brought his evening dress to the prefecture. He locked the office door and removed all his clothing. The basin water was cold. He lathered along his arms, chest, legs and face. As he'd left Paris for Alsace before Catherine returned from the Auvergne, they'd not seen one another for nearly two weeks. He missed her greatly, worried for her safety, hoped her mood had calmed. He was tired and distracted but nothing would make him miss tonight's appointment at the theatre.

Once his ablution and dressing were complete, he sat alone in his office. He needed these few moments of early evening stillness after the confusing and jarring pace of the last few days. He sighed. Who was the corpse? Whilst it was more likely unconnected to the case he felt some beating certainty that it was.

Damn Troppmann. Of everyone, he knew the most and he refused to speak. If Piétri had his way, his head would soon be severed. How many young men had Claude sent to the guillotine? And in what spirit had he sent them? There was always regret, that it was a waste of life, that there was no turning back. He always questioned if it achieved anything beyond the culmination of a case but he sent men to the guillotine with a complete belief in their guilt. He'd done his job.

Yet despite everything he'd found of Troppmann's crime, he lacked this resolve. He looked over some of the pieces of evidence scattered on his desk, the water-stained title deeds to the Kinck house in Roubaix, letters sent by Jean Kinck from Alsace to his wife recovered from the family home along with telegrams.

He would begin again. In his note book, in the pages filled with scraps of evidence, he would write a summary, a list of the most resonant facts, the points of which he was sure. Perhaps the whole business would make more sense on a clean page.

"Alsace," he said.

His thoughts ground to a halt. Someone stood at his office door.

"Desbarolles," he said. "How nice to see you."

"You were so embroiled in your thinking I felt I shouldn't disturb you."

"It's the season for heavy thinking." He was surprised to see him and excused his evening dress, explaining he was to meet Catherine at the theatre. "What brings you to my little office?"

"I was in the area. I thought I'd inquire how the investigation proceeds."

"Not as well as I'd like."

Desbarolles sat and Claude summarized his meetings with Troppmann's parents.

"The father's an alcoholic," Claude said. "The boy and the mother blame everything on an 'evil' society that's destroyed the father, but I wager he's drunk his best fortune away."

"And you think that has some bearing on the boy's actions?"

Claude looked at Desbarolles. Was that a mocking tone he detected?

"He feels he's... owed something. It's a powerful motivation."

"Something much more powerful is at play here. I still say it's not motivation you should look at but disposition."

Claude sighed.

"He maintains it was Kinck and he was just an accomplice. I need to know where Kinck is. In America or Paris or…"

Of course Desbarolles caught the hesitation. But he felt ill-disposed to suggest he may have found Kinck's body in the sewer. Even before Desbarolles, the loose associations seemed folly.

"Or in Alsace," Desbarolles said. "You're thinking of the Poinsot case."

If it had been anyone else Claude would have been surprised. This path, implausible as it seemed, seemed easier than explaining a body in the sewer. And the echoes of this case of the judge and the state secrets battered Claude again and again.

"But the facts of the Troppmann case bear little resemblance to the Poinsot case," Desbarolles said.

Claude thought for a moment.

"But you have also made this connection. Why?"

Desbarolles studied Claude, taking some moments to answer.

"The connection to Alsace," Desbarolles said. "Its public outrage…"

"True. Troppmann's now more famous than a judge of the Imperial Court."

"But what political agenda could there be here?"

Claude shrugged off the question.

"The current political conditions are so different to then."

"Are they?" Claude said. "The emperor has been rocked by the bad showing in the May elections. He's lost support in Paris and needs new support in the provinces. Ten years ago he'd painted a veneer on Paris which bought him great approval and had no support in the provinces."

"He's astute. I'll give you that."

"If Troppmann's guilty, the motives for the slaying are most unclear. Would a young man kill a whole family for a bunch of financial papers?"

"He's intelligent but not urbane," Desbarolles said, "undisciplined in the ways of the world. I'd wager he did think he could liquefy these documents."

"And if Jean Kinck was involved, would he kill his family and entrust all the documents to Troppmann?"

Desbarolles raised his eyebrows. "Would a man kill his *whole* family?"

"Yes. A man killed his family and disappeared without trace for seventeen years. By chance I recognized him in a market in Lorraine and arrested him."

"What could be so ghastly for Jean Kinck to require such slaughter?"

"Perhaps there was some other plan afoot," Claude said, "and something went wrong."

"This was hardly an accident. Why do you wish to prove Troppmann innocent or at least only complicit?"

"Because I can't see him killing the children," Claude said. "And because he's only a young man."

"The jails are filled with young men. And Troppmann is a greedy one."

There was truth in this and Desbarolles had gleaned it from his hand. Claude peeled back the layers of his thought.

"When I entered his home in Cernay," Claude said. "I entered my mother's kitchen. We both came to Paris at the same age. But I took a different course."

"You were born of sterner stock."

"I think he's become involved in something far bigger than he knew and perhaps more complicated than he could understand."

"I think you're giving him far too much credit. He sought money in the basest manner; murder and theft."

Claude looked at the documents, the title deeds and certificates. What worth were they to anyone except their owner?

"You think I'm being naïve?"

"He has the murderer's thumb," Desbarolles said. "You should accept that and conclude. You have experience, after all."

"Arguably my reading Lacénaire's hand correctly separated the course of my life from someone like Troppmann. But I saw the hand as indicative, it triggered my intuition. I didn't see it as evidence. Men are born with free will."

"But they're also born with dispositions. These hands mark people to be monitored. In the future, infants will be typed, the potentially criminal watched. My thesis, once complete, will arrest crime."

Claude considered this for a moment.

"Men are born blank surfaces, and society paints them," he said. "These brushstrokes may be bold colors, poverty, hunger, exploitation. Or finer and paler strokes—desire, regret, failure. Criminal activity is an aid to survival. Isolating the insane in asylums, the criminal in jails… These aberrant activities march on regardless." He cooled his passion. "It's only by understanding the forces that brought a crime about that such circumstances can ever be rectified. The shape of a criminal's hand shouldn't relieve society of responsibility for its role in creating the criminal."

"So you poke about in the past looking to explain this present mess," Desbarolles said. "You dissect the machinations of the mind with the machinations of the mind. You're working with a blunted, biased tool. For examination, the mind needs externalization. This is provided by the hand."

"But if this disposition you read is so complete, Troppmann would murder all the time."

Desbarolles smiled. "How do you know he hasn't murdered before?"

Trust Desbarolles to find the weakness in an excellent point. Nonetheless…

"There's something in Troppmann's psyche, perhaps in his past, some trigger I must find. I'll use it against him, hold a mirror to him. Then he'll confess it all."

"You'll never get that from Troppmann. He may tell more stories, but he'll never reveal the truth. The only security lies in accurate analysis of the hand."

"If I don't find Jean Kinck soon, Troppmann will go to trial and I shudder to think of the outcome."

"Have you no leads on this?"

Claude faltered. Had the news of the body in the sewer already leaked?

"None," Claude said. "Have you?"

"I've not seen Kinck's hand."

Claude smiled. He looked at his fob watch. "I must go. I won't be late for Catherine."

"Of course."

Claude gathered up the papers from his desk and placed them in his case. On the square outside the prefecture he turned to Desbarolles.

"I really do appreciate your time."

"I worry about you—"

"My age?"

"No. Not at all. Your mind is still most active. Your reputation. Resolve this quickly."

He steadied himself. "My assessment of Troppmann is correct—as to what he did and what he didn't do. I just need the evidence."

They shook hands and walked in opposite directions.

This investigation had placed Claude in a nexus of forces beyond his control. He couldn't risk another joust with higher levels of the prefecture.

He had to proceed cautiously.

He must proceed quickly.

CHAPTER THIRTY-TWO

What should she do? Hortense had Emile read and reread the letter, and each reading added nothing to her comprehension. All that money sat unguarded in a Poste Restante. Money sent to establish the business in Alsace. Her bowels roiled at the thought. What kind of foolery was this? There was no time to seek her father's counsel. What was she to do except what Jean asked? She had to rescue the money.

In the morning, she and Gustave took the procurement letter to the mayor of Roubaix. Monsieur Descat was very busy, and although he was a good friend of Jean's, they had to wait. The time was interminable and each minute further lifted her agitation. Gustave grumbled and paced and she implored him to remain calm. After nearly three hours they were admitted to the office, a cavern filled with light and a large desk.

"You've grown," Descat said to Gustave, coming towards them with his hand outstretched.

Hortense had never met this man but evidently he'd met Gustave. She judged him in mid-fifties with grey, wiry hair and an open face that spoke of wisdom. He shook her hand and nodded, motioning them to sit at his desk. He examined the letter, taking his time. Gustave pressed forward, staring at him. She noticed the first of light hair on his chin. He would soon need to shave.

"Before I can sign such a document," Monsieur Descat said finally. "I must verify Monsieur Kinck's signature. Please return in a few days."

"A few days?" Gustave said. "It's urgent."

The mayor glared at him.

"The matter is pressing," she said.

"Jean was foolish to demand this money be sent," Monsieur Descat said. "Cash by mail! I've never heard anything so ridiculous." He checked himself. "I'm sorry, Madame Kinck. Certain processes have to be followed. Monsieur Kinck is a great man, self-made. This is rash, unusual. I would be derelict in my duty not to verify the signature."

She looked to Gustave and felt he was ill-inclined to accept such a delay.

"I understand," she said, standing and raising her hand towards Monsieur Descat. "I'm most appreciative."

She agreed to the delay more to remove Gustave from the chambers before his inexperience thickened Monsieur's annoyance further. She signaled for them to leave.

"You should have demanded it immediately," Gustave said, as they walked home.

"When you're older," she said, "perhaps you'll realize a man like Monsieur Descat will only do something if he feels he has control."

"This is most urgent."

"And if I'd pressed him he would stretch the delay to a full week."

Three days later they'd received no notice from Monsieur Descat. Despite the outward calm she held, she was most fearful for the money and more fearful something had slowed the signing of the procurement note. But what could she do? To return to Monsieur Descat would insult him and play into more delay. She had to keep herself and Gustave busy. Despite her tiredness, she cleaned, set all the children to work. Gustave was anxious to be away on this adventure, his first solo steps in the world. She instructed him to write to Jean's relative in Guebwiller and ask if he could stay with her. Hortense didn't know this woman, but it would be safer if he stayed with a relative. And cheaper.

And then they received a letter from Monsieur Descat. Hortense said nothing but hoped her even nature had brought the result. They hurried to his office only to be told the delays had compounded. He needed the signature of an additional dignitary who was out of town on business.

"I'll not release it until he's returned," he told her.

Gustave set his face to a stern expression but held his tongue. She thanked Monsieur Descat for his help and asked him to contact them the moment the note was in order.

But that evening while she sat alone in the front parlor, Gustave came to her.

"Tomorrow I will go," he said.

"Go where?"

"To Alsace. I'll be there when the document arrives."

Hortense considered this proposition. It might save some time. She had an address to send the procurement letter to. And he was eager to begin.

"Go," she said. "I'll send the procurement note."

"Perhaps I should go as well," Emile said.

"No," Gustave said sharply. "You must stay here."

"But I could help you."

In that moment, Hortense felt how young Gustave was. In the last few weeks he'd worked so hard to be an adult, but he was only sixteen. She couldn't have contemplated such a trip at sixteen, but then, she was only a girl.

"Perhaps Emile *should* go with you," she said.

"You'll need him here," Gustave said.

She looked from one son to the other. Valuable time had been wasted, the money unguarded in Alsace. Tomorrow was the 5th of September.

"I will need you, Emile, to read and write for me."

Gustave left the following morning. He wore his best suit and another vest she'd knitted in haste without the laced colors. He carried a small case as he was to be away only a few days. She kissed each of his checks, warm with excitement.

She felt proud of him. Worried about him. Anxious. On her own, she watched his train recede into the distance.

CHAPTER THIRTY-THREE

The cabs and coaches queued along Boulevard Montmartre. The head of this snake discharged its passengers at the Théâtre des Variétés. Claude was late, but not too late. Three trails of people, in pairs and larger groups, filed into the marble paved foyer through the three entry doors. He managed to slip ahead of the throng through the middle.

Despite the cool of the evening, the foyer was stuffy. Catherine stood to the side of the box office. She hadn't seen him. She was intent on a couple, not three or four metres from her, two men in well-tended evening dress. She stared, unabashed, as he did at her. After so many years she still roused him, especially as he'd not seen her for so many days and especially now when she was unaware he observed her. The silk and lace bodice, the way it hinted at her breasts, sent him tingling. He moved close enough to catch her expression. He shouldn't have fretted. She was as she always was—intrigued, seeking to understand something transpiring between these two men. Some sense notified her of his presence and she turned. She smiled. He shrugged off his fatigue.

"How are you?" she said.

"Splendid, now." He took her shoulders and kissed her cheeks, inhaled her perfume.

"I thought you might not make it," she said.

The statement pricked him.

"And how are you?"

"I'm very, very well."

He dropped his hands from her shoulders. She did indeed look well, a rose blooming in her cheek.

"The Auvergne suits you." He smiled.

"Let's go to our seats. We'll talk then."

She took his arm and they moved across the crowded foyer towards the left-hand side of the double staircase. He wished she was happier to see him. She'd booked their usual seats in the dress circle towards the stage, at the apex of the slight curve that thrust out over the stalls. From this angle there was an intimacy with the performers and yet no obstruction of the view, something Catherine insisted upon. The foot-lights weren't yet lit and not a sound came from the stage. Claude adored the huge central gasolier.

Once they were seated, she turned to him.

"What did you find?"

He stopped himself. "No. You first."

She shrank into the chair's padding.

"I walked a lot. The hotel was lovely. There were many people there so I wasn't short of society. Some of them took up my cause—I was determined to find this land. We walked for miles."

He'd imagined her on her own, not in society.

"Who did you walk with?"

"A woman and her husband, Moubray. They're English. They were travelling with a friend, a Frenchman."

"How good you made an even party."

She continued as if she'd not caught his barb.

"I found a farmhouse, close to Clermont-Ferrand. It's small but it has a lovely courtyard, filled with sun and enough land for a goat and some chickens. And there's peace aplenty."

"And?"

"When this is all over we can go there."

When this is over… Claude saw no end in sight, in fact, he felt a thickening.

"You should have paid a deposit," he said.

"You've not seen it."

"If you like it I'm sure I will."

"Don't be so reckless."

"It will sell before this infernal case is done."

"Then hasten it up," she said. "Tell me your news."

He summarized the hours he'd passed in Alsace and the effect his travel had had on Troppmann.

"So I ask again," she said. "What did you find?"

He shrugged his shoulders. Sighed.

"Nothing with which to save him."

"What were you expecting? A two-headed mother?"

He laughed but her glibness irritated him.

"That would have given the press something to go on," he said. "I can't say how, but I feel restricted. I'm not seeing something. Something is missing."

"Then look closer."

He turned to face her. "You insisted I go to Alsace. I went. I seem to have found nothing of any substance beyond the functions, perhaps dysfunctions, of a normal family."

She returned his intensity.

"Look again. Find another aperture through which to view this young man."

He sighed and turned away, his eyes raised to the higher levels of the theatre, then to the dark boxes opposite them.

"Those two men," she said. "Innocuous men, in the foyer. To most people they were two handsome young men per-haps waiting on two fine women, two men perhaps waiting for three other men. I don't know who they were, but something passed between them. One of them said something, I didn't hear it and I didn't have to, and the other had a look of frustration in his eye, just the flicker that you have with me now. It was obvious what they mean to each other but most people don't want to see."

One by one the gas footlights ignited, the greenish light turning the velvet curtain black.

"Trust your intuition," she said.

"Intuition needs proof."

"Look again."

The auditorium gasolier began to dim and his attention fixed on the drama beyond the proscenium arch. When the married woman onstage began an affair, he did wonder: was it this male friend of the Moubrays, not the Auvergne, that caused the healthy color on Catherine's cheeks? Did he feel jealous? Anxious? Pressured? Yes. All three. He just had to free himself of Troppmann.

Late in the evening, when they arrived at their apartment, Claude still felt irritated with Catherine. He apologized, said he was very tired and went to bed. Sleep came, a delicious anodyne. He woke at a little after three and after lying in bed for a while went to view the case documents by lamplight.

He wasn't long settled when Catherine came to join him with cups of tea. He told her of the body in the sewer and she expressed no opinion to its identity. She looked over the pieces of evidence on the table and picked up the title deeds to the Kinck house in Roubaix.

"The document is unsigned by Madame Kinck," she said.

"She was illiterate."

She read over letters sent by Jean Kinck from Alsace to his wife. Some were incidental. Kinck had arrived safely, the business proceeded, he hoped she and the children were well. Another suggested the business opportunity was excellent. One letter asked her to cash a cheque for a large sum of money and send it to a Poste Restante address. Catherine frowned and looked closely at another letter, this one telling her to send Gustave to Alsace to recover the package of money from the Poste Restante. Catherine examined the title deed of the house.

"The body in the sewer isn't Jean Kinck," she said. "He never came to Paris. Jean Kinck didn't write these last letters to his wife."

"What makes you say that?"

"The handwriting, for one thing." She pointed out slight inconsistencies between the writing in the letters and the title deed. "The grammar of the later letters isn't sophisticated enough for a man of Kinck's standing—you can see that it changes between the earlier and later letters."

"I'm sure you're right," Claude said, quickly casting his eye over them.

"I think… I'm almost certain he's dead," Catherine said. "By the dates these letters were written, I'd estimate—by late August, well before Gustave and well before the others."

Why was he astonished? She was astonishing.

"Then, my dear, we have indeed… to begin with, we have witnessed the last murders first and not, as I'd thought, the beginning of this case. Jean Kinck is innocent."

Her smile showed she was pleased with herself—and with him.

"It's all right. No damage has been done. All study must first establish a secure point and explore in all directions. You must go back now. Step from the mother and children to Gustave and then back to Jean Kinck."

Claude looked over the letters.

"The dates do give a timetable. From the address of the letters, with the shift from genuine to forged… assuming you're right, Jean Kinck was murdered somewhere between Bollwiller and Cernay, in late August."

She looked at the documents and nodded.

Claude sat back in his chair.

"So Gustave and Jean were dead before Hortense. I was right to think Troppmann had other accomplices."

"But who?"

"If I can find the body of Jean Kinck, I'll force the names from Jean-Baptiste Troppmann."

"You must save this boy's life. He's involved but he's not driven these murders. It's too convenient just to cut off his head and be done with him. It's an endless cavalcade. Stop it, this time." "

"I must also find the truth for Hortense. The world must know why she and her children died."

The next morning Claude paced the few available metres in his office, briefing Souvas about the forged letters. Souvas glanced at the samples through a magnifying glass.

"I'm not so sure," he said.

"This real letter was mailed from Bollwiller, this one from Cernay, Troppmann's home. Study them closely and you'll see the Cernay letter's a forgery. I'll wager the murder happened somewhere between."

Souvas looked at the two through the glass, then nodded.

"You believe Kinck is dead?"

"Yes."

"In Alsace?"

"Yes."

"Then, who is the body in the sewer?"

"I've no idea."

Souvas sagged in disappointed. He'd led this charge into the sewer and Claude wanted to encourage him to trust his intuition.

"But I feel it's connected," Claude said. "As yet I've no proof and no idea how."

Claude laid out a map on the center of the desk. Souvas examined it and again the writing samples.

"You want me to leave for Alsace," Souvas said.

"Exactly. The Alsatian police report no sighting of Troppmann and Kinck after late August. This alone makes me suspicious. Troppmann was known. He'd been away for a period. People, shopkeepers, brasserie owners note such arrivals and departures even if only unconsciously. The two men together made an unlikely couple. Someone must remember seeing them." Souvas was jotting details in his notebook. "I want to know who picked up the money from the Poste Restante at Guebwiller. When was it picked up?"

"I'll prepare immediately," Souvas said.

"We'll talk before you leave, once I've had the forgery verified."

Claude would have preferred to scour the area himself. Perhaps he should go? No. He needed to command the investigation. If he left Paris again, Piétri would have Troppmann's head off. Into the breach. He had no other route.

"Work alone," he said. "Don't trust anyone."

Later in the morning, a handwriting expert confirmed Catherine's assertions about the letters. And even later in the day a note arrived from Renard. Nothing on the corpse identified the person. The estimated height of the corpse was a hundred and seventy five centimetres. Jean Kinck was shorter, reported as a hundred and sixty eight. The corpse wasn't Kinck. Renard reported the hands had been tied with the same type of cord as Gustave and with the same handcuff knot, secured by an overhand knot.

When Piétri got whiff of the discovery he called Claude to his office.

"The knots are not enough to say the corpse is involved in this case," Piétri said.

"Not with any certainty, not publically—"

"Then leave it to Renard."

"—but it's enough to ponder." Claude paused. "Why are you so concerned?"

"It's a waste of resource to have two people investigating such a murder."

"I'm not investigating. I'm only pondering. I don't think my thoughts cost the prefecture."

"Don't be sharp."

Did Piétri surprise Claude? No. He was used to economic pressures. But this was different, more intense. Piétri ground some other axe.

Claude dispatched Souvas to Alsace.

Every day he returned to Mazas to interview Troppmann. While he asked his questions, Troppmann, stripped to the waist, exercised incessantly. From any vantage he could gain anywhere in the cell, he pulled himself up, doing push-ups, sit-ups, hanging ape-like—he raised a hand to the cell window, wrapped his fingers around the bars, and latched on. With no strain he raised himself, the play of the trapezius of his shoulder and back and flanks an anatomical wonder.

"You should put your strength to work in a circus," Claude said.

Troppmann said nothing.

"I understand you're strong, but to control three children at one time."

Troppmann removed one hand from the bar yet remained suspended, then slowly turned his body back into the room, the free hand grasping at the air.

"Children move swiftly. You had accomplices."

"Kinck had none." He dropped to the floor, his knees bending to buffer the shock.

"We've found a body in the sewer."

He looked at Claude. "In the sewer?"

"The police believe the victim was murdered near Pantin. The murderer disposed of the body in the sewer."

Troppmann pondered the information. "It's not Kinck. He's in America."

"Really? The body's hands were tied with the same rope as Gustave's"

"That's available all over Paris."

"Perhaps." Claude sighed heavily. "I guess you're right. The hands were tied with the same set of knots, you see. Wounds to the same parts of the body."

Troppmann shook his head. "It's not Kinck."

Claude studied him for a moment. Did he sense an irritation?

"I know," Claude said.

"Then why go on about it?"

"Because you know who it might be."

"I've been locked in here for months…"

"The body was estimated to have been killed around the time of Madame Kinck."

"Paris is a cesspool. Many people were murdered that day."

"Whom?"

Troppmann smiled. "The man in the sewer."

On other days he lay mute on his pallet, lethargic, ener-vated, his face dark. Observing him, Claude tried to conceive of him as Desbarolles did, born evil, as if the soul, the balance of humors was rancid from the start. He could not. There had to be others involved.

As his desperation mounted, Claude wrote to Joseph Troppmann in Alsace, urging him to press upon his son the dire need to confess all he knew. In a matter of days, a letter arrived at Mazas prison. Before it was shown to him, Claude read it.

> *My Poor son,*
>
> *I don't doubt the horror of your situation. Heart broken and without the possibility of writing to you directly, I've asked obliging people to serve me as interpreter.*
>
> *I'm told you refuse to name your accomplices. But if you don't name them, worse for you, you let the entire world believe that you're the only guilty party.*
>
> *In the name of your heart broken mother, of your brothers and sisters who cherished you so, in the name of God who we taught you to fear and to adore, I beg you-name these vile accomplices to the police.*
>
> *Think of your family. It's unfair that we alone bear the stain of your never-ending, hideous crime.*
>
> *Here is the last farewell of a father whose old age is blighted.*
>
> *Joseph Troppmann*

Claude delivered the letter. Troppmann took it from his hand, something absent-minded in his manner.

"What is the day?" Troppmann said.

"It's Wednesday."

"Yes. It's Wednesday. But is there sun?"

His skin was now sallow, paled by the absence of sunlight.

"There's sun."

"I've almost forgotten how its warmth feels."

"We're losing the warmth. The days are shorter and shorter—"

"Yes, the days are short."

Claude swallowed hard. Had he meant the double entendre? He knew each passing day was one closer to his own destruction.

"There's a light breeze from the east."

"A light breeze… How lovely that must be on your face."

"You could feel it again. You just have to tell the truth."

He closed his eyes, as if savoring the memory. His melancholy mood was perfect for such a letter.

"Your letter," Claude said. "You should read it."

Troppmann sat on the edge of his bed and slowly opened the letter. His face neither flinched nor flushed. He didn't cry. He said nothing. Once he'd finished he folded the letter, returned it to its envelope, placed it with his other correspondence and went back to reading a magazine as if Claude wasn't there.

CHAPTER THIRTY-FOUR

Hortense received a message from the mayor: the procurement letter was ready. Why couldn't this have arrived an hour or two earlier before Gustave left for Alsace? Only this evening! Maddened by the whole process, by the whole situation Jean had created, she went immediately to the mayor's office.

"All's ready in due time," Descat said, beaming like an idiot.

"I can't thank you enough," she said, doing her utmost to hide her anger, frustration, and haste.

"Would you like me to address the envelope to Gustave? I understand he's already left."

He may as well have slapped her across the face. She wouldn't be controlled by this man, made to feel his inferior.

"That won't be necessary," she said. "I have the address and will send it myself."

Once at home, she called for Emile to help her. She went to the kitchen and laid the procurement letter at the table's center. Emile hadn't responded to her call so she went to the base of the stair. Since she'd forbid him to go with Gustave, he'd been sullen and withdrawn. She called again and returned to the kitchen. She needed a cup of tea but the fire needed wood. Although Gustave had been gone only a day, no one had been assigned this task.

In the woodshed, she tested that piece of wood, and then this, but she'd used all the smaller ones. She couldn't chop the wood — she had no strength. Emile…? No. He was still too ungainly to wield an axe. It hung on the wall. It was only small. Perhaps she could knock the edge off a larger log. Tomorrow she would ask her neighbor to cut more. She should have asked Gustave.

On her toes, she reached for the axe. She saw something, on the high shelf above. It was fabric, knitted, in a roll. She pulled at it. It was Gustave's multi-colored vest. What on earth was that doing there? There was something inside. With both hands she lowered it to the chopping block. The acrid smell bit her nostrils, her taste. She unwound the vest. What was this doing here?

She dropped the fabric. She clutched her hand to her mouth and looked away. It couldn't be. Despite no wanting, she looked again. The runt. Her small kitchen knife. The bone handle stained red. It had slit the small beast's body from chin to the anus. All, all the internal working were removed, the small carcass a miniature of those hung in the butchers but this one desiccated and uselessly degraded. No dog had touched the kittens. It was Troppmann who'd removed the kittens. Why leave it here?

Emile called from the kitchen. She couldn't discuss this. She rolled it over and returned it to the shelf. In the kitchen her heart beat hard and her tired mind stalled and ignited and stalled and ignited. She must concentrate, deal with what was at hand.

"I understand," she said. "You're sullen because I wouldn't let you travel with Gustave. Well, it's just as well I didn't. Your hour is here."

She handed him the procurement letter.

"You're to write the address to Gustave and then we must send him this letter."

Emile's eyes widened. He followed her to Jean's desk. She stood to the side and he sat in the awkwardly large chair. To her relief, he knew what to do and took an envelope from the drawer, put the letter inside. With great precision, he dipped the pen in the ink and drained the excess.

"What's the address?" he said.

The address. Where had she put that? The damn runt had knocked all sense from her. She went to find her bag, (in the hall? No, in the kitchen) and took out the letter from Jean asking her to send the money.

"This is it."

In his careful hand, Emile addressed and sealed the envelope. He carried it as they marched together to the post office. Hortense sighed with relief once it was mailed. The document would be there soon. The precious money could be secured.

That evening, she asked Emile to bring some of the larger wood into the fire. She would just burn them. The flame would be too high but she couldn't economize, not tonight. And when the children slept, she took the roll of Gustave's vest to the kitchen fire and placed it at the center. It was obvious why he'd left it there. Because he could, to warn her, to frighten her. How foolish she'd been to think her threats had had any effect. Here was his answer. She wanted not to see or think of it. The colored wools smoldered and stunk. It was best removed by fire.

CHAPTER THIRTY-FIVE

Within a week, Claude received a letter from Souvas.

Upon arriving in the area he'd gone to the Guebwiller post office. The postmaster, who hadn't been interviewed by the Alsatian police, said a young man had come a while back to collect a package addressed to Jean Kinck. From a photograph he identified the young man as Troppmann. He didn't have the correct documents and the postmaster refused to give it to him. He returned, insisting that he was Jean Kinck's son, that his father was out of the country and had demanded to pick up the package.

"I can't give it to you unless you have a signed procurement note."

Troppmann finally accepted this, apologized, and didn't come again.

The postmaster found the package for Souvas. It contained the 5000 francs. He then remembered a letter had come to the Poste Restante for Gustave Kinck. He found the letter. It had been sent by Hortense Kinck. She'd sent the procurement note to claim the package from the Poste Restante *to* the Poste Restante.

"The postmaster looked dumbfounded," Souvas said.

Claude realized what had happened. Hortense Kinck had meant to send the letter to the Jean Kinck's relative—the one Gustave was lodging with. She'd made a fatal error.

Armed with this new information, he returned to Troppmann's cell.

"Tell me about the package of money sent by Hortense Kinck."

Troppmann was reclining peacefully on his pallet, flicking through the pages of *Le Magazine Pittoresque*. He let the magazine fall by his side.

"It was sent to the Poste Restante in Guebwiller." Troppmann looked deeply into Claude's eyes. "Surely you know that."

"What was the money for?"

"To establish our business."

"What business?"

"Manufacturing, similar to Roubaix. Kinck had gone to Paris, by now. I went twice to retrieve it."

Claude took great heart in this agreement between the two stories.

"The procurement letter from Hortense Kinck never arrived," Troppmann said.

Claude sighed. "Where was the letter sent?"

"The Kinck woman sent it to the house of a relative. Gustave was staying there, but it never arrived." Troppmann's pupils dilated. "Something pleases you, Monsieur Claude. You understand something."

Claude thought for a moment. Should he lie, keep this information from him? Troppmann was perceptive. He'd know. And the truth would unsettle him.

"I'm afraid Hortense didn't send the procurement letter to the relative. She sent it to the Poste Restante."

Troppmann sat up straight, eyes widening. His breath whistled through his clenched teeth.

"That fucking stupid woman. She deserved none of the good fortune life gave her."

"Imagine that," Claude said. "All the time the money was sitting in the Poste Restante."

"The stupid woman couldn't *read!*"

Troppmann scowled and withdrew to the corner of his pallet, drawing himself into a ball.

"Perhaps you could tell me, why was the money so desperately needed?"

Troppmann wouldn't look at him.

"You and Kinck were spotted at a tavern in Bollwiller, and since then there's been no further information about Jean."

"He'd gone to Paris to order machinery." Now he fixed Claude with cold eyes. "You want to know what we did after we left Bollwiller?"

Claude held his breath and nodded.

"We took lodgings in a castle near Cernay."

From his time in Alsace investigating the Poinsot case, Claude knew there were many unoccupied castles in Alsace.

"That castle," Claude said, "like all the other castles in Alsace, is an uninhabitable ruin."

"What does it matter," Troppmann said, his voice low and hollow, "if there are cellars?"

The hairs on the back of Claude's neck stood as if there were an unnatural presence in the room.

"What would you do in cellars?"

Troppmann stared at Claude, his eyes dilated.

"Coin money." He spat the words. "That was the business. The mine of gold we'd travelled to Alsace to establish."

"Counterfeit?"

"We were to make coins to cure my poverty, my family's poverty, and to enrich Kinck further."

"But Kinck was already wealthy."

"Money makes the wealthy hungry like sleep during the day makes you exhausted."

Claude waited. There would be more.

"But Kinck had scruples," Troppmann said. "He wanted to get rich in a different way. That's what killed him."

He'd said it.

Jean Kinck was dead.

Claude tried to calm his voice for the next question, but it came out sharp.

"Who killed him?"

Troppmann stared down at his belly.

"I'm enough for you."

"What other way did Jean Kinck want to get rich?"

Silence.

"Where is Kinck's body?" Claude said.

"You tell me."

"Somewhere in Paris?"

"Not where you're looking. Not in the sewer."

"Then where?"

Troppmann stretched out on the pallet, covered himself with the blanket, and turned his back to Claude.

"Silver and gold aren't the only coin."

Whatever Claude asked, he said no more, his cooperation over for the day.

Claude was about to call the guard to release him from the cell.

"If you don't know where Kinck was killed," Troppmann said, "take me to Alsace."

Claude strode back to the pallet.

"If I arrange this," he said, standing over Troppmann, "will you tell me the whole story?"

Troppmann made no answer. Claude had to get through to him. What words did he have that he hadn't already used?

"I don't believe you killed them alone. Don't you realize the more you confess the more you're likely to save your life?"

"You must trust me," Troppmann said. "As I must trust you. Take me to Alsace."

CHAPTER THIRTY-SIX

Without Gustave, their lives were changed again. Who would have thought with five children she would feel so acutely his absence? An augmented absence. She fought to place the butchered runt to the back of her mind. The cuts were precise. Gustave had no skill with a knife, of that she was sure. He couldn't have done it. But it was his vest. Jean had given it to Troppmann. He had done it, left it where only she would find it, the vest an added disgust. This chain of logic left her further undone – why would Troppmann so heartlessly massacre something he'd gone to great lengths to foster? And each time the cat pressed itself to her leg, as she hung the washing or dug the garden, she too thought of the other kittens. Troppmann had said the runt would outlast them all. Weak and innocent, what was their fate? Swift, she hoped.

After five days, a letter arrived. Emile was at school and wouldn't be home until the afternoon. It was from Jean or Gustave—she had to know its contents. She thought of her neighbor, Monsieur Dassonville.

He was a caring family man who worked in some facet of the weaving trade. After Jean's sudden departure he'd been concerned at Jean's absence when she was so heavily pregnant, had asked questions. She'd wanted to discuss her dilemma with him but felt she couldn't without revealing the tatty state of their marriage. She knew this letter would bring with it a barrage of well-intentioned questions, but she had no reason to believe Monsieur Dassonville a gossip. And she had no choice. She must know what the letter said.

Madame Dassonville had gone to the market, so they were alone. Hortense sat on the edge of a chair in his parlor. He opened the letter carefully as if not to damage it in any way, put on reading glasses, and read it.

"The letter's from Gustave. A procurement letter hasn't arrived."

She gasped. "How can that be?"

"Don't upset yourself. When did you mail it?"

She told him of its delay.

Monsieur Dassonville frowned and looked over the letter again.

"It's not arrived."

"Oh dear…" Despite all the control she mustered, she began to cry. "I'm sorry."

"Please tell me—what *is* going on?"

She lowered her hands to her lap and met his calm eyes.

"I'm not sure…" She felt herself blush. "It's difficult to explain."

How she wanted to pour forth her heart, clear out all the conflict, hear another man's opinion apart from her father who was so taken with Jean he could see no harm in anything he did. Her body ached. She felt exhausted, this tiredness that mere sleep wouldn't relieve. She looked at Monsieur Dassonville's hands, his long fingers stretched out over the underside of the letter. What was he thinking? What did he really make of this letter? She felt taken over. She wanted to rise from her chair, sit next to him, take his hand and press it to her breast, press his lips to hers. She wanted just to be loved, to inhabit the role her father had made her for, to be cared for in return for her own caring. Jean had ruptured this contract. She had no reserves for all he was demanding. She patted her brow with a kerchief. These thoughts, where did they come from?

"It will turn up." He smiled at her. "If there's anything more I can do, you've only to ask."

When Gustave had been gone over a fortnight she received another letter from him. Her heart sank lower with each word Emile read. He'd given up waiting for the procurement letter and was leaving Alsace to join his father in Paris. The waiting had worn away his youthful sense of adventure. Now a small fortune sat unguarded and unclaimed. She sighed heavily, expelling the air with as much force as she could muster.

For Jean to have done this…

All this was something Jean would never have done.

It was then, only then, for the first time, she realized these actions weren't those of the man she loved. He, that controlled soul, had gone, left, as if that soul had only lived in Roubaix and now out of the cage had changed. What was she to do? How could she go to Alsace and claim all this money? She had five children to care for. She was pregnant. *Damn* Jean. How could he have done this to her? She was powerless, trapped.

A day or two later she received a telegram from Paris. Emile read it to her.

17th September. Just arrived in Paris. You must come. Leave Roubaix Sunday evening at 2 o'clock, second class, bring all the family papers – Gustave.

Why had she doubted Jean? Her fears, her powerlessness were nothing. She felt herself expanding into a void. Her commanding role, her path in all this, was clear.

Jean had become someone else.

And so must she.

CHAPTER THIRTY-SEVEN

Piétri laughed at Claude's suggestion.

"The idea of carting Troppmann to Alsace is costly, too risky—and frankly, absurd. You're losing sight of policing practice."

Claude gazed into Piétri's deep-set eyes.

"Jean Kinck's body must be located—"

"You have only the confession from this raving imbecile that he's dead and a theory based on forged letters."

Claude felt the verbal blow in the solar plexus. Had his ardor to solve this case, in part curried by Piétri, led him astray?

"If his body is found," Claude said, "the investigation would enter its last phase. Troppmann would be forced to confess everything."

"You can't trust him. The newspapers, for Christ's sake... If you take Troppmann to Alsace and they get hold of it the crowds will swell. Control, safety, even simple order, can you maintain that?"

"I've spent many hours with him," Claude said. "Troppmann is clever, hardly an imbecile."

"What if there *is* no body?" Piétri said. "If Troppmann *does have* accomplices, it's highly likely they'll try and rescue him, even kill him."

"They've already tried to kill him with strychnine?"

"You've absolutely no proof of that."

"The medical officer suggested it."

"The emperor needs a public execution."

"What if he's complicit but innocent of the murders?" Claude said.

"He's *far* from innocent."

"What if those truly guilty are still free? They may murder again? The emperor needs the complete resolution, surely?"

Piétri looked down at the documents on his desk.

"Can there ever be a complete resolution?"

Claude sighed heavily. "At the least, there must be justice for Hortense and the children. They were horrendously murdered. We need to know exactly why."

"The woman, the children are dead. Nothing will change that."

"I can't believe you…"

"You look very tired," Piétri said. "You're not thinking clearly. Rest is what you need. The policing work is done. Let the lawyers argue out the rest. Weren't you meant to be on holiday?"

"Is that an order?"

"It's a strong suggestion."

Part paralyzed, Claude stood glaring at Piétri as he returned to the documents on his desk. Rather than run the risk of any further altercation, Claude turned away. He felt stupefied. Piétri's denial of permission to move Troppmann was based on logic. But with this decision, he'd lost any bargain with Troppmann and couldn't help but feel that Piétri knew it. What troubled Claude most was this bizarre idea that the true identity of the murderer was unimportant so long as someone was brought to the judicial system for the crimes, with or without guilt. It was something he'd never experienced before. And now he was ordered on to holiday, a neat euphemism for being removed from the case.

Piétri horrified him.

As he returned to his office, in the corridor he bumped into Renard.

"I just came to see you," Renard said. "We've identified the body from the sewer."

"How?"

"Because of its putrefaction, we couldn't display it at the morgue. But I displayed his clothing. His wife recognized them and came forward."

"The spectacle has its uses."

"I just thought you might like to know. He'd been living in Freiburg—"

"A Prussian?"

"From Alsace, originally, but in Paris to work on the constructions. An Otto Herrmann."

The name meant nothing to Claude. "Many Alsatians labor in this manner."

"I only mentioned it because you were looking for an Alsatian." Renard smiled. "Ironic in a way, how close we can get and yet we're so far away."

"Ironic... Yes." Claude thought for a moment. "Why was he murdered?"

"The wife's no idea. She'd not seen him for months. But she said there was no end to the trouble he'd been involved in."

"What's that meant to mean?"

Renard shrugged his shoulders. "Take it as you'd like."

And that evening, Catherine railed about Piétri's gall and wormwood and disingenuousness and a string of other negatives.

"Go!" she said.

Claude turned to her, somewhat mystified. "Where?"

"Take your holiday. Find Kinck's body. Go to Alsace. Find justice."

He didn't inform the Alsatian police or Souvas of his presence, although he was sure someone in Paris would informed them. But he was, after all, officially on holiday. Souvas was stationed in Cernay so he spent his first few days north of there in Bollwiller, where Troppmann and Kinck had been seen together in a tavern. He drew the tavern's owner into casual speculation but quickly an ennui crept in. He'd clearly repeated his story a number of times and was unconcerned about its on-going accuracy or consequences.

His hotelier proved more open, telling him of a walking track from nearby Wattwiller to Uffholtz. Along the way were the ruins of a castle. Kinck's letters had mentioned a ruin. Troppmann said they'd found a cellar to work in. In the morning, he would walk this track.

The path rose quickly. Ahead he could see it crossed a small hill. He set a brisk walk. He wished Catherine had accompanied him.

"Good morning"

He turned to see a farmer, a younger and more robust man. He too was walking to Uffholtz and Claude let him go on ahead. Claude expected his youthful stride to outpace him but he remained in sight. The straight high pines formed pillars for the clear sky and the morning sun cut through in patches to the earth. The two men hardly spoke, Claude disguising himself as nothing more than an avid walker. It was quiet, save the whorl of wind through the upper reaches of the trees, the odd distant creak or groan from the branches. When he reached the apex of the hill, the farmer was standing slightly to the side of the track. At first Claude thought he was relieving himself but he pointed to the sky.

"What the devil do you think that is?"

In the sky ahead of them a cloud of dark birds circled in the air, thick as maddened bees.

"They're crows," Claude said.

"I know they're bloody crows. What the hell are they doing?"

The farmer started towards them, his eyes raised to the sky as if they might disappear. Claude followed. They took a trail to the left of the main path. The air was damp, the forest floor damp, a high smell of rotting vegetation. As they got closer to the circling crows, the reek of rot increased.

"Look at that," Claude said, walking off the side of the path.

"It's only a dead crow. That's the smell."

"Perhaps, but there's another. And another." Claude looked up to the circling murder. "Do crows mourn their dead?"

The man scowled and pressed on along the path.

Claude advanced quickly but each dead crow entranced him. Most were in advanced decay, the eyes gone, rib cages deflated. With a stick, he turned a bird. There was no puncture wound. They hadn't been shot. Other birds had died more recently, the corpses fresh, the feathers still satin black. In an immediate circle he counted at least a dozen birds.

He hurried on towards the ruins. The farmer stood, his back to Claude, his arms limp at his side. From a distance, in the dappled light, at first Claude thought it was a dead cow.

"Holy mother of God," the farmer said.

It was a man, propped up against a large tree as if he'd simply sat down to rest and fallen asleep.

"Jesus Christ," Claude said.

Although only a few paces, he ran, with fear, excitement and exhilaration. The farmer stepped back, eyes wide with surprise. The clothes were tatty. Torn. No blood. The face pecked away. Was it Kinck?

The farmer groaned. Claude couldn't reveal himself to be the Chief of Police. But he wanted to inspect the body. He looked to the farmer, his face ashen.

"Go to Cernay," Claude said. "Alert the police."

For some moments, the farmer regarded Claude, as if he'd lost all sense of comprehension. He nodded.

"Good man," Claude said. "I'll wait here."

The farmer walked away but within a few steps he began to run, his steps thudding in the quiet forest. He'd not take long to arrive in Cernay. Claude waited till the steps faded and then advanced to the body.

The man's hair was a dark chestnut color. The clothes, although in bad condition, were of good quality. The socks… He crouched. Despite the stench he forced himself closer. They were hand knitted, a low brown color, the same as those the Kinck children wore.

A crow cawed. The loudness startled Claude. He fell back on his bottom. The crow, bold as it was black, strutted over the mat of rotting leaf. Their eyes met. Icy and dim.

"Be gone."

The bird persisted. He waved a hand and then raised himself to his knees. The bird, in no great hurry, unfurled its wings and took the air, only to perch a few meters away on a branch.

Claude stood. The body hadn't been buried. That suggested the crime had been committed in haste. Perhaps by one person. No visible wound to the body. The corpse's head slumped forward, the shirt collar puckered at the rear. He forced himself towards the head, the eyes gone, the bone of the cheek bleached white by the elements. There was something written on the collar. Although written upside down, the name, Jean Kinck.

It was Jean Kinck.

He'd found Jean Kinck.

He inhaled but the height of the stench forced him back and into a fit of coughing. To suppress the need to retch and walked to the castle ruins, little more than mounds of stone. His faith had been rewarded. Troppmann wasn't a liar. This changed everything. By the state of decomposition, Kinck had died as Catherine asserted, before Gustave and well before his wife and the children. But why?

He looked down at the view, quite precipitous, to the farming plains that spread to the east. He could see the village of Cernay and remembered his visit to the Troppmann's house. The crows had pecked at Kinck's flesh—and died because their prey was poisoned. His pulse raced. In his mind, the chemical apparatus on Troppmann's desk surfaced.

"God be damned," he said.

In the evenings, while his mother sat sewing, Troppmann had used those improvised pieces of equipment to synthesize a deadly chemical.

The realization brought wonder, but with that a sadness. What thin tissue separated a genius from a murderer? In another life, perhaps in another time, Troppmann might have put his talents to good use, become successful, even rich. Claude no longer believed he could discern what forces had coached him to this path.

Should he be there when the Cernay police arrived?

It would be complicated to explain his presence and Souvas would feel undermined. They would report the find to the Paris prefecture. He had all he needed. He would return to Wattwiller and Bollwiller and then to Paris and Troppmann. Shock seemed to work on him.

Despite being officially on holiday, the following morning he went straight to Mazas prison. In the main foyer, he was intercepted by the prison governor.

"You've found Kinck's body," the governor said.

"How the hell do you know that?"

"Early this morning, a judge came to the prison and told Troppmann."

So much for Claude's hopes that this new information would be the card that made a winning hand.

"Why would a judge do that?" he said. The governor avoided his eyes. "I intended the information to shock truth out of him. Who ordered this?"

Claude didn't even try to conceal his anger. The governor took a paper from his desk and showed it to Claude.

"Piétri."

This was deliberate interference.

"The judge took a *procès-verbal*," the governor said. "Troppmann confessed to everything. All the murders. Even down to how he strangled the children and then battered them with the spade."

Without more delay, Claude made his way to Troppmann's cell, seething.

"What have you done?"

Despite the ferocity in Claude's voice, Troppmann's gaze remained fixed.

"I'm sorry I didn't speak with you, Monsieur Claude. I realize you'll miss out on the credit—"

"What have you said?"

"They've found Jean Kinck."

Was he taunting him?

"I know," Claude said. "I'm in command of this investigation."

"I've hurt your pride. You're angry."

"What the hell did you tell them?"

"The truth. Everything I did. I poisoned Kinck and then stabbed Gustave and the rest of the family. All on my own. I lied to you. I'm sorry."

"What brings this revelation now?"

"I'm done with lying. It serves nothing."

"I'm done with you," Claude said. "How can you expect me to save you if you'll not help me?"

"I don't expect to be saved. I must pay for what I've done. The guillotine will be swift."

"What are you talking about?"

"I'm not safe here."

"It's a prison—"

"That leaks. I'll not be poisoned again."

So the incident had been an attack, not a warning.

"You think you were poisoned?" Claude said.

"Of course. What do you think it was? I'll not die like that."

"Then tell me the whole truth."

"I see what I've done by speaking to that judge. I've inflamed your dispute with some colleague."

Claude wouldn't be intimidated, wouldn't let his anger rule him.

"I am not a fool," Claude said. "You are *not* telling the whole truth."

He left the prison for the prefecture intending to confront Piétri but after a moment's thought decided against it. What would result but another acknowledgement of Piétri's power over him and further tepid denials?

He ordered a copy of Troppmann's *procès-verbal*. To his horror, the wounds described by Troppmann corresponded all too neatly with those described in his note book at the morgue and the official autopsy.

The morning's mail sat before him, an envelope placed unmistakably at the center of his blotter. It was from Piétri. He ripped it open. His first impression was the briefness of the note. He read it and then counted off the seven words.

Hasten nothing; let things take their course

He almost gasped. His professional pride wouldn't accept this. His pride as a Frenchman would accept it less. Piétri's hand had slapped him, challenged him to a duel.

More was at play. The battle lines had been recast.

Kinck's remains were brought to Paris for forensic examination. Claude met the examiner, Auguste Tardieu. Kinck's viscera were in a state of bad decomposition but Tardieu initial report confirmed death from cyanide poisoning. Further analysis revealed the chemical was of low grade containing impurities.

"It wasn't a commercially manufactured sample," Tardieu said.

"It was made by an amateur?" Claude said.

"I wouldn't say that. The production of cyanide, particularly on a limited scale, is difficult. I'd wager it was made by someone of some knowledge and great inventive ability. In any case, the dose was enormous."

"This would explain the death of so many crows."

"Exactly."

For a week, Troppmann didn't utter a word to Claude—nor, said the prison governor, to his warders. No please or thank-yous, no requests, no letters to his parents. He sat in his cell, on a chair or on the edge of his pallet, for hours at a time.

Late one evening as Claude prepared to leave his office, a note was delivered from the prison.

> *Monsieur Claude,*
> *I beg you to come to my cell as soon as possible. I have a very serious revelation to make to you.*
> *I salute you.*
> *Jean-Baptiste Troppmann*

It was already after eight but Claude left the prefecture building immediately. His coach travelled from the Île de la Cité along the north bank of the Seine. The traffic was heavy and as they approached the Quai de la Rapée, he decided it would be quicker to walk through a series of small lanes close to Boulevard Mazas. He pulled up the collar of his coat against the rain that had threatened all day and now started to fall.

Once off the main boulevard, he turned into a small lane that connected to the rue Audubon and then through to Boulevard Mazas. He was perhaps ten metres along the way when he heard the steps of a horse. He turned and looked back at a Hansom cab. He could see the horse, the driver high on the seat. The vehicle was stationary but the horse shifted its weight from foot to foot, its hooves scraping on the cobblestone. The driver allowed Claude to go first through the narrow alley.

Within two or three paces, he heard the hooves again and the crack of a whip. He broke into a run but knew he wouldn't make the end of the lane before the coach. He stopped at the first doorway, flattening himself into the hollow. The cab thundered, this accelerating mix of hooves and metal and whip. He drew in his girth and breath and felt the heat of the horse, smelt its sweaty flesh.

Then he felt himself fall but not as he'd feared. He fell back into the hollow. The door had given way.

The black coach and horses rushed by. But another force threw him forward into the lane.

He was caught.

Pain burst in on him. And then he felt nothing.

CHAPTER THIRTY-EIGHT

The thought of travelling to Paris on her own with all the children petrified Hortense. For days she'd worked hard to organize the particulars of their journey. After the telegram, Jean had sent letters telling her exactly what train she was to take, what she was to bring but offering no explanation of why she and the children had to travel to Paris. It wasn't like him to omit such a detail. But now it was.

Every task was made more exacting by the heaviness of her pregnancy and profound tiredness. On the Friday afternoon as she was preparing some victuals for the Sunday journey, little Marie came to the kitchen. At first Hortense paid her no attention but when Marie was uncharacteristically silent she turned to her.

"What's the matter?" Her daughter's face was flushed, her poppet hanging slack in her hand.

Hortense dried her hands, knelt down and took the poppet, felt Marie's forehead.

"You're very hot." She pulled the soup from the fire. "We'd better get you to bed." She had enough to worry about, but it wasn't the child's fault she was ill.

Too large to carry her, Hortense took Marie by the hand and led her up the stair to her room, the effort exhausting her. There she stripped her, bathed her with a soft moist cloth, slipped on her nightgown, and tucked her in bed. She placed a small brass bell at her bedside—the sick bell, the family called it.

"You'll ring if you need me. I'll bring you some soup."

Now Emile was in the kitchen.

"We mightn't be able to go to Paris on Sunday," she said. "Can we send your father a telegram?"

"But we have to go." He looked panicky. "We have to meet them."

"We can't travel if she's ill."

"Then I could go on my own."

"You won't be travelling on your own with all our valuables."

"I'll take Henri with me."

"Stop this! Children recover from illness as quickly as they catch them. We'll see how she is in the morning. Please, find out how we send a telegram to your father."

That evening Marie's fever still burned, her brow pinned with sweat. She did as her mother had done, placing cool towels in the child's armpits and groin and sponging her skin with a moist cloth. Perhaps she should send for the doctor? But one of the boys might tell him they were to leave for Paris on Sunday, and the doctor would insist they not do it. Emile was right, they simply had to go to Paris. She'd had enough of this charade. It couldn't go on any longer. She must see Jean and demand to know what he was doing.

She remained at Marie's bedside all night. Although she was exhausted, drained by the baby in her womb, by the child in this bed, by her worry over the whole situation, sleep never came. The sun made its first mark on the day, the morning clouds blushing a vehement color, the birds of the rue de l'Alouette in high song. Marie's fever had broken. By mid Saturday afternoon, she danced and sang for her brothers as if there'd never been any cause for concern.

Hortense had lost a night's sleep and most of the time to pack. She had no time to travel to Tourcoing to consult her father. She packed only one change for each child, otherwise there would be too much to carry. She packed some bread, cheese and sausage for the journey. Despite the excitement the children felt she was sure the moment the train was travelling they would be hungry. She wouldn't pay the fancy prices charged on the train for food.

That afternoon, Monsieur Dassonville stopped in.

"There's nothing to be concerned about," he said, "nothing at all. There's no need to change trains. The train from Roubaix will take you straight to Jean and Gustave. Just ask the guard to tell you when to alight."

"Thank you." She nodded quickly and smiled. Jean and Gustave would meet them at the train station and take them to the hotel. It was a simple plan, no complication. They would be reunited.

"I'm of half a mind to come with you." Monsieur Dassonville looked towards his house. "I don't suppose it would please my wife."

While she prepared, the children ran about the house as wild as gypsies. The journey, seeing Paris and their father and brother, excited them to rapture. She had no energy to discipline them. Although she hated it, they were also excited to see Troppmann.

In all this confusion and uproar, her father arrived.

"What the hell is going on?" he said.

She showed him the telegram.

"You should leave the children with your mother and I, go on your own."

"I'd have to take Emile to read for me." Her father nodded. A roar of cries went up from the children. "They're all excited about the journey. And Jean asked that I bring them all."

"This is strange," her father said. "Why would Jean ask this?"

Why had Jean taken the whole family to Paris to make a photograph? Why had he kissed her in public when they first met? Jean was Jean.

She missed him. She missed Gustave. Choice for a woman was a luxury.

"Jean has always demanded his way," she said.

Her father read the telegram again.

"Indeed he does." He sighed. "You must obey him. And remain calm. Jean will soon explain all the mystery to you. I'm sure everything is all right."

Her father's advice had always been sound. Of course everything would be all right. This was another of Jean's follies. What could possibly be wrong?

CHAPTER THIRTY-NINE

Claude roused to sharp pain in his ribs on the left-hand side, his forehead pulsating. There was no immediate sound save the distant beat of traffic.

He moved his left arm, raised it to his head. His touch made the pain worse. He was bleeding a bit there, the skin split and sticky. He moved his left leg—pain but not severe— and his right leg, which seemed fine. Nothing felt broken. He touched the cobblestones, hard and cold. No rain, nothing above him but the powdered night sky.

He placed his palms on the stones and raised himself to a sitting position, carefully, slowly, but not as painfully as he expected. Then to his feet. He held a handkerchief to his forehead. He was all right. He was all right.

But what had happened to Catherine? They'd been walking together… To the theatre. He'd lost her. His heart raced as he peered into the dark recesses of the lane. Someone slumped against a wall. Catherine? It was just a hessian bag. No, no, no. What was he thinking? Catherine wasn't with him. He was on his own. He was going to Troppmann, not the theatre. He looked more about the lane. No one. The left leg of his trousers was torn at the knee, as was the lapel of his coat which had caught on something in the hansom cab, wrenching him forward. The cab had driven straight at him.

This was an attack. He looked to one end of the lane and then the other. He could hear nothing. He should go back to the main thoroughfare.

He took a few steps. His right leg felt fine but the left smarted. He'd injured a muscle. It was 8:30. He'd been unconscious for only a few minutes. He should go home. Why wasn't Catherine there? He stopped. Perhaps it wasn't Troppmann who sent the note. Would there be another attack? But what did it matter now? Troppmann wanted to see him. He had to continue to Mazas Prison, his gait reduced to pivoting his right leg then throwing his left forward. But how could he concentrate on an interview with Troppmann in the state he was in?

The guards took one look at him and tried to take him to the infirmary, but he demanded to go straight to Troppmann's cell.

Troppmann was seated on the edge of the bed, fully dressed. When he saw Claude he stood up.

"What's happened to you?"

Claude lowered himself gingerly into the chair facing him.

"It's nothing."

"But you're bleeding."

"I tripped. What is it you have to tell me?"

"You're injured. We must get you help. Guard—"

"No! What do you have to say?"

Troppmann lowered his hands and walked away.

"I'm sorry if I seem angry," Claude said. "I'm in pain. Please, what is it you have to tell me?"

Troppmann turned back to face him.

"I'm sorry for your accident. But since the discovery of Kinck's body, I've nothing more to conceal. To deserve the indulgence of the law, I've only to tell the truth."

If this was more tomfoolery, he'd be hard pushed to disguise his anger. The pain made him feel vulnerable and made it hard to concentrate.

"Do you know how he died?" Troppmann said.

"Perhaps you could tell me."

"Don't test me on such trivialities and I'll not insult you." Troppmann paced the perimeter of the cell. "Do you know how I procured the cyanide?"

"I've no idea."

Troppmann glared at him. "You've heard of electro-chemical plating?"

Claude shrugged, feigning ignorance.

"The process is used in counterfeiting. Worthless metals are covered with a small amount of gold and silver. Potassium cyanide is used. From potassium cyanide to cyanide is a small chemical step."

"You did this at your parents' house?"

"Yes."

"With such rudimentary equipment?"

"I improvised."

"Who taught you?"

"A book. People think learning's the domain of the wealthy."

"And yet you claim the empire has denied you easy advancement," Claude said. "Surely with this good mind you have, linked to impressive manual dexterity, you were well set to achieve anything."

"Learning is one thing. Fair application is another."

Claude took a deep breath. The air caught in his lungs. He winced.

"According to your previous confession," he said, "Kinck consented to become your accomplice in counterfeiting. Why kill him when he was useful?"

"In essence, Kinck was an honest man. But his honesty was at war with his greed. To maximize our profits—this was Kinck's phrase—the counterfeiting was to be on a grand scale. But the process is intricate, precise. Kinck was cunning. We needed to involve other men."

"Who else would be involved in this?"

"Alsace is full of unoccupied men who would be suitable. I'm sure you know this. We'd found a secluded castle. Ordered the machinery, the metals. The chemicals. We had the labor we required. Kinck had sent for money to pay for it all. But then he had a change of heart. At the last minute, he refused to help."

"And yet he wrote to his wife that he was certain of making a million?"

"By other means."

Was he irritable from the pain, or was Troppmann drawing things out deliberately?

"For Christ's sake, tell me what!"

"Some of the workers were French." Troppmann passed his tongue over his teeth. "But some were Prussian. Some wanted the easy way to money, but some were involved for… other endeavors."

"Will you stop this game?"

"The Prussians," Troppmann said, "they were involved in the counterfeiting to raise money to support their political efforts."

Claude's heart raced which made his wounded temple throb.

"One evening, Kinck overheard the Prussians discussing a plan to assassinate the French emperor."

"How does this involve Kinck?"

"Like you, he was an honorable Frenchman. He was happy to counterfeit the empire's currency to pad his purse but to kill the emperor was too much for him. The empire had served him well. He'd prospered."

Hortense's parents had spoken of Kinck's avaricious streak. Might he have seen counterfeiting as some victimless crime, his greed tempered by bourgeois notions of patriotism?

"Kinck wrote everything in a notebook," Troppmann said. "The time, the place, the date, all the details of the assassination. By alerting the emperor's authorities, he felt certain of a reward. He fed two desires with one caress, his greed and his patriotism. He had no need for counterfeit. He possessed a state secret."

Troppmann paused—for effect? Claude waited.

"Since I'd wished to join him in the counterfeiting, he promised me a share of the emperor's money. He was that sure he'd be paid."

"How do you expect me to believe you killed a man because he promised you a share in the profits?"

"If you'd let me finish…"

Troppmann began to pace again, which further infuriated Claude. Without thinking he sucked in a deep—painful—breath.

"Kinck told the men he was leaving for Paris."

"But none of the equipment had been paid for—"

"Correct. None of these men are saints, Monsieur Claude. They'd kill their mothers for less. But they're also not stupid. They have honor. We'd made a pact to counterfeit. And they were prepared to die for their cause. Would Kinck report the counterfeiting?"

"So he was a liability…"

"One of the Prussians confronted me, held a knife to my throat. He knew Kinck knew of their assassination plans. They wanted to kill him."

"Who are *they*? Name them."

"I argued for time. The money hadn't arrived from Roubaix. It would only be a day or two. He had to collect it from the Poste Restante. If we could delay him we could at least assure ourselves of the money. But they thought he'd known this information for too long and were afraid he'd written to his wife and family, telling her not to send the money. They said, 'For the security of us all, the secret he knows must die with him.'"

"Who said that?"

"I can't tell you."

"I'm not in the mood for this stupidity. Name them so I can give credence to what you've said."

"I can't."

"You're soon to face trial for eight murders. For God's sake, name your accomplices." Claude took the tiniest of beats to calm himself. "You'll be executed."

"You've seen what they did to the Kinck family. They tried to poison me. It was only that the food tasted so bitter I stopped eating it."

And now there'd been an attempt to kill or injure *him*.

"But you murdered Kinck?"

"I only made the poison. They gave it to him in a glass of wine."

"What happened next?"

"They were running out of time. The assassination was to take place in late September. I cared nothing about the assassination but I was too close to the counterfeiting to lose out. We had some money Kinck carried but nowhere near enough to fund the assassination. They'd have to pay for accommodation in Paris, bribing officials to get close to the emperor, fleeing France. And from my perspective, there was nowhere near enough to fund the counterfeiting."

"Why didn't you just leave them?"

"After what they'd done to Kinck? I knew too much. I'd made an oath. They knew where my family was."

Troppmann inhaled through his nostrils, a soft snorting sound.

"Once the counterfeiting was done, they'd leave for Paris and I'd have a small fortune. First we needed the money the Kinck woman had sent to the Poste Restante in Guebwiller. Twice I went to retrieve it but they wouldn't give it to me. In so doing I'd drawn attention to myself, potentially to the whole operation. The Prussians panicked and we fled to Paris.

"But we had to get the money. The assassination couldn't proceed without it. With two of the Prussians, I travelled to Roubaix. I told the Kinck woman that Kinck was in Paris on business and she must obtain a procurement letter for Gustave to go to Alsace, pick up the money, and bring it to his father in Paris.

"The stupid woman sent the note to the wrong address. Gustave arrived in Paris without the money. His father wasn't there. He became suspicious, told me he was going to report to the police. I led him out to the field, where the Prussians killed him. But he fought back, Monsieur Claude. He fought back hard."

He was facing Claude, his eyes glazed with memory.

"He was strong," Troppmann said. "He didn't want to die."

"Yet you didn't stop it."

He closed his eyes for a brief moment. The pain in them when he looked again at Claude was palpable.

"I regret it all. Do you think I don't?"

"I'm sure you do," Claude said. "But you helped them."

"I had no choice. They'd have killed me but they needed me."

"Then you had something to bargain with."

"I'll not gamble my mother's life."

Yet he'd placed his mother in this precarious position.

"So you called the whole family to Paris," Claude said.

"As you know, he'd told her he was to make a fortune. They thought Kinck had told her of the assassination plot. And as a result of that she'd not sent the money. He was always writing to her despite the fact she couldn't read. They made me forge letters from Jean telling her to come to Paris with all the family's documents. I knew she'd not be separated from the children, so if we painted it as a surprise celebration there was a good chance she'd come."

"Even if she knew of the assassination?"

"Exactly. She was an obedient wife who loved her husband. I collected them from the station, took them to the field, but I did nothing else. The Prussians killed them."

"But why kill the children?"

"The younger ones demanded to go with her. They had seen everything, everyone. If I had not gone back to the cab for the elder ones, they would have alerted the police. For a window of escape, they all had to be silenced."

"Surely you can't think this mere assertion will save you."

"If I name them, they'll kill my mother—my whole family. But I hid Kinck's note book, which contains all the plans of the assassination. Take me to the castle of Herrenfluch."

Claude couldn't tell him he'd been there and discovered the body. Could there have been a note book? It was a forest. The ruins of the old castle contained so many places a note book could have been secreted. The forest floor was covered in decaying leaf. It could be anywhere.

"Tell me where you hid it. I'll protect your mother."

"You can't protect her."

"I understand your concern. She can be moved from Cernay, kept in hiding under guard until these men are arrested."

"Are you joking? Your guards can't even protect *me* in this prison. I was poisoned."

Claude's temple smarted. How could Claude protect her when he couldn't even protect himself? But they could have protected Troppmann had they known he needed protection. Troppmann's silence had cost him dearly. He should point this out—

"You don't even trust your department, Monsieur Claude."

Claude sighed. What could he say?

"Not entirely, not always. But we can protect your mother."

"I must take you to the note book or you'll know nothing. Nothing!"

"You're just playing to have yourself taken to Alsace where you hope to escape."

"And if I do nurse that hope, then I must have accomplices."

Could he have forged this story of Prussian insurgents while in prison? It seemed fabulous on the surface, yet it made sense on more than one level. Claude's instincts told him Troppmann was telling the truth.

Suddenly he launched himself at Claude, stopping his face only inches away. Claude didn't react.

"Take me to Alsace, Monsieur Claude." His breath was hot on Claude's skin. "It's all in Kinck's note book."

Troppmann pulled away. Claude straightened himself but remained seated.

"If you don't believe me, so much the worse for you." Troppmann turned his back on Claude. "If they don't take me to Alsace to prove the truth of what I say, it's because they don't want the truth."

That last sentence stung. Claude needed some peace—his aching head could stand this no longer. Without further word he left the cell and the prison.

Catherine bathed the wound on his head with a vile stinging liquid. When they removed his trousers, his grazed thigh wept. She turned a wide bandage around and around his rib cage, which eased the pain of breathing and calmed him considerably.

"I was sure you were there," he said. She smiled briefly as she continued to dab the graze on his thigh. "I couldn't find you and panicked."

"I was here, reading. I'm safe."

"You know this wasn't an accident," he said.

She looked deeply into his eyes. "I've no doubt."

"The cab followed me. When the chance came, the narrow lane, they took it. I was lucky for the doorway, luckier still it opened."

"Who would do such a thing?" she said.

"You tell me." His loud voice caused her to pull away from him.

"You're in shock. Confused. It will pass. Let me finish this and I'll make you some sweet tea."

Her soft hand calmed him. Once she'd finished dressing his wounds, they returned to the kitchen. She helped him to a chair and started to make tea.

"In Alsace," Claude said, "Kinck and Troppmann connected with some Prussian insurgents."

"I'd be more surprised if they hadn't. I've told you, trouble is coming to Paris. What was their involvement?"

"They financed the counterfeiting. Kinck and Troppmann only wanted to make money. The Prussians wanted to fund their own activities."

"So Troppmann had become involved in something bigger than he thought."

"Much bigger than I expected. The Prussians were plotting to assassinate the emperor."

Catherine poured the tea and sweetened Claude's with honey while he recounted Troppmann's confession.

"If Prussia was responsible for assassinating the emperor," she said, "France would retaliate."

"And would be easily beaten. Prussia is far better armed. Prussia would be seen as the retaliator—the aggrieved, not the aggressor."

Catherine poured the last of the tea.

"This is too intricate for Troppmann to have made up," she said. "You know that, don't you?"

Claude sighed.

"I don't know what to think. I doubt everything. He's a bright young man. He's had access to all the newspapers and their countless theories. Maybe you're right—he doesn't understand, he's too young to care about the ramifications of an assassination of this nature."

For some moments they sipped tea in companionable silence. Claude set his cup down.

"From the first moment I arrived at the Pantin field I believed he had accomplices. He says Kinck wrote the details in a note book."

"Where's this note book?"

"He hid it, near where Kinck's body was found but won't tell me exactly."

"And you believe these accomplices just tried to kill you?"

"I'm not sure. Perhaps they fear he's told me their names?"

"Piétri said to stop advancing the case."

Claude looked at her. She never spared the truth.

"You're thinking of the Poinsot affair?" he said.

"There are too many parallels for coincidence."

"I don't want to think of that," he said. "I can't believe the prefect would resort to… to violence to stop my advancing the case."

"But you must consider it."

He looked into his wife's eyes.

"I have. It's too shocking."

"The emperor has painted the whole of France with this gloss of prosperity," she said. "Think of the Kincks as a pinnacle of his creation. They've been destroyed. On the face of it, the reasons for their destruction hardly matter. He needs this resolved. Swept away."

Claude drew spit to his mouth.

"Then they're willing for Troppmann to answer for it all."

"If the public knew of such plots against the emperor, it would cause great unrest, panic about an invasion. An execution will stop all this trouble, for the present, anyway."

He stared at the table but saw only the bitter truth she was putting into words. Should he just walk away and let this take its course? His head felt so cloudy. Would he be able to live with himself if he just left it?

"I won't let them win," he said.

"You can be sure Piétri's under orders to silence any disquiet."

"Dammit, Catherine, Troppmann bloody well knows who these men are but won't tell me."

"He must. You must make him."

"He's resolute. He says they'll kill his family and he's probably right. I can offer his mother protection but both he and I know I've no control over how effective that will be."

She sighed heavily and looked away.

"What's the matter?" he said.

She turned back to him, sympathy and anger in her face.

"All this. This case is too much. It's fierce, unwieldy, lashing out—"

"Is this the trouble you feel?"

"Not really. This is just savage modernity. It's the first thunderclap of what's to come."

"Do you want me to quit?"

Her silence and stone face caused him to brace himself.

"I have never asked you such a thing and won't start now."

"No, you never have. But it's what you want."

"I just want this resolved. You *must* take more care."

"I can't not go out, you know."

"You can travel only with Souvas."

Did he have a choice?

"But this note book… Souvas must go back to Alsace to find the damn thing."

"Do you trust him?"

Claude, taken aback, said, "Of course I trust him."

"I was making no accusation."

"After this evening, I don't know who I trust anymore but I must cut my coat with the cloth I have."

There was a long silence, this one not so companionable.

"I'm sorry this has delayed our plans," he said.

"Our plans…" She sighed. "The farmhouse has sold."

"I'm so sorry, Catherine."

"There are other farmhouses." Her voice was soft.

"Of course."

"Antoine, the man I met in the Auvergne? Nothing but conversation passed between us. It meant nothing."

He didn't want to discuss this, not now at any rate. But to say nothing would be a slight. Did he believe it was as she said? If it wasn't, could he deny her whatever pleasure had roused that color in her cheek? He'd accepted the odd flirtation in the past, none of which had had any real effect on their marriage. And for himself, his peccadillos had nothing at all to do with Catherine, in fact, they'd only served to reinforce the strength of what he felt for her. This case had made her lonely, more so than many others, a powerful aphrodisiac. One-too-many disappointments.

"Then there's no need to speak of it."

"No, there is."

"I'm in pain—"

"You see, this is the trouble. We speak so much of all this crime—"

"I shouldn't—"

"Let me finish. If I'd been born male... Your work has always stimulated me. It keeps me alive, in a sense. I'm a woman but I don't want to spend my time concerned with shades of lace, soft-hued ivory or white, at best the quality of meat. I've no child. But sometimes I wish for talk of things other than murder."

"And you think I don't? You know a case takes hold of me, becomes an obsession. I can't stop that. But you're right. Completely right. Our conversation needs balance. Yet I can't apologize for this case."

"Of course you can't. It's just circumstance."

"When this is finished…"

"There's one certain thing," she said. "If they'd wanted to kill you, you wouldn't be here. This was a warning, not an assassination attempt." She did her best to smile. "You must rest, my love, and you must take care. Tonight, nothing was broken."

Claude's intuition had been right—these extemporaneous attractions peppered lives but had neither meaning nor substance. The way she said "my love"—so casually, thoughtlessly—showed a sentiment ingrained in her soul. Theirs was a grand affair, he was sure of it. He kissed her, glad he'd never mentioned his suspicion. Catherine was clarion; solve this case.

CHAPTER FORTY

With Emile's help Hortense went through every legal paper they possessed. Emile read each piece, then she placed the title deed to the house, the other properties Jean owned, their marriage license, birth certificates, household leases, and private ledgers in a bag.

"Should we take all these?" Emile said.

"I've no idea." She looked at the mass of paper. She'd had enough of delays and changes. "It's better to take them all than leave some vital piece."

Surely all her questions would soon be answered in Paris by Jean. She pressed on, despite her uncertainty.

On Sunday morning, she woke the children very early. She dressed the boys in their school clothes, gray trousers, black jackets and gold braided caps. Marie was at an age where she must choose her own clothes and she decided on a pale blue silk dress and apron, her favorite clothes for play. Hortense wore her black silk dress. Although she felt uncomfortable with its style and the panels she'd had to add because of her pregnancy, she was travelling to Paris and intended to make as favorable an impression as possible.

She hurried them through their breakfast and the last of the chores, worried they would miss their train.

"You're over two hours early," the station master said.

Hortense felt foolish but looked at the children's faces and started to laugh. The children laughed too, and then the station master.

"You must think me a fool," she said, putting an arm around Emile and Achille.

"It's better to be early than late," the station master said.

She relaxed a little. The laughter felt good.

"There's another train leaving for Paris in the next few minutes," he said. "You may as well take that one."

It was pointless to leave the children sitting on the railway station with nothing to do for over two hours.

The train departed at midday. They had a whole carriage to themselves and although the children were very excited they behaved, happy to take turns with the window seats. Hortense sat near the hall door and watched the world slip by. She could easily have fallen asleep but the children needed supervision. In her lap she held a small photograph of Gustave taken when they'd traveled to Paris for the photograph. She passed her rosary beads between her fingers.

After some hours the guard came to their carriage.

"Your stop is the next. Gather up your things to the vestibule."

The train ground and shuddered to a halt. People rushed across the platform to greet others, none of the faces familiar, the children's no longer bright.

"Don't be disappointed, little ones. We're very early."

What were they to do now? Darkness pressed in on the day, but she'd made her way to Paris! She'd take a cab to Jean and Gustave's hotel and surprise them.

She signaled a coach and the polite driver helped with their few pieces of luggage. As they passed along the boulevards, clusters of people huddled around small bonfires. The noise—clattering carriage wheels, wild banging from inside a building, people shouting everywhere, a woman screaming for no apparent reason, and no one other than herself the least disturbed by the din. She knew she would never want to live in such a place.

When they arrived at the hotel the coach driver jumped down and took the bags inside. Hortense felt proud as she approached the concierge and asked for Jean.

"He went out earlier in the afternoon," he said, looking over the rim of his glasses.

The fault was hers. They were early.

"Could you show me to our rooms?"

The concierge looked down at his register book, ran a finger over the page.

"No rooms are reserved."

The four words hit her like a blow. Jean was scrupulous about details. What had become of her husband who controlled every aspect of their lives?

CHAPTER FORTY-ONE

After not quite a week, the skin on Claude's temple knitted and the headaches stopped. The scab on the leg graze hardened and began to itch. His ribs no longer hurt so much but his body felt fatigued, older, and the pain in his leg resulted in a pronounced limp. He'd always healed quickly and each day brought new strength, but at night he woke in a cold sweat, reliving the moment he fell into the doorway.

Who was behind this?

No amount of nocturnal thought could resolve this. It could have been worse. A limp he could live with. Nothing broken. Still, the nightmares and lack of sleep compromised vast tracts of the day.

From Alsace, Souvas reported finding no sign of a notebook even though he'd overturned every stone anywhere near the site where Jean Kinck's body was found. Dammit. *Could* he trust Souvas? Had he gone himself, his eyes might have seen what Souvas had missed. Had he not fled the site before the Alsatian police and Souvas arrived, perhaps he may have found it. How could he now hobble around Alsace? So bloody frustrating. Perhaps this note book simply didn't exist. Should he try to obtain permission to take Troppmann to Alsace? He had to do something. Time was running out. He had to do something.

That involved making a decision – a simple act that for the moment seemed beyond him. Had he been right to try and befriend Troppmann? Should he have taken a harder line? Should he have demanded Troppmann's father come to Paris and confront his son? Perhaps his mother would have had better success.

Enough! He went to Piétri.

"First you want to take him to Alsace to show you Kinck's body," Piétri said after Claude had brought him up to date on the counterfeiting, the Prussians, the assassination plot. "Now he's going to show you where he hid some confounded note book. Don't you see a pattern here?"

"He had accomplices. I believe he became involved in something far bigger than he understood. Justice will not be served if—"

"Without names, these accomplices don't exist."

"He won't give them. If the note book is found, it will at least corroborate his stories."

"Have the Alsatian police search for it."

He wouldn't confess he'd sent Souvas.

"Searches have been made. Nothing's been found as yet, but—"

"Then where has he hidden it? In mid-air? It doesn't exist. He wants to escape."

Claude exhaled his frustration.

"If there is a political agenda here," he said, "it must be brought out. Surely you can see that."

Piétri looked down at papers on his desk. "The trial date is set."

"What do you mean? I've not finished my investigation. You can't—"

"December 28th. The date, the lawyers, everything is fixed."

"But there's still evidence—"

"There's nothing more to be done." Piétri's gaze was unflinching. "You'll remove from your *procès-verbaux* any references to these supposed political associations and assertions as to assassinating the emperor."

"Troppmann is not the only one. I'm sure of it."

"The case is closed. The emperor's moves to further liberalize society have enraged the conservatives. There's unrest. This case is a source of unrest—"

"Doesn't it hurt your professional honor, your pride as a Frenchman? Does it matter not at all to you that Troppmann didn't—"

"It doesn't matter what I feel." Piétri's voice was shrill. He brought it down. "We have a job to do, a greater job than just right or wrong. Order. And this job will be done."

"You really don't want to know the truth."

"It's a little more complex than a singular truth."

"Is it? Then tell me."

Piétri looked into Claude's eyes. He tapped his finger slowly on the desk. He said nothing.

"I'll not tolerate this," Claude said.

"You've no choice."

"Using haste to precipitate an execution is a sure sign something in the state is foul."

"You know you're being watched, as I am."

"All this secrecy… What do you mean?"

"The random act is planned. We are controlled, constrained."

Claude all but spit his next words.

"And you're prepared to allow this?"

Piétri sighed. "Look at yourself. You look terrible. Exhausted. Go back to where all this started. Go with your wife to the Auvergne."

"Am I now being suspended?"

Piétri met his gaze and he felt clearly that this man wasn't his nemesis. That was someone far more occluded.

"*We* have no choice," Piétri said. "If you disobey, the sting you've felt in the past will become a punch."

Claude swallowed. No one had ever put his suspicions into words.

"We'll see about that."

The case was going to trial. His role was effectively over. He'd been told, not suggested, to go on holiday. How patronizing! He'd be assigned new cases. Nothing he could do would save the young man. He set his features hard so as not to give any emotion away to Piétri but the effort was in vain, his chagrin all too clear.

He walked across the Pont Saint-Michel to the Left Bank, hoping to clear his head. He continued along the Boulevard Saint-Michel until he realized he was near Desbarolles's apartment. He stepped into the building, climbed the stairs, and knocked. Desbarolles appeared in the doorway of his apartment.

"Have I disturbed you?" Claude said.

"You look terrible, my friend. So disturbed. What's happened?"

"Nothing new. All's well."

"You'd better come in, as I'm sure all is not."

As Claude limped through the hall of the apartment, his confident stride hobbled, as if he wore shoes not quite his size. In the heated parlor, Desbarolles prepared an aperitif while Claude explained the incident.

"The trial date has been set," Claude said. "December 28th."

"You still believe he has accomplices? That he's their scapegoat?"

Claude told him Troppmann's new revelations.

"I have no proof of the political assertions he's made—"

"And you can't run the risk of stating them publicly."

Claude sighed. "It would be damaging, without proof."

"No one will believe him. He's lied too often."

"I'm not sure of anything," Claude said, "but my instincts tell me he's not lying about the accomplices."

"You must remain silent. Your professional reputation demands it."

"It galls me. Piétri is a stooge." Then, after some moments of silence, "What do you seek from Troppmann?"

"You're as sharp as ever." Desbarolles smiled, which calmed Claude a little.

"You'll not get your confession," Desbarolles said. "Troppmann may tell you bits and pieces but he'll never tell the out-and-out truth. The mind is faulty and cantankerous and cunning. The secure proof is in his hand. If my work was aided, given support, it would be completed."

"What do you mean?"

"The irony of this case is that neither of us has reached a satisfactory conclusion."

"I couldn't agree more."

"Perhaps it's not Troppmann who has to confess but I. My interest in this case has not been entirely… pure, although you've already deduced this. If Troppmann doesn't confess, then you've lost. His lawyers will appeal the case, they may even appeal to the emperor for clemency, but he'll be executed."

Claude sighed and nodded.

"If he remains mute, un-divined, all will be lost. The moment the guillotine blade falls, the machinations of the criminal mind are lost, forever. You'll never record it for future reference."

"What is it you want?" Claude said.

"I wish to make a cast of the hand, to preserve it. The cast will provide a point of reference, a perfect exhibit, against which other murderous hands can be compared. The criminal mind will deteriorate but the hand can be preserved. I'd remove the hand immediately after the execution, make the cast, and replace it to the coffin. No one would be the wiser."

"And if he confesses?" Claude said.

"If he confesses their names, you win. You'll have your accomplices. He'll save his head. The authorities, every discipline of criminology, of science, will keep him alive for more questioning until every little detail in his mind is dissected and there's nothing left."

"At least one of us will have success."

"Then we have… a gentleman's agreement? If he doesn't confess, I may make the cast of Troppmann's hand?"

"He will confess. The pressure of the trial will break him."

"And Piétri will lose. Unless there's simply nothing to break."

The idea agitated Claude.

"It pains me to see you so tormented," Desbarolles said.

Claude chose not to answer this assertion.

"My dear, Claude. You have such faith in the good of human nature."

"My wife asked me to save this boy."

She did want that, didn't she? But she's also wanted it solved quickly. Yet another contradictory mix.

"I must know the answer," Claude continued, "if not for its own sake for the sake of the murdered family, both the living and the dead. Justice. And though he's far from good I believe he's innocent of what they want to kill him for doing.

There's more to this. He could be the lynchpin, the only connection to the subversive ranks in Alsace."

"Do you really believe that?"

"Yes, but there's something more." Claude sighed. "I'm tired of the stain of the Poinsot case. By not pursuing them, Piétri virtually colludes with these insurgents. It's treason. If I can prove Troppmann's assertions, I'll have proved my own assertions about the Poinsot case. If I get the names of Troppmann's accomplices, the rest will fall into place."

"But you'll disrupt the prefecture, publically humiliate the empire."

"I can't help that. The truth is the truth. The consequence of truth cannot be disdained."

"You can't do this. It will ruin you."

"If I destroy Piétri—"

"You will be destroyed."

"—so be it."

"Then your stakes are very high. You have a greater bargain than our trifling wager. And it all hinges on him confessing some names."

Claude had come to like, almost depend on Desbarolles.

"Your welcome presence will act as an astringent, a distraction, something else to focus on. If you win, you can make your cast. But now I must redouble my efforts. I will use what I have-the trial-to break Troppmann."

CHAPTER FORTY-TWO

For some moments, Hortense couldn't think. If it hadn't been early evening she would have damned Jean and taken a train back to Roubaix. The children were fractious and she was tired beyond belief. It was too late to take another train.

"I'm hungry," Henri said, and soon they were all saying the same thing with the same tone. They'd eaten almost everything she'd packed almost before Roubaix was out of sight. What was she to do?

She dragged her mouth apart in an attempted smile. She closed her eyes, not so much to wish the whole scene away as to find some moment of private clarity. She had nothing at her disposal other than to repair more of the wreckage of Jean's reckless behavior.

"Could I please book a room?"

The concierge's face showed his contempt. Damn him— she would *not* be judged. She paid for the room. Once their cases were taken to it, she asked the concierge to recommend a restaurant near the train station. A hackney-coach driver took them to Ronda-Point de la Station at Rainy. She ordered nothing for herself, too roiled to eat.

"What time is it?" she said.

Emile looked at the restaurant clock. "It's a quarter to."

From the restaurant, they'd walk to the station to meet Jean and Gustave. Damn Jean! Why had he summoned them there? Why wasn't he at the hotel?

The children ate their meals. She reminded herself that he wasn't expecting her until the later train. Gustave and he must be enjoying some Sunday folly. There would be a simple reason why he'd not yet booked a room. She felt certain of it.

She chided herself for her error in the timing, for her lack of trust—and then, as there was no real damage done, praised herself for having travelled so far and without any major incident. But still these thought bought little calm.

When the children had finished, Emile reminded her again of the time. They returned to the station. She could hear the rhythm of the train they should have taken approaching now. Walking onto the platform, waves of fatigue and expectation left her dizzy.

Her heart stopped. The children ran away from her and swarmed around Troppmann. She felt her head go so light she thought she would faint.

CHAPTER FORTY-THREE

Two days before the trial, the sound of running footsteps in the hall was followed by an out-of-breath assistant at Claude's door.

"A young man has come forward. He says he saw a man and a woman with two children walking across the Pantin field on the night of the murders."

"And?"

"They were followed at some distance by three men."

The young man, Frerin, was only fifteen, the son of a Pantin factory worker. They lived in one of the newer workmen's cottages along one side of the field. He was accompanied by his uncle.

He'd been in the back of the house around eleven when he saw a lamplight moving through the field. He thought nothing of it until he saw by the full moon that there were actually two groups of people in the field.

"The first man—the one what carried the lamp—he was walking ahead of a woman and two children. The three men stayed behind, out of the circle of the lamplight. "

It had been a full moon, but thick clouds had plunged the whole field into darkness.

"How long?" Claude said.

"Maybe a few minutes. I weren't really paying attention. When the moon come back, there wasn't no one on the field. I mean the women and children."

"Can you describe the men?"

"He's a child," his uncle said. "He's invented this story."

"Can you describe them?"

"I was a long way, but it were three men. They wore white shirts. There ain't nothing more I can say."

Claude and Souvas had found a blood-stained white shirt in the hotel cupboard. Rigny, the hotelier, had said two men returned to the room.

"What did you hear?"

"Didn't hear nothing."

"No cries or screams?"

Frerin thought, cast his mind back.

"I think I heard a cry. A woman."

Hortense Kinck's larynx had been removed, cut expertly from her throat. But perhaps she had cried out when she was first struck.

"Why has it taken you so long to come forward?"

Frerin's chin quivered. He looked quickly to his uncle.

"Because he thought nothing of it. We don't read newspapers, but a neighbor talked to us about the murders this morning so we thought he should come in."

"As indeed you should have," Claude said.

There wasn't anything more to be had from this boy. At least he'd confirmed the existence of the accomplices. Claude thanked Frerin gravely, as if he were an adult, and they left. Claude ordered all the occupants of the houses at the edge of the field to be re-interrogated but this new information prompted no other memories.

On the morning of Tuesday, the 28th of December, Claude stood on the pavement of the Boulevard du Palais, opposite the east-facing façade of the Palais du Justice. In anticipation, the gates of the Court de Mai were closed, causing the tight press of people to spill from the footpath to the street. The crowd's density alarmed him. Vendors sold photographs and postcards of the Kinck family, even one of Troppmann in his cell. Christ knows who'd authorized it.

"Tickets!" a hawker yelled. "Good tickets."

There were 600 places in the court's public gallery and sources had gauged the demand to be as high as fifteen thousand, skyrocketing the black-market price. This fan of tickets the hawker displayed were most likely forgeries but Claude wouldn't respond.

Claude crossed the vast courtyard, entering the east foyer and walking one of the long southern corridors to the new west vestibule. It was breathtaking, the black and white geometric marble floor beneath the high-vaulted roof. The street's chaos would surely spill into the judicial realm, sooner rather than later. Already too many people crisscrossed the floor, filled the perimeter alcoves. These grand extensions of the Palais de Justice, the pride of the empire, hadn't anticipated this fevered interest.

Claude made for the lower levels of the building, the cold of the corridors cutting through his coat. Troppmann was in the holding cells, transported from Mazas before dawn—though even at that hour an angry mob had gathered, banging on the van and yelling insults.

Following a week in which every attempt to break Troppmann had proved futile, for his own peace of mind Claude had stayed away from him. He'd been assigned new work, aware his seniors watched him, but the break had caused Claude nothing but more agitation. He'd hoped his absence would cause Troppmann to reflect, even panic, and name his accomplices, there'd been no word from him and no reports on his condition from his warders.

Claude peered through the cell door's observation slot. Troppmann lay on a pallet. He opened his eyes, sensing someone at the small aperture, and motioned with his hand for Claude to come in. A good sign? Should he just leave him be? Would talking to him achieve anything? Claude felt it was too much to hope for. His clothes, the ones he'd been arrested in, were freshly laundered. His hair had been cut, the fuzz shaved from his cheek. The prison governor had done well. Dire as the day was, his face held that blush of youth Claude had first noted.

And he was smiling as if he'd not a care in the world.

He couldn't have done it all. He was too young and just naïve. To hell with indecision. Claude motioned to the guard to open the door. Troppmann sat before him, contained within his solitude.

"What brings you here?"

"Are you prepared?" Claude said.

The smile faded, and Troppmann closed his eyes for a moment. The light touch of youth drained from him.

"I'm tired of it all. The sooner this circus is over the better."

"Someone has come forward and said they saw you and Madame Kinck on the field followed by three other men."

He deflated, his confidence sapped.

"That may be but I'll still not name them."

"Tell me the names of your accomplices and everything will change."

"Don't you listen? I said, I'm tired. The more I say, the more people twist it and make what they want of it."

"What do you mean?"

He rose to sit on the pallet.

"What is it you want, Monsieur Claude?"

"I want you to confess the whole truth. Name your accomplices. Be spared the guillotine."

Troppmann shook his head slowly. "You want what everybody wants from me, to make your name."

"My name is already famous."

"You want to be the victor over the Pantin murderer."

"We both know that's not you. The guilty must pay for their crime."

"I am guilty."

"You were involved, seduced by the easy money of counterfeiting. You had no care for the assassination of the emperor. The major guilt lies with others."

"It's very kind of you to care—"

"I do care. I want to save your life. Name your accomplices. I just want to save your life."

Troppmann looked at him with pity, the silence pungent.

"You're trapped," Troppmann said. "Imprisoned."

"I don't want to see you destroyed."

"Innocent blood has been spilt. I was involved. I made mistakes. It's enough that I should pay."

"The charges will be reduced. You'll live if you—"

"I'll live, Monsieur Claude? How will I live? I won't last a year in a prison. They'll kill me. Even if I did walk from this prison, there's not a person in France who doesn't know my name and what I did."

"Others must take the major part of the blame."

"It's gone too far. I am to blame."

"You can—"

"I'll never walk in a field again."

"You'll be alive."

"But my mother will die."

"I told you, we can offer her protection."

"My silence is better protection."

Claude fought to keep the panic he felt from his voice.

"How do you know that once you're dead, these accomplices won't think you revealed them anyway? I'm determined to find them."

"You won't find them, not now."

"Once you're dead, you'll have no control. You'll not gain anything by being a martyr."

"Oh, but I will. People have traded on my fame for far too long."

Already, Claude had betrayed him. Desbarolles's cast would ensure his hand would be immortalized, referred to again and again as a perfect example of a murderer's thumb.

"My wife asked me to give you this."

From his coat, Claude took a small paper package. Troppmann slid off the red ribbon and opened the bag, which contained six pieces of chocolate. He looked up at Claude and smiled. It wasn't a broad smile but it was generous, his eyes moist.

"Will you thank her for me, Monsieur Claude?"

"Of course."

Claude stood. "She would like you to confess."

How gauche the remark sounded.

"If the guillotine doesn't kill me, my accomplices will," Troppmann said. "Either way I'm dead."

"That's suicide."

"Like the canal, like the knife, it's suicide."

"I'm not accustomed to do this, but I beg you—name them."

Troppmann placed the paper parcel of chocolate on the floor. He looked at Claude, lay down, and turned his back on him. There was nothing more to be said.

Claude made his way through the dark corridors. Perhaps it was as Desbarolles asserted and Troppmann couldn't help himself.

No. He wouldn't, he couldn't accept it. The stress of the trial would shatter Troppmann's resolve.

And in this thought Claude would invest his hope.

Despite the cold wintry day, the crowded conditions in the public gallery made the courtroom hot and humid. Adjustments had been made to the seating, the benches pushed closer together and supplemented. Some of the women, dressed in velvets, lace, and silks, carried generous hampers.

Once the gallery was filled to capacity, the lawyers appeared from the public end of the room, parading through the crowd to their positions in the bar, dressed in black robes and toques. The court attendant rapped on a door behind the judge's bench. The court rose. The magistrates in their red robes with white fur trim moved to the bench, the jurors singled out to the stand. A tense quiet came over the room, broken only by the occasional shuffling or cough.

Troppmann appeared in the dock, a stair delivering him from the cells below. The public heaved forward. Troppmann stiffened, his eyes darting about the room. The women raised opera glasses and a grumble of voices rolled like low thunder, the crowd disappointed. He wasn't a monster, not this rather small boy. Troppmann recovered his calm, his face almost handsome, his pugnacious body somehow frail.

The first day's proceedings started with the details of the murders. Having seen them hashed and rehashed in every journal in France, anyone present could have recounted them verbatim. The vivid descriptions of the attacks conjured the mouth of each gaping wound, flowing with the innocents' blood. Lurid morgue photographs circulated the jury, rendering their faces pale and slack-jawed.

The prosecution's interrogation of Troppmann lasted four hours and twenty minutes. Troppmann was limp throughout, answering briefly. In an exaggerated movement, he repeatedly smoothed out his thick chestnut hair as a cat might groom the top of its head and behind its ears.

President Thévenin questioned Troppmann over the substance of each of his confessions. First he'd said he was an accomplice to Jean and Gustave, then he accepted responsibility for the murders, then he'd retracted, saying he was only an accomplice to others.

"You claim to have accomplices…."

"Why won't you follow up my clues?" Troppmann said.

"How can you expect us to take your clues seriously when you lie habitually?"

Having led Troppmann exactly where he wanted, he itemized the inconsistencies between the three confessions. Thévenin made no mention of the Prussian insurgents. He bludgeoned Troppmann, forcing him to admit over and over that he'd lied.

The confession of the coachman, Bardot, created the only discernible difficulty with Thévenin's argument that Troppmann was responsible for all the murders. It left Troppmann with only twenty minutes to complete the first round of murders and bury the corpses. Thévenin met this obstacle head on.

"I ask the jury to examine his hands," he said.

Troppmann had just placed his hands on the balustrade of the dock, his long thumbs gripping like a falcon's talons. For him to have moved them from view would be tantamount to admitting guilt. He left the fingers spread wide over the rail.

"You can see for yourselves the strength and size of the hands that enabled this man to murder all the children, even to strangle two at a time. They are hands of unnatural strength."

On the second day, the prosecution introduced handwriting experts who confirmed the letters, crucial to the entrapment of all the Kincks, were by Troppmann. Witnesses told stories of Troppmann's avaricious nature which had coveted the goodly fortune of the Kinck family—a family, some witnesses gave the impression, at the pinnacle of France's industrious society.

Monsieur Dassonville spoke at length of his neighbor Madame Kinck. The newspapers had at some points portrayed her as unsettled, open to the clutches of carnal and material weakness. Dassonville's testimony worked against this grain, resurrecting her as a frugal, devoted wife.

Thévenin had Hauguel, the caulker who'd rescued Troppmann from the canal, ceremoniously led into the court.

"You sought to arrest a criminal."

"I only thought to pull someone from the water who was surely going to drown."

"Here, we have a living example of French honor and manliness, strapping, quick-thinking, courageous. He placed his own life in great peril to rescue Troppmann."

Expert doctors spoke of the strength in Troppmann's hands.

"It's well above the normal. His profession as a mechanic has made him accurate and precise with his hands."

A chemist asserted Troppmann had the knowledge to synthesize the cyanide that had killed Jean Kinck. On and on it went against the boy.

In his summation of nearly three hours, the procureur général, Monsieur Grandperret, warned the jury that Troppmann had tricked his victims.

"Don't be duped by one who knows how to compose his features," he said.

And the prosecution rested.

As Claude crossed the court's main foyer on the third morning, an attendant handed him a message from Lachaud, Troppmann's defense lawyer: *Come to my chamber.*

That morning Lachaud was to take the stand. Claude had always found him capable and highly controlled, but this morning he seemed anxious.

"What on earth's the matter?" Claude said.

"A woman has presented herself. She claims to have new information."

A weak light came through high windows of the room, bare but for a bookcase and a table holding Lachaud's notes. The woman, wearing a black hooded mantle, sat in a chair against the wall.

"Madame Braig owns La Taverne de Londres, a hotel near the Pantin field," Lachaud said.

"Madame," Claude said. She made no gesture in return.

She was in her mid-fifties, slight of frame and stature. She wouldn't look at the two men who stood gazing at her, her concentration fixed on a small white handkerchief held in her lap.

"I have taken great risk to come here," she said in an insistent whisper.

"Why?" Claude said.

"I've been threatened with death. I'll only talk if you promise to keep me safe."

Lachaud looked into her eyes, his face expressing all the concern Claude felt. She seemed to relax just a bit.

"You'd best tell us what you know."

Lachaud took the courtroom floor, presenting facts that strongly suggested Troppmann had accomplices.

"He couldn't possibly have dug trenches, murdered all the victims, and buried them in the allotted time."

To shore up his thesis he interviewed Frerin, the young boy who claimed to have witnessed Madame Kinck and Troppmann followed by three men. But the boy soon cracked in the witness box, rendered incoherent and unconvincing by clever cross-examination that moved too fast for him to follow properly.

Lachaud laid out intimate details of Troppmann's difficult childhood and extrapolated to the effect this had on his development and expectations. He called to the stand Dr. Amédée Bertrand, who had published a small medico-legal pamphlet which argued that in the Troppmann case he detected a mental disorder.

"Troppmann hoped his father's invention, the funnel, would become a national wonder and assure his family fortune," Bertrand said. "This fixed idea provoked congestion of the blood, increasing the size of his brain while diminishing its circulation, flattening the convolutions of the brain. It's a phenomenon observed in pregnant women."

"And what effect would this produce?" Lachaud said.

"The changes in the brain provoked a cerebral compression which gave rise to an insane monomania."

"But the man presented to us now seems quite sane."

"The compression was reversed, cleared if you will, by the saline purge undergone by the defendant in the Le Havre canal. It restored his reason."

Claude questioned Lachaud's wisdom in calling this witness. Was he hoping the jury would think reason "restored" meant Troppmann wouldn't murder again? That would hardly save him.

"I have a deposition from a woman," Lachaud said. "She came to my rooms this morning, here at the courthouse."

Claude watched Troppmann's face. For the first time that day he looked directly at Lachaud, his expression puzzled. Claude's pulse quickened.

"She's the owner of a hotel near the Pantin field. She can't appear in court as she's received letters threatening her with death if she testifies."

A noise ruffled through the crowd.

Lachaud read Madame Braig's deposition, maintaining she saw Troppmann and two men, possibly a third, at her establishment the morning after the murders. They were drinking, huddled round a small table and talking quietly. She remembered Troppmann particularly because he was continually watching her.

Lachaud had wanted to present this deposition to Troppmann, but Claude insisted it be pressed upon him in court, hoping against hope that the shock of this new information would break him. Yet Troppmann was frowning in concentration, as if trying in vain to retrieve a memory.

"I know of no such hotel," he said. "The woman's mistaken."

Claude wanted to scream at him: You might as well join the prosecution! And yet Troppmann's failure to seize upon evidence that would help him was no surprise in light of the threats he'd received, the poisoning in jail.

"You had accomplices," Lachaud said, his gaze fixed on Troppmann.

"I had accomplices. I won't name them."

A loud roar erupted. The judge banged a hammer but the roar barely died down. Claude rose from his seat and frantically waved his hands at the gallery for silence while court ushers dispersed through the crowd, demanding order and silence. Lachaud's gaze remained fixed on Troppmann.

"Why won't you name them?" he said.

"I'm bound by an oath. They'll kill my family. That's all you need to know."

Claude felt the possibility of Madame Braig's deposition slip through his hands. Lachaud could do nothing but proceed to his conclusion.

"There were four murderers," he said, "and you're trying only one of them. In God's name, in the name of law and justice, the whole truth hasn't been presented here."

The defense rested. And quite suddenly, in the early evening of the third day, the jury received their instructions and retired to decide Troppmann's fate.

Claude paced the foyer, his stomach rumbling. He'd been unable to eat all day.

"The trial hasn't forced him to name them."

Desbarolles had come up to Claude, who wished he hadn't been spotted just now by his friend.

"The sight of the guillotine will," Claude said.

"Am I to assume you've put off my claim to victory?"

"There'll be no victory."

Desbarolles smiled and left. Claude chewed his thumb nail, tried to be hopeful but nothing had occurred to sway opinion his way. Back in court he waited for the verdict, unhappy that it was but a few hours in coming. At nine-thirty p.m. the jury reconvened in the courtroom. In near silence the public, journalists, and dignitaries hurried back in. The artificial light in the courtroom was low and yellowy and gloomy.

"Guilty."

The verdict didn't surprise Claude, nor did Troppmann's reaction to it. He stood perfectly still in the dock, his face coldly composed. Claude attempted the same expression but doubted he achieved it.

The judges retired to decide upon sentencing. They returned quickly to the courtroom.

In public, Troppmann would be guillotined.

The courtroom erupted in applause, shouts, thunderous cheers. The court ushers did all they could to restrain them, but the verdict leapfrogged to the roaring mob gathered outside the Palais de Justice. The noise was deafening.

Claude had no chance to gauge Troppmann's response—he was led immediately away from the dock, back into the bowels of the building. As the commotion continued, Claude collapsed to his seat. He raised his hands to his face to hide his anguish. He had failed, completely. Barring a miracle, the crowd would get what it wanted. The blade would fall. The young man would die.

CHAPTER FORTY-FOUR

Hortense remained frozen, unable to move her feet. She should silence the children, they were making so much noise others on the platform glared at them. Little Marie struggled in her arms. But where was Jean? Where was Gustave? Why was this loathsome man here, no longer in the fine clothes he'd worn in Roubaix but again wearing heavy, coarse clothes, ungainly boots?

Troppmann turned to her, one of the few glimpses of concern she'd ever seen on his face.

"Everything's all right," he said, before she could gather any protest.

Marie squirmed from her arms to his. The other children rose on toes to embrace him, shooting quick questions about where he'd been since he'd left Roubaix. Hortense moved to a nearby bench.

"My little ones, your father and I have been working. Very hard, in Paris."

He took a paper parcel from his pocket and gave it to Emile, who took one large boiled lolly—swirled colors, the brightness of which Hortense had never seen— then handed out more to the other children. They filled their mouths and stopped their questions. He turned, even took a few conciliatory steps towards her bench.

"Where is Jean?" Her throat was dry and she sucked for spit. "And Gustave?"

"I'm here to take you to them."

But he was dressed in coarse fabric, his boots large and heavy. Where could they be?

"He said he'd come to meet us."

Troppmann turned on her. She recoiled but only Alfred saw the exchange and came to take her hand.

"Have you brought everything he asked?"

She patted her bag. Troppmann glanced at it, then looked down at the children and opened his arms wide and smiled.

"Then let's go and meet them."

He walked away along the platform. The children's light steps fell in behind him. *Stop!* She wanted them to stop so she'd have time to think but no words would come. And what was she to do? Jean and Gustave weren't at the hotel. The night had closed in. She felt blinded—no, blind-sided, that was it. She didn't trust Troppmann, didn't think following him was safe. What choice did she have if she was to see Jean? He had changed, changed the game again. She had *no* choice.

She stood, smoothed her basque, held her bag with both hands over her stomach and followed Troppmann.

CHAPTER FORTY-FIVE

On January 18, 1870, Claude walked away from La Roquette Prison along the Boulevard Prince Eugène towards the statue of the prince. Although his leg had healed, his gait was still impeded, perhaps a bad habit he needed to break. So what should have been an easy stroll became a chore. It was a bitterly cold evening about a quarter to eleven. The moon, being only two days past its full, augmented the artificial light, giving the boulevard a silvery aura, bled of color. He stopped, surveying the square and stamping his feet against the pavement and the cold. At some distance a younger man stood. For a moment he returned Claude's stare, then turned from the ring of light. Piétri's minion. He was still being monitored.

Men and women, a clutch of priests, passed by. Claude shivered—best keep his blood moving. He walked away from the statue. Never in his career had he needed to hide his own actions from his superiors. Troppmann's appeal to the emperor for clemency had failed. He would be executed in the morning.

Since the trial, crowds had gathered at the Pantin field. Where practical, convicted murderers were guillotined at the site of their crimes. But for Troppmann the venue would be La Roquette Prison, transporting him to the outskirts of Paris having been deemed too dangerous. The shift pleased Claude. The field would have been nothing short of a free-for-all.

La Roquette would force some dignity to the occasion, though huge gore-hungry crowds were anticipated. Officials had distributed guides to the best viewing spots. Extra military had been arranged to assist the police.

Claude had invited a group of writers, journalists, to witness the event. He still held hope the shock of the day would force Troppmann to speak the names of his accomplices. Once the names were uttered, they'd be published. Claude's superiors could do nothing to stop it.

Desbarolles approached from the direction of the prison.

"Good evening," he said. "We come to the eleventh hour."

"You grow arrogant. He may yet confess the names."

Claude's other guests appeared from the dark, near the axis of the statue. Maxime Du Camp, tall and imposing, strode towards him. The writer's hair, still dark and thick-waved at fifty, fluttered above his thunderous brow.

"Good evening," Du Camp said, extending a hand.

Du Camp introduced each man he'd invited, amongst them Albert Wollf, the drama critic Jules Claretie, and the Russian writer Ivan Turgenev, who loitered at a distance. The police spy he'd observed at the base of the statue was in fact the opera librettist and playwright Victorien Sardou. He breathed to calm himself – he shouldn't see everything so suspiciously. There were eight men in all.

Du Camp and his followers carried hampers of breads and ham and numerous bottles of Bordeaux.

"You shouldn't have brought food," Claude said. "The prison governor has catered for all."

"One doesn't wish to overplay one's welcome," Du Camp said.

"Crowds have started to gather about the gates of La Roquette," Claude said. "If we arrive late, we mightn't be able to force our way through."

The walk to the prison was about a kilometer. The night's cold having seeped to Claude's bones, he set as brisk a pace as he could ahead of the others, but Du Camp caught up to him.

"Do you expect Troppmann to resist?"

"Resist?" What an odd word. "What could he resist?"

They turned into rue de la Roquette. Claude half expected the carnival to be in full swing but it was still only a little after eleven, and there were relatively few people on the streets. The dim lights within the alehouses and cafés showed silhouettes and shadows at their frosted windows. Vendors had started to erect stalls at the sides of the main corridors. Within a few hours, their tables would be filled with mass-produced curios. The air smelt of something building.

Soldiers were lined four deep across the mouth of La Roquette Square, fortified by another row about sixty metres within the square, also four deep—an impenetrable human fence. The small throng gathered around the outskirts of the prison were controlled, their voices just a low mumbling. The women clasped knitted shawls and watched their small children run through people's legs.

At the main gate Claude approached an official and the party was escorted into a guard room. Once the metal door was bolted, there was silence. A prison, to a writer, was a romantic place. These motherless walls forced them to silence. They marched across two bare courtyards, noiseless save for the drumming of their feet. The prison governor, de La Roche d'Oisy, stood in the doorway of his apartment.

"Good evening, gentlemen—welcome!" he said with the alacrity of a host welcoming guests to a milestone anniversary, toying with the ends of his imperial moustache. "The whole apartment has been given over to you."

Servants helped the men remove their coats. A long table strained under the spread of stuffed turkey, *foie gras*, breads, punch, and tea. A servant took Du Camp's offerings and shuffled the table to accommodate them. Already plates were filled, writers were eating and drinking. The sight repulsed Claude.

"Troppmann has eaten well," d'Oisy said, rubbing his hands together, "and has been soundly asleep since nine this evening."

"Does he know?" Wolff said.

D'Oisy shot him a look of surprise.

"He's no idea his appeal has failed."

The assembly moaned. Their host raised his eyebrows and hands.

"That's simply the way it's done."

"Does he continue to proclaim he had accomplices?"

"Yes, but he'll not name them."

A distant clatter of cart wheels on the courtyard flagstones silenced d'Oisy.

"The guillotine has arrived," d'Oisy said.

A diabolical mix of faint hope and sharp regret bubbled through Claude. He wanted to hold the boy as if he were his own, ask him to divest himself of the truth as a father would ask a son. This intimacy couldn't be achieved now that the wood and the blade had arrived in the square, aimed squarely at Troppmann's destruction.

CHAPTER FORTY-SIX

By the time Hortense had caught up with them outside the station, the children were huddled in a group on the pavement with Troppmann at the center. With great flair, he hailed a hackney coach. The children were so excited they wouldn't have noticed if she wasn't there.

"I can't carry you all," the driver said. "I'm not licensed to carry so many. You'll have to get two coaches."

Hortense looked around but there was no other coach in sight.

"They're children," Troppmann said. "Most of them quite small."

"It'll be worth my license if we're caught."

"Then I'll make it worth your while."

Jean had evidently spared no expense in this venture. Troppmann and Emile, Henri and Achille sat on the back seat, facing the driver and opposite herself, Alfred, and Marie. She had her arm through the handle of her bag and around Marie, who she clutched on her knee. Wind beat at the side of the coach. A silvery light extinguished and reignited as thick clouds scooted over the sky.

The children gazed out the window.

She couldn't bring herself to speak to Troppmann even though so many questions shot about in her mind. Were she to ask them, it was as if her position as Jean's wife would ebb further away.

"They're waiting at the Pantin field," Troppmann said. "They've something very grand to show you."

With this statement, their little faces were torn away from the view and back to him, faces full of anticipation. Hortense couldn't look at him. She held Marie tight on her knee and each time he said something she wanted to shield her ears and eyes.

"Faster!" Troppmann yelled out to the driver. How could he command someone in such a coarse manner? And in front of the children. But their excitement accelerated along with the coach's speed.

After a time he called out again to the driver.

"Make a stop at the Quatre-Chemins."

Slowly, the coach ground to a stop. Troppmann turned to her.

"We're to walk," he said.

"Walk? Where are we to walk in the dark?"

He turned towards the children.

"We're going to meet your father and brother and bring them back. You don't mind waiting here, do you?"

The children sagged. They turned to her. Why did they look to her? She felt destroyed by decisions. What to do, what to do? Her head told her not to get out of the coach. But her heart wanted to see Jean and Gustave, wanted all this to stop.

The absurdity of this was Jean. He was close. He controlled this riddle, turned her again and again until she was giddy. She felt sure of it.

She didn't trust Troppmann. The children looked at her with eyes as innocent as kittens.

She must exercise control.

She must follow him.

CHAPTER FORTY-SEVEN

Even at this relatively early hour, beyond the prison's high walls what could only be called a mob was building, the air heavy with alcohol. Men clumped together, peering like schoolboys, jostling one another.

The heavy van pulled by three horses stood in the square, where a half-dozen men strewed its contents—haphazardly, it seemed, but Claude knew their orchestration, finely tuned. The mouton, a large block weight to which the blade would be attached, sat to the side. The blade lay on the flagstones, framed in wood to protect the pitiless edge.

"Why is there another van?" Turgenev said.

A similar van stood some metres away.

"To take the body away," Claude said, his voice thin.

Turgenev walked away.

Jean-François Heidenreich, a tall, thin man with a stock of gray hair, strode about directing the guillotine's construction. He was the executioner of Paris. The writers, who knew his role, asked him how the mechanism of the guillotine worked, how many executions had he supervised, on and on. Heidenreich's assistant, Nicholas Roch, followed him about the square.

"Is his presence by default or design?" Desbarolles said.

Claude turned towards him. "What do you mean?"

"Heidenreich is Alsatian, is he not?" Desbarolles raised and dropped his eyebrows. "A symbol of… fraternity, perhaps, or a final stress to Troppmann."

"His expertise is celebrated," Claude said, turning back towards the maturing guillotine. "In such a case, it's only natural he should take command."

They watched the seamless construction for a few moments.

"It's a master stroke," Desbarolles said, "inviting these… writers."

"Your cynicism runs high this evening."

"Come, Claude, you know as well as I these men will snipe and gripe about what they see but they earn their living through writing. And there are so many of them, no authority could censor them."

Claude resented feeling unmasked. "You afford me more cheek than I deserve."

"I'm most sure I don't. Listen to them, their inane demands. Next they'll ask the executioner of Paris if he enjoys his work. But there's one oversight."

"What's that?"

"Even if Troppmann does confess the names in these last moments, you'll be hard pushed to stop the law from proceeding."

"I have a mechanism," Claude said.

In the haste to leave the governor's apartment, he'd forgotten his heavy coat and excused himself. The governor had foreseen the night chills and was serving mulled wine, which pleased the other men who'd retreated from the cold square. Claude couldn't stomach it.

It was now nearly 12.30, which meant at least another six hours had to pass. Some chattered feverishly. Turgenev draped himself on a small settee, his eyes closed. D'Oisy showed off a pile of letters sent to Troppmann, some begging him to confess, some promising him the eternal fires of hell. A Methodist abbot had sent a twenty-page thesis on Troppmann's guilt from the Protestant prospective. Troppmann hadn't opened it. Many writers claimed to be his accomplices.

"If these accomplices were given credence," d'Oisy said with a smile, "Troppmann was in league with half of France. Women express undying devotion, some love."

"Darwin would say they are naturally drawn to his strength. He would make a good mate."

Claude had bitten his thumbnail to the quick. To distract himself he would return to the square. The stage for the guillotine was set, ten steps to finality. Against the cold and his thoughts, Claude walked the square's perimeter. Desbarolles had been as astute as ever with the reason Claude had invited the writers. Nothing would stop the writers from unleashing the truth. Claude had only a few hours and a faint hope that his plan would loosen his tongue.

The noise had increased considerably, as had the cold. One police officer estimated there were twenty-five thousand people outside the gate. Despite the lines of guards, the crowds had inched forward. A man hawked a leaflet: "Troppmann's last words!" The air smelled like a brewery. People perched in the trees for better views. A drunk man had fallen from a tree and died. The crowd took no heed.

The guillotine rose from the stage—thin and frail-looking, considering its purpose. Heidenreich invited some of the party for a closer inspection.

"Why is the blade cut at an angle?"

"Basic mechanics," Heidenreich said. "One side of the neck is pierced. The apparatus is less likely to jam, and the cut is cleaner."

At the rear of the device, the flat wooden bascule stood at attention. Troppmann would be leaned against it, strapped to it, then lowered into position. Finally, a lunette—a wooden collar—would close around his long neck.

Heidenreich asked everyone to leave the stage. Alone, he walked around the machine, eyed it from diverse angles like an illusionist teasing tension in his audience. Claude's body tightened. His remaining nails dug into his palm. The public fell quiet, and into the silence he dropped the release.

The sound the blade made was brief, a fraction of a second, but the crowd roared as if Troppmann's head were already separated from his body.

Claude stood, cold, his mouth parched. He turned away and returned to the rooms. Finding an unoccupied one, he settled to read *Le Monde Illustré*. He could concentrate only on the engravings and even they failed to absorb him.

The governor announced it was six o'clock. Claude smelled hot chocolate. What was usually a pleasure was nauseating.

"Fortify yourselves," d'Oisy said. "The morning air is very cold and may be harmful."

"Is he still asleep?"

"Yes"

"In spite of the racket?"

"His cell is behind three walls."

Claude closed his magazine. At some point, he'd chosen to believe in the nature of Troppmann's involvement. Why couldn't he simply choose to feel as everyone else did, that he'd butchered a family and should pay for it? It was like being in love: once the faucet was turned on it couldn't be turned off, the well simply had to run dry.

It was time to act as he'd planned. Nothing else could be considered. Too late now.

He walked to the main room and stood in the doorway, looked around slowly at all present. One by one their faces turned to him.

"We must wake Jean-Baptiste Troppmann."

CHAPTER FORTY-EIGHT

"Perhaps we should all leave together," Hortense said.

Every face in the carriage turned to her. Emile and Achille gave out a small cheer and made their way to exit the coach. Henri started to rise.

"The children must stay here," Troppmann said.

He put out his hand and pushed Emile, Henri, and Achille back into their seats. He changed his stern expression to a smile.

"We must walk through the field. It's dark." He looked directly at Hortense, something he did infrequently. "It'll be easier without them." He smiled at the children. "We won't be long."

The older boys nodded their heads and relaxed into their seats. They would agree to anything he suggested. But little Marie and Alfred, tired and disoriented, began to whine. They'd heard there was something of a surprise, something exciting, and begged to go.

"You must stay here," Troppmann said.

Perhaps Marie was only frightened by the force of his voice, but she began to wail. From her bag Hortense took a piece of sausage, unwrapped it, broke off a piece and gave it to her. It did nothing to quiet her cries—she wanted to go with Mommy. Alfred took up this call.

"They can't come with us." Troppmann turned to the children. "We'll bring you back a surprise."

The older boys nodded their heads but the younger two were now beyond any reason.

"Come along, then," he said. "Just you two."

They left Emile to watch over Henri and Achille. Outside the coach, Troppmann looked at her.

"You have your bag," he said. "Good."

Her pregnancy made it difficult but Hortense carried Marie in her arms. Alfred walked at her side, holding the folds of her skirt. His small steps made it hard for her to walk, harder still as her feet stumbled on the uneven ground. Troppmann moved ahead with the only lamp. Although she wouldn't have accepted, he could have offered to carry Marie if he was in such a hurry. But he was an inconsiderate boy. Such a thought wouldn't cross his mind.

Once her eyes had grown accustomed to the dark, she could make out the silhouettes of factories and at a distance from them rows of workers' cottages. From the rich loam scent in the air and sough of the wind, she assumed they were on a rough path in the middle of a cultivated field of lucerne. Ahead of them, glowing in the occasional bright patches of moonlight, was a high white wall.

Jean had found a factory. Why had he bought a factory in Paris when his desire had been to move to Alsace? At no time had he ever expressed an interest in living in Paris—in fact he'd told her he considered Paris fickle and no place for children. But then, many vital things hadn't been discussed. What had changed so greatly in his desire in the past few weeks they'd been apart?

She heard noises, the wind punctuated by a hard footfall. She felt rather than heard people moving not far away. She peered beyond the circle of light thrown by the lamp but could see no figures against the sky. She imagined it was Jean or Gustave, skipping about in the shadows. At any point they would jump into the small circle of light and surprise her.

She was about to yell for Jean to stop frightening her and come out of the shadows when a sharp gust of wind snuffed out the lamp. She stopped walking, fearful she would trip on the path. She waited for her eyes to adjust to the bare moonlight. A billowy cloud moved over the face of the moon, plunging her into darkness to which her eyes would never adjust.

For the life of her, she couldn't move or speak. Her heart thumped at a rate to burst it from her chest. Seconds passed like lifetimes. One hand clutched Marie so tight she began to whimper, the other hand grasped Alfred's shoulder. He tried to bury himself in the folds of her dress.

She heard someone move in front of her. Troppmann? She heard a voice, not so far from her but out of sight.

"Hortense."

CHAPTER FORTY-NINE

Indian file, the men marched through a maze of cold corridors and stairwells. In front and behind, guards unbolted and bolted doors, sending echoes bouncing about the stones. They stopped in front of a cell door. A guard released the door and Claude entered, followed by the party.

Troppmann stood in the middle of the room, gently rocking from left to right. He gazed out with huge round eyes. He wore a straitjacket. Claude searched for signs of disorientation in his face. Troppmann returned the intensity of his gaze but kept rocking. Back and forth. Back and forth.

Claude took off his hat, placed it on a small table, and stepped forward until he was but a meter from Troppmann. He smelt his breath, slightly sour with fresh sleep.

"The emperor has dismissed your appeal," Claude said.

Troppmann's face showed no sign of surprise or fear. He said nothing.

"The hour of retribution is near."

He regretted his formal tone but it caused Troppmann's rocking to cease. He tilted his head slightly to the right and leaned towards Claude as if he hadn't understood. He said nothing. Claude searched his eyes in vain for tears, fear, acceptance—anything. He wracked his brain. What could he say? What would unfurl this boy?

"My child," the abbot said, stepping silently towards them. "Take courage."

Troppmann's gaze remained with Claude. Was he trying to tell him something without words, delivering him absolution? The abbot placed his hand on Troppmann's shoulder but took it back when the gesture had no effect.

Now Troppmann began looking from face to face, as if he'd only just realized the presence of men crowded into the cell.

"I'm not afraid," he said, looking back to Claude. "I am not afraid!"

His voice was lower, an even baritone.

"Won't you have a drop of wine, my child?" From the folds of his cassock the abbot produced a small metal hip flask. He unscrewed the lid and placed it to Troppmann's lips.

"Thank you, no," Troppmann said with a small polite bow of his head.

The sense of time running out made panic Claude couldn't discern in Troppmann rise in himself. And he was in a quandary. Was it best to allow the boy to endure the full complement of shocks all at once or should he dole them out, try at each turn to loosen his tongue? He didn't want to force the issue. Yet the stakes were too high not to do it. What was the best course of action?

"Go ahead, Monsieur Claude," Troppmann said.

He knew exactly what was coming, but it must be said.

"You're not guilty of the crime for which you have been condemned. We both know that."

Troppmann squared his eyes to Claude.

"I didn't strike the murderous blows in the Pantin field."

"And Gustave? Jean Kinck?

"I struck no blow. I made the poison but I didn't administer it."

"And you still assert that you had accomplices?"

"Yes."

"You can't name them?"

"I can."

A collective gasp issued in the close cell. Claude steeled himself.

"I can name them, Monsieur Claude. I would like to name them. But I will not."

Claude waited through an odd moment of intimacy, both of them knowing he wouldn't try again to elicit a confession.

"Can I do you any last service?" he said finally.

Troppmann nodded. "In the drawer, there's a letter for my mother." His voice quavered. "You'll have to stamp it. I haven't a sou."

It seemed to Claude that every man in the cell looked away from this vessel into which the public's hate had run, seeing for a moment the child he had been, once held in the arms of a mother who wanted for him a life blessed with hope and possibility.

For his own sake, to keep steeled to the task, Claude quashed the sentiment.

"Undress, please."

Troppmann's arms, covered by the overly long sleeves, were crossed over his chest. Two guards untied the arm restraints. Once the rear was undone he freed himself in one graceful movement, unfolding his arms like wings from a cocoon. Quickly he removed his undershirt and then his trousers, standing completely naked at the center of the room.

In the chilly air, in front of so many scrutinizing eyes, he seemed uninhibited, as if long imprisonment had eroded all sense of privacy. He stretched. He extended his hands above his head and slowly milled each arm a few times, his breathing deep and steady. The guards presented him with clothes and boots, the same ones he'd had on when he was arrested, the same ones he'd worn through each day of his trial. He put the clothes on quickly, casually, stamping his feet into his working boots as if he had miles to walk in them.

The straitjacket was replaced.

"Can everybody please leave the cell?" Abbot Crozes said, preparing to take Troppmann's confession.

"Do you expect the abbot to break the rule of confession and tell you who the prisoner named?" Du Camp asked Claude while they waited outside the cell.

"Of course not."

It was the opposite of what he hoped for but no sooner had he finished the sentence than the abbot emerged from the cell, shaking his head ever so slightly. Nothing of any consequence, if anything at all, had passed between him and the boy.

The guards brought Troppmann from the cell and they moved off, single file with Claude at the head, moving quickly despite his labored gait. Desbarolles was at the rear, behind them all. Partway up a spiral staircase, the night lamp failed, plunging them into darkness. They froze on the stair.

"Everything is under control," Claude said.

The light was restored. Troppmann walked quickly, taking the steps two at a time, as if eager.

They filed into a large cold room furnished only by a leather stool in the center, occupied by a black-suited Heidenreich and his assistants standing to one side. Troppmann stood near the stool. From the corner of the room, the abbot started to read.

"On this mountain, the Lord of hosts will prepare for all peoples a banquet of rich food. On this mountain…"

His voice droned, the words fading in and out. Heidenreich's assistant, Roch, began to bind Troppmann's legs with rawhide straps. Troppmann moved his foot, stepping on one of them.

"I'm so sorry," he said with a little bow to Roch as he moved his foot. "Please forgive me."

Two assistants removed the straitjacket. Roch used more straps to bind Troppmann's hands behind his back. Heidenreich inspected their work, tugging, pulling.

"The straps are too big," he said. "They won't do."

Troppmann scrutinized Heidenreich's face. Claude looked at Desbarolles, who nodded. Troppmann had recognized the executioner's accent and now they looked at one another, two countrymen. Claude hadn't foreseen this potentially destabilizing influence on Troppmann. This was fortuitous. But Troppmann inclined his head slightly, releasing Heidenreich from any association he may have felt.

Roch was handed an awl. Troppmann stood at attention, unperturbed by the delay. Once new holes were forced into the leather, his hands were bound on top of one another, behind his back.

Apparently the straps were deemed sufficiently tight, for he was then placed on the stool. Left alone, he swayed. An assistant came from behind, pushed his head forward and scooped up the thick mane of hair from his collar.

Heidenreich inspected Troppmann's swan-like neck.

"Cut off the collar," he said.

With scissors, Roch cut away the freshly laundered collar.

"Deeper."

He cut again, a deep gouge that revealed not only the nape of the neck but the taut, sinewy trapezium in the shoulders.

With one cut, Roch severed the hair at the nape. Troppmann flinched, then stood and shook his head.

D'Oisy stepped forward.

"Is there a last request? Any money or debts to be discharged?"

"No."

"Is there a last note or a strand of hair to be sent to your relatives?"

"No."

"Do you wish to thank your warders?"

"No. I wish only to thank Monsieur Claude."

Claude felt a poignant sentiment rise in his throat but it was short lived. Heidenreich ordered a short black tunic to be thrown over his shoulders, then moved to grasp his elbow.

Claude advanced.

"A moment, please."

Heidenreich stepped as far back as he could with his hand on the prisoner's elbow—to the point that in the midst of all this Claude felt he and Troppmann had a kind of privacy.

"In a few minutes," he said, "everything will be at an end."

Troppmann raised his face. Many times Claude had looked into the eyes of a man about to die. Often the eyes seemed withdrawn, hollowed back into the face. Some were filled with tears. Some lost all color, just the white framing dark circles, others' eyes went wide and became nothing but color. Troppmann's were clear.

There was nothing to say. What could he do? All his planning and strategies came to nothing. His mind raced but was blank. As a last resort, he thought to embrace him as he would any other boy he cared about but he couldn't. Not in these circumstances, not in this cold room, not now.

"What a pity the children wouldn't stay behind," Troppmann said.

"It's a grave pity."

His eyes fell from Claude's face to Heidenreich's hand at his elbow.

"They knew nothing," Troppmann said. "Nothing! But they insisted on accompanying their mother. I hope they didn't suffer long."

"The autopsy report suggests they died instantly," Claude said. It had actually been inconclusive, but this was something he could do, something he could give Troppmann.

Heidenreich tugged at his elbow to move him forward. It was better to leave him like this. Claude bowed his head and stepped from their way, ceding control. In single file, the abbot and the governor leading the party, they walked out of the bare room towards the prison courtyard. Claude looked back into the room. The locks of chestnut hair lay in clumps, destined to be someone's souvenir.

Claude had one last card to play.

The sight of the guillotine.

CHAPTER FIFTY

The call came in front of Hortense, urgent like a warning bell but nonetheless soothing.

It was Jean.

Jean!

Every fear, all confusion evaporated. She couldn't hold these grudges. She wanted only to see him, hold him, know there was something of the old in this new life. She steadied, drew her breath to call back to him—

And felt an excruciating pain between her shoulders, then the heat of someone exhaling over the nape of her neck as if he'd just performed some great exertion.

She cried out and held Marie still tighter. Her left hand let go of Alfred and reached over her right shoulder. Her coat was wet. She started to twist. The same pain struck, only lower.

She moved forward, trying to flee, but staggered from the force of another blow. She tripped and fell to the ground. Something scraped on her backbone. Searing pain.

She opened her mouth to scream but had forced out only a small cry when a blow struck her face, forcing her head back against her shoulders. With this pain she let go of Marie, something a mother should never do, tumbled away from her into the pitch dark. Marie managed a small cry silenced immediately with such sharpness Hortense was sure she'd been hit across the mouth.

CHAPTER FIFTY-ONE

Row after row of military checked any further advance of the mob. But not their savage noise. *La Marseillaise* rose in uncoordinated rounds. As Troppmann emerged from the building the crowd erupted into a ceaseless roar that reached an ever higher pitch, crescendo piled on crescendo. Claude shook. He'd never heard anything like it and could only imagine the effect it had on Troppmann.

In the only vestige of solemnity, Abbot Crozes walked in reverse along the narrow passage, facing Troppmann, holding a large cross of sufficient size and weight to require two hands to keep it aloft. He pushed his right foot back behind him, then the left, measuring each uncertain step backwards.

The further the prisoner and his entourage proceeded, the more chaotic the scene as soldiers held back the crowd, whose screams and shouts became even more frenzied. Claude couldn't see his face, but the cause of it all seemed to be taking it in stride —considering that the leather bindings reduced Troppmann to small, childish steps. Perhaps the necessary concentration on the simple act of walking diverted his thoughts from anything else.

Despite the biting cold of the morning, beads of perspiration formed on Claude's forehead and above his lip. He clenched and unclenched his hands as he walked behind Troppmann and the abbot. The boy's hands, bound behind his back, stayed calm.

For some few moments, Troppmann's eyes were fixed not on the guillotine but on the abbot and the crucifix. But when they were a good way into the triangular enclosure, the abbot stepped aside.

Claude moved around Troppmann. Despite his bindings, his knees bent and his body bowed as though someone had punched him in the midriff. He froze.

"I can yet stop this," Claude said, "if you tell me their names."

"Goodbye, Monsieur Claude." And with that Troppmann moved forward, his steps firm though hobbled.

Through some theatrical contrivance, Heidenreich appeared suddenly on the left side of the guillotine. Under instruction, Troppmann began to separate from the abbot, the governor, from Claude. He shuffled up the ten steps. At the pinnacle, he glanced at the apparatus but made no effort to raise his eyes to the blade.

He turned to Heidenreich.

Two assistants appeared from the right and the left. Each took Troppmann by the arm and shuffled him towards the vertical bascule. Troppmann looked each directly in the eye before they strapped him to the upright flat surface. Once secured, the contraption swung forward to the horizontal position.

Troppmann kicked the heels of his working boots together. Anticipation held the crowd in its grip, rendering them all but silent for a moment.

An assistant snapped the lunette closed around his neck. Troppmann's body flinched. So tense, Claude felt as if a shot had been fired.

All was set. Claude couldn't see his face. What could he be thinking?

Troppmann breathed in, as if to steady himself—then suddenly forced his head sideways in the lunette until it no longer sat properly in the contraption.

"Straighten his head," Heidenreich said.

Troppmann persisted, forcing his eyes up so they were fixed on the blade. Claude stepped forward towards the base of the stand but was blocked by a guard.

Roch moved to seize Troppmann's hair—his mouth snapped, gnashing down on the fingers. Roch yelled, pulled his hand free, making the wound worse. Yet he persisted, his bleeding hand grabbing the hair further back on the head, forcing it back in place. For a fraction of a second Claude's eyes met Troppmann's. He saw the fear in them.

There was a moment.

Heidenreich secured the loaded machine.

"Name them!" Claude yelled from the base of the stand.

The swooping sound of the descending blade began. Troppmann forced his head back and looked up.

"The—"

The blade sluiced, no sound of bone crushing or flesh cutting clean. Just a snick.

The head thumped into a box.

Blood splattered against the shield.

The crowd thundered.

Blood gushed, steaming in the cold air. Time stopped.

Claude launched himself at the scaffold, mounting the stage in one smooth leap. The boy's head lay face down. He grabbed the hair, felt the warmth of the scalp, and rolled the head over, a mist rising from the clean cut, the white stump of the spine visible. Blood drained, no longer pulsing, from the severed veins. Troppmann's eyelids fluttered like butterfly wings, his mouth pursed and relaxed, pursed and relaxed as if for a final kiss.

"Troppmann! Tell me who they were!"

Heidenreich's assistants were trying to pull Claude away but he fought them off.

Troppmann opened his eyes, slowly, evenly. His mouth quivered slightly, as if engaging to speak. Claude leaned into his face—closer, ear to mouth—

But of course a set of lips disconnected from lungs cannot make sound.

Claude pulled back. The edges of Troppmann's mouth had lifted, the surrounds softened to a peaceful smile. The eyelids closed gracefully and would not reopen, no matter how loud and many times Claude shouted his name.

Heidenreich yelled orders from the rear of the machine. The straps were released, the body tipped into a suitcase.

Roch, his hand covered with his own blood, grabbed the head by the hair and returned it to the box, closing over the lid and whisking it away.

Two men from the crowd lurched forward and soaked their handkerchiefs in the pools of blood.

The Paris Chief of Police, kneeling at the base of the guillotine, rose to his feet.

It was over.

The horses, startled by the crowd's deafening roar, sped from the courtyard, drawing Jean-Baptiste Troppmann's corpse behind them.

CHAPTER FIFTY-TWO

She'd lost little Alfred, his hand torn away from her skirt. She hoped he'd run but to her left she heard more thumping and could only imagine the blows were to his small frame. Only the child she held within her was safe.

She tried to sit up despite the excruciating pain but could coordinate no movement, none at all.

"Jean…"

She felt something cold at her throat, heard a popping sound and escaping air. Warmth spilled over her chest, her skin, inviting against the cold, covering everything. She tried to yell. She couldn't make a single sound. The most human of functions was gone.

Then she realized she could hear no noise save those of nature, the rattles of the wind, her own whistling breath. Some streaky silvery clouds blew slowly between the moon and her. There was quiet. Nothing would take the pain away. Until she heard a voice.

"Where are we going?"

And then another.

"Where is our father?"

And another.

"Our mother?"

Dread engulfed her.

She heard three thuds and then she heard no more noise around her, save the rustle of the breeze through the field of lucerne.

CHAPTER FIFTY-THREE

No one looked at Claude when he stepped away from the base of the guillotine. Blood stuck to his hands. He'd lost control. He clamped his jaw and lowered his eyes to the flagstones.

D'Oisy accompanied him to the governor's apartment. He said nothing and Claude appreciated the silence. He showed Claude to a vacant room.

"I'll have warm water brought to you." He closed the door. Claude wanted nothing more than to be home with Catherine. A maid brought a pitcher of warm water, another a basin. Once the water was poured, they left him. The water jiggled, slowly coming to rest. He caught his undulating reflection and winced. He looked a hundred years old.

"I wish to leave immediately," Sardou said, in the next room.

"I'm afraid it won't be possible for some hours," d'Oisy said. "It's not safe. The crowds on the street are out of control. It will take time for them to disperse."

Claude plunged his hands into the water, which was too hot. But he pressed them deeper, watched red ribbons trail through the water, the stubborn stains clinging to what was left of his fingernails. He wrung his hands with soap, the suds coloring strawberry. His state was unbecoming. He must pull himself together.

Despite the hour, d'Oisy ordered coffee and cognac, which no doubt accounted for the outpouring of opinions Claude heard from the next room. He couldn't identify all the speakers, nor did he care.

"This act was as barbaric as the acts performed to the Kinck family."

"At least justice has been achieved."

"At least they didn't know they were to be executed. Whatever occurred that night, Madame Kinck was led to her death thinking she was soon to meet her husband. The stress we have put that poor boy through leading up to his execution was worse than the blade."

"It's only Troppmann's mother who'll suffer. She must live with this the rest of her life."

"This execution won't stop further murders."

"It's four months to the day since Madame Kinck was murdered."

Claude took a towel and sponged the knees of his pants. They were ruined. He couldn't clean them. He dried his hands and went to join them.

The room fell silent. He stood motionless, ignoring them, his posture limp. Turgenev had draped himself over a chaise longue. Desbarolles sipped cognac.

"A society shouldn't answer violence with violence," Claude said.

The room erupted in praise—he was a hero, after all. Congratulatory hands were thrust towards him. He took none of them, in fact remained immovable.

Turgenev approached him.

"You lost control," he said. "It's understandable. I'll not write of this."

Claude had no wish to discuss anything and with considerable stress walked to Desbarolles.

"Will you follow me?"

Desbarolles nodded.

The two men walked slowly through a series of passages towards the prison morgue, deep in the cool recesses of the building. Desbarolles made no attempt to speak. The air in the morgue was bitterly cold and reeked of antiseptic, the room a series of strong arches covered with white tiles. The day was still early, perhaps only seven-thirty, and the light in the room was low.

Four marble slabs stood like tombs, evenly spaced at the center of the room. The severed head sat on a shelf. The eyes were closed, the expression blank and benign.

In that last moment, what had Troppmann been thinking? What had he started to say?

"Ignite the lamps," Desbarolles said to the attendants as he started a burner to melt wax.

Claude was still looking at the head.

"It happens often," Desbarolles said. "The eyes, the mouth move as if still alive but I wouldn't read much into it."

"No," Claude said, still regarding the head. "You're wrong. Life doesn't leave a body in an instant. He tried to speak. I know there's no way he could have formed words. But in that moment… I believed he was trying."

"It was merely autonomic movement. What do you suppose he was trying to get out?"

"I have no idea."

Claude turned towards the blunted body on the far slab, covered by a white sheet stained red around the neck. To the side of the slab, an empty coffin stood open.

Desbarolles took Troppmann's large hand in the palm of his own. The hand still held tension, having clamped shut in the last seconds. With some effort, Desbarolles prized open the fingers and thumb and turned it over to view the palm. The skin was dry and creased

"Your secrets will now be preserved," he said.

Claude stood on the opposite side of the slab and watched Desbarolles work.

He severed the hand with the skill of an experienced surgeon, sawing through the forearm a few centimeters below the elbow. He then worked Troppmann's hand quickly and with grace, striking a demonstrative pose, the fingers bending up at forty-five degrees from the flat surface of the palm, the long thumb pulled up straight, parallel to the clutch of fingers.

"I've no hard feelings that you've won our small contest," Claude said.

Desbarolles didn't look up from his swift movements.

"You're a fine investigator," he said.

"But I've failed."

"No." Desbarolles gasped the word back into his mouth on an inhalation, then sent it out again. "No. You've not failed."

CHAPTER FIFTY-FOUR

Billow, billows, billowing white sheet. Hortense felt familiar waves, this lifting and falling, the gossamer falling and lifting and floating, a freshly laundered sheet held at the corners and hurled into the air. It took the air, held itself aloft, then fell, drawn down and folded over, over and over. Pain for pleasure. Pain for life. All too human these contractions, thickening into darkness. She tried to breathe in more air, but there was all this dirt on top of her...

What would happen to the child? How could she suckle here, deep in earth? What fate would it have?

Why hadn't Jean come to their aid? Had he seen what was happening and run to alert the authorities? The air was foul, what there was of it, burning her lungs. What would her wise father advise her now?

But she couldn't move. Her muscles no longer obeyed her. She could open her eyes but she was terrified of what she would see, could still hear the thuds, could still not hear the children...

What was that?

Added pressure on her chest. Central. As if to further thwart her breathing.

Breathe. Much harder to do now.

Someone was walking. Slow steps over her. Over her grave. Step. Step. Stop. Still.

Silence.

Gone again, but the dirt had shifted. Heavier on her chest, off her face. The morning was fresh on her cheek. Air had never tasted so sweet. She opened her eyes.

And saw them—men, some at a slight distance, some close enough to see her, their faces grave and contorted. She was a horror–but she was in labor! She tried to cry out, to scream, alert them as they went about their business, but there wasn't anything left within her

No sound, no cry.

No pain now.

Someone touched her, lifted her splayed arm up by the sleeve of her dress.

A kind sir. Her arm was full of pins and needles.

He touched her hand, patted it for comfort. She couldn't remember such a kindness.

"She's warm," he called out. "Her flesh is warm!"

She heard the thrumming of feet.

"The flesh is warm!"

Another face. Another man.

"She's alive. But only just."

A man with a lovely face, intelligent eyes, took her hand. Pressed it gently but firmly. In her mind she pressed back but he released his grip. He lowered his ear towards her mouth.

"Who are you?"

She tried to say her name but nothing would come. Nothing would come.

CHAPTER FIFTY-FIVE

In Paris, the bleak winter of 1870 was followed by a glorious spring, cloudless and calm days.

The emperor and Emille Ollivier, the Minister of Justice, devised a new liberal constitution. The emperor hoped he'd crafted a way to release some power, just enough, to the legislative council to entice the younger Parisians to ongoing support of the empire. On May 8th, seven and a half million citizens endorsed the document. The empire was safe, the emperor's continuance ensured. He and the empress soon retired to Saint Cloud to escape the summer heat of Paris.

These tender months of spring treated Monsieur Claude less tenderly. His limp finally gone, Catherine and he walked the Auvergne but found no land that suited them. With Souvas's help he'd moved to new investigations, work nowhere near as demanding or protracted as the Troppmann case. The High Court acquitted the emperor's nephew Pierre Napoleon Bonaparte of murdering a journalist, Victor Noir—thanks to nepotism and vast capital expenditures, according to many newspapers and a public outcry. All interesting stuff, but less interesting to Claude than the entrails of the Troppmann case.

Others might lavish him with praise, but he felt he'd failed, not only with Troppmann, not only for justice for the family, but in vindicating his conclusions in the Poinsot case. The case had pushed him past his limits, as an investigator but more over his personal limits. These thoughts were crushing. Piétri had said nothing, as there was nothing to say. Without the accomplices' names, Claude had proved nothing. But scorn seeped about him, never enough to confront, only a drop here and a drop there.

"The damn note book," he said in the office one afternoon.

Souvas looked up from a document. "I looked everywhere. I don't think it existed."

Of late, Souvas's mood had been volatile.

"I wasn't suggesting you weren't thorough. Would you, only when you have time, draw me a map of the site, where you looked in relation to Kinck's corpse?"

"Of course." Souvas squared the pile of papers he was reading, stood and turned to leave.

"One other thing," Claude said.

In the doorway Souvas turned.

"You never told me what you thought of Desbarolles's and Madame Thérèse's reading of your hand. Whilst both drew similar conclusions, they seemed… at odds with your character."

In the hall light, Souvas looked pale.

"I thought nothing of it. I don't believe in such frippery."

Souvas walked away, his quick, irregular gait resonating down the long hall. What made him rush?

At a cramped desk in the dark police archive, Claude laid out the Troppmann documents, the morgue photographs of Madame Kinck and her children, then a close photograph of Madame Kinck's hand, the nails shattered and torn.

There was only one photograph of Troppmann—seated in a chair, hands resting on his thighs, eyes frightened but looking defiantly at the photographer's machine and all subsequent viewers of the photograph. Claude peered at the infamous hands.

Claude's arrival at Desbarolles's apartment was unexpected but he couldn't wait till the morning.

"Monsieur Desbarolles is out, but he should return—before ten."

It was only half an hour.

"I'll wait in the workroom." She walked with him across the hall, lit three lamps in the perimeter, and left the room.

The low light grayed the flesh of the specimen jars on the workbench. Three completed casts of hands lunged forth from solid bases to which small name plaques were affixed. Two were unknown to him, but there it was: the cast of Troppmann's hand.

To his credit Desbarolles had preserved all the detail, the finesse along with the brute, muscular strength. Claude touched the large teardrop muscle that enervated the thumb—the thenar eminence, he'd read in a physiology book. This hand was made for manual labor. It was wrong for its owner to have seen anything else in it.

He inserted his hand down into the cast as if greeting Troppmann, something he'd never done in life. The hand seemed to grasp his, the grip firm yet delicate. He jerked his hand free, the sensation too intimate.

He'd brought a book of Catherine's, an old book of Cabalistic chiromancy. It drew heavily on the work of Rabbi Abraham ben Ezra, linking astrological signs to those of the hand. He turned the pages, comparing the intricate engravings, in themselves fine works of art, to the cast of Troppmann's hand.

"Good God."

He heard the apartment door open and shut. He moved back from the cast just before Desbarolles entered the workroom. The months had been kind to him, his suit of finer material and the cut more current. He'd put on a little weight.

"I'm surprised–happily surprised–to see you," he said. "I've been at Saint Cloud, reading the emperor's hand." As he talked he looked intently at Claude. "Despite his recent win, he'll die in exile, mark my words… Are you all right? You're still terribly thin."

Claude made no attempt to soften his expression.

"Facts require duplication."

"But of course." This with a wry smile.

Claude walked alongside the cast of Troppmann's hand and regarded it for a moment. Desbarolles followed suit.

"Describe the thumb," Claude said.

"What are you—?"

"Describe it."

Desbarolles's gaze fixed on Claude.

"The thumb is long," he said, "muscular, almost a finger in design."

"My wife has an old Cabbalistic book of chiromancy." He nodded toward the book, lying open on the workbench.

"I see."

"A murderer's thumb is short and squat. The distance from the top joint is very short, somewhat abbreviated." Claude demonstrated on Troppmann's hand, pointing between the last knuckle and the tip. "The nail is broad. Clubbed, it's sometimes called." He looked back at Troppmann's slender thumb. "This is not a murderer's thumb."

"My chiromancy theories are more precise than you can know," Desbarolles said. "You'd not verified your information. That's the fault of it."

"The *fault* of it…" He wouldn't lose control. "For you the hand is a metaphor but in this case it stood as a distraction. Correct me if I deviate. Kinck had uncovered a plot to assassinate the emperor. When the procurement note for the money didn't arrive in Alsace, the Prussians panicked, thinking Kinck had told his wife. He hadn't, but we have the forged letter in which he summoned her to Paris—for a celebration with the children, or she wouldn't have left Roubaix. Unfortunately at the field, the younger children were tired and fractious and demanded to go with Troppmann to see their father, sealing their own deaths at the Prussians' hands."

Desbarolles remained impassive, his eyes turned down.

"All this I couldn't prove without Troppmann's naming the Prussian insurgents or finding Kinck's note book."

"Neither of which happened."

"But what's more shocking," Claude said, "is that higher authorities blocked my finding these people. I believe they knew the truth. I believe Kinck had already written to them with the details of the planned assassination."

He looked at the cast of the hand.

"The Minister for the Interior knew of our associations," Claude said. "In the past, I'd expressed… cautious support for your work."

He was looking Desbarolles straight in the eye but he didn't flinch, his gaze unwavering.

"You were hired to distract me," Claude said. "Report on me, lead me astray from the truth."

"Why would I do that?"

"Don't toy with me. You've won. Enlighten me. When did they approach you?"

Desbarolles sighed heavily.

"Just before you were to bring the young man from Le Havre to Paris—"

"How much were you paid?"

"These bourgeois women are given more money than they can spend. Some visit gigolos, some cabarets in Montmartre but others visit me. Until I can establish my criminal theorem, I wouldn't bite the hand that feeds me. The empire feeds me well."

"You reported on me, distracted me from other lines of investigation."

"They didn't want a repeat of the Poinsot affair. The emperor isn't a complete fool. He knows of the plots against him. But what he fears more is public knowledge of such plots. Yes, Kinck had written to the emperor's guards, outlining the assassination attempt. When the bodies of Madame Kinck and her children were identified, the emperor's minions put two and two together. They knew it had the potential to all come out. There had to be a swift execution. Don't you see you smell sweet in this arrangement?"

"But your drawing of his hand, given to me outside the morgue... At that point you'd not seen it."

Desbarolles smiled. "It was... what shall I call it? Given what I knew, an educated guess."

The two were silent.

"You knew the truth. You occluded it. You helped drive me to the brink of madness. I considered you a friend."

"Your work is far easier than mine. You present evidence and you're believed. I present evidence and I attract nothing but further criticism."

"A vendetta?"

"Not aimed at you."

Desbarolles closed his mouth part covering it with his thumb and forefinger. Claude seethed with anger. How could he not take such deception personally?

"Do you know their names?" Claude said.

"Long live the emperor," Desbarolles said, his voice far from convincing. "Long live the empire."

Claude moved away from the work table. He had his answers, but to what end? With no proof, Piétri would deny it all.

"Show me your hand," he said.

Caught off guard, Desbarolles simply opened out the fingers and palm of his right hand and raised it.

"You must cast this hand," Claude said. "It's murdered a young boy."

Claude closed Catherine's book and left Desbarolles's apartment for what he knew would be the last time.

Left alone, Desbarolles paced the work table. After a dozen circuits he walked to a side bookshelf, took down a large reference book, opened it, and removed a small black leather-bound note book. Inside, Jean Kinck had written everything Troppmann maintained in his final confession. He also named the three Prussian accomplices; Frederick Kotzebue, Wilhelm Lange, and Otto Herrmann whose corpse was found in the Paris sewer.

Desbarolles flicked through the tatty book. As the dose of crude cyanide was about to cut off his life, Jean had scrawled a parting:

> *What have I done? And now, what can be done? My heart aches – I cannot catch my breath. My dear Hortense – that you should find this – that this should find you. I was wrong*

to leave you — You're right – we're all cast at birth. My fate was Roubaix and you – I recognized that at Monsieur Noël's — we are parts of a pattern.

I've made a grave mistake — We are — now, every one of us — cut adrift. My dear I wouldn't harm

Desbarolles uncapped a lamp, opened the diary. The flames rose. The leather binding cracked and twisted, knotting itself. The truth burned in a shallow crucible.

EPILOGUE – 1874

FOUR YEARS LATER

Whiskers of lucerne swayed back and forth in the afternoon eddy as they walked a narrow road between hedgerows. Catherine stooped to pick spiky blue cornflowers from the carpet of sulfur and scarlet and violet at the side of the road.

Claude watched her, entranced. Wide-brimmed hats cast broad shadows across their faces.

For far too long, they'd been planning this walking trip to Alsace, but a year after the Troppmann murders, Catherine's prediction came true. At the height of the summer of 1870, a diplomatic crisis over the ascension of a Prussian Prince to the throne of Spain erupted. Napoleon III declared war on Prussia. In an unequal contest, Bismarck invaded Alsace. On September 19, 1870, exactly a year after Hortense and her children were slain on the Pantin field, Bismarck's army advanced on the capital. The Siege of Paris began. The emperor and his family fled to exile in England. Paris descended into *L'année terrible*, then came the Paris Commune…

Through all this inhuman conflict, a walking holiday any-where would have been ill advised. But today, wonderful peace prevailed. When he'd approached the castle, all those years ago, he'd come from the other side of the hill. This side was unfamiliar terrain. On the outskirts of Cernay, Claude stopped to speak with a farmer at the edge of his field.

"Good morning. Is this the path to the castle of Herrenfluch?"

"*Ich kann kein Französisch!*" the farmer said, then turned his back on them.

A wave of cicadas, feverishly drumming their abdomens, erupted in the fields. How quickly the words of this area had evolved, as if for years these new ones had been coiled beneath the earth's surface, just waiting to be released from the war-tilled soil. He was about to deliver a bit of abusive German, but Catherine took his arm and moved him on.

"I'll soon retire," Claude said once their walking pace had resumed its companionable rhythm.

"I know."

Claude stopped walking.

"How do you know?"

Catherine, a few steps ahead, returned to his side.

"Lately you've talked of your work amongst an orchestra of sighs." She smiled. "Your interest in policing has waned. I believe you *will* retire. This time." Another lovely smile. "When?"

During the war he'd burnt many of his files, fearing details could be turned on him. The alliances in the prefecture he couldn't predict.

"The sooner the better. I'll tell the prefect in the next few weeks."

Catherine nodded, then looked around her.

"This is the castle," he said.

Claude looked up into the air, recalling the circling murder of crows. All he could see was the clear powder blue sky. They took the trail the farmer had walked, into the forest, dark and considerably cooler. Multi-colored butterflies bounced on the air, the drone of the cicadas receding.

"The body was positioned here," Claude said.

He walked to the base of a thick tree.

"And according to Troppmann," Catherine said, "the note book was left under a stone, beneath a bush. Here."

On their knees, they peered under the bush. A flat stone lay on the earth. Claude lifted it easily but found nothing underneath. He scuffed the leaf and topsoil away.

"It must have been there when Souvas was here."

"How could he have missed it?" Catherine said.

"Perhaps he didn't."

For some time the two sat silent in the dappled light of the forest.

"You can't let this go on haunting you," Catherine said.

"I failed the boy."

"Can you imagine a life in prison?"

How she loved to throw him a comment he was ill prepared for. But he would meet her obliquely.

"It would be worse in my case than Troppmann's—a life without you."

She ignored him.

"Even if you'd succeeded with him and found these accomplices, I doubt he'd ever have been released. The memories must have haunted him. He didn't want to live. You have to respect that. And you didn't fail. You knew Troppmann's involvement was cursory. Your faith in his nature was vindicated."

"You're far too easy on me."

"Not at all. What we have lived through, the war, the commune… in his own way, Troppmann foretold it all."

"I've thought that. If only Desbarolles had seen that in Troppmann's hand."

She smiled.

"What do you feel at this moment?" she said.

He screwed up his face. "Frustration, regret, a touch of melancholy—"

"But more immediate. What does… the sunlight make you feel?"

Claude looked up to the sun pouring through the leaf canopy to the forest floor in sticky streams.

"Warm. Happy." He closed his eyes and moved his face in and out of a stream of light. "Relaxed."

"The sunshine is outside you and yet you feel it, profoundly. It affects something as nebulous as your mood. Troppmann was neither made by the world nor predestined."

Claude opened his eyes and turned to look at her.

"I don't understand."

"Neither you nor Desbarolles are right or wrong. There's some far more subtle interaction, some interplay. We're born and we inherit things. But the world acts on us, the sunlight, the food we eat, the kind or awful words we hear, uncovering perhaps even covering these facts of birth." She sighed. "We are who we are by a complex interplay, an unknowable dance of forces."

Claude moved his face in and out of the stream of pleasing light, then took her hand. He kissed the palm. She knitted his hand to hers. They dovetailed perfectly.

AUTHOR'S FINAL NOTE

Révélations complètes was duly published though it didn't prove to be the instructive "scientific" manual Desbarolles intended, nor did it contain a reference to the Troppmann case.

Chiromancy continued to gain favor well into the next century. Across the English Channel, Count Louis Hamon, known professionally as Cheiro, made a fortune reading the palms of the rich and famous. No reputable scientific study was ever made into the claims of chiromancy before it withered as an art, as a science, in the 1930s.

Soon chiromancers used smoked paper to record the details of their subject's hand and then printer's ink formed accurate images to circulate between practitioners.

The cast of Troppmann's hand was never used professionally. More or less an abandoned curio, the cast of Troppmann's hand now stands in the Musée des Collections Historiques de la Préfecture de Police in Paris.

END NOTE

If you enjoyed *The Cast of a Hand,* please consider writing a review and posting it on shop websites, Goodreads, or your own blog. As an independent author, I'm reliant on word-of-mouth recommendations, dependent on the kindness of strangers, so if you feel you could oblige, I'll be eternally in your debt.

Please drop by my website www.gsjohnston.com.

If you are a book club looking for an author to meet with you via Skype, I never sleep so I'm on all time zones, truly global.

Also, please feel free to contact me, either via
www.gsjohnston.com Contact Page or
on Twitter – @GS_Johnston
www.facebook.com/GSJohnston.author

ACKNOWLEDGEMENTS

Biggest and warmest thanks possible to –

My editors, Renni Browne and Shannon Roberts, at The Editorial Department (editorialdepartment.com). Also Catherine Hill for her analysis and ideas. Karen Vegar, Avril Carruthers and Marie Tisci for their support and many ideas.

Evan Shapiro for the neat type set (greenavenue.com.au)

Ian Thompson for the snappy cover design.

Clearly, our presence at Troppmann's execution relies heavily on Ivan Sergeevich Turgenev's evocative description and transcription of this bizarre evening. I was also greatly aided by Joanne Brogan, astute genealogist and distant relative of Jean Kinck. Palmist historian, Andrew Fitzherbert, supplied me with many references and erudite responses to many questions concerning the 19th century practice of chiromancy and the life of Desbarolles.

And to you, the reader. All blessings be upon you for reading this far.

And especially to John who puts up with me and all these damn characters in this novel rampaging around the house for years on end.

SWEET BITTER CANE

GS JOHNSTON

An Italian–Australian World War II saga

PART ONE

1920 – 21

Love's gentle spring doth always fresh remain
Venus and Adonis – William Shakespeare

CHAPTER ONE

The Madonna flew from Jerusalem. Like a gyre she rose, wingless, from the Church of the Holy Sepulchre, passing over the sea, over Crete and Sicily, between Capri and Vesuvius, close to the sun, amongst the starlings and swifts and the shrieking seabirds. She swept along the coast of conquered pasts, above the dusty aqueducts, the chipped and crumbling buildings, olive groves and grain fields and winter-gnarled vineyards, never once losing her way, full of grace.

She glided over the cobblestones of Tovo di Sant'Agata in far northern Italy, past the stirring baker and the sleeping cobbler, through the village square, over the water well and barking dogs and prowling cats and shivering rats. She touched down, crimson and sapphire robes fluttering, her lips and cheeks a healthy rose, at the end of Amelia Durante's bed.

For the first time in many years, this vision returned to Amelia uncourted. While staring at the Madonna to the side of the altar in the parish church, blood pulsed the statue's white marble to flesh, her lips alive, her weeping robes the same deep colours. The questions came again to Amelia: What did this vision mean? That she was blessed? That she would travel? Or that she would never leave the village? The Madonna cared for her? What else could it mean? The Madonna beckoned her.

Taken over, she extended her right hand, splayed her fingers. They hung in midair, a featherless wing. The air, heavy with frankincense, scorched her eyes. Amelia gasped, snatched back her hand and raised her left. What kind of fool gave the wrong hand? She swallowed her doubts and watched the gold ring slip over her knuckle. How innocent it looked, this self-joined circle, and what power it held. Even through the white film of her veil it shone, sun-gold.

The priest began. '*Confírma hoc, Deus, quod operátus es in nobis.*'

With her free hand, she rotated the ring, just a single turn, this key to freedom.

'*A templo sancto tuo, quod est in Jerúsalem,*' the small congregation responded.

Amelia looked beyond the priest to the white-lace altar and the risen god above. She inhaled the incense.

'*Et ne nos indúcas in tentatiónem.*'

'*Sed líbera nos a malo,*' she said.

Had she made the right choice? So much was still to be resolved.

'You may kiss the bride.'

Giuseppe turned to her. So strange to see him in a suit, with a tie and white shirt. With infinite care, he gathered the bottom of her veil as if raising the curtain on a theatre performance. His eyes didn't leave hers. He leaned forward, moving his mouth towards her lips. She pressed up on her toes, as far above her mere 150 centimetres as she could muster, but turned so his lips touched her cheek, then the other. It seemed natural to kiss her brother like this. He was just her proxy groom.

She relaxed to her soles and smiled. He returned the gesture, then took her ringed hand in his clammy palm and turned her towards those assembled. Above, the bells clamoured their silver celebration. He walked her along the central aisle, towards her family.

Her mother and father, Velia and Emilio Durante, were in tears, but they gathered smiles as best as they could. After all, this church ceremony was for them, though they could ill afford the expense. All that was legally necessary to complete her marriage to Italo Amedeo could have passed in a notary's office.

To her left, Italo's mother, Signora Pina, stood glaring at the altar. She was painfully thin, fierceness etched into the lines on her face, her greying hair oiled and pulled to a tight bun at her nape. In the row behind her were Italo's aunts, Zia Fulvia and Zia Francesca. Amelia smiled at them, and they dabbed their eyes and bowed their heads and nodded in fervent supplication. Neither woman had married, the Great War, poverty and their hesitations rebuffing the few available suitors.

Outside the church, the humid air prickled Amelia's skin, unusually warm for February in the far north of Italy. Wreaths of olive branches entwined with white roses and lilies – peace, transience and purity – lay wilting in the sun, after a morning funeral.

'You're married,' Giuseppe said, smiling.

She smiled but felt no difference.

Her mother rushed from the church, squinting in the harsh light. She was in her mid-forties and still a proud woman. She smiled but her lips trembled. She embraced Amelia. 'Don't ever regret this,' she whispered.

Her handsome father and her elder brother, Aldo, nodded as Zia Fulvia and Zia Francesca hurried to her.

'You make such a beautiful bride,' Zia Fulvia said.

'If only Italo were here,' Zia Francesca said.

'Soon I will be in Babinda with him,' Amelia said.

She liked the word – Babinda – the bold play of vowels sounding Italian even though it was far away in Australia.

The gay party started towards the Durante home. The villagers smiled and waved, every heart so easily drawn by a wedding. Even the uniformed officers left over from the war – who, two years later, still spilled from the town's cafes – raised their open hands high above their heads in celebration. The war had left them idle. Each bomb and bullet and bayonet had torn the fabric of the village to ribbons, killed the youths, left only scarred old men and babies. But they all smiled, dulled and weary. Who were they to know all wasn't as it appeared? Her marriage rebutted everything they'd fought for – she'd married to leave rotting Italy.

In the main piazza, a man sang a nursery rhyme, his voice unsure and quavering.

> Garibaldi was wounded,
> He was wounded in the leg …

Signor Gregorio slept under the lip of the main fountain. Amelia often brought him food and, in winter, without her father knowing, ushered him into in their barn to sleep. Every piazza in Italy had an eccentric, a religious zealot or political conspirator, and he was theirs. She unlinked her arm from Giuseppe's and went to him.

'It's my wedding day,' she said. 'Why do you sing of Garibaldi?'

Gregorio looked at her, his face crushed and wrinkled, an oval frame of wild hair and wiry grey beard. She'd no idea how old he was, but it was said he'd fought for Garibaldi.

'He commands us to be one,' he said. He raised both arms in an arc, his hands aloft as if about to conduct an orchestra. He blinked both sparkling eyes. 'He brings all to all.'

He'd a large tear in his coat's side.

'What have you done?' she said, pointing to the hole. Clearly, the magnanimous legacy of Garibaldi hadn't made provision for its repair. 'Take it to my mother. She'll sew it up.'

Deflated, he lowered his arms and nodded. She smiled at him. She'd always appreciated his views of the world, which ran counter to most people's. She turned back to the party. Gregorio began to sing again.

> Mamma, don't cry that it's time to leave
> I go to war to win or die.

Amelia's family home was small and typical of the village, built many years ago of roughly hewn limestone with small windows to the world, no shutters. It was kept as well as poverty would afford, the terracotta tiles in strict rows and plumb lines, the sills buffed and whitewashed, the path stones free of weeds. The ground floor consisted of a stable and a low-ceilinged living room, with a kitchen and a chimney. They all slept in this main room, below a hay-filled loft. For this special day, they'd moved the table to the street so there was room for their guests.

'To those who were,' Amelia's father said, raising his glass. 'To those who are.' He smiled at his daughter, his eyes bright with tears. 'And to those who will be.'

Tonight, Amelia would leave her family and her village, as a bride should do, and return to the hamlet of Bovegno with Italo's mother, some hundred kilometres to the south. But it would be Signora Pina who'd share her wedding bed, not her husband, who was on the other side of the world in a small town in Far North Queensland, Australia.

Signora Pina snored all night, whistling on the inhalation and whining out. She lay on her back but, as if to taunt Amelia, occasionally rolled to her side and ceased snoring. In these moments of quiet, Amelia imagined Italo's breathing, firm and regular, water lapping at a lake's shore. But the peace was a momentary aberration. Signora Pina would growl pungent farts, slump to her back and begin snoring again. Signora Pina had slept far too many years on her own. When the first cock crowed well before light, Amelia rose.

The prior evening, Signora Pina had given her a wooden spoon, a traditional gift from a new mother-in-law. Amelia took it from the table but wondered at the sincerity of the gesture. How many hours had she dreamt of her wedding day? It was over, so quick it hadn't really begun. She rekindled the fire and made coffee, the oily brew in a tiny cup. She hardly ever used sugar, such was its price, but while Signora Pina continued to snore, Amelia stirred in a heaped teaspoon, taking the bitterness away.

In Australia, Italo grew cane. Was this his sugar?

From her diary, she took her one photograph of him. Although fifteen years older than her, he had dark hair and in unison his aunts had said, with a dreamy air, 'His eyes are as blue as the sea.' Hers were like her brothers', plain hazelnut, but she'd seen eyes like Italo's in the faces of Bovegno. She searched the photograph again to find something new, something she'd never noticed. He was seated in a Savonarola chair, in a studio, stiff and dressed in a vest and a jacket, a light collarless shirt to fight against the Australian heat, with a white bow-tie.

How was your wedding night?

But a photograph can't reply, and she knew Italo had had no ceremony. Only a woman's virtue was at risk, only a woman's family honour. A man would laugh out loud at such a suggestion, but such was the world. Now a married woman, she could travel to Australia, but even a married woman couldn't travel alone. On the boat, she'd have a chaperone, the only demand her father had made, to be paid for by Italo. Italo owned his land. Imagine that. She'd never even heard of anyone she knew owning land—

'You think it will be different there.'

Signora Pina's hoarse voice made her jump. The death of a husband soon after the birth of an only child had cheated Signora Pina, each year harshening her tone, frightening off any man who may have been interested. And when Italo was only twenty, he emigrated to Australia. For fifteen years, Signora Pina hadn't seen her only child, her only son, her only notion of family.

'I've made coffee,' Amelia said. 'It's still fresh.'

Signora Pina continued to stand in the doorway, glaring at her.

'You're right,' Amelia said. 'It's grown bitter. I'll make some fresh.'

She poured the older coffee for herself and began again, but under Pina's scrutiny what was second nature became foreign. She concentrated, ground only the beans needed, watched the water to assure it would remain just off the boil. The silence rang.

Signora Pina, stern, harsh and angry beyond belief, annoyed her. Amelia was forced to live with Pina and had no choice but to honour her elder and Italo's mother, but she didn't understand her. All she could do was hasten the remaining immigration paperwork and count the days until she could leave. Amelia fought not to show her discomfort and, without a tremor, placed the fresh coffee on the table. Signora Pina made no move to acknowledge it, less still any intention to drink it. Amelia sat opposite. Pina lit a cigarette, the first of the day's chain. They remained so, silent.

'Why would you marry someone you've never met?'

Why would she ask this now? Was this the heart of Signora Pina's resentment?

'Other girls have married this way. Travelled to Australia, some to America ...'

'And what were their fates?'

'Zia Fulvia and Zia Francesca assure me ...'

'Two spinsters.' She spat the words. 'They've never even tasted love. What do they know?'

Perhaps her judgement was that Amelia Durante, the daughter of a peasant apple farmer, wasn't good enough for her son.

'What are you running from?' Signora Pina's voice was tight. 'A mother who'll never be pleased? A father who beats you?'

'Signora …' Amelia breathed deeply to choose her words. 'The facts of this courtship—'

'What courtship? A few letters … You put too much confidence in words.'

'But the facts remain.' Signora Pina recoiled at Amelia's force. 'Two years ago, Zia Fulvia and Zia Francesca approached my parents. The delay wasn't mine. My parents begged me to forget this, forced every delay.' She steadied herself. 'I am *not* running away.'

Signora Pina was silent. Perhaps Amelia had won some ground.

'I love Italo …' Amelia said.

'You've never met him. You don't know him.'

'We will learn to love—'

'You don't even know what love is.'

'I'm not a foolish girl.'

'Do you think he's not loved? He's thirty-five. If you think this is true, you're more foolish than I first thought. Look around you. He has no fortune.'

'We will make one together. It's possible in Australia. A peasant in Italy can never hope for such a thing.'

There. She'd called herself what she was.

Signora Pina sighed and looked away. 'Men think only of themselves.' Signora Pina stopped. 'He's only married you because there are no suitable women in Australia.' She sighed. 'What's done can't be undone, but you'll promise me one thing.'

Amelia breathed out. 'Of course. Whatever you wish.'

'No doubt, God willing, you'll soon have children. You must bring them back to me.'

What did she think? To reach Australia was months and months of travel. Did she think they could travel like the Madonna flew from Jerusalem?

'I'll not die alone. You must return to care for me.'

And then Amelia understood. Pina resented the marriage as it was another statement, perhaps the firmest statement yet, that Italo wouldn't return for an even longer time. He would now have a wife, and an Italian wife, and soon a family in Australia.

'Promise me. Or I'll curse you.'

Amelia resented this corner into which she'd been forced. She stood, picked up her cup. She had no choice. 'All right. I promise.'

How was Amelia to bear this? If only Italo were there. He would know what to say, what to do.

'Can't you be happy for me?' Amelia said. The words fell from her mouth, too late to catch them.

Signora Pina's face hardened further.

'In Italy, people toil for more poverty,' Amelia said. 'I've escaped.'

Signora Pina blew smoke at the untouched coffee. Amelia had spoken out of turn, had rubbed her nose in her own lack of courage to follow her son to a new land with greater expectations. The unification of Italy and the Great War had brought huge waves of change. Amelia knew men who were unemployed. Italo had left for this reason. She could see the villages destroyed. And yet there was no will to rebuild them, no-one who could see what had to be done.

She thought of a line in a letter from Italo that had won her heart.

In Australia, the sky is so large and clear and blue. Nothing can hinder a man, and anything is possible.

It wasn't just the sentiment but the play of words. He put them together with a poet's measured touch. But she wouldn't tell Signora Pina about his letters. She'd said too much. Though in many ways she hadn't said enough.

She had to leave the confines of this hot kitchen. She'd go to the water well. She picked up the wooden pail. Signora Pina made no move to stop her. Outside, the morning was still cool, and she grasped her shawl at her chest, tightly around her shoulders. The sun, low in the winter sky, came down the street. She was amongst strangers, something she had to get used to. She exhaled her frustration. Did Pina have no consideration for her? She'd taken a great gamble and now the dice were thrown, spinning in the air. She was married but had never felt so alone. Through the sun's rays, she caught a person's silhouette, something familiar and heartwarming. She squinted.

'Mamma,' she said. 'What are you doing here?'

'Aldo went to the market in Ghedi. I wanted to see you.'

Amelia threw her arms around her, and although she exerted all control, she started to cry and then to sob. How would she bear life without her mother? She inhaled the scent at the base of her neck, as soothing as warmed milk. After some moments, Velia took her hand, pulled back from her, smiled and led her away, through the square towards the church. They sat in front of the Madonna, Pina's empty bucket at Amelia's side, and she poured out what Pina had said.

'She's small-minded,' Velia said. 'Don't reduce yourself to that.'

'She should be happy.'

Her mother said nothing. What an insidious position Amelia had put her in; for Velia to say she was happy would be a lie.

'You've never said anything about Italo,' Amelia said.

'It's not for me to judge, but from what you've told me from his letters he sounds a fine man.'

'But you think it's foolish to marry someone I've never met.'

Her mother said nothing, just kept her eyes fixed to those of the Madonna. Amelia pushed back the quick of her thumbnail to make it hurt.

'I'm so scared,' Amelia said. 'Isn't that silly, now that it's all done?'

Velia squeezed Amelia's hand, and they were silent. 'My parents didn't want me to marry your father. He was only a farmer, and they'd worked hard in their shop for so long. They knew a farmer's life … They wanted a better life for me. But every morning he came to the bar next to the shop before he travelled out to their land.'

'So far out of his way.'

'I know.' Velia smiled. 'And when I saw him … When he looked at me, I felt something so strong. I couldn't describe it.' Her eyes shone. 'He was so handsome. What hope did I have?'

Amelia had never heard her mother speak of this. 'Do you regret it?'

'I married him for this feeling, despite everything my mother said. But with time, the feeling faded. Those things weren't so important anymore.'

Amelia swallowed hard. 'Don't you love him?'

'Of course I do. But there was a time … It lasted for many years. Even with all of you children and all the work, I felt very lonely. As hard as it is for me to say this, in my heart, I feel you have made the right choice. Your father doesn't understand, but I do. But I'll miss you. You're my child.'

Amelia looked away, into the face of the Madonna, so open and tranquil.

'I've brought you a present,' Velia said.

From the bag, she produced two packages wrapped in brown paper. One was flat and the other rectangular, a small box. Amelia smiled and opened the flat, softer one. Inside was a silk shirt, a light mauve.

'Mamma, it's so expensive.'

'You'll need it, to make a good impression.'

She pulled it free from the wrapping.

'So beautiful. Your stitch is so fine—'

'It's not my stitch. I bought it.'

Amelia gasped. Such extravagance.

'Open your other gift.'

She pulled back the thick brown paper. Inside was a book, an Italian–English dictionary, large with a strong binding of red leather and the pages with gilded edges, the paper as thin as tissue.

Amelia laughed. 'Where did you get it?'

'I had your uncle send it from Bologna. Despite all our poverty, I always bought you any book you needed.' She stopped herself. 'Your reading has led you to this marriage. It carried you away. Your brothers don't see the point of it but from the moment I started to teach you, you read everything anyone gave you, newspapers, even pamphlets on the street. You're like me – you believe it.'

'Do you remember, years ago, my vision that the Madonna flew from Jerusalem to me? I think the vision was about being carried by reading.'

Her mother smiled. 'Despite our lifetime of hard work, your father and I are no better off than when we first met. I'm bone-tired. But we were lucky – your brothers were too young for the war.' She turned and looked at Amelia, grabbed her forearm, her nails digging into the flesh. 'Go.' Her eyes widened, the black discs at the centres flared. 'I give you my blessing to fly. Break this cycle. But don't just fly – soar, as close as you can to the sun.'

Her mother said goodbye, demanded she not follow her. She watched her walk the aisle, the tap of her sole uneven on the marble floor. Once she was gone, Amelia turned to the Madonna.

'Please, Holy Mother, keep me safe.'

But the Madonna remained, calm and impassive.

For now, Amelia would fill and empty Signora Pina's buckets.

Chapter Two

Plans hardly ever go as willed. Despite Amelia's rush, spurred by her dislike of Pina, the final stages of the bureaucracy took months. And once all the document leaves were in place, booking a steamer proved full of headaches. The closest port was Genoa, but these boats travelled only to Sydney. Italo couldn't be away from the farm the length of time required to travel to meet her in Sydney. And her father disapproved – it wasn't possible for a young woman to make her own way from Sydney to Brisbane and then to Cairns.

But spring unfurled some good news. In July a British ship, the *RMS Orvieto*, would leave London but passing through Naples, sailing to Brisbane. Brisbane was closer; Italo could meet her there. And then Zia Francesca found a married woman who'd also make the voyage and act as a paid chaperone. And so all parties agreed, and the ticket was secured.

In Amelia's rush to say hello to Italo, she'd pushed from her thoughts the final goodbye to her family. In early July they left the cooler air of the north. In a last-minute gesture, Italo paid for the whole family to take a train south along the Adriatic coast and then overland to Naples, into the parched heat. Bologna, Pesaro, Ancona – such cities flew past the window. Amelia's head spun. Those last moments together, the heat in the train, the uncharacteristic silence that would just not remit, the scratching for the last few words so she could hold the sound of their voices in her heart. Her brothers made no attempt to tease her. But even the knowledge she'd finally see Italo did nothing to quell the running tide of anxiety pulling and releasing in her belly; what had she done? This was folly, this was folly, complete, miserable and unanswerable folly.

Finally in Naples, they stayed in a pensione near Piazza Dante, on the fringe of the oldest part of the city, the thick walls so high no sunlight graced the narrow streets. They could understand nothing of the Neapolitan dialect, which bore little resemblance to standard Italian and even less to theirs. They ate pizzas covered with tomato and mozzarella and basil and olive oil. She'd never tasted something so rich. Her brothers ate three each.

And the next morning, in a single file, they walked towards the port. They passed the church of Gesù Nuovo, the austere façade protruding grey pyramids. She excused herself and went to the church's centre door. An old man, his clothes tatty and soiled, his scent rancid, sat on the portico step. He raised his shaky palm. It lacked the two central fingers.

'Signorina,' he said. 'Just a coin, just a coin.'

Amelia stared into his eyes. He opened them wide. His left leg was missing. She opened her bag, found a few humble *centesimi*. She had no need of this money anymore and didn't stop to count it – her last Italian transaction.

Inside the church, her eyes burned with the thousand colours of inlaid marble, the gold and frescoed ceiling forming another sky, held high by square pillars that dwarfed men. She walked towards the altar, massive gold candlesticks and apricot marble columns pointing to heaven, past row after row after row of low wooden pews. At the centre, the

Madonna stood, massive and white and bold, her clasped hands held to the side of her chest, her face and eyes lowered in diffidence. Amelia knelt on the cold marble and prayed – Hail Mary, Mother of God.

Once she'd finished, she moved into the Holy Mother's gaze. She gasped. This was the face she'd seen in her vision, so many years ago. She bowed, pressed her heated cheek to the cool marble floor. She'd not made a rash decision. Her path was long and slow, unromantic perhaps, but it was her own.

'It's time for me to go,' she said.

She raised herself, walked the central aisle, out into the powerful Neapolitan sun. Her mother smiled. In silence, they continued to the port. These were her last steps with her family, her last in Italy. She could find no words. Perhaps none were needed. The voices on the street, the clatter of traffic, rang too loud. She cowered, covered her ears. But Aldo took her arm, his strength encouraging her. This just had to be endured.

Amelia guessed the salty tingling in her nostrils was the sea. They followed a chicane of signs, joined long lines, heard the babble of immigration. This was real. This was happening. And then they were there, on the dock, standing near a tower of metal that somehow floated. The black hull, scored with rows of portholes, gave way to the white upper decks, crowned by two white funnels with lazy trails of dark smoke. The hull bore patched sections of paint, rust and brown stains, old, worn, almost uncared-for. Two masts and booms bookended the vessel, should the steam motors fail.

Single men danced to the gangplank, whole families waddled like ducks, and young women on their own or in pairs, pulled themselves free of their parties. The moment had come. Monday the twelfth of July, 1920.

First, she hugged her brothers, tall Aldo and then Giuseppe, who always smiled but now wept. They were good brothers. What more could she have asked for? Then her father.

'Don't go,' he said, his voice cracking. 'You'll have to work so hard. You can't speak the language. You don't know him. I'll miss you. I love you.' He broke into open cries, his lips trembling. She'd never seen him so and searched for words to allay him but could find none. 'You'll see things I can't even imagine. I can't protect you.'

She couldn't look into his eyes, still so filled with confusion. And lastly her mother.

'You carry my dreams,' Velia said. 'I will miss you.'

She held her mother's warmth. 'I will miss you too.'

Would she ever see her again? Italo was her fate.

She stepped away, but her mother held onto her hand; her father cried. She pulled, but her mother's grip was tight. She opened out her fingers. Her hand began to slip and then jolted free. Her mother wailed. Although her portmanteau was hardly heavy, she carried it with both hands – no brother now. Her steps on the gangplank, the bridge between the land and the sea – all these moments she etched on her brain. She turned to her family, still on the dock and now so small and far away. The ant-like figures waved, and she waved her hand above her head, stretched it as high as she could so they could see. Another group arrived on the deck and she moved into the shadows, gave her papers to a uniformed man who glared at the information. She had tears now, her vision blurred, her cheeks hot and wet. When she looked back to the dock, her parents and brothers were nowhere in sight.

Their pain had been too great, and she exerted incredible effort not to drop her portmanteau and run through the crowd to find them. Cries rose in her throat, but she swallowed them whole.

Her third-class ticket sent her to the lowest deck, each step along the long corridor heavy. In all the strain she'd given up trying to stem the tears. She found her cabin. Already there were two women, the cabin cramped. The elder, a squat woman of at least sixty years, came to her with open arms. Amelia raised her portmanteau like a shield but allowed herself to be taken by the soft folds of flesh. No words passed between them. Amelia stayed in the embrace until the woman released her and held her by the shoulders. The woman's eyes were blue and soft, her flaxen hair now mainly grey.

'Are you all right?' she said, in Italian but with an accent, heavy, German. Her large eyes changed expression constantly.

Amelia nodded.

'I am Frau Gruetzmann.'

Amelia could find no words.

'And this is Clara Sacco.'

She recognised the name. This woman was her chaperone. She was only a few years older, taller than her with a fine figure, her nose straight and proud. Amelia offered her hand, but Clara embraced her.

'This needn't be formal,' Clara said, and smiled. 'And this is my son, Cristiano.'

Amelia looked around the small cabin. A little boy of only five or six, his dark hair cut short and his eyes fine and inky, sat in the shadows on the lower bunk. He walked to her, stretched out his hand. The prim gesture made her smile and pushed at her gloom. She took his small hand. The three women and the boy stood together, Amelia still holding her portmanteau but now at her side.

'And who are you?' Frau Gruetzmann said, and smiled.

Amelia laughed. 'I am Amelia Durante …' She stopped herself. 'No … I'm no longer her. I am Amelia Amedeo.'

With this error, she'd told this woman not only her name but her position, the purpose of her travel, where she was going. She felt the ring on her finger.

'You're from the north,' Frau Gruetzmann said. 'Your accent.'

'Tovo di Sant'Agata.'

The Frau narrowed her eyes and nodded.

'Cristiano can move to the top bunk,' Clara said.

There were two sets of bunks. The top bunk seemed its own world, and after sharing a sleepless bed with Signora Pina for nearly three months, its privacy was appealing.

'It's easier for him to stay below,' Amelia said. Clara made to protest but Amelia cut her off. 'I insist.'

Clara nodded. Under Cristiano's watchful eye, Amelia raised her portmanteau to the upper bunk and unpacked her few clothes into a small cupboard at the bunk's foot. He was most impressed by her Italian–English dictionary, though the book brought thoughts of her mother and fresh tears. Frau Gruetzmann smiled and chatted away, soothing the pain. She was from Innsbruck, which explained why the Frau had noted Amelia's accent. She'd joined the boat in Toulon, two days before, and already knew where everything was. She was travelling to join her son, who lived in Melbourne. He'd been interned during the war in a prisoner of war camp in Victoria but was quite free now and making his way. Amelia felt the pathos – just two years ago Austrians and Italians were sworn enemies, and yet here they were, sharing a cabin, leaving Europe behind, a heavy underscore to the futility of war.

Frau Gruetzmann spoke of Clara as if she weren't in the room. She was to join her husband, Paolo Sacco. They lived in Bologna and had married in 1914, just before the war. He left for Australia and eventually settled in Brisbane. Amelia reckoned the years – Clara hadn't seen her husband for six.

'Cristiano, how old are you?'

'I'm six.'

Amelia nodded. 'You're a man now.'

Cristiano nodded. His earnest face warmed her heart, but she doubted he'd ever met his father. She couldn't imagine the full weight of the sorrow accompanying such separation. Suddenly her path seemed common.

The ship's horn blew, three times. They looked at the ceiling of their cabin. Cristiano grimaced and covered his ears. No-one said anything. The departure hour, the moment inscribed on all their documents, had become real. They were leaving Italy.

'You two go to the deck,' Frau Gruetzmann said. 'I'll mind the boy.'

'I want to go too,' he said.

Clara reached out her hand to him. Amelia didn't want to watch Italy fade and craved solitude. But Frau Gruetzmann wasn't going to leave the cabin. As much as she appreciated her distracting talk, she felt a great need of peace. Clara smiled. Cristiano offered his hand. They were kind. Perhaps the fresh air would lift her spirits.

The three walked together, the floor rippling under her feet. The ship's horn blasted three more times. At the deck's railing, Amelia took in the bite of brine. Below, men ran to the gangplank, raggedly dressed peasants waving hands and papers above their heads, their belongings wrapped in newspaper in their other arms. They were no better off than Signor Gregorio.

'It would appear they too have missed Garibaldi's promises,' Amelia said.

Clara glared at her. 'Careful – you sound like a Bolshevik.'

Amelia had read this word in a pamphlet but had no clear idea of what it meant, except people spoke of it in harsh tones.

'The rising fascists,' Clara said, 'would strike you down.'

Clearly, Clara was better educated, and Amelia should learn to hold her tongue.

Finally, the gangplank was hauled away, the thick ropes unleashed, withdrawing like snakes into their holes. Amelia checked the dock one last time but there was no last glimpse of her family. The *RMS Orvieto* was dragged from the port by two tugboats. Italy began to slide away. With the other passengers, Clara and Amelia and Cristiano walked to the rear deck. Fishermen in their two-sailed boats bounced across their wake. Clara looked back towards the shore. Her face bore no clear emotion, neither pleased nor sad to be leaving.

'You must be excited,' Clara said.

The tension rose again, lodged bitter cries in her throat. Amelia raised her hand to her mouth. Clara raised a comforting hand to Amelia's shoulder. She nodded, though she felt no sense of excitement. But Clara was trying, and she shouldn't be ungenerous.

'Your husband must be excited,' Amelia said, wincing at her awkward deflection.

Clara exhaled. 'If it weren't for Cristiano, I'd be like you. The truth is I don't know him.'

'Then why did you marry?'

Clara narrowed her eyes. 'The truth?'

Amelia hadn't meant to pry. But she nodded.

'Yes, I'm tired of deception. Let's start this voyage with the truth,' Clara said. Her voice had a soft, wooden register. 'I was pregnant.'

Amelia sucked her bottom lip. She turned her eyes from Clara to the Bay of Naples. Only then she saw, to the side of the bay, brooding Vesuvius, a plume of dark smoke lazing in the sky as from a sleeping winter house.

'And a piece of paper and a ring made everything all right?' Amelia said, glancing back at Clara.

'In some eyes….'

'But why did Paolo leave you in Italy?'

'When we met, he was about to emigrate. He couldn't – well … wouldn't – alter his plans. I was to join him in a month, two at the most. Naively, I hoped I might even get away with no-one knowing I was pregnant. But then the war came, and we thought it was unsafe to travel, especially with the baby.'

'But the war's been over for two years.'

'Once it was clear I was pregnant, I couldn't work—'

'You worked?'

'I was a teacher. So without work, there was no money to live, even less to travel.'

Amelia looked back to the smoke from Vesuvius and then the two trails from the steamer's funnels. How often hopes crashed without money.

'We've lived with Paolo's parents for six years in Bologna. Paolo found work with a building company and started to send some money. But it wasn't much, especially after I paid for our living. It took years to save for our passage.'

'Paolo and Cristiano have never met, have they?'

Clara turned to Amelia. 'You're smart.'

A comfortable silence fell between them.

'And you?' Clara said. 'You've taken a larger gamble. At least I've met Paolo. There must have been someone in Italy?'

'In my village and the next village and the next, there are hardly any men left. Those the war hasn't picked off, immigration has won. There are just frail old men and babies.' She shuddered, breathed in the enormousness of what she'd done, tried to shake it off. 'Perhaps it's better to marry someone like this. My friends in the village … The men failed them.' She stopped, aware of Clara's scrutiny. 'I've taken a great risk. And I'm frightened. I've no idea how this will end.'

Clara turned to dimming Naples. 'But there's something far more dreadful that's made you leave.'

Amelia looked back towards Vesuvius, unsure what she wanted to say to this woman she'd only met. Her honesty unnerved her.

Clara searched her face. 'Why are you so scared to tell the truth?'

Clara had trusted her with a story she doubted many knew. So Amelia would tell a story she hadn't even told her mother.

'I had a friend, Emma Veronesi,' Amelia said. 'She was a very beautiful girl. We'd known one another all our lives. She only had to smile … But that's not fair to her. She was so much more than just her smile.

'During the war, the son of the feudal lord came home on leave. Each day he rode through the streets on his fine horse in his fine, fine uniform. How could Emma not notice him, this Raffaelo Mancuso?

'One afternoon she was filling the water buckets at the fountain. He rode by and she stared at him. The next day, he met her eye. He stopped, dismounted and came to the fountain. She stepped back to allow him to drink, but he wasn't thirsty. He talked to her. And I've no doubt she smiled her smile.

'Each day he'd come and dismount. Until one spring day, he asked her to meet him, in the early evening, in the forest. I begged her not to go. But she went. And they met. And he told her he loved her, and kissed her, and had his way with her.

'And of course, she believed all his promises, as did I with each passing day. Raffaelo returned to the war but said once it was over he would marry her, and she would have everything. What fools we were. The fighting against Austria in the Veneto was fierce. She feared he'd not return. But she was pregnant. And when she told him, when he finally returned, he denied knowing her. Before anyone else knew, Emma threw herself from the church spire.'

'My God.' Clara breathed deeply. 'How awful. I'm sorry for you.'

'And the day she died, when I stood at the well, he rode past. He raised his buttocks from the saddle, took the horse to a canter, but I knew what he was showing me. His ass. And he knew that I'd say nothing. What lets them take whatever they want?'

'*Jus primae noctis* – the right of the first night – medieval laws.'

'Beautiful Emma. He threw her away as if she were muck.' Amelia looked out at the dark, breathed in the sea air. 'The priest refused her a funeral mass. She burns in hell, he said.' The priest was wrong. Amelia knew. Emma was with the Holy Mother, who saw and felt and understood everything. 'I don't want to die poor while someone who owns the land I work is made wealthier. I want something more, free from the stain of poverty, free from fief.'

'And this is it?'

'Italy is barren with its old ways. Australia is new. New ways.'

Clara was silent. 'You're right; Australia is a young country. Let's hope it has new ways.'

The deck vibrated below their feet.

'I've never told Emma's story to anyone. People think Emma was possessed by the devil or there was madness in the family. Only Mancuso and I knew the truth. And no-one would believe me …'

'I do.' Clara took Amelia's hand.

'Will we ever return home?' Amelia said.

'Italy isn't our home anymore.' Clara continued to look to the horizon.

Amelia observed her. She had warm eyes and an open face. All that was left of Italy was the dark trail of Vesuvius, cutting through the salt air and the blackening sky. She would miss her parents and her brothers; just to think of them squeezed her heart. What were they doing now? How long until they returned home? Would they go that evening with the others of the village to Veronesi's large stable for *la veglia*, the evening party? The men would play cards, the women's never-idle hands spinning wool and their voices telling stories to the young. Shouldn't she be there with them?

She breathed in her last glimpse of Italy. Signora Pina had made her promise they would return. She shook her head. The sea was black, capped here and there with white peaks, not a drop of blue to be seen. She felt pulled apart, as if she'd shed an old skin. She made a promise to herself: from now on, she'd go only forward.

The *RMS Orvieto* had no second class, just first and steerage. A steerage ticket restricted the passenger to the lower decks, a mix of Italians, Germans and Irish. Amelia listened to all the voices she didn't understand, but the Irish – their hefty rhythm, their broad smiles and laughing – she liked the most. The first-class passengers, a mix of English and Scots, were free to range to the lower decks, but Amelia and Clara's daily walk was restricted to the lower.

'Why can't they stay on their own deck?' Amelia said.

'There's space for everyone—'

'They just want to ogle us.'

In an effort to tire themselves, they repeated circuits of the decks many times, but the crowds slowed them. Amelia linked her arm through Clara's. Whilst they kept to one another's company, they saluted the other walkers and passed small amounts of information. Some were families, some single men and even two others brides by proxy.

'Do you speak any English?' Clara said.

Amelia winced. 'There are many Italians in Babinda. Italo said I don't need it.'

'You won't have any independence without it.'

Amelia thought. 'Do you speak it?'

'Not a word.' Clara smiled. 'Let's start together in the morning.'

And so each morning after breakfast and their walk, they studied. They made lists of every item in the cabin, and Clara found each word in Amelia's dictionary. Every morning all four of them would repeat the words – bed, porthole, floor, ceiling, chest of drawers (three words where they had one). Amelia was years from her schooling, which had been snuffed by her work on the farm and then the war, snuffed by her just being a girl. She swam in a head-aching confusion, but her love of Italian words soon carried over into an interest in these clunky and abrupt ones, sounds that had no rhythm or rhyme she could find but that somehow made meanings. Clara was a steady teacher and mixed the work with much laughter and courage. Three days later, when they'd crossed the Mediterranean to Port Said, they'd all, even Cristiano and Frau Gruetzmann, made headway with the nouns of their cabin.

Each evening the Italians ate at one long table, the men at one end and the women at the other. The noise – plates and cutlery, the men's opinions and counters, glasses knocked together and over – made eating vibrant. The wives kept an eye on their husbands' plates and, if they finished their food, a stodge of potatoes and meat, they would hurry to replenish it.

'And you wonder why I want to leave Italy,' Amelia said.

Clara regarded the wives and their husbands. 'What would you have them do?'

'Serve themselves. Serve their wives, God forbid.'

Clara laughed. 'I wish you luck.'

Would Italo expect her to wait on him? Surely, a man who'd lived on his own, far away from Signora Pina, would be able to serve himself food. She looked at the other unmarried women. They too watched the wives, but they watched as if learning how to be, rather than how not to be.

'I'm glad you're teaching me English.'

Each day brought more heat, landscapes she could never have dreamt of seeing. There was an excitement to this, but at the same time she wished the voyage would end. The land of the Suez Canal was ceaselessly flat, and each hour the air became hotter and drier. Along the shore camels toiled, carrying goods, carrying people. They passed steamers returning to the Mediterranean, so close they could see the passengers on the deck, waving and smiling. And on the shore, trains passed them effortlessly.

Five young boys, dressed in what appeared to be long white shirts that brushed the ground, waved to them from the canal's edge. Amelia and Clara waved back. In unison, the boys turned, pulled up their shirts to reveal their round, bare bottoms, which they proceeded to wiggle. Clara and Amelia gasped in shock and then bent over with laughter, drawing the scowls of those on deck who'd not seen the show.

Each day grew more stifling, as much as forty-two degrees Celsius by midday. To avoid the heat, they took their walks earlier and earlier in the morning. Soon they'd left the calm waters of the Suez Canal and were moving through the long Red Sea, a place from the Bible, where Moses had parted the water – and she, Amelia, was seeing it.

With only a taste, Amelia was now keen to further her English studies. Clara began the verbs, starting with the conjugations of 'to be'.

'There's so little difference between them,' Amelia said.

Clara patted her hand. 'Don't listen to the end of the verbs. Listen to the beginning.'

'This language is upside down.'

They added new verbs – to eat, to sleep, to want, to feel, to hear, to touch. They made small sentences, peppering them with the nouns they'd learnt. She would listen to those who spoke English, concentrating on the sounds. How flat they all seemed, how lifeless, as if everyone who spoke English were sad. In her sleep, verb conjugations pounded like galloping hooves. By the time she'd memorised the verb 'to eat', they were free of the Red Sea, moving into the Gulf of Aden, the horizon free of land.

On the first morning in the Gulf, the blue sky washed over with fierce dark clouds. A storm was coming, the tail end of a typhoon, and the passengers were asked to secure their cabins and remain below decks. They hoped it would last only a few days, not all the way to Ceylon. The winds picked up, the dark water rose, the crest broke open, sounding like shovelled gravel, white spilling over the slope of the wave. The ship rolled. Amelia gripped the railing. The wind moaned through the decks and open passageways. She turned back to the cabin.

Clara and Frau Gruetzmann had put themselves to bed. Clara lay flat on her back, her face pale but heavy about her eyes, staring at the ceiling. Cristiano sat on the top bunk. Amelia took his hand to relieve his fear and to assess what she could do. Both women had vomited into buckets, the stench nauseating. Amelia drained one into the other and took it to the deck. The engines strained up one side of a wave, but then the propellers broke free of the sea, whining high as the ship slid down the swell.

Day and night, this pendulous action remained. Luckily, both she and Cristiano remained unaffected. Cristiano worried about his mother and helped where he could. The cabin reeked of vomit, but it sat so low in the water it was impossible to open a porthole. The ship surgeon, McCausland, examined Clara and Frau Gruetzmann and instructed Amelia to give only small amounts of water. Amelia held Clara's head from the pillow to sip from the glass, but whatever she managed to swallow soon returned to the bucket. After two days, despite the unrelenting motion, Frau Gruetzmann recovered a little, enough to sit and drink some weak black tea.

Amelia had reports; they would see Ceylon in three days, if they were lucky. And the reports were good to their word. They sailed into Colombo on Monday, the twenty-sixth of July. With each metre they advanced, the sea calmed and the sky brightened until there was full sun. The port was busy, all manner and size of craft crisscrossing. The boat was surrounded by a sea of black hair as the native boys yelled to the passengers from rafts, trying to sell trinkets, diving for the coins the passengers threw into the blue sea. For the first time in days, Clara, weak and shaken, came to the deck.

'The nausea won't stop until I'm on dry land,' she said.

And so they arranged their passes. On land, Clara's legs wobbled, drunk from the sea. They walked her to a shaded bench. Amelia looked at this strange place. The men, lithe and tall, wore long swathes of fabric, almost dresses, white turbans covering their dark hair. Some women wore rings through their noses. Men, indentured like beasts, pulled small single-seat vehicles, tooted at by cars, swerving past long carts drawn by oxen. Others, their heads shaved, were swathed in orange or maroon robes. Amelia tried to take it all in, but her eyes saw things she didn't know how to understand. The ground was covered in gobs of red, the droppings of some exotic bird, and she instructed Cristiano to avoid them. But the men chewed something and then spat it to the street, leaving their mouths and the street stained red.

Once Clara felt less nauseated, Frau Gruetzmann and Cristiano walked ahead towards the steamer. Clara smiled for the first time in days, which warmed Amelia's heart. A heavy squall came over. Clara took Amelia's arm, and they walked the long portico to the ship.

Now they'd reached the equator, their morning walk was accompanied by a humidity that became higher and more oppressive until it broke into rain. And even then, the cool relief from the closeness, the exhaustion and the sticky skin was only brief as the steaminess rose again.

'You'll need to get used to this,' Clara said. 'Babinda isn't so far from the equator.'

The thought of such sultriness was unpleasing.

This was the last leg of their journey to Australia. Each morning they would stop at a map that charted the ship's progress.

'Is Brisbane near Babinda?' Amelia said.

Clara pointed to Australia. 'Brisbane is here.' She ran her finger north, along the coastline, higher, higher and higher. 'There's Babinda.'

'It's not so far ...'

'Look at Italy. It's the same distance as ...' She opened her thumb and her forefinger. 'From Munich to the heel of the boot.'

'That far ...' The distance flattened Amelia. Her only friend in Australia would be so far away.

'We can write,' Clara said.

'But it won't be the same.'

Clara smiled. 'Nothing is ever the same.'

Amelia looked out to the clear horizon. What an irony – to have wished these days of travel to pass quickly. She wanted to pitch the ship's anchor overboard, halt any more progress. In Clara, she'd found the friendship she'd had with Emma. She looked at the distance between Babinda and Brisbane.

'Come,' Clara said. 'We've many verbs to master before Fremantle.'

Chapter Three

Australia rose on the horizon, shone at them. The passengers crowded the decks, two, three deep at the rail, jostling for their first glimpse of the port town of Fremantle at the mouth of the Swan River. It was a Friday morning, the sixth of August, 1920.

'It's so small,' Clara said with a note of disgust but couldn't take her eyes away.

People started to yell to their loved ones, who were so far below Amelia doubted anyone could understand.

'I'd be happy with a single hut,' Amelia said.

Clara continued to stare at the shore but raised her lips to a smile. 'What have we come to?'

Amelia bent next to Cristiano. 'What do you hope to see first in Australia?'

He looked to the shore. 'A kangaroo.'

She smiled. Men walked along the dock in time with the ship, beyond them carriages for coal and rows of warehouses. There was industry. Clara was too harsh.

Frau Gruetzmann packed a small day bag and they joined the long immigration queue. The day was indifferent, neither hot nor cold, but the sun shone, the sky a profound blue. They watched huge cranes haul the cargo from the hull. Cristiano had it on good authority there were three British automobiles to be unloaded. A mix of people of all ages stood at a distance.

'What do you suppose they're looking at?' Clara said.

Both the men and women wore hats, the women dressed in lightweight fabrics. And then Amelia remembered. It was no longer summer, as it was in Italy. In Australia everything was upside down; it was now August, almost *Ferragosto*, the celebration for the height of summer, yet it was the middle of winter. But the women dressed like it was summer.

'They've come to see the "new chums",' Frau Gruetzmann said. 'I was told about it. That's what we are.'

Frau Gruetzmann used the English words, and Amelia had no idea what they meant. But once Clara explained the term, it was evident to Amelia that 'new chums' was what they were. From the stern looks on the mob's faces, Amelia was unsure what favour that classification afforded. Everywhere was English, all the signs and all the people speaking it.

They began to walk. Amelia sucked the air deep into her lungs, fresh and clean but dry. Cars moved along the street, but there were also horses pulling drays. They passed a café and Clara asked for a table but couldn't make herself understood, so Amelia took her coat sleeve and pulled her back outside, and they erupted into laughter. The streets were wide and bore so few people. They walked into a park and found a bench, part shaded by a tree. Even Cristiano was without words.

Men and women lay on the grass, some seated. A noise, almost human, roared in the treetops. Cristiano covered his ears. Frau Gruetzmann's eyes bulged. Clara looked to the canopy.

'It must be a kookaburra,' Amelia said. She looked at Cristiano. 'It's laughing at you.'

They continued to look up but couldn't spot the bird. What a wondrous sound, so different from a nightingale's. But what had amused it? The other people paid it no heed. They were drinking from tall brown bottles. Italo had written of the Australians' love of beer, and she presumed this was what they were drinking, the empty bottles left lying on the grass. But in a park and at this hour of the day?

A man stumbled towards them, saying something. Amelia looked at Clara, but she hadn't understood his meaning either.

'I not know,' Amelia said to him, in her brittle English.

The man stopped walking and glared at them. He smelt of alcohol.

'He's drunk,' Clara said, in Italian.

The man's red eyes swelled.

'Dagos!' He yelled the word, spat it. 'Dagos. Dagos. Dagos.'

Clara pulled Cristiano to her and they moved away. The man repeated the word and many more with much the same tone again and again until he began to laugh, leaving them to retreat towards the boat.

Amelia felt unsettled; why was there a need to drink in such a manner? And why were there no police to stop such behaviour? And the man appeared angry with them. Why was he yelling? She'd not challenged him. But what could she say? Every defence she had was in Italian. She had no power. And with no common language, nothing would ever be understood. She vowed she'd never retreat again, and she'd master this upside-down tongue.

Their voyage along the southern coast was without inci-dent. At Port Adelaide, more cargo was unloaded. Melbourne was a true metropolis, its gateway a large working dock. Here, Frau Gruetzmann left the boat. Her son, a middle-aged man with her large eyes, came to meet her. Amelia cried as she remembered Frau Gruetzmann's first kindnesses, and they promised to write long letters with every detail of their new lives. Without her, the cabin seemed large and excessive. They lost sight of the coast again until they passed Botany Bay and then moved north, entering the magnificent headlands of Sydney Harbour, which Clara thought missed only the Colossus of Rhodes. They were only a few days from Brisbane.

'Zia Amelia,' Cristiano said. 'Will you and Zio Italo stay with us in Brisbane?'

It was the first time he'd called her his aunt, and she felt she should correct him, but she liked the sweetness of his thought.

'Only for a few days.'

A gloom came over his face, and he withdrew into his thoughts.

'Zia Amelia,' he said again. 'How will you know what Zio Italo looks like?'

She smiled. 'I have a photograph.'

'Will he be with my father?'

It warmed her heart that, to Cristiano, his father and Italo were already friends. She couldn't bring herself to tell him the truth. 'I'm sure your father and Zio Italo will be there together.'

They sailed into Moreton Bay through a series of small islands on Friday, the twentieth of August, 1920. She wore a dress saved for the day, but it was woollen, too heavy for the heat, yet she had to make a good initial impression. The few remaining passengers crowded onto the deck, each having a position at the rail and a clear view. Amelia kept her eyes to the shore, her small portmanteau over her belly. Clara and Cristiano stood next to her.

'You won't be able to see him yet,' Clara said.

'Aren't you excited?'

Clara was silent. 'I don't know …'

Amelia breathed deeply. 'I'm scared, more than anything.'

'Why fear?'

'God knows what will happen. You'll be so far away. I never thought to have another friend like Emma.'

Clara's eyes teared. 'You're a strong woman. You'll overcome everything.'

Amelia swallowed her tears. And the two embraced.

www.ingramcontent.com/pod-product-compliance
Lightning Source LLC
Chambersburg PA
CBHW070746120726
47910CB00001B/178